Reviewers

"Melissa Brayden has be[come] [a master] of the genre, writing hit after hit of funny, relatable, and very sexy stories for women who love women."—*Afterellen.com*

Love Like This

"All the best traits of Brayden's books are present here: great dialogue, banter, humour, a well laid plot, multidimensional characters and, last but not least, a good old romance."—*Lez Review Books*

"It's sweet and sexy, with enough angst to keep things interesting, but not enough to hurt you. It's a totally enjoyable romance that would be a perfect beach read."—*The Lesbian Review*

Sparks Like Ours

"Brayden sets up a flirtatious tit-for-tat that's honest, relatable, and passionate. The women's fears are real, but the loving support from the supporting cast helps them find their way to a happy future. This enjoyable romance is sure to interest readers in the other stories from Seven Shores."—*Publishers Weekly*

"*Sparks Like Ours* is made up of myriad bits of truth that make for a cozy, lovely summer read."—*Queerly Reads*

Hearts Like Hers

"*Hearts Like Hers* has all the ingredients that readers can expect from Ms. Brayden: witty dialogue, heartfelt relationships, hot chemistry and passionate romance."—*Lez Review Books*

"Once again Melissa Brayden stands at the top. She unequivocally is the queen of romance."—*Front Porch Romance*

"Autumn Primm and Kate Carpenter are my favorite Brayden couple to date. This book had me laughing, crying and swooning like never before."—*Les Reveur*

"*Hearts Like Hers* has a breezy style that makes it a perfect beach read. The romance is paced well, the sex is super hot, and the conflict made perfect sense and honored Autumn and Kate's journeys."
—*The Lesbian Review*

Eyes Like Those

"Brayden's writing is just getting better and better. The story is well done, full of well-honed wit and humour, and the characters are complex and interesting."—*Lesbian Reading Room*

"Melissa Brayden knocks it out of the park once again with this fantastic and beautifully written novel."—*Les Reveur*

"Pure Melissa Brayden at her best...Another great read that won't disappoint Brayden's fans. Can't wait for the rest of the series."
—*Lez Review Books*

Strawberry Summer

"The characters were a joy to read and get to know. Maggie's family is loving, supportive, and charming. They're the family we all wish we had, through good times and bad."—*C-Spot Reviews*

"The tragedy is real, the angst well done without being over the top, and the character development palpable in both the main characters and their friends."—*Lesbian Reading Room*

"*Strawberry Summer* is a tribute to first love and soulmates and growing into the person you're meant to be. I feel like I say this each time I read a new Melissa Brayden offering, but I loved this book so much that I cannot wait to see what she delivers next."—*Smart Bitches, Trashy Books*

"*Strawberry Summer* will suck you in, rip out your heart, and put all the pieces back together by the end, maybe even a little better than they were before."—*The Lesbian Review*

Praise for the Soho Loft Series

"The trilogy was enjoyable and definitely worth a read if you're looking for solid romance or interconnected stories about a group of friends."—*The Lesbrary*

Kiss the Girl

"There are romances and there are romances...Melissa Brayden can be relied on to write consistently very sweet, pure romances and delivers again with her newest book *Kiss the Girl*...There are scenes suffused with the sweetest love, some with great sadness or even anger—a whole gamut of emotions that take readers on a gentle roller coaster with a consistent upbeat tone. And at the heart of this book is a hymn to true friendship and human decency."
—*C-Spot Reviews*

"An adorable romance in which two flawed but well-written characters defy the odds and fall into the arms of the other."
—*She Read*

"Brayden does romance so very well. She provides us with engaging characters, a plausible setup with understandable and realistic conflict, and ridiculously fantastic dialogue."—*Frivolous Views*

Just Three Words

"I can sum up my reading experience with *Just Three Words* in exactly that: I. LOVED. IT."—*Bookaholics-Not-So-Anonymous*

"A beautiful and downright hilarious tale about two very relatable women looking for love."—*Sharing Is Caring Book Reviews*

Ready or Not

"The third book was the best of the series. Melissa Brayden has some work cut out for her when writing a book after this one."
—*Fantastic Book Reviews*

By the Author

Waiting in the Wings

Heart Block

How Sweet It Is

First Position

Strawberry Summer

Beautiful Dreamer

Soho Loft Romances:

Kiss the Girl

Just Three Words

Ready or Not

Seven Shores Romances:

Eyes Like Those

Hearts Like Hers

Sparks Like Ours

Love Like This

Visit us at www.boldstrokesbooks.com

BEAUTIFUL DREAMER

by
Melissa Brayden

2019

BEAUTIFUL DREAMER
© 2019 By Melissa Brayden. All Rights Reserved.

ISBN 13: 978-1-63555-305-5

This Trade Paperback Original Is Published By
Bold Strokes Books, Inc.
P.O. Box 249
Valley Falls, NY 12185

First Edition: July 2019

CREDITS
Editors: Lynda Sandoval and Stacia Seaman
Production Design: Stacia Seaman
Cover Design by Jeanine Henning

Acknowledgments

I've always wanted to live in a place like Dreamer's Bay, a small town on the water where everybody knows everyone else. Perhaps that's why I gravitated to telling this particular story, because I'd get to spend a little time there in the process. It's my hope that you'll enjoy your stay as well. Eat a donut. Play some cornhole. Watch the tide come in.

The writing of this book in the midst of so many life changes was truly something! I want to say thank you to every single reader who offered kind words, support, and well wishes on the new little addition to my life, and patted my proverbial head after many a sleepless night. I was blown away by the response, and truly touched.

Thank you to my fabulous editor, Lynda Sandoval, my amazing copy editor, Stacia Seaman, and the entire team at Bold Strokes who have so many important things to do to make this book arrive in the hands of a reader. Jeanine Henning has turned out another cover I love that resonates with the story I told, and I'm so grateful.

The friends I've made in the writing community continue to make my job fun, interesting, and never solitary. Thank you Georgia, Rachel, Nikki, Carsen, Barbara, Kris, and so many more for the laughs along the way.

My family is amazing and it's even a little bigger now. Love abounds. Alan, you get me in a way no one else does. My rock. The adventure continues!

For All Those Still Searching

PROLOGUE

Elizabeth Draper sat on the edge of the pier with her light brown hair up in a ponytail and her plaid shirt tied around her waist by its sleeves. With her jeans rolled up to mid-calf, she kicked at the water with her big toe as she scanned the memories of the past eighteen years like a wistful montage. So much had happened in just this small five-mile stretch.

Dreamer's Bay was what you would call a blip of a town along the coastline of South Carolina that not a lot of people knew about. With Hilton Head to the north and Wilmington Island to the south, a lot of folks skipped right over the Bay should their foot rest too heavy on the gas pedal. Elizabeth liked that about her hometown. She preferred it small and elusive, like a hidden treasure you had to uncover, all their own. Once you found it, however, why would you ever want to leave? It was the kind of place where good things happened and people were there for their friends and neighbors. Beyond the beach itself, the lightning bugs in the summer were just one of the many beautiful spectacles you encountered in Dreamer's Bay. The breathtaking Fourth of July fireworks display was another. She smiled imagining last year's awe-inspiring design, not to mention the best damn funnel cake you could find for hundreds of miles.

Not only that, but Elizabeth had been blessed with a batch of fantastic memories all her own in this place. There were the Easter egg hunts in Bountiful Park. Nights spent playing flashlight tag with the neighborhood kids until her dad finally called her inside at her nine p.m. curfew. She shook her head and grinned when remembering her stint as Twin #2 in *Peter Pan*, which they'd performed in the school's underequipped cafetorium when she was twelve. The entire population of the town had been in the audience. Only her mother had been missing.

She didn't think about that part too much. On purpose. Instead, she'd fondly reflected on the time she'd scored second place in the annual bake-off with her grandmother's recipe for chocolate mint pie with homemade whipped cream. The win had come with a pretty significant trophy she'd displayed on the shelf in the living room.

In just a few hours, she would carve out another memory as she graduated from high school, leaving her youth firmly behind her. The next day she'd be on her way out of Dreamer's Bay for the first time in her life, headed to the University of North Carolina, where she'd start summer classes right away. Her stomach hummed uncomfortably at the thought of leaving everything she loved. Elizabeth had never really known life anywhere else, and the idea that she was about to explore the wider world left her excited and terrified. There was nowhere like Dreamer's Bay. What was she going to do these next few years without it?

That night, as she clutched the portfolio that contained her high school diploma, the emotion of the monumental event overcame Elizabeth. With a lump in her throat and tears welling in her eyes, she surveyed her classmates as they gathered outside the auditorium following the ceremony, wearing their matching blue and white gowns. Hugging, cheering, and well-wishing abounded, but also the understanding that they would part ways now, bound for different places in life, their futures uncertain, their hopes and dreams still to be realized. Some would stay. Some would go. But they would never be the same group again, who'd grown up together and experienced so many of the same things. She hugged her English teacher, Mr. Webb, then turned and hugged her best friend KC and kissed her buddy Dexter's cheek. She turned around, looking for the next hug, and came face-to-face with Devyn Winters, another classmate. They'd not spent a lot of time together in high school, running with different crowds. Devyn was co-captain of the cheerleading squad and Elizabeth was, well, just Elizabeth. She'd heard Devyn was bound for Penn State, having always been the good student. Extra popular, too. Elizabeth wasn't.

"Hey, congratulations," Devyn said, with a polite smile. She was gorgeous, with blond hair and hazel eyes, and in that moment, she was haloed perfectly by the outdoor lights overhead.

Elizabeth beamed back. "Congratulations to you, too." They stared at each other a moment, and for some reason it mattered more than it should have. They reached for each other and shared a tight embrace, only it didn't feel obligatory. It was probably the gravity of the day, bonding two acquaintances who would then drift their separate ways again, back on their rightful trajectories that had never included the other. That's what it was, right? Yet it felt like so much more.

When Devyn released her, Elizabeth placed a hand over her heart, wondering about the intensity of the pang that struck her chest.

"Elizabeth. Over here."

She raised her gaze and there was her father, rushing toward her with his arms open and eyes misty. That was her rock, right there, the person who always had her back. The pride in his gaze meant everything tonight. "Congratulations, little girl, you did it."

With her cap clutched in her hand, she fell into his arms, happy to share this moment with the one person she could always count on. "Thanks, Dad." She laughed in wonder. "I can't believe it. I'm a high school graduate."

"I can. You worked hard and it paid off. I've never been prouder of you."

In the midst of that crowd and the continued well-wishing, Elizabeth couldn't help but glance around for Devyn and wonder about the moment that still tingled. She scanned the faces around her, but to no avail. Devyn Winters was gone.

CHAPTER ONE

Present Day

"Happy birthday, dear Donna. Happy birthday to you." Devyn Winters stared at her happily singing coworkers as they held that final note of the song for several moments longer than necessary. She raised her eyebrows and smiled as she did her best to look as happily engaged in this whole feel-good moment as the rest of the office did. Did she have to read their lips to remember the birthday woman's name? Why, yes, yes she did. She was awful when it came to remembering the admins because there were so many of them. She'd like to be better, but honestly, who had the time? She'd done her job, appeared for the requisite singing, snagged some vanilla cake with bright purple icing, and now worked on crowd-surfing her way out of the overrun break room while balancing her cake over her head.

"Devyn? Hey, Devyn?"

"Yep?" she tossed over her shoulder as she continued to dodge and weave like a pro. Time was money.

"Can I grab you to talk about the McMahon property at 803 Financial? If you have a spare sec, I mean." She glanced back at Redheaded Ricky, who meant well, always smelled pleasantly of soap, but rarely ironed his work shirts. He was a decent enough broker at the firm but was known for being a softie and often late to the negotiating table, missing out on the really high-end listings because he'd decided to have a life on the side of his job. She didn't blame him. Everyone's priorities were different, but there wasn't a lot she could do for a guy like him who wasn't available when the big deals went down over drinks after hours.

"Sure. Can we walk and talk?" she asked reluctantly. With

an afternoon stacked to the brim with listing appointments and two additional meetings with developers, she didn't have a lot of downtime to talk shop. Plus, she'd just given away three minutes of it to Donna-somebody and her confetti-vanilla birthday cake, which she decided mid-bite was not bad at all. The three minutes might have proven beneficial in the end.

"Definitely," he said, matching her stride. "Walkin' and talkin'."

She glanced over at him, waiting for him to speak. "So…803 Financial? The McMahon building?"

"Right." He nodded. "Three units on the fourteenth floor are about to hit the market. I want that listing, and I was hoping you could offer me some insight. Advice, if you will, on how I might land it. Everyone knows you're a pro when it comes to working with the top developers."

She whistled low because that property was out of Ricky's league. In fact, countless brokers had been vying for a meeting with the developer, Randy Thibedeux, for weeks. "Have you ever worked with a developer?"

"No."

She high-fived her assistant Karen as they passed her desk. "Messages?"

"Twelve. And check your email. Two offers came in on Eighteen Lexington. One is an international buyer."

"Full ask?"

"One at full ask. The international offer is slightly under but all cash. I think you can get them up."

"I love it. My client will love it even more. Thanks, Karen." Then she remembered Ricky, who was still on her heels.

"So, what can I help you with exactly?"

He had a hungry look about him. "How do I move from private listings to developments?"

Well, wasn't that the million-dollar question, literally. She tossed him a glance. "You want to work with developers?" It didn't shock her. There was nothing in the world like being handed a fifteen-million-dollar building and selling out the entire thing single-handedly. The dollar signs from the commission alone sent her a thrilling chill. That didn't even begin to cover the street cred.

Ricky came farther into her office and sat in the oversized leather chair across from her desk. There were times she slept in that chair when it made more sense than going all the way home. "Yes, very much, and you seem to have it all figured out."

"I do okay." She flashed a smile, knowing it was an understatement. She played hardball in the big leagues with her name on the tip of everyone's tongue and loved every minute of it. It came at a price, though. She couldn't slow down for so much as a millisecond or she'd lose it all to someone who was willing to schmooze harder or stay up an hour longer. Good thing she loved the grind.

"How did you get started?" Rick asked.

"With high-rises? You start with a single listing in one building, prove yourself by knocking it out of the park by bringing in a killer offer, and hope the developer is so stoked that they give you another shot, then another, followed by an entire building of high-end inventory."

He nodded along enthusiastically.

"Then their developer buddy sees that their multimillion-dollar building sold out in three months and wants to know who they used. It's all about your track record and forming strong relationships. Prove yourself, and there's always more."

Ricky stared at her like she'd just invented electricity. "That's amazing."

"It can be." She grabbed a Red Bull from her bottom drawer for herself and slid one to Ricky, who happily scooped it up. "New construction in Philadelphia is up twenty percent. It's a good time to get your feet wet if you're serious."

He blinked hard as she spoke as if committing her wise words to memory. "I am. Very serious, in fact."

Despite her schedule, Ricky's obvious sincerity snagged her attention, prompting her to make an uncharacteristic decision. "Listen, I have a four o'clock this afternoon with a known wheeler-dealer. The guy never stops. In fact, I don't think he sleeps with all the buildings he's got going up. Do you want to sit in on the meeting? He's three-quarters of the way into construction on a building on Walker Avenue, and I'm angling for it."

"The whole building?"

"Of course the whole building."

His face lit up in admiration. Bless his heart. "Yeah. Yes. I would love that. If you're sure you don't mind."

"I don't. We'll likely do drinks after a tour of the property. There's a bar around the corner he likes."

Ricky paused. "Just so I'm clear, this might be a late workday?"

Devyn understood that Ricky would likely need to let his wife know that he wouldn't be home for dinner. She couldn't imagine being tied down like that. To her, every day was a late workday, but that was the kind of pace that got her fur up and made her excited to get up in the morning, to get out there and sell. She didn't live by the clock, and that had paid off in spades. Financially, she was set. She lived in an upscale condo in the heart of downtown Philadelphia and reaped the rewards of her hard work, as evidenced by her round-the-clock concierge and large staff of various assistants both at work and in her personal life. "Yeah, Ricky. We might go past six. You still up for it?"

He grinned and rolled with the punch. "Definitely."

"Great. Meet me downstairs at three fifteen. I have a slice of cake to finish now while I present these new offers to my client."

"Best of luck," Ricky said, shooting her two enthusiastic thumbs-up.

She smiled and leaned back in her leather desk chair. "I won't need it."

❖

Elizabeth Draper and Hank the hound dog were getting along splendidly that morning. In fact, as far as Elizabeth was concerned, Hank was always a pleasure to walk, tongue hanging out the side of his mouth like a calling card. They rounded the corner onto the last tree-lined street of their weekly Wednesday-morning walk. With winter melting into spring, the green was reemerging in the grass, trees, and bushes after months of dormancy. The brighter colors inspired a bouncy spring in her step that she swore translated to Hank, who she'd decided months ago was an incredibly intuitive doggo.

She paused the walk to let Hank and his nose investigate the suspicious crevice in the sidewalk, while she took a deep inhale of fresh air. Someone nearby was brewing coffee with the windows open, and it only added to Elizabeth's enjoyment of the morning and the happy reminder that she still had the whole day stretched out ahead of her.

"Almost home, big guy," she said to Hank as they neared the red brick one-story where he lived with his owner, Pam. The reminder was unnecessary, however, because Hank was already pulling on the leash and whining softly. He knew exactly where he was and was anxious to lap up some water before falling onto his side on the cool kitchen floor for his late-morning snooze. Dutifully, she let them into the house with the key Pam had provided, made sure Hank had plenty of water, and retrieved the weekly payment left for her on the kitchen counter. "You have a good day, Hank," she said with a final pat and kiss to the side of his big, sloppy cheek. "Be nice to your mom when she gets home from the office, and I will see you on Friday morning."

With a thud, he fell onto his side to absorb the cool from the tile. She smiled as he let out a long and contented sigh. They'd had a good walk that day, and for the first time in quite a while, she'd been able to leave her jacket and car at home where she worked from her converted garage that she'd turned into a functioning office for On the Spot, the errand and odd job company she owned and operated. True, there was only one full-time employee: herself, but she did employ a wide variety of part-time workers all categorized by their dependability and particular skill set. The community college kids had been a great resource for the kind of work she did, and as she grew, so did her Rolodex. And they did continue to grow. The town of Dreamer's Bay had truly embraced the business, and Elizabeth was beyond grateful.

In fact, in checking her phone after Hank's walk, she learned she already had three new requests for tasks that very day. Mrs. Belmont was under the weather and looking for help picking up her dry cleaning and ingredients for fresh tomato sauce. The Hubbard family wanted to hire either her or one of her vetted childcare workers to take the younger two Hubbards to the park for some exercise once school let out for the day, and that grumpy Mr. Ivers wanted McDonald's for lunch again, even though his doctor had told him countless times that his cholesterol was too high and salty foods should be avoided. She sighed and shook her head at that one. It wasn't her job to evaluate the requests of her clientele. Though, when she delivered the Big Mac and large fries, she would certainly have trouble holding her tongue entirely about his continued high sodium consumption. She happened to care about him, grumpy or not.

She did a quick calculation. She could easily handle those requests herself, as they were staggered, but as more requests came in, and they likely would, she'd call KC, her best friend and favorite outsourcer, to step in and handle a few. As the mother of a young child, KC appreciated the part-time work that got her out of the house but never overwhelmed her schedule. The fact that she brought Grayson, her two-year-old, along with her on tasks had turned out to be a bonus. Her clients loved little Gray, the company's new ambassador, which only added to KC's tips.

"Busy afternoon," Elizabeth said, as KC answered. "I'm pretty much full on my end, so can I put you on standby should we receive any more bookings?"

"Consider me standing by. We're currently eating Cheerios with banana and discussing the need for more cookies at breakfast and maybe why that's not a good idea. Done with Hank?"

"He's exercised and snoozing in a sunspot."

"That's my favorite dog."

"I'm in agreement with Gray, though, in case you're counting," Elizabeth said. "There can never be too many cookies, and the morning hours seem like a great time to sneak a few more in. He's seizing the opportunity and there's a lot to be admired there."

"No, no, no. Don't encourage his junk food fixation. He's obsessed with food as it is."

"While you two battle it out, I'm headed over to Jill Winters's place. She wants me to see if I can fix that stubborn hinge on her back door. Got my tool belt all ready to go." She sighed wistfully. "I wish Thalia could see me with it on." Thalia Perkins had been Elizabeth's crush ever since she'd moved to town and set up her own massage and facial spa just outside the square. Dark hair, gorgeous lips, and a body she had to fan herself over. While Elizabeth had made it clear in every way she could that she was every bit as gay as Thalia—in case she didn't pick up on that readily—she hadn't exactly had the courage to make a move. She'd never really been the forward type. Okay, that was a lie. She was actually lame as hell when it came to moves. She had no game and owned it.

"One day you're going to be over this whole Thalia thing and I'm going to fall to my knees in relief for both of us. That woman may be beautiful, but she's trouble, and I don't like the way she treats you, like you're some flavor of gum that she likes some of the time."

"I think it's the some of the time that keeps me on the Thalia hamster wheel."

"Exactly, which is why she needs to stop leading you on."

"Unless she's not, and one day we might live happily ever after." She was only half kidding.

A pause on the other end of the line. "So, you've seen Jill?"

"What do you mean seen her?" Elizabeth asked. "I've seen her a lot. Medium-length brown hair, brown eyes. Cheerful disposition. Hangs out with eight-year-olds a lot."

"I mean recently, weirdo."

"I passed her at the grocery store on Saturday when she asked me about the hinge job. Then a few days before that at Morning Glory." She really did love the breakfast specials there.

"Not at all today?" KC asked. "Because when I stopped in for coffee and a dozen jelly-filled, Lulu at Amazin' Glazin' said folks were looking for Jill because she didn't show up at the elementary school this morning." News, even the most mundane, always traveled at incredible speed in the Bay.

Elizabeth shifted her phone to the other ear as she walked, nearing her one-story house on Whippoorwill Way, the shady little cul-de-sac she called home. She frowned into the phone. That was weird. Jill was a fourth-grade teacher and incredibly reliable. Everyone knew that. It wasn't like her to not show up...for anything. "I haven't seen her *today*, no. I bet she just overslept. It happens to the best of us. But you know what? Just to be proactive, and because I'm a little worried, I'll head over to her place and see what I can find out. Maybe she'll answer the door, bleary eyed and embarrassed, and we can all exhale."

"I'm all for that."

"She'd do it for any one of us." Jill Winters, only slightly older than Elizabeth's thirty-two years and a couple grades ahead of her in high school, was someone she considered a friend, a bright spot in the community. Elizabeth sincerely hoped all was okay, yet she felt an uncomfortable gnawing in her midsection. Jill wasn't a wild child. This could be bad.

"So would you," KC said. "You're a good egg, Liz."

She shrugged. "Just doing what I can to help. With the divorce from Ed, Jill's on her own now. We all have to look out for each other, right?"

"She doesn't have any family nearby?" KC asked. "I'm trying to remember her story."

"Her mother died several years ago."

"Right, right. I remember."

Elizabeth pulled a leaf off a low-hanging branch as she walked. "And then of course there's her sister, Devyn."

"Who's dropped off the face of the planet. I don't even think she has an Instagram."

Elizabeth grinned ruefully. "She's probably too cool for social media, KC. I mean, c'mon."

KC laughed. "My bad. Can't expect the sought after to mix with the commoners in a public space."

"Can you imagine?"

Devyn Winters had been their classmate back in the day, but Elizabeth hadn't seen her at all since. Last she heard, Devyn was some kind of hotshot real estate broker in Philadelphia and hadn't looked back. She'd swooped into town for their mother's funeral four years prior and swooped back out again without much in the way of a hello to anyone other than her circle, which included Jill and likely Devyn's fellow cheerleaders, who unfortunately still lived in town, clinging to their glory days and too much Botox. Apparently, the two went hand in hand. She hadn't seen a frown line on Cricket Johansson's face since the eighth grade, and it frightened her.

"Well, let me know if there's anything I can do to help. Dan is on call at the hospital, but Gray says he's game for On the Spot gigs as long as there is music in the car," KC said over Gray's singsongy voice in the background. He'd been on a Justin Timberlake kick recently, soaking up whatever he could from the radio. KC was going to have to keep an eye on that one and his burgeoning two-year dance moves.

"I will, and stand by for the afternoon rush. Dreamer's Bay is just waking up and I have a feeling there's a lot these people need."

"We already have our sneakers on," KC said. "Hit us up and we'll be on our way. I wouldn't mind if someone needed a liquor delivery. We're low on fun juice and I haven't danced in a while."

"Any liquor requests are prioritized for you. Don't forget to check their IDs. And don't drink with them while on the job. Get your groove going later."

KC sighed. "Fine, Killer of Joy."

"That's me. Always. Owning it. Purchasing stock."

She didn't say goodbye as she clicked off the call. She didn't have to with KC. They had an impressive shorthand that went all the way back to kindergarten, when KC Makowski—now KC Collette—and her family first put down roots in Dreamer's Bay. Elizabeth had been born there. She liked to tell herself that the place was in her blood for that reason. While it was true that not too many people had heard of their town, they'd snagged a decent enough tourist uptick after *American Leisure* listed them as one of the small towns you should visit before you die. The handful of bed-and-breakfasts couldn't accommodate the influx, and several more had sprung up to sustain the visitors, who still came in clusters during the warm weather months for time on the beach. The Bay had a group of pretty darn good restaurants, a couple of supermarkets—one big, one small—a movie theater with three screens, and a recently renovated bowling alley where Elizabeth participated in the Tuesday-night league in the winter months. Go Ball Busters! The stretch of water along the coast and the quaint little boardwalk were their claim to fame, however. You could buy ice cream and watch the tide come in.

With concerns about Jill still on her mind, Elizabeth let herself into her modest but, in her opinion, very charming home on Whippoorwill Way. She was the third house on the bend of the cul-de-sac and knew each of her neighbors quite well. What she loved most about her home was that it felt entirely hers. She'd decorated in a decidedly rustic Southern motif, embracing sunflowers and overturned tin pails and faded wooden signs that hung on the beige walls. She'd used a variety of lavender accents because, well, she adored lavender and all its purple relatives. She smiled at the pair of wooden ducks on her mantel and nodded as she passed. In her refrigerator, she found the fresh-squeezed orange juice she'd made just the night before and poured herself a luxurious glass, which really did hit the spot after her long walk with Hank.

She checked her appearance in the mirror and found that her longer-than-she-was-used-to brown hair sported even more natural highlights than it had just a few weeks prior when the sun had been less present. Now she could spot hints of blond, red, and light chestnut mixed in with the everyday brown, culminating in a hodgepodge of color. She'd been told the natural highlights brought out the green in her eyes. Whether that was true or not, she embraced the compliment, enjoying her hair's jumble of shades. What else could she do? Elizabeth had never considered herself a beauty, but she was attractive enough and, for the most part, comfortable in her own skin. Of course, she secretly wished Thalia Perkins noticed her more, but then she couldn't have everything she wanted in life. She ran her fingers through her hair, giving it an informal fluff. Good enough, she thought, and set out in her car for McDonald's and Mr. Iver's overly salted lunch, just as a new flood of requests hit the app on her phone. She checked her watch and did a quick calculation on time. Her phone buzzed again with a request for a grocery delivery. And another for a ride home from the auto shop. It was going to be a busy day for On the Spot, and Elizabeth was up for it. But first, a stop at Jill Winters's place. She wasn't religious but rattled off a quick yet sincere prayer that all would be okay. This was Dreamer's Bay. It had to be, didn't it?

❖

By 8 p.m., Ricky was glancing furtively at his watch, probably wondering how much longer they were going to go. Devyn ignored him and focused her attention on Wyatt Lowe, the shrewd developer at the helm of Twenty-Four Walker Place, an art deco tower going up in Streeterville on the north side of Philadelphia. The sixty-seven-story high-rise was one of the most expensive construction projects in the city's history, and any broker worth their salt was angling for a piece of the pie. Devyn wanted the whole damn thing. First, she had to convince Wyatt, who was known for his perfectly coiffed dark hair, high-end wardrobe that bordered on perfection, and risk-taking business sense. He'd raked in millions like Monopoly money and had a lot to show for his forty-five years on the planet.

Wyatt studied Devyn over his bourbon neat. "We're thinking twenty-two hundred a square foot."

Devyn wanted to spit her drink across the table. Instead she swallowed carefully, then regarded him. "That's insane."

"That's not what your competition is saying. In fact, Tom Morelli thinks it's doable."

Devyn leaned forward. "Morelli will tell you whatever he has to in order to snag the listing. If you listen to him, you'll be shooting yourself in the foot."

Wyatt glanced at the ceiling, then took a drink.

"I'm a straight shooter, Wyatt, and you know it. Two thousand a square foot, and I'll sell the thing out with my team."

"Can't do it," Wyatt said. Ricky looked on as if engrossed in a complicated tennis match. "Twenty-one."

She hesitated, took a hit of her drink, and placed the glass on the table. "Fine. Twenty-one hundred a foot."

He raised an eyebrow. "In three months."

"Nope." She shook her head. "The building is still under construction and won't show the way it needs to. People can't fill in the blanks. All they see are hard hats and unfinished kitchens."

"What do you need from me to make it happen?" Wyatt asked.

"A high-end showroom at the very least, a model, technology, or get me more time."

"No showroom. Do you know how much that will cost?"

"Do you know how much you're asking me to accomplish in a short time period? People need to see what they're laying down money for in order to cough it up. You're investing over two hundred million dollars in this building. Surely you can take one final step to be sure you get a high return on your investment." She stared at him good and hard. "Come on. Let's set a Philly record with this one."

His eyes lit up at the prospect, and he ran a finger around the rim of his glass as if weighing his many millionaire options. Ricky, who sat to her right clutching his Blue Moon like a handful of pearls, held his breath in anticipation.

Devyn stared at Wyatt, and Wyatt stared back. She waited.

"Fine," he said, once it felt like all of the air had been sucked from the room. "We'll get you your showroom and you sell the building out in *four* months at twenty-one hundred a square foot or I'm pulling the listing." That would kill not only her ego but her reputation among other developers. She couldn't fail. She wouldn't.

Devyn sat back in her chair with a satisfied smile, riding the kind of high only an opportunity like this one could inspire. It felt like sitting at the top of the roller coaster, waiting in anticipation for that rush that would blow your hair back and release the endorphins, only to have it hit so much harder than you had even anticipated. So fucking satisfying. "You're on."

And that was that.

"You're amazing. I can't even believe that happened," Ricky said, running a hand through his red hair as the two of them waited on the curb for her car service. He was practically leaping out of his skin next to her. "That high-rise is ridiculous. I've never seen anything like it."

"It's definitely a head turner," Devyn said, more conservatively.

"They have a movie theater for the tenants. And an amazing gym that is certainly better than the one I pay for monthly."

Devyn grinned. "Yeah, well, there's more where this one came from. When I sell out this one, there'll be another waiting." She passed him a glance. "You think you're up for it? The McMahon listing is going to take a lot of finesse, especially if you're used to smaller, more intimate listings. These guys want a lot of high-profile marketing and a lot of attention. Phone calls at three a.m. if they feel like it."

"I understand and I'm up for it. Yes." A pause as he gathered his gusto. "I mean hell, yes."

She clapped him on the arm, just as the car arrived at the curb. "That's the spirit."

"Beyond just McMahon, though, how do I get that first listing with a developer like Wyatt? Someone huge," he asked as they rode back to his car, the lights of downtown Philly glimmering.

Devyn whistled low. "That's on you. You gotta be ready to scrap. Make a hundred calls. Arrange a few hard-to-get meetings, and follow rule number one: schmooze your ass off."

"Schmooze my ass off. Got it. Do you think that if you had pushed, that you could have gotten another month? I mean—"

Devyn held up one finger and gestured to her phone. Oddly enough, the incoming call came from the area code she grew up with in South Carolina, but it wasn't a number her phone recognized. She clicked onto the call anyway.

"This is Devyn."

"Hello, am I speaking with Devyn Winters?" a female voice asked.

"Yes." She rubbed the back of her neck, which ached from the long day. "What can I do for you?"

"This is Marlene DuBois. I don't know if you remember me, but I'm the assistant principal at Bay Elementary. We met at your mother's funeral."

Devyn blinked several times, trying to keep up. Her sister, Jill, was a fourth-grade teacher at Bay Elementary in the their hometown. What the hell? She sat up a little straighter, her attention crisp and focused. "Yes. How are you, Marlene? Is everything okay?"

"We're hoping so, but I'm cautiously concerned." A pause, while Devyn's heart hammered away. Her sister was her best friend and pretty much the only family she had.

"Jill didn't come into work today, and didn't call in either. It's unlike her."

Oh, God. She blinked and tried to make her brain work. "No. Um, I completely agree. Jill wouldn't do that." She checked her watch. It was getting close to nine at night. Why were they just now calling her? What if Jill needed her? What if she'd been taken? There was a depth of stillness present in the car. They were stopped at a traffic light. The world had slowed down around her, yet her mind raced out of control, bolstered by adrenaline.

"We sent an officer to her home for a wellness check, but we weren't able to locate her there either. Her car is gone, however."

"Doesn't matter. Something's wrong," Devyn said automatically. Her voice didn't sound like her own, strangled and desperate. "Trust me on this. Tell the police she wouldn't just take off and not show up for school." She felt Ricky's eyes on her and noted that the car was still stopped at the traffic light. She fought the urge to exit the vehicle, knowing that there would still be nothing she could do from the side of the road. Yet that nonsensical pull to do something, *anything* overrode all other instincts. She couldn't stand being this far away.

"We think so, too, and since she has you listed as her emergency contact, I thought it might be time to give you a call."

"I appreciate that." Devyn's take-charge side emerged. She willed it forward, along with a command to speak slowly, directly. "What do we need to do?"

"We're making some calls, and some friends of hers have started a search," Marlene explained. "Is there anyone else in the family she might have gone to visit?"

That was the thing. There was no family. Just the two of them since they'd lost their mother to a short bout with cancer four and a half years back. "No. There's just me, and I'm in Philadelphia, but I'll hop on a plane as soon as possible. Tonight." After Jill's divorce from that idiot Ed, she was all Jill had, and vice versa. If something had happened to her sister, she was damn sure going to show up.

Her mind flooded with all the things she had on her schedule that week. Of all the times for something like this to happen, this was definitely one of the least opportune. She pinched the bridge of her nose as the details swirled in a jumble. She'd make this work with help from her assistants and then make sure Jill was okay. She just had to be. There was no other option.

"Let me give you my cell number so we can keep in touch," Marlene said. "Elizabeth Draper, who's a friend of Jill's, is actually the one who suggested I go ahead and give you a call. She's been a great help." The name rang a bell, but Devyn's brain wasn't functioning properly. All she wanted was to hear Jill was found, safe and sound.

"Great. Thank you so much for calling, and let me know of any updates. I'll keep my phone on."

"Of course."

They said goodbye and she clicked off the call, then pressed the phone to her chin as she mentally rearranged what she thought the next twenty-four hours of her life would look like. That was hard to do in the midst of swelling fear. She placed a hand on her chest as if that would somehow assuage the exponential worry. *Focus.* She would need to distribute appointments among her staff and reschedule the ones she'd need to be there for in person. Karen could help with those. Then there was her personal assistant outside the office, Sheldon, who would keep things in her condo and personal life afloat. This was really going to decelerate her momentum on a variety of projects, but that took a strong second place to her need to fix this, to find her sister and make the world turn again. God. This was Jilly she was talking about. The girl who'd given Devyn the good chocolate chip cookies and kept the burnt ones for herself and who'd attended every football game, a sport she loathed, just to watch Devyn cheer with the rest of the squad. Jill was only two years older, but her maternal side exaggerated their age difference to the point that Devyn really had looked to her as a second parent, next to their single mother, in many ways.

"Everything all right?" Ricky asked, after a long stretch of silence.

She shook her head. "No, it's not. I think my sister needs me right now. I'm headed home to South Carolina."

"I'm sorry to hear that. I hope she's okay." And then, "What part?"

"Tiny little place called Dreamer's Bay. Right there on the water."

He squinted at her and tilted his head. "Can't say I've heard of it."

She nodded. "Most people haven't."

CHAPTER TWO

Devyn blinked as she stood in line for her rental car at the Charleston airport. Holding a subpar cup of airport coffee that tasted a lot more like burnt popcorn, she stared out the large windows that showed her it was not yet daylight in South Carolina. She didn't understand why time moved so slowly, why the attendant did. She tapped her foot. Adjusted her bag. Looked at her watch. All of it a helpless little dance to keep her from coming out of her skin. In a little over two hours, she'd arrive in Dreamer's Bay for the first time in just over four years. In addition to the panic she waded through regarding her sister, the idea of being back home had her nervous and uncomfortable. Nothing but Jill could have brought her back. It wasn't an awful town, quaint enough and easy to navigate, but she didn't have too many fond memories, having hidden who she was the entire time she'd lived in the Bay. Worst of all now, the person she associated most with the town, her mother, wouldn't be there. It made her resent the place even more.

"We're out of luxury cars," the gum-chewing rental agent told her as she tick-tacked away on her keyboard, glancing at her phone between hitting the Enter key.

"Midsize is fine."

"No go." More tick-tacking and phone checking.

Devyn sighed. "Compact, economy, whatever you have. Something with wheels would be fine. I'm in a hurry."

"I have a Chevy Spark."

"Sold."

It turned out that the Chevy Spark was the smallest car Devyn had ever laid eyes on, and getting her Louis Vuitton suitcase into its microscopic back seat—forget about trunk space—was an ordeal requiring two hands and a well-placed foot. She gave the thing a last kick for good measure, blew the wayward strand of blond hair from her eyes, and swore. Why were little things getting in the way right now? She glanced at her phone for the million and ninth time for any message from Jill, willing one to be there. Nothing. She'd left countless voicemails for her and sent just as many texts. She blinked back her tears and slid into the driver's seat for the short journey to her hometown. The drive left her alone with her thoughts, and that meant a million terrifying images. Jill bruised, battered, or tied up in the back of some guy's car, hoping someone would find her. She punched the steering wheel in frustration and blared the radio to drown out her cruel brain.

With traffic nonexistent on the highway that early, she and her Spark made it just in time to see the sunrise over the water as she drove along the coast into Dreamer's Bay. If her heart hadn't ached, she might have been able to enjoy it. She pulled in a steadying breath as the familiar sights sprang into view, inspiring a nostalgic pang laced with dread. She took in the two-pump gas station on the outskirts of town where Mr. Henry could be seen doing his morning sweep with the newspaper rolled up in the back pocket of his baggy pants. She passed the rust-colored library, still wondering why they chose that shade but happy to see someone had purchased the building and marquee. According to the scrolling message, there would be a children's book fair that week. Farther down Center Street, the main drag, she came to the heart of the town. The Circle, as they called the town's roundabout, was outlined by a variety of businesses including an Arby's and a McDonald's that must have moved in since she'd last been home. Even Dreamer's Bay was susceptible to big business invasion. The center of the Circle was made up of benches surrounded by large potted plants, offering a nice spot for folks to take their lunch hour and greet their friends and neighbors. She stared at the very bench where she remembered sitting with her mother, who had purchased both her and Jill a warm chocolate croissant. They'd eaten them there together, the three of them. Devyn felt the sharp rising of sadness almost immediately, like a chemical reaction. She gave her head a shake and pushed past it, sliding a strand of hair behind her ear—her own special game-time gesture. It always bolstered her confidence. This time it didn't work. The town made her think acutely of her mother, who she missed desperately, but also of her youth, when she'd played the part of someone she barely recognized now. Both pulled at her chest, as if opening a long-put-to-bed wound. None of it was relevant. It didn't matter whether she wanted to be in this town or not, she was here for Jill and should stay tuned into her.

She'd be back home in Philly and living her life in no time, once she knew her sister was okay. And she would be. Devyn hated that she was even considering the alternative. Yet how could she not? Bile rose in the back of her throat as she banished another series of graphic images from her mind.

She arrived at the nondescript one-story brown police station and opened her mouth to speak to the young woman seated behind the first desk she came to. The woman beat her to it.

"Devyn Winters?" The small station looked empty behind her. Where were all of the people who were supposed to fight crime? The grim realization that she was in a tiny town with very few resources settled uncomfortably.

"Yes. I'm Devyn Winters, and I'm here about my sister."

"Right this way."

She followed the short brunette, dressed in business attire rather than a uniform, down the hallway to a large conference room with a long table in the center. The smell of stale coffee hit her hard. Someone around here liked it strong. She scanned the faces of the small group gathered. She knew most of them.

"Ms. Winters, I'm—"

"Officer Bertaw." She remembered him from those high school safety presentations in the gym. He'd arrived each year with stickers, bookmarks, and stern reminders about the dangers of drinking and driving. She'd mostly daydreamed.

He smiled conservatively. "*Detective* Bertaw these day."

"Congratulations," she said, as sincerely as possible, given the occasion. Honestly, who the hell cared about his promotion right now? "Do we know anything more?" She glanced around the room. The redheaded woman with the bun and brightly colored skirt was likely the vice principal she'd spoken with. She nodded a hello. Next to her sat that Elizabeth Somebody from high school. No clue why she'd be there. Small towns were weird. Hadn't Elizabeth been in charge of the high school food drive? And why was her mind supplying unnecessary details in this moment? She blinked and focused.

Detective Bertaw gestured to a dry erase board. "We know Jill went to karaoke in Halper's Glen last night. Mike's Sports Bar does a thing every Tuesday evening. What we don't know is if she made it back. We do know she's not home at this point and did not report for work yesterday or today."

Devyn closed her eyes momentarily at the rudimentary information. "And that she's not answering texts or calls, which is nothing like my sister. That means something has happened to her. Trust me. Someone has her or she's hurt somewhere." She gestured to the space around her. "So, can we get out there and find her? Now?" Her throat tightened with anguish.

"We have patrol on it."

"Pardon me." She held up a pleading hand to Bertaw. "I say this with nothing but respect, but in the city limits, doesn't that amount to approximately two people and one patrol car?" She glanced around for some kind of lifeline. Someone she could shake and make them understand. They all just blinked back at her, making her feel both powerless and determined to change that. She knocked on the table to wake everyone the hell up. "Let's make some phone calls. Call in some police friends. I'll pay for whatever you need. Money is not a problem."

"It doesn't exactly work that way," Bertaw explained. He was losing his hair. On top and in the front. Little brown wisps clung as if using one another for comfort. Another unnecessary detail her stupid brain thought mattered. Now she wanted to shake *herself*. Her neck ached, her mouth was dry, and she felt shaky all over. She hadn't had anything to eat or drink since the call came in about Jill, not that she could have. Her stomach roiled.

The redheaded woman met her gaze. "I talked with the two women who went with Jill to karaoke night. They're both teachers at the elementary school. I'm Marlene Dubois," she said, her hand to her chest. "We spoke on the phone."

Devyn nodded, waiting for her to continue.

"They said Jill took her own car and left the sports bar before they did, somewhere just after ten p.m. They recalled her being happy but a little tired."

"That's because she doesn't stay out late. She's a homebody," Devyn supplied, and looked to Bertaw to be sure he'd heard.

"I don't mean to interrupt." Elizabeth stood and came around the table. She had big green eyes that, in this moment, carried warmth.

Devyn latched onto her, because she needed that warmth.

"I've made some calls around town, and folks are meeting in the Circle in half an hour. We're going to fan out and see if we can't help aid the search."

"I appreciate that," Devyn said. Those food-drive organizational skills were working in Devyn's favor today, and she was grateful for Elizabeth, someone who was *doing* something. "How can I help?" she asked the room. "I have a key to the house. Jill and I share ownership."

"Great." Bertaw said. "We did a wellness check, and nothing seemed overturned or disheveled. No sign of any kind of struggle, but you might see something substantial that we wouldn't know to look for."

Devyn felt a surge of purpose. The idea of proactivity quelled the dread that crawled all over everything like the vines of an untended garden. "I'll head over there."

Elizabeth turned to her. "How about I pick you up at the house in an hour, after the volunteers have been organized? We can drive some of the back roads, see if we spot any sign of her car."

Devyn's hands shook as the reality of the situation came into focus. They were assembling *volunteers*. This was really bad. If she wound up alone in this world, what was she going to do? Jill had always been there for her. She felt more than saw ten-year-old Jill's hand brushing the hair from her eyes that time she skinned her knee while roller-skating in the driveway. How had Jill only been ten then? She'd seemed old and wise to Devyn at the time. "Yes. I'll be ready."

"See you soon." As she passed, Elizabeth gave Devyn's wrist a supportive squeeze. She wasn't naturally a tactile person and her instinct would normally have been to bristle against a stranger's touch. She didn't. She needed reassurance in that bleak moment and drew strength from it, in fact, fleeting as it was. Devyn would take back every dismissive thought she'd ever had about Elizabeth in high school if she and her volunteer squad could make all of this stop. She fought the urge to fall to her knees and beg for that. She was already bartering with a God she hadn't spoken to since adolescence, desperate to trade what she had, promising to be a better person. Anything.

On the drive to Jill's, her mind shifted to how in the hell they'd gotten here. Twenty-four hours ago, she was in a startlingly different reality, going about her fast-paced morning, landing a big deal, and heading home for the night. How could someone be so content in one moment, celebrating a career victory, and so terrified the next with just the push of a button on a cell phone? Everything felt raw and ruined, and it just might stay that way forever. All Devyn wanted was to fast-forward to a moment when it would all be okay again.

Her breath caught when she pulled into the lazy S-shaped driveway that led to the well-cared-for one-story home she'd grown up in. Yep. Right there was the spot in the grass where she'd accidentally started a fire with a magnifying glass when she was eight. She'd been feeling bold and scientific that day after watching Bill Nye do something similar on TV. Her mother, instead of chastising her, had agreed that learning about science could be fun, just maybe not the kind that involved actual flames. Jill had laughed but eventually consoled her with a piece broken off her candy bar. The once burned patch of grass now grew green and vibrant again, the incident just a sepia-tinted blip in Devyn's memory. She blinked through her windshield up at the house. Pretty blue shutters now adorned the window. The color reminded her of Jill. In fact, all of the new little touches were straight out of Jill's stylebook. A cheerful gnome with a gray beard on the front step. An arrangement of potted plants with spring flowers already blooming in a cascade of colors. The pair of wooden rocking chairs on the porch. All new. All Jill.

Her hands were a jumble as she attempted to put the key in the door, shaking and causing her to miss the keyhole. She closed her eyes and bit the inside of her lip as she pressed her forehead against the wooden door, gathering her sense of purpose once more. She had a job to do here, a goal, and that meant shoving her own emotions to the side and drawing on the finely honed set of skills that she used in her everyday life. Calm, collected, and in charge. That seemed to work. She exhaled and let herself into the house. Jolted back fifteen years, she could still see the younger version of herself and Jill streaking through the entryway into the living room after school, waiting at the kitchen table with their afterschool snack—prepared by Jill—for their mother to get home from the insurance firm at which she'd been the office manager. Burying her face in her mother's shoulder, Devyn would inhale her scent when she arrived home, Oil of Olay moisturizer and a little bit of peppermint from the sugarfree gum she often chewed. Devyn could smell the wonderful combination now just by closing her eyes.

She picked up one of the many knickknacks that now decorated most every surface, a mixture of new and old, and smiled at Jill's homey approach. Devyn, on the other hand, had fallen far from the tree with her own decorating style: open floor plans, hard lines and planes, and clean surfaces. A lump made its way to her throat as she thought about her sister and how much like their mother she'd turned out to be. A surge of love hit. She didn't get sentimental about much, but her sister was different.

Shifting back to project mode, she shook free of the all-consuming sentimentality and moved about the space, which consisted of a living room, breakfast nook, dining room, and two bedrooms down one small hallway, separated by a bathroom. The master suite was located directly off the living room.

First impression: Jill kept the place neat and well organized. There was a calendar on her refrigerator with the Tuesday she'd gone missing marked with only a *K*, which she imagined stood for *karaoke*. In her bathroom, her medicine organizer still held Wednesday's thyroid medication, which meant Jill hadn't been there Wednesday morning to take it. Devyn's stomach dropped and her palms went clammy. She flexed them uncomfortably. Jill's bed was neatly made. Her car was gone. Her school bag was discarded next to the door, along with a pair of heels she'd likely stepped out of the second she'd arrived home from work. She pictured it happening.

At a loss, Devyn curled up on Jill's bed, running her hand across the blue and white quilt she used as a bedspread. There was a photo of the two of them, from the weekend Jill had stayed with her in Philadelphia, framed on Jill's nightstand. Jill smiled at the camera while Devyn smiled at Jill as they stood in front of the Rocky statue, arm in arm. "Where are you?" she mumbled, and touched Jill's face in the photo.

Tears rolled sideways from her face to the quilt. She didn't try to stop them.

No, Jill hadn't made it home Tuesday night. As she cried on her sister's bed, letting the sobs overtake her, Devyn had never felt more alone. The edges of hope began to fade until she had nothing left.

CHAPTER THREE

"Tony, take your group to the northern corner of the map and check out the park."

Elizabeth peered over his shoulder as he circled the area on his map.

He chewed his lollipop stick and nodded. "Got it."

"We have no idea what she might have done that night," Elizabeth pointed out. "Maybe she took a walk in the park."

"What about me?" Charlie asked, clearly eager to get started. He rubbed his forehead as he spoke, as if comforting himself. He then gestured to the men with him. "I got my guys from the store here and we'd like to help. What do you need?"

Charlie owned the liquor store in town, and that meant he knew lots of folks. Okay, make that everyone, and that was an asset to their cause. "Maybe talk to the local business owners in the Circle. See if anyone saw Jill in town Tuesday night after ten, even driving through."

"Yes, ma'am," Charlie said, and placed a backward cap on his head as if newly energized.

Elizabeth met with each and every group in the park, offering a different colored area on the map for them to check out. She moved quickly, spoke in simple terms, and with a grateful smile, headed to the next group. She was on a roll. Yes, this was a job generally handled by someone in an authority position, or at least someone with experience when it came to missing people, but in the absence of either of those resources in the present moment, Elizabeth felt called to act. That had always been her. She was someone who took the initiative when it needed taking and dove into even the most difficult of tasks headfirst, sometimes without knowing what the hell she was doing. She'd figure it out as she went, which was a lot like the position she found herself in now.

With Jill Winters missing for a second day and the police department woefully understaffed, she'd rattled off a quick message on the town's Facebook page, put On the Spot jobs on hold, and met over a hundred helpful folks ready to see what they could find out about Jill and where she might be. Her heart swelled at the outpouring of support. They might not have been the most professional of search teams, but they were present and willing, and it was so much more productive than just waiting around for Bertaw & Co. to eventually get around to calling in the cavalry.

"Great. You're all set," she said to the final group. "You all have my cell phone and a direct line to the detective working the case should you come upon anything helpful. Don't hesitate to reach out."

An abundance of overlapping answers floated back.

"Thanks, Lizzie."

"Will do. Don't you worry."

"If anyone can find Jill, it's us."

"Thanks for organizing, Liz."

As the groups headed off in their respective directions, Elizabeth hopped into Shug, her blue Ford F-150, and headed to Jill's house to retrieve Devyn, who she had to say was the same, yet different than the last time she'd seen her some years back. She now carried herself with a certain level of authority that made people pay attention. She was also just as beautiful as Elizabeth remembered, probably more so. Blond hair just past her shoulders. Hazel eyes, but not the soft kind. No, Devyn's were more piercing in their beauty, which only added to the melancholy all over her face earlier today. Elizabeth hoped they could change that soon. She'd always been an optimistic person, and she was clinging to that tendency now, willing it to prove beneficial. Yet it was hard. Jill was out there, and time felt like it wasn't on their side. She pushed past the sudden nausea and rang the bell to Jill's house. Devyn answered promptly.

"Hi. Are you ready?" Devyn asked, and stepped from the house onto the front porch.

The whites of her eyes were red, the lids swollen, and her hair didn't fall into place the way it had earlier. She'd been crying, hard. Her skin was pale. Elizabeth felt nauseated again.

"All set. I thought we'd take the most common route to Halper's Glen and see about any possible turnoffs or detours."

"Okay. Let's do it." Devyn followed her to the truck, pausing briefly as she looked at it.

"What?" Elizabeth asked.

"Just didn't peg you for a truck person."

Elizabeth quirked her head. "Didn't know you pegged me at all."

They hopped in and rode in silence. Elizabeth stole an occasional glance at Devyn to be sure she was all right. She felt strangely protective of her, given the situation and her role in leading the volunteer search. In many ways, it seemed like it fell to her to shield Devyn from some of the fear that must have been eating away at her. When she saw tears roll down Devyn's cheeks in the silence of the truck, she handed her the package of pocket tissues she kept in the center console. Devyn accepted them, yet said nothing.

"Do you have enough air?" Elizabeth finally asked. "If not, I can—" She reached forward toward the controls, but Devyn waved her off.

"I'm fine."

"Would you like some water? I have a case in the back seat."

"No, thank you."

"Or maybe—"

"Elizabeth. I'm fine. Really." A pause. "What's your last name again?"

"Draper," she said, placing a hand on her chest. They came from a graduating class of under a hundred and had been in school together for over a decade. How was it that Devyn didn't even know her last name? Ouch. Was she really that inconsequential? Not the time for it, she reminded herself.

They drove on, stopping on each side street, exploring each turn in the road with hopeful curiosity, pointing out possible glimpses of white, the color of Jill's Mazda. Each time, the glimpses proved disappointing, dropping the women's morale more and more as the drive went on. The forty-minute drive had stretched to two hours by the time they reached Mike's. The freestanding building, painted green with bright yellow lettering, was closed, and not set to open again until the evening. But there was a car in front, and that meant someone was gearing up for tonight's crowd. When Elizabeth killed the ignition, Devyn didn't hesitate. She walked like a woman on a desperate mission, leaving Elizabeth to walk double-time in order to catch up.

"Hey there, wait a minute."

Devyn glanced behind her. The wind lifted her blond hair and blew it across her face in a messy jumble. It was like the weather had shifted to mimic the chaos of the day, scattered and haphazard. Devyn didn't seem to care or notice. "Sorry." She paused for Elizabeth to catch up while blinking impatiently.

Elizabeth met her gaze. "Do you know what you want to ask?"

"I want every detail they have and then more details, and I plan to get them. If they have camera footage, I want that, too. I can't believe the police wouldn't already have it, but with Podunk Bertaw at the helm, who knows?"

Elizabeth nodded, impressed with the new determination behind Devyn's eyes. She stood next to her as Devyn banged loudly on the door to the bar. "Excuse me. Can you open up for a moment?" She exchanged a glance with Elizabeth just as an older guy with a gut appeared wearing a stained white apron. Mike. Elizabeth had seen him before on one of her own trips out to the bar. It was a popular place, and a great spot to hit up when the same old Dreamer's Bay locales felt monotonous.

"Yep. What can I help you with?" Mike asked. His big, bushy eyebrows cast a shadow on his face.

Devyn leapt right in. "I'm looking for my sister. She was here two nights ago. On Tuesday." She flashed a photo on her phone and handed it to him.

He nodded, chewing the inside of his cheek. "Already talked to the cops. Sorry about your sister, but I can't say I remember her. We're packed when there's karaoke." He moved to close the door, but Devyn stepped forward.

"Well, we know she was here for sure, because she came with friends." Devyn paused and offered him a smile, which seemed to slow everything down. It was highly effective, making it clear to Elizabeth that Devyn knew how to handle people and turn it on when it benefited her. "Would you mind taking another look?" she asked softly. Mike fell for it. Who wouldn't?

He studied the phone. "I don't know her, but she comes in a lot. Sometimes with other women. They sit together and drink wine, a group of them." The other teachers. Elizabeth nodded. "And sometimes she comes with a guy."

"A guy?" Devyn's ears seemed to prick and Elizabeth passed her a look.

"What did he look like?"

Elizabeth didn't hear the answer because her phone was ringing.

With volunteers out in the field, she couldn't ignore the call. She clicked the Accept button and covered one ear in order to hear better. As the news was relayed to her from the very last team she'd sent out, she closed her eyes. Harris, who worked at the mail supply store, was speaking a mile a minute, and though Elizabeth struggled to understand each detail, she absorbed enough to understand what they'd found. No, no, no. She looked to Devyn and attempted to figure out the right words. Her heart sank and her limbs felt like tree trunks.

"What is it?" Devyn asked, noticing her expression. She abandoned her conversation with Mike and moved to Elizabeth, who could only stare at her. "Why aren't you saying anything? Say something," Devyn said, squeaking out the words. Her arms wrapped around her body. She was clutching herself, as if braced for a blow.

Elizabeth took a breath. "They found her car about fifty yards from the road, under a branch. That's why we missed her. She'd hit a tree. Hard. They say it looks pretty bad."

Devyn took Elizabeth by the shoulders and squeezed, her eyes going wide. She was hanging on by a delicate thread that was likely to snap. "Is she going to be okay, though?" The voice no longer sounded like hers. "What did they say?"

Elizabeth placed her hands on her own shoulders, on top of Devyn's. Anything to let her know that she wasn't alone. Devyn's eyes searched Elizabeth's for answers, and in that moment, she would have given anything to tell Devyn what she wanted, what she *needed* to hear.

Unfortunately, those weren't words Elizabeth could deliver.

CHAPTER FOUR

They didn't know much. The volunteer who'd found the car couldn't get inside. But Jill was in there, either gone or clinging to life. Two days without food or water, and exposed to the elements. God.

As they sped to the scene, just three and a half miles outside of Halper's Glen, Devyn braced herself for the worst but in the same breath refused to accept it as a possibility. If Jill was dead, if she had been the past two days, Devyn would have felt it. Wouldn't she? She stared at Elizabeth's profile and wondered if this woman, who'd been so unnecessarily kind, would be the last image she'd see before her world turned upside down. She memorized the profile so she could hold on to it, remember it forever. Elizabeth was beautiful, more so than she'd realized. Somehow, if she could anchor herself in that beauty, then surely the worst wouldn't happen to her. It couldn't. She released the image and allowed her shoulders to fold onto her chest as she cried, clenching her fists in worried anguish.

Elizabeth pulled the truck alongside the two other civilian vehicles. Two men and a woman stood nearby with a white dog, who whined quietly off to the side. They must have been the volunteers, but no one Devyn recognized. The trio who'd found the car nodded to them. Devyn blinked back, fear holding her hostage. Farther down she saw the emergency lights flashing. Two police cars and a fire truck. She walked toward them automatically, but Elizabeth caught her by the arm.

"We need to wait here," she said quietly in Devyn's ear.

"No. Let go. I need to go to her."

"Not yet," Elizabeth said, holding on as Devyn pulled against her.

Then Devyn understood. Elizabeth didn't want her to see Jill's body, to have that image forever burned into her memory.

"You need to let them work. Can you do that?"

Devyn stopped resisting as the reality of it all hit her like a freight train. She moved right past terror to hysteria, shoving her fingers into her hair. She whined or hummed quietly, not a sound she had any control over. These were crucial moments, and she had a sinking feeling that her life was about to be changed forever. She looked helplessly at Elizabeth for a lifeline, but the darkness in her expression communicated so much, none of it good.

Behind her there was the wail of a siren approaching. She turned in time to see the ambulance pull off the road. The sob she heard tear through the early evening air was one she recognized as her own. She felt for the hood of the car and found it, using it to keep herself steady. She was shivering but felt the warmth of Elizabeth's arms around her and sank back, letting them hold her more fully. If they'd run the siren, there was still hope. They didn't run the siren if it was too late. With Elizabeth's arms still offering support, she watched as the EMTs exited the back of the ambulance in a hurry and raced past them to the scene she could only glimpse through the trees. In a *hurry*, she reiterated to herself. Devyn squinted through the wash of tears. Her heart jackhammered. The wind rustled. How could it rustle so normally in a moment that was anything but? Who'd allowed that?

"Hold steady. Maybe that's a good sign," Elizabeth said quietly in her ear. She didn't want to get Devyn's hopes up. She'd used the word *maybe* to shield her. Devyn wanted to run down the short hill to the car and see for herself, yet she was too afraid of what she'd find, what she'd see. Instead, she carefully reminded herself to breathe, focusing all of her attention on doing just that until shouting erupted from the scene. There were several voices, and each one muffled the other. What were they shouting about, damn it? She craned her neck and Elizabeth released her. Her skin prickled uncomfortably and time seemed to have stopped moving forward.

"She's alive!" a male voice shouted up to them.

Devyn dropped to the ground and was left sitting there in a pile of moss. She held her head in her hands and cried tears of relief and gratitude. She held her eyes closed and thanked any and all higher powers. Jill was all she had left, and she was still with them. She'd worry about the rest later. For now, her world didn't have to end, and that felt like everything. When she opened her eyes, she was face-to-face with the white dog she'd seen earlier, who promptly dragged its tongue across her cheek. She was too numb to react. When the dog continued to lick her, someone pulled it away.

"Yours?" she heard a voice ask.

"Nah. Was alongside the road when we stopped. She's the reason we did. That dog was some sort of beacon. Led us straight down to the car."

She made note of the words but couldn't quite make sense of them in this moment.

"Hey." Devyn blinked at the quiet voice as someone raised her chin. It was Elizabeth and her soft green eyes offering her a reassuring smile. "We found her," she said quietly, and wiped away Devyn's tears. "We have her."

Devyn nodded and squeezed Elizabeth's hands. She tried to speak, but her voice wasn't there. She swallowed in an attempt to find words. She tried again, meeting Elizabeth's gaze. "Thank you." In response, Elizabeth's palm found her cheek, and it was the most comforting touch she'd ever encountered and it happened in the midst of the most impactful event of her life. She felt her limbs return to her, and the blood slowly came back to her face. With gathered strength, she stood next to Elizabeth, ready to face whatever lay ahead.

❖

Devyn's right leg bounced as if it had a mind of its own as they made their way back to town. Night fell around them, little by little. People would be making dinner, calling their kids inside for the day, or wondering what was on television. How odd to imagine regular activities in the midst of their crisis. She took comfort, however, in the knowledge that Jill wouldn't be out there alone in the darkness tonight. They had her. It had taken more than half an hour to free her from the crumpled metal. Devyn had only glimpsed Jill from afar. Pale and bruised and who knew what else? The ambulance had left ahead of them with its siren on, barreling toward the hospital at a high rate of speed. She stared up at the sky and prayed they'd gotten there in time.

Elizabeth made a right on Loveline Street, which would lead them to the hospital that serviced not only Dreamer's Bay but the four other neighboring small towns. While it wasn't enormous, the facility was up to date and staffed with a team of well-respected physicians. She knew because she'd spent her time on the plane researching the place just in case they needed it.

"I'll drop you here and park the truck," Elizabeth said. "Are you okay to go in on your own?"

Devyn nodded. "I'll be fine. Thank you." She exited the truck but glanced back. She'd been in town a day, yet it already felt like she and Elizabeth had been through so much together. She blinked in amazement. How odd the way trauma brought people together, acting as a shortcut for their relationship, which now felt so much older than just a few hours. Elizabeth had been her person through all of this, and because of her and her search teams, they'd found Jill.

She made it to the hospital reception desk, placed her bag on top of the counter, and took a deep breath. This wasn't the time to be nervous or jittery, this was a key moment where she needed to remain in control. "I'm Devyn Winters and I'm here for my sister, Jill. She was brought in within the hour."

The woman nodded as if they'd been expecting her. "Emergency room is down the hall. Check in with the nurses' station and take a seat. They'll update you when they can."

More waiting. Devyn wasn't sure that was going to go well for her.

Ten minutes later, Elizabeth appeared with two cups of coffee and took the seat beside her. She didn't have to stay. She'd done her part, pitched in, and now that Jill was in the hands of the medical professionals, Elizabeth could easily slip back to her own life with a job well done. Yet she seemed to be settling in.

Devyn glanced at her phone to find messages from her staff, checking in on Jill. There were also messages from her assistants Sheldon and Karen. None from friends, because she didn't really maintain any. She ignored the messages and stole another glance at Elizabeth, who hadn't read a magazine or picked up an electronic device. Instead, she sat there, peacefully waiting.

"You don't have to wait," Devyn finally said.

"Oh." Elizabeth seemed surprised. "Do you want me to leave? I don't want to make you uncomfortable and can—"

"I'm not uncomfortable, but it's getting late." Devyn looked to the exit. "I imagine you have a life to get back to. People waiting on you. A husband."

"Nope, and I'd like to see how she is," Elizabeth said and seemed to return to her own thoughts. What an interesting human being she was. What Devyn could recall of Elizabeth from high school was scarce, but the memories mainly surrounded clubs, fund-raisers, and maybe the student council? She wasn't sure, but Elizabeth was probably on it. She'd been a go-getter, though. Not shy about answering questions in class either, to the snickering of Devyn's friends on the cheerleading squad. An academic herself, she didn't participate, but she didn't put a stop to it either. Guilt gathered in her stomach, just a little too late.

At the one-hour mark, a blond male doctor in blue scrubs found them in the waiting room and took a seat in the empty chair across from them. "She's hanging in there," he said to both Devyn and Elizabeth. "You're her sister?" Devyn nodded. "Nice to meet you. I'm Dr. Collette. I work in emergency."

"Nice to meet you," she said, obligatorily.

Dr. Collette continued with a frown. "Unfortunately, I can't give you too many specifics just yet. We're still assessing the extent of her injuries from the accident and exposure. Once we do that, we'll come up with a plan for treatment."

She rubbed her wrist. "But she's okay? That's the part I need to know."

He nodded. "For now. It's clear she has significant trauma to that left leg, and the rest of her is pretty banged up. Her vitals gave us a scare for a while there, but with some fluids, she's rebounding. We'll know more in a few hours."

"But she's gonna pull through? Beyond everything else, she's going to live, right? That's the part I need to understand." Devyn held her breath as she waited for his response.

He smiled hesitantly, and she noticed the lines under his eyes that marred his otherwise good looks. Must have been a long day. "She's stable, and that's a very good thing." It was noncommittal, but still encouraging. She felt the pain in her chest recede slightly. She would take that tiny bit of encouragement and hold on to it with all she had. They'd build on it little by little until all was right with the world again.

Devyn thanked the doctor, whose name she'd forgotten to memorize, and then watched in surprise as Elizabeth stood and wrapped her arms around his neck for a quick squeeze.

"You know him?" she asked, once they were alone.

Elizabeth gestured to the swinging door with her chin. "That's Dr. Dan Collette. Married to my best friend, KC. He's a great guy and an even better doctor. Jill's in the best hands now."

"I remember KC." Devyn sat up taller as the untouched memories from years ago drifted back. "She played volleyball, and we cheered for a few of the games. She was good."

Elizabeth nodded. "She still plays on the rec team. We're currently in the off-season."

"Good for her."

Their conversation trailed off and Devyn sipped the now cold coffee as a fluorescent bulb flickered in the overhead light across the room. She'd missed the window for hot coffee. Didn't matter.

"I'll freshen it up," Elizabeth said, reaching for Devyn's still full cardboard cup.

"No, no, no." Devyn scooped it up first and took Elizabeth's, too. "You don't have to do that. You've been helpful enough and can pass the baton. I'll get us both fresh cups." She headed from the waiting room and then turned back, feeling the need to ask the question that tugged. "Was I ever mean to you in high school?" Lord knew she'd had her awful moments that she very much wanted to distance herself from now. She hadn't been the happiest, which mostly stemmed from self-doubt and realizing she wasn't like her friends, boy crazy and planning their future dream weddings.

Elizabeth shook her head and Devyn exhaled. Thank God. "We just existed in different social stratospheres. Everyone wanted to be you. Not a lot of people noticed me."

"I'm sorry I didn't more. You're a good person. You've proven that today." Devyn wasn't warm and fuzzy. She didn't claim to be and she didn't try for it. But Elizabeth and her selfless efforts since she arrived not only made a difference to Devyn, who'd felt supported and taken care of, but likely saved Jill's life. She would never know how to thank Elizabeth for that. She'd start by being the one to get the damn coffee.

CHAPTER FIVE

The animal shelter was closed for the night when Elizabeth drove past on her way home to Whippoorwill Way. She stared at the building, hidden behind a grouping of live oaks, and noticed the warm light coming from what she knew to be the administrative offices. If that light was on, it was likely Greta Martin was inside finishing up some paperwork. Elizabeth occasionally volunteered at the shelter and knew Greta's workload—it never seemed to end.

She was exhausted, emotionally drained, and should really just go home. She'd sat with Devyn for a couple more hours until they moved Jill to a room in ICU with a comfortable recliner for Devyn.

Somehow Elizabeth couldn't drive away from the shelter. Not until she knew more.

Making a last-minute left turn into the shelter's small parking lot, she sighed. She'd only stay a moment, find out what she could, and then leave. She grabbed the bottle of Crown and two plastic cups from her stash in the truck. She didn't love the stuff, but she knew Greta did.

Greta squinted at her through the window of the locked door, which prompted Elizabeth to stop knocking on it. She held up the bottle and cups, which earned her a grin.

"Well, to what do I owe the pleasure?" Greta asked, swinging open the door.

"I was driving past and thought maybe you'd like a nightcap." Elizabeth smiled her most friendly smile and walked past Greta. The normally boisterous shelter was now mostly quiet. Once the lights went off, the dogs seemed to settle in with the giant dog biscuits Greta tossed into each run.

"I'm always up for a nip," Greta said. She closed the door behind

Elizabeth and followed her to the small office behind the reception desk that was overrun with papers, photos, and a variety of knickknacks. Maybe too many. Elizabeth turned to face her friend, who appeared tired. Greta was a good fifteen years older than Elizabeth and her shoulder-length brown hair was newly streaked with gray. Elizabeth thought she wore it well.

"Did you hear the latest about Jill Winters?"

"Everyone's heard. Such a blessing she was found in time." She accepted the plastic cup from Elizabeth, and they took a moment to toast. "You did good, Liz."

"Not all me. The search team never would have found the car without pulling over for that white dog. She's the reason Jill's okay." She glanced behind her, projecting that an idea had just occurred to her. "Oh, hey. Did they bring her here?" Yep, nonchalant. That was her.

Greta tossed back the rest of her whiskey and turned to her antiquated laptop, the screen attached to the keyboard with the aid of a little bit of blue duct tape. "They did. Sweet girl, too." She pulled up her intake form and turned the laptop to face Elizabeth. A photo of the dog she'd seen at the accident site lit up the top right corner of the screen. Her heart squeezed.

"Would you look at that." Elizabeth would just swear the dog was smiling at the camera. She had the kindest eyes that seemed to say, "Hello, want to cuddle with me?"

"No microchip. No collar. The little girl's pretty thin. I'm thinking she's been on her own for a while." Greta swung the laptop back around. "I have her pegged at maybe four or five years old. Probably a Lab mix, though she's smaller than a Lab. Why? You in the market for a best friend?"

"No," Elizabeth said automatically, then took a sip of whiskey. "I mean, I *wasn't*."

A pause as they stared at each other. Greta smiled a knowing smile and grabbed her keys. "Why don't we just say hello? Can't hurt to introduce the two of you."

Elizabeth shrugged. "Yeah, okay. Hello couldn't hurt. She's a hero, right? She deserves a little attention."

"And she loves it."

Elizabeth followed Greta through the locked door to the dog wing and down the short hallway of indoor/outdoor dog runs, waving and allowing the dogs they passed to lick her hand through the metal mesh gates. The wing was now alive and loud again.

"Sorry to wake you all," Elizabeth said, out of an innate need to be polite. After all, this was their quiet time she was invading.

At the end of the hallway, Greta paused at the last run and turned on the small night-light above. "Hey there, precious girl. I brought you a visitor," she said. The dog stood from her blue dog bed and walked toward them, tail wagging slowly. Elizabeth smiled. So did the dog. "Why don't you go inside?" Elizabeth hesitated, but when Greta opened the door to the run, she slipped through.

"Hi, there," she said, and instinctually took a seat on the concrete floor. The dog slowly approached and climbed directly into her lap, taking up the entire thing, and curled into a ball. Elizabeth's heart swelled and melted as she stroked the soft fur of the dog's neck.

"I think that means she likes you," Greta said with a laugh.

"I like her, too," Elizabeth admitted, reluctantly. She really hadn't planned on anything like this. Maybe she should get a hold of herself and slow down and think. Yes, thinking was generally a good idea.

Greta shook her head at the pair of them. "I think you're in trouble now."

She covered her eyes with one hand. "Greta, what am I doing here right now?"

"I think something larger than you might be responsible."

"Maybe," Elizabeth said, and then frowned. "I don't like thinking about her out there all on her own."

Greta leaned against the wall outside the run. "I imagine she didn't like it much either." She paused. "Something about this one, though. She's special."

"She is, isn't she?" Elizabeth said. The dog looked up at her and sighed, her whole body going slack, as if she realized that she could finally relax.

"Does this mean you're taking her?"

"Oh," Elizabeth said, caught. She'd stopped at the shelter on a whim. To make sure the dog was okay. She looked down into the big brown eyes that blinked back at her, and relented. No, that wasn't true. Greta was right. Something had pulled at her, *made* her stop. But that didn't mean she was instantly equipped for a pet. "I'm not sure about that. I'm…a little confused on what I should do here. Today was very unexpected, and I'm tired and emotional and—"

"Why don't you take her for the night?" Greta offered, gently. "You could both use a little rest, I think. Maybe in the morning, you'll have a stronger grasp on where your head is at."

"I could do that? Borrow a dog?"

"Sure. I'll fill out the paperwork for a foster." There was a sparkle in Greta's eye as she said it. Yep. She was playing matchmaker, which was what she did best. "Just need you to sign it on your way out the door. I'll handle the rest."

"Okay." The word was out before Elizabeth had considered it. But honestly, one night wasn't going to hurt anybody. Greta passed her a leash from the wall and Elizabeth slipped the loop around the dog's neck. "Wanna get out of here with me?" she whispered. The thumping of the dog's tail against her leg was a good enough answer.

"What should we call her?" Greta asked, opening the door for them.

Elizabeth had no clue. She was already so far ahead of herself. She stared at the happy dog, now turning in slow circles in the hallway, anticipating her freedom. She was getting sprung and knew it.

"What about Scout?" Elizabeth asked. "Not only one of my favorite literary characters, but also? That's kind of what she did for us today."

"Looks like a Scout to me," Greta said.

Scout shook her entire back end in agreement and smiled once more. It was the most peculiar thing, the smiling. She'd never seen a dog do that before.

They followed Greta back to the office, where she loaded Elizabeth up with tons of temporary supplies. Food, bowls, toys, and a blanket. "Call me with questions and we'll see where your head is at tomorrow. Sound good?"

Elizabeth realized she was a crazy person with no business taking a dog home in the middle of the night on an emotion-fueled whim, but that was apparently who she was now, a lunatic. "Um...sure. Sounds good."

Greta put her hand on Elizabeth's shoulder. "You're going to be fine."

Just twenty minutes later, she wasn't sure she would be. There was an actual dog in her bedroom. With her. She loved dogs. Adored them, but had never had one of her own before. She changed into her pajamas. Scout still stared. "Should we get some sleep?" she asked.

She fluffed the blanket she'd earlier folded into a fluffy square beside her bed. Scout eyed it and whined quietly, not moving. "It's really comfy. Why don't you give it a shot?"

Elizabeth pulled back the comforter for herself and slipped into bed. She hesitated before turning off the light, hoping Scout would settle in. The dog blinked but still didn't move. "No?" she asked, looking around for ideas. Anything to make Scout feel more comfortable, so maybe she'd curl up and they could both get some much-needed sleep. She didn't get very far, because Scout approached the bed tentatively and pawed at the side. She was asking permission, Elizabeth realized, and her heart was gone. Given in earnest to the four-legged white ball of love that wanted to sleep next to her.

She scooted back from the side of the bed, leaving a space, and patted the spot next to her. Without delay, Scout jumped up on the bed, stretched out alongside Elizabeth, and let out a long-contented sigh. "Okay. So, it's going to be like that? You like people, and you're a cuddler. I'm learning you."

They stayed like that, snuggled up and warm, until Elizabeth felt her eyes grow heavy. She did her best to release the stressful events of the last twenty-four hours. She found it easier to do so with Scout there with her. She gave the dog the smallest squeeze and kissed her head.

"I think you might be home," Elizabeth whispered, and felt herself drift into peaceful oblivion.

Chapter Six

This was too difficult to wrap her mind around. Devyn squeezed her eyes closed and opened them again, desperately hoping that the image in front of her would shift from the crumpled person in the bed with tubes and monitors coming off her from several locations. It didn't. She bit the inside of her cheek and blinked.

Jill didn't look like herself, and the horror shook Devyn into an emotional puddle. Her sister's face was swollen and red and purple, as were her hands, which looked a little too big. Devyn picked one up and held it to her chest, listening to the beep, beep, beep of the nearby monitor while fear vibrated off every inch of her. Her older sister, always so calm and happy, in control of any situation, now lay lifeless and battered in the dim light of an intensive care hospital room. It seemed so impossible, yet here they were. The unthinkable had happened. The hospital staff had told her Jill wouldn't wake up until probably the next day. They'd sedated her, which would allow her injuries to heal, while they assessed if there'd been any major trauma to her head.

A few hours later, the imaging showed that, thank God, there hadn't been. At least that was what the doctor, KC's husband, had explained as he'd gone over the large volume of scans in way too much detail for her brain to follow. She'd looked around for Elizabeth to help her translate, but she'd given Devyn some space to spend time with her sister and had gone home for the night.

Bottom line, Jill was in bad shape, but she would heal.

Her wrist was sprained, and three of her ribs were broken. Her body was marred with cuts and bruises in various spots. However, her left leg and hip had taken the brunt of the trauma. She would need surgery the next day and pins and screws and many months of rehabilitation to be mobile again, and even with all of that, she might never regain full function on that side. Devyn anxiously tapped her foot. She didn't like what that would mean for Jill, a very active elementary school teacher who spent most of her days up and around the classroom, and she liked to go for jogs on the weekends. Devyn moved about the room overnight, walking the darkened space, and decided those kinds of details could wait. Right now it was about getting her sister through these next few days as comfortably as possible. She'd very seriously considered having her moved to Philadelphia, to one of the top hospitals in the country, but Jill would hate the idea of being moved out of the Bay. For reasons Devyn didn't share, she felt bonded to the slow-paced little town and loved it there.

She'd been at her sister's bedside for only a handful of hours that morning when the first floral delivery arrived, followed by an additional arrangement, balloon bundle, or stuffed animal every hour or so. The deliveries were unending, and the back table of the nurses' station where they were stored overflowed. Word must have spread fast throughout town, but then that's how it had always been. Jill was loved by so many that of course her friends and neighbors would show their love in the face of such an awful accident. The sentiment was nice, but the space was small. Devyn distantly wondered where they'd put all the stuff.

As the day moved forward, she couldn't go over the details of the accident anymore. They haunted her and left her feeling helpless. To counterbalance the grim thoughts, she checked her phone for any bites on the property she'd listed just three days before, a penthouse in one of the most sought-after buildings in downtown Philly. With a private outdoor space most would kill for, she knew it wouldn't last on the market for long.

Just as she would have predicted, she had a nibble from a potential buyer she'd shown the place to just days before. The agent wanted her to call him. Somehow, she had to get herself together enough to sound like a human on the other end of the phone, a successful one who couldn't be fucked with when it came to negotiating. She didn't feel like that person at all in the present moment.

"Knock, knock," a voice said from across the room, in place of actual knocking.

Devyn glanced up to see Elizabeth entering, carrying a small basket. She was in a new set of clothes, slim-fitting jeans and a green Henley, and looked brighter, refreshed. A shower and some food will do that. Her hair was pulled partially back and fell from the clip a little to frame her face. Light brown with highlights of blond and what appeared to be shades of strawberry mixed in, a most intriguing and beautiful color combination. It was too intricate to be anything but natural.

"Hi," Devyn said, standing politely and smiling. She held up one finger and, with the phone to her ear, tried to make it clear that she was engaged in a call.

"I hope this isn't a bad time," Elizabeth whispered, and looked over at Jill.

Devyn watched as the image of her sister, battered in that bed, took hold of Elizabeth. She knew the feeling and almost forgot herself on the call. "Jared? No. No, I'm here. I hear you have an offer for me on Eighteen Park."

Elizabeth opened her mouth and closed it again. While Devyn worked on Jared to come in with a thirty-day close, Elizabeth quietly made her way to Jill's bedside and took her hand. Devyn swallowed at the caring gesture. Jared promised to see what he could do, and she clicked off the call. With a hand on her hip, she studied Elizabeth.

"You look like a person again."

"Yeah, I got a few hours, but thought I'd head back up here. See how things were."

"I was thinking overnight about how quickly you came in and took control yesterday. If you hadn't done that..." Devyn realized there were tears in her eyes, but then there had been constantly for the past forty-eight hours. She couldn't stop them.

"She's okay, though." Elizabeth's arms were around Devyn's neck immediately. "Sorry. I just have this thing about people crying in my presence. I can't not hug them." She'd said it with an enthusiasm that Devyn was beginning to understand was her default. She'd not seen it while Jill was missing, but she vaguely remembered the exuberance from high school. She was someone who worked to bring cheer into almost every room. Those kind of people generally exhausted Devyn.

"It's okay," Devyn said, with Elizabeth pressed up against her. She let her hands rest on Elizabeth's waist lightly.

"She's here and she's safe. Keep telling yourself that." She couldn't see Elizabeth's face, but Devyn had a feeling she was smiling.

Devyn nodded as the tears flowed freely, landing in a smudged circle on Elizabeth's green shirt. The warmth and steady feel of her body in Devyn's arms was like a much-needed anchor. Cheerful or not, she didn't want to let go of Elizabeth. Yet, after the weighted moment passed, she forced herself to.

"I'm sorry about that," Devyn said, and absently smoothed her jeans. "I'm apparently getting used to you comforting me."

"Stop that. It's okay to be emotional."

"I know." Devyn wiped her face and stared at the ceiling. "If there's a time to cry, this is probably it. Still. Not like me."

"That's okay, too," Elizabeth said, as Devyn put some space between them. "You can't be a badass all the time. No one can. And I was happy I was able to help with the search. It's kind of what I do. I'm basically a professional when it comes to chairing committees. I'm a people person."

"That part I remember about you."

Elizabeth began ticking off one finger at a time. "Student council, Spanish club, Neighborhood Outreach, Big Sisters, and prom committee. Not to mention the yearly food drive. That was me in high school."

Devyn smiled. "All of that while my friends and I were learning to do back handsprings, hanging out in the sand pit on the beach, listening to music, and drinking cheap wine. I think your time might have been better spent."

"I don't know about that. You guys were out living life. It's a little embarrassing, my mundane résumé."

"Well, I, for one, am grateful for it. Did you do a magic show at some point, or am I making that up?"

"Sixth-grade talent show. I was Electrifying Elizabeth."

"Oh, wow. You were. I remember now." A pause. "You weren't bad, but your costume—"

"Was a bit much." She nodded. "I made it myself out of found fabric and glitter and newspaper. Not a lot of help on the parental side of things. My dad worked a lot."

"It served its purpose." Devyn made sure not to share the less-than-kind things she and her friends had had to say about the costume.

"And I won third place in the talent show, so I chalk that up to a win."

They exchanged what could only be categorized as a small but important smile. The occasion didn't allow for much more. "Anyway, it's very nice of you to come by." Devyn ran a hand through what had to be disheveled hair, but this woman wasn't here for her anyway, so why should she care?

Elizabeth stared at her. "Are you trying to toss me out?"

"Of course not," Devyn said.

"I'm here to relieve you for a bit. You need to take a little break. Eat something. Rest. Shower. I thought I'd come up and sit with Jill."

"No, that's not—"

But Elizabeth was still talking. "I know it's technically against the rules. Family only, but I talked to Jimbo at the nurses' station, and he said they'd turn a blind eye since you seem to be on your own."

"Jimbo?"

Elizabeth gestured behind her. "Charge nurse. We're on the same bowling team. Oh." She glanced at the basket she'd set next to her chair and thrust it forward, walking it to Devyn. "I almost forgot. This is for you. I brought it with me just in case you were still here, and you are."

"Oh, you didn't have to go out of your—"

Still no pause. "There are some baby wipes, and hair ties, and snacks both savory and sweet, and a couple of crossword puzzle books, and a *Cosmo*." She shrugged. "I had to guess about the *Cosmo*, but you seem, in many ways," she paused, "well, glamorous. Other than that, just about everything you'd need to survive time with a loved one in a hospital."

"Wow." Devyn glanced through the basket, surprised by all the little details Elizabeth had thought of. "You've done this before. Is there a hospital committee? There is, isn't there?"

Elizabeth's eyes went wide. "No, but there should be. That's a great idea. I should write that down." She gestured to Jill. "Do you mind if I sit with her and—"

"No. Go ahead." Elizabeth took a seat in the chair next to Jill's bed and left Devyn to her own thoughts.

Spending time with Elizabeth reminded her that she really didn't know much about Jill's world in Dreamer's Bay. That hurt, but it was all on her. She had a way of getting caught up in the hurricane of downtown Philadelphia and her adrenaline-laced job. She would ask Jill more about her day-to-day life, who her friends were, what she did on a Tuesday night. In the past, most of their phone calls and texts were quick check-ins, or worse, calls from Jill that she never got around to returning. She deeply regretted that now. In fact, the thought brought on near-physical pain. Fuck. She'd almost lost her sister, for God's sake, and she wouldn't take her for granted again.

The writing on the wall was clear. This was her second chance.

Across the room, she heard Elizabeth begin to speak quietly to her sister. "Oh no, Jilly." Elizabeth sighed. "This isn't fair at all. I'm so sorry this happened to you, but I want to say this. Don't you worry about a thing. Do you hear me? You're going to get better and be back to your old self in no time. We're all going to rally together and make sure of it." Elizabeth nodded enthusiastically. "Everyone is thinking about you and pulling for you. Understand? Your sister is here, too, and she made sure we found you. You would have been so proud of her." Devyn bowed her head at the words. Elizabeth made her feel a little less alone in all of this. That was for sure. "All the folks in town send their love, which is why the nurses' station looks like an out-of-control flower shop on mushrooms right now. Not that you've ever done mushrooms. I honestly don't know if you have, but I feel like you understand what I mean."

Devyn's phone began to vibrate. A glance told her it was Jared, the agent with an offer for her. In this moment, she didn't care, and slid it back into her pocket.

That was certainly new.

The tender moment at Jill's bedside squeezed her heart, which was also new. In addition, it made her slightly nervous, reminding her that she was an outsider in the quiet moment, just like she was an outsider in this town. At least nowadays. It didn't feel like hers anymore, but then it never really had. She reflected on the teenager she'd been the last time she'd spent any real time in the Bay: lost, confused, stifled, but refusing to let on. She was none of those things now, but she was *still* a visitor. She shifted uncomfortably. "I'm going to grab another cup of coffee from the shop in the lobby. I'm practically mainlining the stuff. Can I get you anything? Cookie? Candy bar? A new committee?"

Elizabeth smiled and tucked a strand of hair behind her ear, and that was when it struck Devyn that she'd really blossomed since high school. Not that she'd been unattractive, but now? Yeah, very pretty. "I'm okay. Thank you, though. I'll sit with Jill while you're away. We'll chill together. Maybe I'll even perform a magic trick or two," she said proudly.

"I appreciate that. And pull as many rabbits out of a hat as you can. We could use a little magic." With a final nod, Devyn left the room feeling overwhelmed and not at all like herself. These were the moments in her life, the difficult ones, when she turned to Jill for comfort and advice. Jill was her soft place to land and always knew exactly what to do. It was up to her now to figure all that out on her own. And she would. Somehow.

❖

"So, here's the deal," Devyn said, as she juggled the phone and the car door handle at the same time. She squeezed herself out of the ridiculous Spark and passed it a glare just because she thrived on their adversarial relationship. "I got my client down to ten point five million, but he's not going a cent lower. This is a steal for skyline views and we both know it. Best and final, Greg."

He hesitated. "C'mon, Dev. You know that's not enough of a drop. Your client needs to be reasonable or lose a killer offer. My guy is prepared to walk. The property is not worth a dime more than ten. Hell, that view is partially obstructed."

"Get your client up." Devyn was going to close this deal if it killed her. Even if she had to do it from thousands of miles away. The property had been on the market for three months now and was starting to get stale. This was her shot. Though her personal life had fallen apart around her, she had to keep her professional world propped up as much as possible in the midst. She wasn't going to back down.

"If you'll consider a sixty-day close, you have a deal," he said.

"Done," she said with a smile, knowing her client had already consented. "Let the paperwork commence."

Devyn hadn't left the hospital for thirty-six hours, becoming numb to the harsh fluorescent lighting, sterile smell, round-the-clock chatter from the nurses' station, and awful coffee no human should ever actually consume. But having been advised that Jill would likely wake soon from sedation, she wanted to steal what time she could to freshen up and grab a quick bite so she'd be ready and able to assist in any way needed. She let herself in for the second time to what she still saw as their family home from years ago, despite the transformations. When their mother died, she'd let her portion of the house go so Jill could move in. It only made sense given she had no interest in living in town herself and definitely didn't need the money from a potential sale. Since that time, it was clear that Jill had practically remodeled the entire interior, updating the fixtures, the kitchen counters, and cabinetry. Not bad at all, she thought, as she moved through the house, still not quite used to being inside again. In broker mode, she quickly calculated the likely resale potential, knowing full well Jill would never in a million years consider selling. While she had a handful of good memories from the place, she wasn't the type to get mired down in sentiment the same way.

She hopped in the shower and lost herself beneath the stream of hot water, allowing it to cascade over her skin for an extra five minutes of heaven before forcing herself to towel off, get ready for the day ahead, and rejoin the world. She fed Jill's five fish and headed back out to her rental just as her phone vibrated in her pocket. A local number she didn't have programmed in her phone. She slid onto the call, nervous something had gone wrong at the hospital. Not the case.

"This is Devyn."

"Who knows where the action's at?" an enthusiastic female voice sang into the phone. Devyn was instantly sixteen years old again. Nostalgic and tingly.

"Who knows where the parties are?" she sang back with a slight smile.

"Who jumps, and jives, and is made up of five?"

She knew the answer like it was yesterday. "The senior Dreamer Stars."

"You bitch, I hear you're back in town and didn't call. I don't really mean the bitch part. Well, maybe a tad." Cricket. They'd been part of the same five-person friend group and were co-captains of their high school cheer squad. "And I know it's not under the best circumstances. Bless your sweet heart. We were all so sorry to hear about Jill's accident. She's going to pull through, right?" She said the words in that overly earnest voice people sometimes employed to communicate their abundance of sincerity.

"She will," Devyn said. "Recovery is going to be an uphill climb, though." She scratched her forehead, still not quite sure what lay ahead but knowing it would be a lot.

Cricket made a clicking sound at the back of her throat. "I just feel so awful about that. On an unrelated note, I have spin this afternoon, but maybe we can grab a bite after. You'll need to get out of the hospital to keep your sanity. Lisa, Heather, and Coco are all free and dying to join us. We've all secured babysitters. You in?" Devyn dropped her hand from her forehead, leaning into the head trip it was to be talking to Cricket and hearing those names all said in a row together. They had been a tight group back in the day, the senior girls on the squad. The Senior Star nickname felt so ridiculous now.

Devyn hesitated. "I'm not sure it's a good idea for me to be away from Jill right now." In fact, she couldn't imagine it.

"Well, shoot," Cricket said. "Rain check, then. We'll put the babysitters on standby and later this week we can revisit this possibility. We're all just dying to see you and hear about all you've been up to."

Devyn took a breath. "I feel the same way and I'm confident that at some point we can make that happen." Hell, she'd probably be here long enough to need a night out.

"This will be insane." Cricket crowed. "The Senior Stars back together again in the same place. Just think of the trouble we can get into in this town. Get ready, Dreamer's Bay. We're coming for ya."

"Pretty crazy," she said, finding it hard to match Cricket's excitement level or her strange overconfidence. Devyn wondered about her own ability to find enjoyment in shallow get-togethers and gossip. She lived a faster-paced life these days and rarely slowed down enough to eat, much less shoot the breeze. Did she even remember how, outside of schmoozing a client? Still, there was a part of her that was curious about her old friends, who held a special place in her heart for those playful memories.

"I'll give you a call soon, sweetie. Love to Jill. We'll send over a basket of something to munch on."

"Oh, no, no. No need. You don't have to do that."

"Already done, so don't you fuss one little bit. Bye, now."

Devyn was left holding the phone to her ear after a call that felt a little bit like *The Twilight Zone*. She climbed into the tiny Spark, her own personal clown car, and on the drive back to the hospital, surfed the local radio stations, of which there were three. She learned that Dr. Dan and Loud Louise, the morning show hosts from back in the day, were still on the air after all these years. How was that possible? She thought of all she'd done in that time—college, fledgling career, advancement, real estate domination—and Dan and Louise were still spouting off on the airwaves every day. She wondered if Loud Louise had ever snagged that husband she so often pined for publicly, or if Dr. Dan ever really admitted that he was not, in fact, a doctor at all.

"Gonna be a warmer one in Dreamer's Bay today," Dr. Dan exclaimed. "You got your kiddie pool all set up, Louise?"

"You know it, Dan. Now if I can just get my eight-year-old to watch the little one and someone to watch that husband of mine, I can get in it." Sounded like Louise now had a loud little family of her own. Well done, Loud Louise.

"Don't forget, Dreamers, we've got the Springaling coming up next month in Bountiful Park, and you simply do not want to miss out. Dig out your killer recipes for the bake-off and get to work. I, for one, will be there with a fork and bib ready to try everything fried before I cool off in the dunking booth."

Devyn shook her head and smiled. Of course the Springaling would still be going strong, full of food and games. This town loved their cookies, brownies, and cakes and made sure any and all events revolved around them. It seemed that hadn't changed either.

When Devyn arrived back in Jill's hospital room, she was shocked to see a nurse standing over her sister, who blinked back up at her.

"You're awake," Devyn said, much louder than she'd meant to. That wasn't supposed to happen for another couple of hours. She moved quickly to her sister's bedside and smiled down at her as warmth and relief took their turns. It was Jill. God, it felt good to see her. The nurse took a step back and allowed Devyn her space.

Jill stared back at her in mystification, almost as if she didn't believe what she was seeing. "Dev? You're here?" Her voice was weak, but she was *there* and she recognized Devyn, which was everything.

Devyn misted up right on cue, feeling a lump in her throat. "Yes. I'm here. I hopped a plane as soon as they called. Do you know where you are?"

Before answering, Jill gestured to the nearby tray and the cup of water the nurse had left. Devyn put the straw to Jill's lips and held it as she drank. "Hospital," she said finally. "The nurse said...an accident."

Devyn nodded and ran a hand through her hair to distract herself and channel the coursing adrenaline. Somehow, talking to Jill made it all so very real. "A pretty bad one."

"I'm hurt."

"Yes. But you're going to be okay. I promise."

Jill blinked and glanced down at her own body with her eyes, apparently not strong enough to raise her head fully. The bruise beneath her eye was now a painful-looking mixture of purples, blues, and reds. "My legs?"

Devyn swallowed. "The left one took the brunt."

"Oh, God." Jill started to squirm, which was alarming because Devyn wasn't sure what damage that might do. She was out of her depth here and wondered if she should ring for the nurse to come back.

"Listen, don't worry about that right now," she said, scrambling. "You just rest and let me handle everything. I'm on top of it, okay?"

"But I'm the big sister," Jill mumbled and closed her eyes, drifting off once again. It seemed the short conversation had taken up a lot of her energy.

"Not today." Devyn smoothed Jill's hair softly. As she sat there alone in the quiet hospital room, she'd never missed their mother more. She wished for her nurturing superpowers now and stared skyward with a heavy heart for guidance. She needed tips to get Jill through this, to make her feel safe and protected.

"Is this a bad time?" a voice asked in a whisper. Devyn turned to see a giant yellow chicken looming in the doorway. That had to be a hallucination, right? She squinted, recognizing the face that peered at her through the open orange beak. Elizabeth Draper. This time dressed as a human-sized barnyard animal.

"What's going on?" she whispered back. "What's with the outfit?"

Elizabeth glanced down. "Oh, you mean this? I just came from delivering a singing telegram to Genevieve at the post office. Do you remember her from the field trips we used to take there in elementary school? She always let us mail a postcard?"

Devyn did, and nodded.

"It's her birthday today, and her coworkers wanted to surprise her."

"I'm sorry. With a chicken?" Devyn asked, trying to piece it together. She abandoned the whisper altogether. Jill could always sleep through the loudest of thunderstorms, a true gift.

"Yes. Well, it was that or the Stay Puft Marshmallow Man, you know, from *Ghostbusters*? And then I have to figure out his singing voice, which is harder than it sounds." She ran up the scale in a strange, low voice as a demonstration. "See? Just not quite there. I'm gonna work on it. So, as you can tell, my character options are limited. I could do a clown, but who wants that walking into your job on your special day?"

"No one."

Elizabeth pointed at her. "Exactly. How's the patient?"

Devyn opened her mouth to answer but was distracted by the visual of Elizabeth attempting to walk into the room while maneuvering her giant orange feet. "She's hanging in there. She woke up just a little while ago and was herself and alert and asking questions."

"That's fantastic," Elizabeth said, beaming. It really was a beam, too. Her smile lit up her whole face, and the beak surrounding it.

"It was really nice to hear her voice, if only for a few minutes."

Elizabeth nodded and made a circular gesture. "Is it okay if I stick around a little bit? Even if she doesn't wake up again for a while, I think she'll know that I was here, and when people come to visit you, it matters." Cue the big, bright smile. It was like a ray of sunshine had landed squarely in the room. On one hand, it was kinda nice. On the other, a little irritating, given her work mode. She was in the zone, and not up for sunshine, rainbows, and chickens, as nice as Elizabeth was.

"I think that's true, and you're welcome to stay. I'm just going to be working remotely." She gestured to the corner of the room where she'd set up her laptop earlier.

"Thank you, and go right ahead. Don't let me and my chicken-self get in the way." A pause. "I heard the other fourth-grade teachers stopped by before school."

Devyn glanced up warily. "That must be where the smiley face cookies came from. I must have missed them while I was getting cleaned up at Jill's place." She returned to her laptop.

"Hasn't she just done so much with the house?" Elizabeth gushed.

Yes, gushed.

She was easily impressed, but this morning it was a bit much. Hopefully, Elizabeth and her good deeds would be needed elsewhere. She appreciated the help and all Elizabeth had done, but maybe space would be better today.

"It looks great." She opened her email.

A horrible thought seemed to occur to Elizabeth. "Not that your childhood home didn't look nice, too. I'm sure that it—"

"It's fine." Devyn held up a hand, attempting to tamp down her frustration. "I translated you, and Jill's made some great improvements." Ah, look at that. There were several inquiries about Twenty-Four Walker, Wyatt's building, sitting right there in her inbox. Right on schedule. Apparently, word was out that she had the listing, and agents were hungry to get their clients in the door first. She didn't know how she was going to make this all work from Dreamer's Bay, but she had to see if she could figure that part out. She rubbed her forehead, trying to ease out the creases that had been there for the past three days. She took a slow, deep breath and prepared to dig in.

"Good, because I wouldn't want you to think I thought less of the original house."

Good God. She paused. "I don't." To keep from having to force further conversation, Devyn turned away from Elizabeth and lost herself in her work. In the middle of her broker email was one from Wyatt Lowe himself, with a series of questions about her plans for a brokers' open. He also wanted to know about her international contacts, of which she had hundreds. Not that she'd had time to reach out to any of them, given her current predicament. Nor was she in the headspace of the go-getter she was known to be. This was going to be a balancing act.

"You're not a fan of small talk. I can tell."

Elizabeth again. This was becoming a problem.

Devyn rolled her lips in and glanced up to see Elizabeth peering over with those wide, curious green eyes. She stole a second glance. She reminded Devyn of that little skunk from Bambi with the eyes. What was its name? "I'm fine with small talk. I just have a lot on my plate and need to buckle down while I can."

"Busy day at work? I mean, I'm guessing."

"Yes." She began typing to demonstrate. Surely, she'd get the message. Elizabeth had come to visit Jill, not *her*, so there was no reason for extra added small talk. Devyn stole another glance. She was also just a little too perky, sitting there in her chicken suit, as if her main goal in life was to deliver light, happiness, stars, and hearts. As nice a thought as that was, there was too much going on right now for blatant cheer. Who had the time? She had Jill, and Wyatt Lowe, and units in a high-rise she should be closing on that very second, not sitting here in Dreamer's Bay, of all places, with a green-eyed Pollyanna impersonating poultry.

"You're a Realtor, aren't you?" Elizabeth asked, pulling the head of the chicken away from her face like a hood, leaving it resting on the back of her shoulders.

If that had been an option, why in the world would she wait so long? Next, she pulled a bottle of water from the oversized bag she carried with her. Devyn couldn't imagine what kinds of things she carried in there. What was so important that she couldn't leave a few of those items at home?

"I'm a *broker* in Philadelphia," she told Elizabeth, matter-of-factly.

Elizabeth nodded. "You prefer the term 'broker.' Got it."

"I do. Thank you."

"Selling houses must be an interesting line of work." She was smiling again.

"Not houses. I mainly sell buildings. In their entirety."

Elizabeth paused mid-drink and lowered the bottle of water. "Even better. That sounds lucrative. Is it?"

"I do okay." She leveled her gaze on her laptop and attempted to focus yet again. She had a feeling this was going to be a long and very social afternoon.

"I'd love to hear about it."

Devyn sighed and closed her laptop, accepting defeat. "What do you want to know?"

CHAPTER SEVEN

I like this dog," Dexter Whitby said, popping a malted milk ball into his dude-sized mouth. Scout raised her head from the new fluffy dog bed Elizabeth had purchased for her at the pet store, along with only about five hundred new toys all tossed into a basket in the corner for her to pick and choose from.

"I think you lucked out," KC said. "So many dogs gnaw on the drywall in the house and hide your strappy shoes."

After a long day of work, Elizabeth was happy to entertain her friends around her kitchen table. She'd put out a bucket—yes, a literal bucket—of Sam Adams lagers for them to pull from willy-nilly. It was past five, and she, for one, felt it. She'd never been a partyer or heavy drinker, but this was how Elizabeth Ann Draper liked to cut loose. A beer and her closest friends. More specifically, Dexter and KC.

"No wall eating at all. I'm surprised at how little trouble she is." Elizabeth smiled at Scout, proud of her and their newfound bond. "She really just wants to be around people, I've found. I've taken her out on several jobs, and everyone just dotes on her. She eats up the attention."

"Well, of course they do," KC said, emphatically. "Have you seen her soulful doggy eyes and those eyelashes? Have you?"

"I have. They're one of the reasons she's here."

"Speaking of here," Dex said. "I heard Devyn Winters is back here in the Bay."

"You are correct. She is back," Elizabeth told him, helping herself to his oversized box of candy and stealing a handful. "I mean, as expected. Her sister went missing, and now she's pretty banged up."

"Her much *nicer* sister," Dexter said, nodding. "I remember when the Senior Stars mistakenly invited me to their end-of-the-year blowout and then rescinded the invitation when they noticed their mistake." He shook his head and took a pull from his bottle.

"Sorry they did that to you, pal," KC said and touched her beer to Dexter's.

Dex had been a good friend of Elizabeth's for most of her life but had moved more firmly into her inner circle alongside KC once Elizabeth moved back home after college. A skirt chaser in theory and practice, he was known for his impressive biceps, bald head, and generous spirit. Despite his borderline obsession with the gym, he always carried some form of snack food with him at all times. Purely a bonus, as far as Elizabeth was concerned, and it made her like him all the more. She didn't believe in diets or anything at all related to them. Snacks made life better.

"As for me"—KC grabbed a handful for herself, popped a couple into her mouth, and mused—"I was never a Devyn fan, myself. The whole Senior Star tribe was insufferable. Shallow. Yes," she said, nodding confidently. "That's the word I'm looking for, and self-congratulatory for being beautiful and popular, which requires no skill set."

"Well, if they had to be mean, at least they were hot," Dex added.

KC chose to ignore that comment. "They were like this vortex of vapid. Devyn was right there in the center of it, despite the fact that she was smarter than the others. She was head cheerleader, right?"

"Along with Cricket. She hired On the Spot to wax her fleet of vehicles and asked for Kevin, the twenty-year-old with the abs, to be the waxer. That's the God's honest, absolute truth."

"Not at all surprised," KC said. "Devyn likely isn't any better."

Elizabeth agreed wholeheartedly with their assessment of younger Devyn. She'd all but ignored Elizabeth in high school in favor of the more exciting types. She'd always gotten good grades but never really engaged with study groups, nor had she ever traded more than five words with Elizabeth at a time. Yet Elizabeth was hesitant to say anything bad about Devyn, given the difficult time she was having. Somehow, it just didn't seem right. "You never know. She might be entirely different now. People can change as they grow."

"Do the other Senior Star cheerleaders seem different to *you*?" Dexter asked, scrolling his phone, likely for the most recent Braves score. The aggressive punching gesture he made silently in the air meant they were winning. "The only reason they give me the time of day now is that they're bored with their husbands."

It was true. The women of Dreamer's Bay found Dexter easy on the eyes and took turns flirting with him to pass the time—and, okay, propositioning him on the sly, too. Though Dexter had grown up to be ridiculously handsome, with a fitness model's body, he hadn't always had an easy time of it. His family had moved to the Bay when he was in the sixth grade and he was the gangly kid with thick glasses. Elizabeth winced at the memory of his reception the day the principal first introduced him to their homeroom class. "They called you Poindexter."

"Yeah, and it stuck for the next six years. I was a pointy-headed nerd. I can admit that shit, and when we moved to town there were, what? Five black families? I already felt like a fish out of water being the sixth. To be labeled awkward, too?" He shook his head. "Damn, man. Not my favorite years."

KC leaned over and swung an arm around his broad shoulders. "You're a total glow-up story, Dex. Just look at you now. Muscly and chiseled and with that little dimple right there." She touched it with her forefinger.

He pumped his eyebrows. "You're into me."

"I'm not. I'm married."

"If you weren't."

She shook her head. "I'd let you down easy."

"Yeah, well," he shifted his focus, "Liz would be into me if she weren't gay."

KC laughed. "You don't know that."

His face fell, so Elizabeth patted his forearm. "If that's what you want. Sure. You're very handsome in a cue ball kinda way, and if I were all up in the man business, I'd probably be drooling right now. There. How was that?" She stole another milk ball, thought better of it, and stole three more. She was a candy whore on the take and happy about it.

Dex sat a little taller, nodding about his false victory. "Well, so long as there's a chance." A pause. "Speaking of gay. Devyn Winters is. You into *her*?"

Elizabeth frowned. "She is not. And just because two people are gay, it doesn't mean they will automatically be into each other. Look at Linda from the movie theater. She's gay, and I can't stand her. Then there's Raven from the mini-mall. We barely speak, except in passing. There's Tammy and Lindsay, who are both very attractive and from what I understand single, but you don't see me chasing them down just because. There's not a secret club."

"You left Thalia off that list," Dexter said blandly. Her friends were not fans.

KC nodded. "That's because she's writing love poetry about her in her head as we sit here."

"I am not," Elizabeth said. "I'm an awful writer." A pause. "But I would if I thought she'd like them." She sighed at how pathetic she was.

"I don't get why the one woman you're into has to be such a dick. Ironic, man."

"Listen, she's got a lot of things going on," Elizabeth offered, in what felt like a lame defense even to her. Thalia Perkins did have a track record of canceling their plans or ghosting her altogether for weeks at a time after flirting with her here and there until she got bored. Somehow, though, Elizabeth couldn't seem to shake the crush she'd developed. Just when she did something to make Elizabeth say *no more*, Thalia would toss her dark hair or bat her gorgeous dark eyes and reel her right back in. Then there was the way she sort of half smiled that would just make everything okay again. Yep. Elizabeth kept coming back for more. She didn't really like what that said about her.

KC raised her hand and yanked Elizabeth back from the wonderful and confusing land of Thalia Perkins into the fold of the conversation. "I think Devyn is, though. Gay. I googled her at some point when I was on my 'where are they now' kick last year. She's had what looked to be girlfriends."

Huh. Not only did that surprise Elizabeth, but it rattled her, intrigued her, and turned her mind into a hamster wheel of energy that honestly surprised her. Why would she care enough to react energetically? Plenty of people were gay. Millions. Beyond that, how the hell had she missed this?

KC leaned in. "I think we only point it out because your pond is a little small in these parts, and maybe that's one detail that would be… of interest to you."

Elizabeth balked at the idea. "You think I'd be into Devyn Winters? Popular and shallow, and oblivious to my existence for our entire adolescent history? Yes, she seems nicer now, but still." She left off *beautiful* on purpose, but Devyn was definitely that. Even more so these days, in her adult sophistication and the way she carried herself with such *authority*. The authority part was really nice and sent a shiver down her back. She shrugged it off as she chewed her milk ball.

"Besides, she's here because Jill needs her, and the least we can do is make her feel welcome. Senior Stars snobbery or not. Is 'snobbery' a word?"

"Yep," KC said. "But the thesis statement remains. You're a bighearted goober, always have been, and you deserve more in your life than Thalia, for God's sake." She stood reluctantly and shrugged. "But I can't count gay people all afternoon, nor reminisce with you two any longer. My child needs to eat, and that means I have to forage. That's who I am now," she said with a heavy sigh and pulled her curly brown hair into a ponytail as if preparing for battle. "Not sexy and alluring, but a forager."

"There's a dreamy blond doctor who thinks you're sexy and alluring," Elizabeth pointed out. KC's husband was a transfer from Charleston. She'd snagged him within months of his arrival in town, much to the chagrin of every other single straight woman in a thirty-mile radius, and the two of them still had goo-goo eyes for each other—sigh-worthy on many levels.

"That he does," KC said. "Thanks for that reminder. Now I just might have sex tonight." With that, her shoulders went back and her boobs went up, and she sashayed right out of Elizabeth's kitchen.

"She just needs a little encouragement," Elizabeth informed Dexter once they were alone.

He nodded. "You're good with encouragement, Liz. You make people feel better about themselves. Your gift."

"Thank you." She shrugged. "When someone needs a confidence booster, I think it's nice to give it to them. Devyn, for one, could use a friendly face. I don't care what history says about her, I plan to continue to be just that."

"Cool."

They stared at each other.

"Do you want me to get out of your kitchen now?" he asked.

"Unless you want to help me do laundry, dishes, and balance my bank account. Actually, it could be really fun if we did it together." She made a show of brightening like it was her best idea yet.

"I'm outta here. Meeting Misty from the gym for dinner," he said, and hightailed it to the back door. His place backed up to Elizabeth's, making the travel time between houses about twenty seconds from back gate to back gate.

"Isn't this your second date? You haven't had a lot of second dates lately. This is big news in Dexter-land."

He laughed. "Dude, I don't know what's going on. I don't even recognize myself. She's a nice girl. What can I say?"

"You gonna marry her?"

He pulled his face back. "Let's not get crazy. But my plans beat the hell outta yours."

"I wouldn't be so sure," she said, scoffing.

He blinked at her. "Don't take this the wrong way, but your Friday night to-do list is depressing as hell. Don't forget to live a little, okay? Maybe put the checkbook calculator away and head out on the town."

"Hey, I'm living. Living the glamorous *laundry* life." She did a little dance that seemed to fall flat. "No? Not the laundry life?" She danced a little more. "Nothing?"

He shook his head in sadness. "Never say that sentence to anyone. And secondly, nah. You don't live the glamorous life either. You're too busy making everyone else's life better. Consider doing the same for your damn self. That's all I'm saying."

"I do. I bought that geranium for myself last week. You're forgetting."

"When is the last time you got laid, Liz?"

Her mouth fell open. "I'm not answering that."

"You don't have to. It was that hook-up over a year ago with the woman from the painting class, and that's way too long."

She shrugged. "I guess it's been a little while. Yeah."

"My advice? Get your head out of the clouds and your clothes on the floor. If you need some tips on how to score chicks, just let me know." He smiled his contagious/annoying smile, popped a milk ball, and headed out for his own exciting existence. Women, late nights, and shots at the bar. That's what drove Dexter these days. She wondered what it must be like to be sought after the way he was. What was so great about Dex was that he'd known the other side of that coin. He remembered what it was like to be picked on, less than popular, and was thereby always kind, and never took his good looks or universal appeal for granted.

Once he left, she ruminated on his comment about her boring life, balked, shrugged, and glanced around her empty kitchen. "I live. I do." She finished the last sip of her beer and shot the empty can in the direction of the garbage, achieving the perfect arc…and then watched it fall limply onto the kitchen floor with a bang. Huh. Surely that wasn't a metaphor. Surely.

She sighed and shifted her lips to the side in defeat.

Maybe she should start some sort of club. Chair a new committee. She thought of Devyn, who would poke fun at her and roll her eyes. She smiled and got to work on that laundry, and then replayed that daydream of Devyn all over again.

❖

Devyn had memorized the nurses' names, though it was hard to predict who they'd have on which days. Their schedules didn't seem to follow any rhyme or reason. Because some were more helpful than others, she made a point of always being there first thing in the morning in case Jill needed extra assistance with anything. When Jill rested, Devyn worked, often not seeing the outside again until late each night.

"Are you working?" a voice asked, quietly.

Devyn swiveled in the recliner that Tuesday morning to see Elizabeth standing there with a brown bag. She blinked, her brain caught in a fog of paperwork and email. Jill slept nearby. "Hey. Yeah, I was."

Elizabeth held a palm up in warning. "I will not bother you. I promise." She walked into the room with slow, overexaggerated steps, as if walking on literal egg shells, and handed the bag to Devyn before backing away toward the door in the same, weird fashion.

"What is this?" Devyn asked, opening the bag. When the smell of fresh bread hit her, she all but melted into a puddle.

"A warm turkey, cranberry, and cream cheese sandwich from McConnell's Deli. I was picking up lunch and thought you could maybe use a sandwich yourself. You tend to work through meals from what I've seen."

"You didn't have to do that." But Elizabeth had, and the food smelled so good that Devyn practically wept.

"I wanted to. Oh, and there are some fresh-cut fries at the bottom of the bag. Now I will leave and not bother you with my chatter." She zipped her lips and turned, showcasing a killer pair of jeans that looked like they'd been cut to showcase her specific shape.

"Wait." Devyn sighed, owning that she hadn't always been the friendliest when caught up with work. "You don't have to go."

Elizabeth gestured behind her. "Actually, I do. Got a couple of poodles that need grooming and I'm in charge of making sure that happens. I'm thinking a rainbow Mohawk."

"Please tell me you're not serious."

Elizabeth pointed at her and broke into a grin. "I'm not. In fact, I'm simply driving the duo to Margie Urbina, who's accredited. I'll be back on Thursday to spend time with Jill. Bye, now." And before Devyn could answer, Elizabeth was gone.

Left to her thoughts in the quiet room, Devyn stared at the warm bag in her lap and smiled. Okay, so maybe stars and hearts went a long way after all.

❖

"So, we put in an over full-ask offer and still wound up in a bidding war for the ages," Devyn said. "It was honestly one of the most exhilarating deals I've been a part of when repping a buyer."

"In what way?"

"Well, for one, the eccentric millionaire seller asked that each potential buyer submit a paragraph stating what they would do with the property should he sell it to them. Was totally in love with the place like someone would be a pet and had no intention of selling it to someone with big renovation plans for the place."

Jill chuckled. "Sounds like something off one of those reality shows on HGTV."

"It honestly felt like one," Devyn said, sliding her chair closer to Jill's bed. It was just after three in the morning and Devyn had decided to stay the night at the hospital after noticing her sister's spirits seemed to have taken a dip. She'd grown noticeably quieter and had a difficult time sleeping. Her normal "look on the positive side of things" disposition had been nonexistent the past two days, and it was obvious that this whole ordeal was beginning to drag her under. Devyn couldn't stand it, and tonight, she didn't feel right leaving her alone. She sat forward. "I was fielding calls left and right from the seller's broker with counteroffers, contingencies, and of course, the essay evaluation. He sent notes."

"Notes?" Jill laughed.

"Notes," Devyn said, laughing along with her. "Grammatical corrections and everything. The guy was comma obsessed and sent apostrophe tips in the footnotes. Yes, there were footnotes. We had to resubmit like some sort of reprimanded sixth grader."

"Now, those, I'm familiar with. So, what happened?" Jill pushed a hand behind her and sat up with a wince, blinking at Devyn in the dimly lit room. It made her happy to see Jill captivated by the story, a small distraction from her painful recovery. She'd tell her a thousand more if they helped at all.

"In the end, my guy got the condo, and I've learned a valuable lesson about proofreading my client's work ahead of time."

"Victory," Jill said, with her less bruised hand in the air. They smiled at each other for a moment and Jill softened. "I'm really glad you're here, Dev. Not because I need your help, and I do, but it's just nice to see you, you know? Spend time with you."

Devyn nodded. "It's really nice to see you, too, Jilly. We shouldn't wait so long next time."

"I'm going to hold you to that." Another pause, but the comfortable kind. "Remember when Mom used to make us warm toast with extra chunky peanut butter when we were feeling sick or sad or low? To this day, I love peanut butter warm."

"God, yes. Nothing ever tasted so good, and it worked, too. Life felt…manageable again when you had that warm toast on a plate in front of you. You let your problems just slide away."

She could make out the tears glistening in Jill's eyes in spite of the darkened room. "I could go for some warm peanut butter toast about now, ya know?"

Devyn smiled, her heart squeezing unpleasantly. She stared at the ceiling as guilt engulfed her. "Mom would have been so much better at this than I am. I keep asking myself what she would do and I know I'm falling short."

"No," Jill said, firmly. "You've been so wonderful, dropping everything to be here for me." Jill met her gaze firmly. "I know that was hard for you. You're incredibly driven, Devyn, and I admire that about you so much. But you put me first." She placed a palm over her heart. "It matters so much."

Now she was the one battling the tears. She wiped one away and pushed beyond the painful lump in her throat. Jill meant everything to her, and she should know that. "Of course I did. You're my Jilly, my big sister, ya know? We're family, and no matter what I have going, you come first. You can believe that."

"I do." Jill nodded, and a thought seemed to hit. "It has been enlightening, though. Seeing you do business from here and stealing a little glimpse into what your life must be like. Phone calls at all hours, a million emails to return. Don't even get me started on trying to keep track of your myriad of assistants." She squinted. "I've been eavesdropping on those calls, trying to translate it all, by the way."

Devyn raised a shoulder. "You could always just ask."

"No. I like observing it all more. You're an important person."

Devyn moved her head from side to side. "I like my job, but it takes a village to make it all come together. It's a hustle."

"My existence seems so much slower paced compared to yours."

Devyn balked. "Doubtful. You have twenty-five fourth graders to wrangle. I can't even imagine. The runny noses alone would stress me out."

"You'd survive. You'd have them organized into competitive teams ready to take on the other classes." Devyn had to laugh. "The pay is a little less, though."

"Pshhh," Devyn said. "Who cares about money?"

Jill leveled her gaze. "You do. You have enough."

"Fine. I love money. It gets my fur up but I'm glad there are people like you in the world, willing to fight the good fight so I can be cold and calculating." It was a joke, but not entirely. Hearing her words out loud struck a chord. Sigh. Maybe she had gotten caught up.

"Hey, I didn't mean anything by that," Jill said, picking up on her deflation. "I'm driven by people, and my connection to them. You're not, and that is one hundred percent okay."

"I didn't take offense." Devyn shook off the feeling that she'd sold her soul, knowing it was only a temporary impression anyway. She loved her life in Philadelphia and was crazy about her job. Did it matter that she wasn't exactly warm and optimistic and out to change the world like Jill or Elizabeth Draper? No. She made charitable donations on the regular. She did her part. "We're just different. That's all."

Jill tucked herself back into bed more fully. "And different makes the world go 'round."

"Yep," Devyn said, still trying to shake that self-assigned hollowness that encroached.

"Thank you for sitting with me tonight." Jill tapped her pillow. "I think I'll try and get some sleep."

"Anytime." Devyn killed the small lamp across the room and returned to the recliner, her bed for the night. Alone with her thoughts, she stared into the darkness, now defenseless to her own self-recriminations. Her life had purpose. It did. It had meaning. She had friends and colleagues to enrich it further. Wait. No, she didn't.

She sighed. Self-awareness could be a total bitch.

❖

"I don't understand why Dexter doesn't just dive in?" Jill asked. She moved her right arm in the circular gesture the way the physical therapist had demonstrated an hour earlier.

"Eight more to go." Elizabeth bit her lip as she thought on how to explain. "He can be a man child. On one hand, it's endearing, but when it comes to love and this new woman, he's just being dumb. He needs to stop dating other people and make her his forever girlfriend. Two more to go."

Jill winced at what must have been a hit of pain, finished the final two rotations, and slowly lowered her arm. "What about you?"

"I have no love life," Elizabeth stated simply. "I'm a boring woman who watches too many game shows."

"What about Thalia Perkins?"

Elizabeth sighed. "She's...Thalia. She's a hard one to pin down."

Jill leaned back against her pillow and allowed her eyes to close. The workout had likely tired her. A smile graced her lips. "But you wouldn't mind pinning her down."

"Jill," Elizabeth gasped, sitting forward and laughing. "Really?"

Jill was laughing now, too, and Elizabeth handed her a pillow to place against her ribs. "I'm sorry. I just call 'em as I see 'em."

"Am I that obvious?" Elizabeth asked. "It's possible I pine for her a little. She's...gorgeous."

"I know it. At the Valentine's Day dinner, you couldn't take your eyes off her."

Elizabeth nodded. "She wore that red dress."

"That showed off her amazing rack." Jill grabbed her own boobs and Elizabeth laughed louder this time. It wasn't so much *what* Jill said and did, but the fact that it was prim and proper Jill saying it.

"What has happened to you?" Elizabeth asked. "It's the pain meds, isn't it?"

Jill nodded, joining her in laughter. "More of those things, please. Keep the good drugs flowing."

And then a voice from behind interrupted them. "Well, someone's having a good time."

Elizabeth glanced behind her and saw Devyn enter the hospital room. She wore jeans, heels, and a plaid blazer. Much too dressy for a hospital, but that was Devyn, she'd found. Dressed and ready for the day, even if it meant working from nowhere. "We were just gossiping a little."

"Elizabeth's life is complicated."

"Is that right?" Devyn asked.

"No. Your sister is being kind. My life is basic at best. Can I steal you for a minute?"

"Of course," Devyn said.

"Don't forget eight on that other arm. Be right back."

Once they were safely in the hallway and out of Jill's earshot, Elizabeth turned to Devyn. "First of all, how are you holding up? Did you get the book I dropped off for you?"

Devyn smiled and leaned her shoulder against the wall. "I'm hanging in there, and yes, I read it in a day and half. I called Trevor being the killer, by the way."

"Then you're smarter than I am." Now that she was up close and personal, she couldn't help but notice the tiny flecks of gold in Devyn's hazel eyes. Her jacket was nicely starched, too. "Listen, I had an idea for when Jill goes home."

"Okay," Devyn said, frowning. "It doesn't involve singing or dancing, does it?"

Elizabeth swatted Devyn's shoulder. "No."

"I'm sorry. You just never know with you."

Elizabeth reined in her excitement, because she had a lot of it about this concept. "I want to have her students in front of the house to cheer for her homecoming. What do you think?" She braced herself.

Devyn tucked a strand of blond behind her ear. "It sounds great, but that might take some effort. You think that's doable?"

"Please. Do you know who you're talking to? You don't worry about a thing. Just keep me updated on a possible release day, and I'll do the rest."

"Are you sure?"

Elizabeth swatted her a second time. "Stop saying that." She leaned against the wall, mirroring Devyn. "I'm definitely sure."

"Then let's do it."

Elizabeth lowered her voice. "Level with me. You really saw the killer coming?"

Devyn blinked. "Oh, sweet Elizabeth. How could you not?"

CHAPTER EIGHT

A m I out of here today?" Jill asked her nurse, with hopeful eyes. She and Devyn had spent the morning prepping for the possibility. Devyn had assisted Jill in the shower, using the special chair, she'd blow-dried and styled her sister's hair and even applied a little bit of makeup to her otherwise pale face.

Her nurse today, Eileen, held a folder full of paperwork, which had to be a good sign. They waited for the verdict. "The doc just signed on the dotted line," she said. "Which means…" Devyn did a drumroll on the side table. "You're free."

"You don't know how wonderful those words are," Jill said, sitting up straight in bed. While her mobility was still compromised, her strength seemed to have returned, and she was anxious to get back into the real world. Devyn didn't blame her. She was anxious herself.

She accepted the folder and listened to Eileen's instructions about following up with physical therapy folks the next day to jump-start Jill's recovery, which would take time. She accepted the prescription for pain medication and list of activity restrictions, of which there were a lot. Jill faced an uphill battle, but this was a big moment and a victory to celebrate. They were leaving this damned hospital once and for all.

It had been three weeks since Devyn had arrived in Dreamer's Bay, but it had been hard to tell. She'd spent most of that time in Jill's various hospital rooms, making one day blend into the next. She'd been there with Jill through two back-to-back surgeries, the therapeutic exercises that all but killed Jill with pain and many a sleepless night, and now it was finally time to put this chapter behind them. While she'd been counting the days until Jill would be released, she was also sad to see their one-on-one time come to a close. They honestly hadn't spent this much time together in years, and now that Jill was on the mend, Devyn would start making plans to get back to her own life.

"We should call Elizabeth," Jill said, of her most frequent visitor. "Let her know I'm sprung, so she doesn't stop by."

It just so happened that Devyn was way ahead of her and had already dashed off a text to Elizabeth. She'd actually turned out to be rather useful, bringing Devyn the odds and ends she needed to get through the long days, even taking her lunch order a time or two and dropping it by the hospital as a treat. Say what you want about an overly upbeat woman, sometimes in a chicken suit, but they really did come in handy. Elizabeth, she already knew, had plans that morning, and they were good ones.

Devyn nodded. "I will be sure to do that just as soon as I have you safely home."

"Home," Jill said with a big smile. "I can't wait. It's still the same, right? You haven't renovated with your own space-age style?"

"I was tempted, but the plans for your aluminum foil kitchen complete with a mural of Elon Musk were scrapped last minute. Sorry to disappoint you."

"Look at me, dodging eighteen-wheelers *and* terrifying design projects."

"This is your year, Jilly. I can feel it in my bones."

On the drive, while they both basked in the freedom that lay ahead, Jill turned to Devyn from the passenger's seat, outfitted with soft pillows to make the bumps in the road hopefully less excruciating. She shook her head in disbelief. "It's all still here. Look. The town, the people. In the midst of all I've been through, the world kept turning. They're still living their regular lives." She waved at an older couple walking hand in hand down the sidewalk. They waved back with a smile.

"Look, though. They're happier now," Devyn said. "The Bay was just waiting for you to return, so all could be right with the world again."

That sentiment was confirmed when they turned onto Jill's tree-lined street. This was the part Devyn had been waiting for. Elizabeth Draper, along with twenty-five fourth graders holding homemade Welcome Home signs, began to cheer loudly and jump up and down right there in Jill's front lawn. Devyn glanced over happily for her sister's reaction, which was one she'd never forget.

"I don't believe this," Jill said, covering her mouth as they pulled into the drive. "I'm going to cry. Oh, my God. Yep, crying in progress. Look at these guys. Devyn, these are my kids."

Devyn grinned at Jill's happiness. "Well, don't go leaping out of the car. Let me come and help you. We still have to be careful, small people or not."

She hurried around the car, and once Jill was safely in her new set of wheels, namely the wheelchair they'd rented, she wheeled Jill over to her students, who each took turns covering her in gentle hugs, well-wishes, and love. In their midst, Jill simply beamed. It was the best medicine possible.

"I'm so glad it worked out," Elizabeth said quietly, taking her spot next to Devyn as they looked on. She folded her arms across her chest and let out a happy sigh, wearing a cute pair of denim overall shorts that looked great on her. "The kids were thrilled to welcome her home."

Devyn held out a hand in Elizabeth's direction. "All the credit goes to you. I had my doubts about putting you guys on call without knowing the exact time we'd be discharged, but you did it. This just made her day. Her year. I can tell."

"You doubted me?" Elizabeth's jaw dropped playfully. "I had those kids occupied with art supplies and pretty much any and every Hostess product on the market. I'm no rookie."

Devyn laughed. "I won't doubt you or your company ever again." She frowned. "I forget its name."

"On the Spot. You should write that down. In fact, here's a business card. We have a fantastic website you need to take a look at, too. Tell your friends. We're getting busier by the day." Elizabeth lit up when she talked about On the Spot. She clearly took pride in her work, as random as the work might be.

"And how much do I owe On the Spot for this particular task?"

Elizabeth balked. "No, no, no. This one was for Jill. On the house. Plus, it was my idea. I'm not gonna hire myself."

"Then allow me to make a donation." Devyn pulled a handful of bills from her pocket and thumbed through some twenties.

"Put that away," Elizabeth said, swatting at it playfully. "We're all squared away here. Jill is happy. The kids are happy. And you and I are happy. There's no need for money to change hands when the world is at peace." With that, she flitted away to wrangle the kids with Devyn staring after her and those overalls.

She might not have been much of a businessperson, refusing

payment, but Elizabeth's actions spoke to her character, and Devyn could certainly not fault her. She also came with a certain lighthearted optimism. It was...nice, and maybe "nice" deserved more credit than she'd previously assigned it.

Three hours and a lot of slow maneuvering later, Devyn had Jill comfortably on the couch with an audiobook and her pain medication administered on schedule. Now she needed to figure out dinner and the near future beyond. "So, what's on your list of requirements for an at-home nurse? I mean, if we were to hire your perfect Mary Poppins."

Jill pressed pause on her phone and turned from her spot on the couch. "What do you mean?"

Devyn found a bag of heat-and-serve frozen pasta to pop onto the stove for the two of them. Perfect. "I'll do the legwork to make sure they send us the right person, but since you're the patient, you should get a say in what they're like. What qualities are you looking for?"

"I don't understand. Why do we need a home nurse?" Jill stared at her quizzically. "You're here and doing a great job. Don't second-guess yourself."

Devyn paused mid-bag-rip. "It's just that I'll be heading back to Philadelphia soon." She was already pushing it. Her team was doing the best they could with Twenty-Four Walker and had sold six units, but that put them way behind schedule. *She* was the closer and *she* was the one the other brokers wanted to do business with.

Jill took a moment. "What are you talking about? You're leaving already?"

"I figured you understood that I'd have to get back to work."

Jill nodded but didn't say anything. The best way to describe the look on her face was distant and devastated.

Devyn hated that. "I'm sorry. I thought we were on the same page about that."

"It's just that there's just so much rehab ahead of me still, and I can barely get myself off this couch." Now she just looked terrified.

"That's why we get you the best home health nurse possible."

Jill shook her head in sad disbelief. It was clear her coping skills were taxed, and who could blame her? "I just can't imagine having a stranger in my house, doing those kinds of personal things for me."

Devyn hesitated. What was she supposed to do with that? She had to sell out that building in *three* months instead of four or lose the biggest listing of her career. The one that would put her at the top, where she'd worked tirelessly to be. It would be pulling a rabbit from a hat, but she had to try. "Jill, I can't work effectively from here."

"Okay. I guess I'll be all right, and of course you need to go home. Your life shouldn't be put on hold. I just misunderstood is all."

Like a knife in her heart. She'd never seen her sister look so dejected, and it just wasn't fair after all she'd already been put through. If Devyn stayed and devoted the same kind of attention to Jill as she had thus far, she'd never get anything done. What was the compromise here?

She set the bag of pasta on the counter and rounded the counter into the living room. "What if I stayed a little longer. Another few weeks?"

Jill seemed to perk up. Her green eyes glimmered again. "That would be wonderful, if you could manage it."

"What if we had someone part-time, though, which would give me the chance to steal away and still do my job?"

Her sister nodded, taking what was offered. "I don't love the idea of a stranger, but I suppose I could get used to it."

Devyn remembered the business card in her back pocket. "What about Elizabeth?"

"Liz?" Jill considered this. "You think she'd be up for it?"

"Doesn't she do this kind of random request for a living? Plus, you guys have great rapport. You laugh together like lunatics, and she's well versed on your condition because of how often she visited."

Jill considered this. "If she'd be game, I'd love that."

Devyn ripped open the bag of pasta with gusto and stared at Jill in determination. "Leave this to me."

CHAPTER NINE

Elizabeth had been born in the mid-eighties and wished to hell she'd been old enough to fully enjoy it. To make up for it, she passionately embraced the time period now. With Duran Duran in her earbuds, she rode her longboard to Jill Winters's home that Thursday morning, waving to the neighbors she passed along the way, high-fiving that ninth grader, Jimmy Rodriguez, as he set up his family's sprinkler near the curb.

"Lookin' solid on that board, Ms. Draper."

"Thanks, Jimmy. I'm not great at it, yet, but I'm working at it. Life's too short to walk everywhere, ya know?"

"Preach," he called after her.

The longboard was something she'd picked up on a whim once she noticed folks on the boardwalk whizzing by on the things. They looked like fun, and she was always up for extra fun whenever she could find it. She'd taken a few informal lessons from teenagers at the beach and hopped on her own board whenever possible to keep her newfound skill set intact. Today seemed like the day for it.

She arrived at Jill's house and leaned her board against the brick wall of the porch, smiling at the spring flowers that Jill had meticulously spaced and planted in the garden out front. Perfect color combination of pinks and purples and yellow. She took out her phone and snapped a photo.

"Are you stalking the flowers? Some sort of flower paparazzi?"

She turned and smiled at Devyn. "No. It's just that they're beautiful. I'm putting them on my Instagram so more people can see them. Anyone who needs to be cheered up could use a dose of these colorful guys."

"Instagram cheer, huh?" Devyn asked, stepping back from the doorway so Elizabeth could enter the house.

"It's really very effective." A pause. "Wow. You look…nice." She blinked and took a moment to absorb the image of Devyn in front of her in dark, slim jeans with a sharp plaid blazer with a tapered waist. Her blond hair was down but had a little tousle to it. The look was… okay, a really, really good one. Elizabeth swallowed and smiled. "Well done."

Devyn glanced down. "Thanks. Not too dressy, but put together enough to make me feel 'on' while I work. It's a whole psychological thing. Don't get me started."

"Whatever it is, I'm sure it will work out just fine for you, looking like that. I mean, in your snazzy work outfit." She covered her face and hoped to die right there.

Devyn regarded her with a curious smile, and Elizabeth hoped she hadn't been that obvious in checking Devyn out, emphasis on *obvious*, because she had been checking her out and tended to wear any and all emotion on her face.

"So, what's on tap for this morning?" Elizabeth asked, with too much gusto, attempting to rebound. "I can stay until noon." When Devyn had called and offered her the temporary job of caring for Jill, she'd immediately said yes. It meant she'd have to delegate more of the incoming jobs to her small staff, but KC had already stepped up to the plate and offered to play point person and assign tasks to the runners during the first half of the day. She'd also pulled in two extra runners to cover the gaps.

Devyn flashed a smile. "First of all, thank you for agreeing to help out."

"You don't have to thank me. I'm happy to help Jill. You know that. Plus, you've officially hired me, so no volunteering required."

Devyn chuckled. "That part's true."

"And you're paying me really well."

Devyn met her gaze. "Well, I wanted to be sure you said yes."

"You could have negotiated if I'd balked," she said light-heartedly.

"Money's not really that big a deal to me."

"Well, well," Elizabeth said, with a raised eyebrow. "You don't hear that every day in the Bay."

"Shit." Devyn paused. "That sounded pretentious as hell, didn't it?"

Elizabeth held her thumb and forefinger closer together. She clapped Devyn on the side of her arm. "I'll let it slide."

Devyn picked up a set of instructions and handed them to Elizabeth. "Jill's on the back deck, getting a little sun. She'll need help getting back inside. We've been using the wheelchair, but the physical therapist will be here in an hour and he can probably show you some other techniques for mobility. The contraption around her knee is the most tender area."

"Got it. Where will you be?"

"Second bedroom down the hall doing some work. I have some calls set up throughout the morning with some potential international buyers, but if you need me, just pop in. I'll take over when you have to leave."

"We have our plan. Go, team." She held up her hand for a high five and Devyn obliged.

"Sorry," Devyn said, with a laugh. "It's been a while since I've participated in an actual high five."

"Thank God I'm here, then," Elizabeth said, letting the partially judgmental comment slide right off.

"Yes, thank God." Devyn glanced around. "You good? Anything I can get you?"

"I'm good," Elizabeth told her, and then dropped her voice to a whisper. "Plus, I work for you, so maybe don't cater to my every whim. Just a friendly employee-to-boss tip."

"Right, right. I guess I'll get to my calls, then." Devyn made her way to the bedroom that would serve as her office, but not before pausing and offering one last lingering look back.

Hold it right there.

Was Elizabeth crazy or had Devyn just given her a once-over? A checkout from head to toe? Huh. The information from Dexter sat on her shoulder like an annoying little canary, but the truth of it certainly resonated. Devyn was so incredibly gay. How had she not picked up on it herself earlier?

She shook herself out of the moment, and the tiny shiver she got from the sexy once-over, that may or may not have happened.

Devyn was Devyn, and not someone with the qualities she looked for anyway. Yes, she was hotter than hot on a hot day, but she was fast paced and sophisticated and pretty much out of Elizabeth's league. That wasn't a bad thing. Elizabeth liked her two-jalapeño league. Not too mild, but not too hot. Devyn came with at least four out of five in the jalapeño-ranking game. Probably five, and who could keep up with a five? And why was she thinking about jalapeños when she could be spending time with Jill? She remedied that quickly.

"How's the patient?"

Jill turned and smiled serenely, which was a great way to describe Jill, in a nutshell. "Great, now that you're here." She was the poster child for everything calm and warm in the world, which was why she was known for having great patience with her students. Of the sisters, Jill had been blessed with the darker hair from their mother, and Elizabeth had always admired the way it fell in natural layers to her chin. She could only imagine that Devyn's blond hair had come down from their father's side, though Elizabeth had never known the man.

Elizabeth plopped down next to Jill on the comfy sofa on the covered patio and looked out over the well-taken-care-of lawn. It wasn't a large outdoor space, but what they had was covered with beautiful, mature live oaks. "Nice out here."

Jill had her leg propped up on the coffee table, and she gestured with her head to the yard. "Devyn had a lawn service tend to it while I was up the river. They did a great job taking care of all my babies out here."

"Up the river? Isn't that jail?"

"Is it?" Jill looked thoughtful, and then shrugged. "Felt like jail. Do you realize I was in that hospital for over three weeks?" She sat back and waved off the comment. "Of course you do. You were there for much of it, which, I have to say, makes you a saint."

"Not a saint. Couldn't let you get all the attention is all," Elizabeth said, and adjusted the pillow under Jill's injured leg. "Better?"

"Much. You're a good nurse." A pause. "Devyn seem okay to you today?"

Elizabeth glanced behind her to the house. "Yeah, she seemed… driven. From what I learned in the hospital, she's pretty much always that way, no?"

"The total truth. I feel like she's staying in town because I guilted her into it." A cloud seemed to settle over Jill, and Elizabeth hated that. She shouldn't feel like a burden to anyone, and the look on her face made Elizabeth want to say something to Devyn about it privately, and right away. Jill sighed. "She has a million things going on in Philly and she's stuck taking care of her burdensome sister."

Elizabeth shook her head resolutely. "Nope. Impossible. You should have seen the way she looked after you in the hospital, how worried she was." It was true. Elizabeth couldn't count the number of times she'd popped in to find Devyn next to Elizabeth's bed, holding her hand, or curled up in the chair nearby, choosing not to go home for the night. "Nothing about her said forced responsibility. I promise."

"Yeah, well, now is different. She's got some giant building she's gotta sell, and the clock is ticking." She took a deep breath. "But I'm grateful to her. That she stayed. It's nice to have family here when I need them."

"Isn't that the truth? If Dexter, my pseudo family, didn't show up for my car accident, we would have some serious words. I already know KC would be there."

"Dex would be there in an instant. Though he'd be sad if you were hurt. He used to have the cutest little pout when he was a kid."

"Still does. Now he just uses it to pick up women."

Jill sighed. "Men."

"Can't say I mind dodging the man bullet." She studied Jill, who shifted uncomfortably. "Want to go inside? We can get you set up on that comfy couch like a kept woman."

That earned a laugh. "Sold. Would you mind helping me?"

Following the instructions in the hospital paperwork and what she'd witnessed from the nurses firsthand, Elizabeth delicately helped Jill maneuver her way inside to the couch. After a late breakfast, physical therapy, and lotion application to keep her skin smooth and awesome, the two of them settled in for a session with the Game Show Network before Elizabeth had to head out for the rest of her workday.

"Speaking of the man bullet," Jill said, between episodes of *The Price Is Right*, "are you still seeing that girl from Hilton Head?"

"Pam the trust-fund baby? Nope. We fizzled two and a half years back."

She deflated. "I'm way behind on my town gossip."

Elizabeth grabbed the remote and paused mid-prize-reveal. "You've come to the right place. I know all of it. I mean, I don't generally spread the negative stuff, because that just hurts pretty much everyone, but I'll happily dish out the good stuff. In recent news, Mr. Connor from security at the strip mall is also stripping down with Elaine the florist."

"No."

"Yes. I couldn't make this stuff up, and she's all glowy. I love it."

"That makes me so happy."

Elizabeth smiled. "Right? Me, too."

"What's everyone so happy about?" Devyn asked, entering the living room with a tired smile. It was the first they'd seen of her since she'd shut herself away to wheel and deal, or whatever it was she did during her working hours.

"Security guards and florists hooking up," Jill told her matter-of-factly. "It's all the rage."

Devyn raised an eyebrow as she collapsed onto the love seat. "That's celebration-worthy?"

Jill tossed a pillow at her sister. "Small-town celebratory, yes. Get on board."

"With small towns?" She winced. "Been there. Done that."

"Biggest mistake you ever made was not embracing this place," Jill said, with a wink. Apparently, Dreamer's Bay was a point of disagreement between the two. Elizabeth couldn't imagine anyone not loving their town. But she had more friendly gossip to report and turned to Jill. "And Darlene, the assistant librarian, is going back to school to get her master's so she can be *head* librarian, and the lizard in the waiting room at Dr. Piedmont's dermatology practice is apparently a girl and not a boy as they thought, which has opened up all sorts of breeding issues with the other lizard, who remains male."

"How do you know all this?" Devyn asked, the edges of her mouth tugging in amusement.

Elizabeth shrugged. "I do odd jobs for a living. I'm everywhere throughout the week. Plus, people think I'm unassuming and speak freely in front of me."

Jill pointed at her. "They trust you."

"And they should." Elizabeth pointed right back. "Remember. I don't pass along any of the negative stuff."

"How can you not?" Devyn asked, incredulous. "That's the fun part. C'mon. Tell us something bad about someone, Elizabeth. Who's having a torrid affair with their next-door neighbor? Live a little."

She sat up straight and laughed outright at the notion. Devyn was bold, that was for sure. "I most certainly will not divulge that kind of tawdry gossip. Plus, I'm saved by the clock and need to run." She kissed Jill's cheek with an affectionate smack, and turned to Devyn. "Walk me out?"

"Yep," Devyn said. She got up and followed Elizabeth to the front porch.

Once they made it outside and the door was safely closed behind them, she turned to Devyn. "It's about Jill. She thinks you don't want to be here."

Devyn's eyes went wide, understanding crossed her features, and she sighed. "No. It's not that. I want to be here for her. I just…have a lot going on, and my home is in Philly, and…" She glanced behind her and swallowed, regrouping. "She said that?"

Elizabeth nodded, feeling the concern crease her features. "And it's not necessarily my business, except that my heart aches for her and what she's working through, ya know? And then for her to imagine that her sister is anything but happy to step into her life for a while? Gotta be rough."

Devyn nodded and rubbed her forehead. "You're right. Of course, you're right. I'll talk to her."

"No," Elizabeth said. "Then she'll know that's what we were talking about out here, and everything you say will feel inauthentic."

"Inauthentic."

"Right." Elizabeth stepped in, and dropped her voice. "The best thing to do is find little ways to show her."

Devyn stared at her as if she'd spoken another language. "I'm awful at this sort of thing. I'm a go-getter. I barrel into things headfirst. I don't do subtle. I'm results oriented."

Elizabeth took a moment, caught off guard by Devyn's show of weakness, and the true remorse that radiated. "Okay. That's fair. Can I make a suggestion, then?"

"Please."

"Spend time with her. Maybe find ways to point out that you're enjoying that time. Less preoccupation with work when you're together. You seem really focused on email specifically. Also, less glancing at your phone every five minutes as if something more pressing is looming."

"Well, I have a job back home," Devyn pointed out.

"You also have one here." Elizabeth delicately placed a hand on Devyn's shoulder.

"Fine," Devyn said, closing her eyes momentarily. "I'll give it a shot. Less phone. Stay present."

"There ya go. That's all I'm asking. For Jill."

"For Jill." Devyn gave her head a shake. "Elizabeth Draper. Unlikely voice of reason."

Elizabeth gasped. "Unlikely? Excuse me. More like the *most* likely. I have this town and the people in it figured out."

"That include me?" Devyn raised an eyebrow, and Elizabeth's entire midsection squeezed.

"Duh."

"Duh? We're back in high school now?" But she said it in jest, and jesting Elizabeth could hang with. She enjoyed it, even.

"Does that mean I should kiss your popular feet, then?"

"No, but maybe we could talk about my ass." With a wink she headed back inside, leaving Elizabeth standing there gaping, unable to reply, and not at all thinking about Devyn Winters's perfectly shaped ass as it sashayed its way through the door.

Okay, so that just happened.

She blinked and turned to the street, cheeks aflame and libido firing without even consulting her. Yeah, maybe she had time to find a bottle of water before heading to her next job.

Her mouth had gone unexpectedly dry.

CHAPTER TEN

Ronnie Roo's was packed like a dented can of plump sardines when Devyn arrived. Now that she was back in town, she was actually reverting to sentences like that one. Comical and tragic at the same time, but she decided to roll with it.

The familiar smell of freshly fried onion rings and sizzling burgers smacked her in the face and transported her in time. Years back, she and her friends had patronized Roo's, the sloppy and wonderful burger joint, after each and every football game, still in uniform and riding high on their teenage high horses. They were good days, if a little stunted in the depth department. She'd felt happy and confined at the same time back then, wondering about the great big world beyond their town. She'd always been an adventurer at heart. But Roo's was a welcome sight that evening. She smiled and took in the room. The cluttered walls hadn't changed. License plates, traffic signs, fishing poles, coffee mugs, musical instruments, farm equipment, and pictures of the four celebrities who'd passed through town were all thrown together in a series of endearing collages that flanked the room.

She scanned the bustling dining area until her eyes landed on the table of women near the bar, seated around a high-top. They turned as she approached, breaking into an identical four-way grin. Cricket was the first to call out to Devyn. She'd gained about twenty-five pounds over the years but still looked as glamorous as ever with her red hair piled on top of her head like a soft and flowy billow of smoke. Devyn glanced at her gaping neckline and blinked. *Hello*. She'd also had the girls done. Maybe twice.

"Well, look who just waltzed her way into Roo's looking drop-dead gorgeous and successful," Cricket said loudly. Several nearby tables turned and smiled. She recognized Mrs. Hudson from the Laundromat and nodded hello, before turning back to Cricket.

"Shut up and hug me," Devyn said. She pulled Cricket into a one-armed tight embrace and turned to Lisa, who she'd heard was a Mary Kay consultant now. Made sense, as her makeup had always been perfection. "Good to see ya, Lees. It's been too long."

"We wondered when you'd shuffle back to the little ol' Bay." She frowned. "Sorry the circumstances had to be what they are. We were all sad to hear."

"Me, too. But Jill's doing better each day. Slowly on the mend." In fact, after some tips from her PT instructor, Jill felt confident enough to spend the evening on her own, freeing Devyn up to get together with her old friends. It was a big step for Jill, but Devyn would make sure to text her several times throughout the evening to be sure she was okay.

"We're so glad to hear that," Lisa said, in a hushed tone and emotional hand to her heart. "Bless her heart, she's been through so much."

Coco, the short and spunky one of the group who used to top their cheerleading pyramids, hopped off her barstool, offered a salute, and grabbed Devyn around the waist for a playful bear hug. "You haven't lost your strength," Devyn said with a laugh, hugging her old friend as she shuffled side to side.

When she released her, Coco tossed her shoulder-length dark hair and flexed. "CrossFit four times a week, inspired by two kids and a messy divorce. Working on getting back in the dating saddle and thinking about that one over there." She nodded to a blond guy in an Armani shirt at the bar, nursing a beer. Most likely a tourist. Very few locals wore Armani in a beach town.

Devyn winked. "I have faith in your comeback."

Heather was the last to greet her. Always the most beautiful and judgmental of the group, she gave Devyn a calm once-over. "You're looking good," she said cautiously, as they hugged, never one to dish out too many compliments. In Heather's eyes, doing so made her relinquish control. She'd confessed as much growing up. Seemed things hadn't changed.

"I appreciate that. So do you," Devyn said. Heather's dark blond hair fell a little longer than was customary for a woman over twenty-two, but Heather wore it well. She still looked great. Coco's guy-at-the bar passed Heather a glance, and she smiled demurely and turned away.

Same old Heather. A friend to your face and stealing your boyfriend the very next minute. Coco hadn't seemed to notice.

"Sit, sit," Cricket said, kicking out a chair at their table.

"What can I get you?" the waiter asked. Devyn surveyed the four pink Zinfandels already on the table, and felt the pressure to conform. What was that about? She was back in town a few weeks and already losing her identity. It felt eerily familiar and awful.

"Scotch, neat," she told him, finding her footing. "The good kind." He nodded and scurried away, probably to find out if they even carried scotch. Dreamer's Bay, in its simplicity, was more of a beer and wine kind of a place.

"Since when do you drink straight whiskey?" Cricket asked, seemingly shocked and impressed.

Devyn smiled, her polite muscle in place. "Just a thing I picked up."

"Very city girl of you," Lisa said, and sipped from her wine. "My husband, Len, drinks scotch when his week's been a rough one."

"Elliot, too," Cricket exclaimed. "Though he prefers bourbon. When he gets home and pours the bourbon, I just know. Steer clear."

Devyn resisted the urge to wince as the conversation shifted to the three remaining husbands and their feelings about alcohol, sports, lawn care, and parenting. If they'd somehow slipped back to the 1960s, she wished someone would have notified her. Ten minutes later, they were still at it.

"Elliot can't stand it when people traipse across the lawn when there's a perfectly good sidewalk right there. Drives him insane. He does that thing where he huffs a lot about it." She demonstrated the huffing.

"Talk about inconsiderate," Coco said, nodding earnestly along with the demo.

"Len is the same way," Lisa said. "What gets him going is when the ice cream man comes ting-a-linging along well past eight in the evening. Who needs ice cream once the kiddies start going to sleep anyway?" She shook her head in Len solidarity.

Devyn smiled blandly, feeling more and more numb to the conversation. Was this all these four really talked about? Had it always been this way? It had, she realized. They'd always been boy crazy, and though she'd played along, she'd secretly been dreaming of so much more than snagging a man and settling down. That's what this town did to you, though. These women were the perfect, sad examples. What about their own hopes and dreams?

"What about you, Dev? We're going on and on and you're pretty much the main attraction here."

She swallowed her scotch and let it burn. She gave her head a slight shake as it made its way down. "Me? What about me?"

"You seeing anyone?" Heather asked, leaning her chin on her palm casually.

"Yeah, what are the men like in Philadelphia?" Coco asked.

"The men are fine," Devyn said, nonchalantly. "I just don't date them." She glanced at the faces and realized they honestly knew very little about her. Well, it was time to fill them in. "I'm gay. You guys knew that, right?"

Coco blinked, and Lisa sputtered over her pink wine as discreetly as possible, but Devyn didn't move a muscle. This wasn't a big deal. This was just her life, only now the details were a little different from what they'd previously known.

"I'd heard a rumor," Cricket said. Aha. So, apparently Devyn just confirmed what they'd already suspected. She watched Cricket rebound from her initial, uninhibited reaction with a festive burst of energy. "Well, that's just fantastic. Really exciting. We needed a lesbian in our group, and now we have one. Diversity rocks." Devyn studied the faces of the others, who nodded enthusiastically along like overly made-up bobble heads. Did they? Had they been longing for a lesbian friend all along? She tried not to smile patronizingly.

"Any special lady?" Cricket asked.

"Nope," she said, setting her glass on the table. "Been living the single life for a while now. I go out. Nothing too serious. Not a lot of time for romance with my job. Maybe someday, though."

"Maybe someday." Heather nodded like she'd beat Devyn at some sort of cool contest, which was fine because Devyn realized she seemed immune to what Heather thought, a big improvement over the time she'd worn flats to the school dance when Heather thought heels would have been the more sophisticated choice. She'd chastised herself for that decision for months afterward, and just thinking about it now made her uncomfortable.

The table switched to talk of the holiday auction, which seemed odd, as it was still late spring. But maybe they started early these days. In the midst of chatter about catering, donated excursions, and silent auction items that just had to be bigger this year than last, Devyn's eyes roamed the restaurant. Then paused. Because standing in the doorway, looking for a table, was none other than Elizabeth. She had on slim-fitting jeans with a hole in the knee and a plain white T-shirt. A very basic outfit that looked way too good for what it was. Her brown-blond hair—she still couldn't decide which it was—was down and a little tousled. She'd wondered if that had been on purpose or a happy accident. She shook her head at what an interesting character she was.

"What do you think, Devyn? Do people enjoy shrimp or steak more at a gathering?" Lisa asked, and pursed her red lips in anticipation of the answer. That was a lot of lipstick right there.

She blinked. Replayed the question she'd missed the first time. "Uh…I'd say shrimp, but a combo couldn't hurt. Depends on the chef."

"She makes a valid point," Coco said, and they were off again on their event planning. Devyn drifted back, locating Elizabeth sliding into a booth with a bald man with really impressive biceps.

"You remember Dexter," Heather said, following her gaze. She then signaled the waiter for more wine.

Devyn squinted and looked again. "*That's* Dexter? What in the world happened?"

"A total success story," Cricket said, and fanned herself like Scarlett O'Hara in the heat of the day.

"With pillow lips to boot," Coco added. Everyone turned to her.

"I knew it," Lisa said, and shook her head. "I just knew it, you blatant whore."

"What?" Coco grinned proudly and then pretended to wave away the attention. "I'm single now. I can mingle."

Devyn tried not to cringe outwardly at that line. "So, are they a thing? Dexter and Elizabeth?" Somehow that just didn't seem to fit for her. Especially the way Elizabeth had leaned into her harmless flirting.

Heather laughed quietly. "No."

Cricket leaned in. "No, Dexter's a man about town, and Elizabeth's gay, though I've never actually seen evidence of that."

"Not true," Coco said. "She follows after Thalia from the little spa like a puppy dog. It's cute, if it weren't so sad."

Lisa raised a finger. "Oh, and she had a girlfriend a couple of years back. Remember? The one with the really loud car that went vroom, vroom, chugga, vroom?"

"Oh, that's right," Cricket said vaguely, as if tasting something unpleasant she couldn't place. "And the unfortunate slicked-back ponytail."

"Always a ponytail with those girls," Heather said, taking another delicate sip.

Devyn squinted and swallowed her offense at the judgmental and inaccurate statement. Some battles weren't worth it. Her thoughts returned to confirmation that Elizabeth Draper was gay. This was entirely helpful information. She turned back to Elizabeth and smiled. Good for her. It wasn't easy to be yourself in a small town like this one. She knew firsthand and had failed miserably. Apparently, Elizabeth had conquered the fear in a way Devyn hadn't been able to, years back. Given, things were different now, sure, but still. "Excuse me for a moment. I'll be right back," Devyn told her friends, who all exchanged a knowing look. Gay people were gathering. Imagine that.

When she approached Elizabeth and Dexter's table, they were laughing at something on Dexter's phone. There was a lightness to their banter, a warmer vibe from where she'd just been, almost like stepping out of an uncomfortable rainstorm into a ray of sunshine. She exhaled and felt the tension melt away.

Elizabeth turned as Devyn landed at their table, and her green eyes lit up. "Devyn, what the what? Hey. Wasn't expecting to see you at Roo's."

She felt her features slide into an authentic grin. Elizabeth's nonthreatening persona had a way of putting her instantly at ease. "Hi. Didn't mean to interrupt."

"You're not," Elizabeth said. "Just me and Dex."

Devyn shrugged. "I just saw the familiar faces and thought I'd say hello." Her gaze shifted from Elizabeth to Dexter. "Really nice to see you again, Dexter. It's been a while."

He smiled and, without so much as a pause, stood and offered her a friendly hug. "Good to see you back in town. Hey, want to join us?" He slid over, making room in the booth.

Devyn passed a glance to her friends in the bar. The thought of returning to them wasn't high on her list, though an inevitable social responsibility. "No, I couldn't. You guys are having a nice meal together."

"Which happens at least several nights a week," Elizabeth informed her. "We're an unconventional couple. We have a third wheel, but she's married with a kid and at home right now."

"Really. Huh. Lot of women in your life, it seems," she said to Dexter with a playful smile.

He rolled up his sleeve to display a tattoo on his forearm that read *Blessed*. "It is what it is."

"Are you sure?" Elizabeth asked. "We'd love to have you. You can share our onion ring pile. It's why we come here."

"An onion ring pile is hard to pass up." She wouldn't have expected herself to want to hear about Elizabeth's day of odd jobs, and "only positive" gossip from the field, but here she was, wishing she had the night free for an onion pile and just that. The perky weirdo had apparently worked her way onto the endearing list. How had that happened? "I can't, but I'm gonna take you up on it another night."

Elizabeth followed her gaze to the bar and recognition landed. "Oh. It's the whole gang of you. A squad reunion?" She said it delicately, as if the idea didn't thrill her but she also didn't want to be obvious. Devyn didn't blame her. She saw how their group must look to others, then and now, and retroactively hated her younger self for it.

Devyn shifted uneasily, now aware of the fact that she didn't necessarily want to be lumped in with the women who used to be her very best friends. "Yes, just catching up, as they say. We don't really stay in touch."

Dexter raised his beer and offered a lazy grin. "Send the ladies my best."

"Will do. They'll love it. Trust me."

Devyn smiled one last time at Elizabeth, nodded, and took her leave. A final glance over her shoulder showed the duo back to whatever fun conversation she'd interrupted.

"Did you see the heels on Melinda Masters at the firemen's pancake breakfast last weekend?" Cricket was asking the table when Devyn returned. "Horrendous. I was embarrassed for her and all her extended family."

Heather laughed quietly. "Not only did I see them, but I snapped a photo so we could all never forget." She located said photo and turned it around so the table could gawk. The heels weren't that awful, and it was now clear to Devyn that these women were looking for any shred of evidence that they might be superior to everyone else. She cringed internally and buckled in for a night of catty judgment. Not far away, a kinder table with an onion ring pile offered a nice distraction. The view wasn't a bad one either. She stole a glance at Elizabeth in that simple white T-shirt that was anything but, and smothered a smile. Nope, not a bad view at all.

❖

"What time do I need to hit the road?" Dexter asked, and reached for one of the awesome onion rings.

Elizabeth glanced at her watch, remembering her text exchange with Thalia. "She said she'd meet me here for drinks at nine. So maybe I should make myself free by eight forty-five."

"That gives me a few more minutes to devour these bad boys," he said, dunking one of the rings in the specialty sauce Elizabeth adored. Ronnie Jr., the head chef, was killing it these days.

"Do you remember your plan for tonight?" he asked, in coach mode now.

Elizabeth sighed. "Just be myself, and not get caught up in the excitement of what could be. Thalia is…Thalia."

"And?"

"Let her chase me for a change." She glanced down at her outfit. "I kept it completely casual tonight for that very reason. I didn't want to look like I was trying too hard."

"Excellent. That's what I'm talkin' about." He tossed back the rest of his beer and stood, giving his arms a traditional flex. Several women from nearby tables turned their way in unison. Elizabeth smiled at her lap. He really did have an amusing effect on the ladies.

"Have a good night, Dex, my good buddy. You seeing Misty?"

He grinned big and bold, which told her everything she needed to know. He was into this new girl, and she was witnessing a whole new Dexter. He rubbed his chin. "Outlook is good."

"I was hoping you'd say that. I like the way you sparkle when I say her name."

"Nope." He dropped his hand in protest. "Dudes don't sparkle."

"They do, too."

He exhaled. "Fine. Maybe I do. What do I know? I don't recognize my damn self, so anything is possible." He pointed at her. "You be good to yourself."

"On it," she said, to his retreating form.

On her own now, she settled back into the booth and checked her watch. Fifteen minutes to Thalia. She should figure out what drink she'd order, imagining that it probably said something about her. She didn't enjoy that she cared as much as she seemed to about the way Thalia viewed her, but some things are just best embraced. Elizabeth flipped through the folio, admiring the photos of various cocktails she knew very little about. Yes, something more sophisticated than her go-to IPA would surely set the right tone for "You really want to get to know me better. I'm not a total doofus." She flipped the small booklet to the back cover and stared at a martini with a trio of olives on a stick. Would you look at that? She could be Bond. Elizabeth Bond. Perfect, because Ms. Elizabeth Bond could be sexy without trying too hard. She smiled at all the right moments, but not too much, and knew how to toss her hair with barely a gesture. Feeling inspired, she raised her hand for Irene, the server and part-time library attendant.

"Figure out something you'd like, Liz?" Irene asked. She looked super cute today.

"Did you get highlights?" she asked.

Irene beamed and lightly touched her head. "You're the only person who's noticed."

"They look great. I'm not just saying that. You have a whole new pop to you."

Irene smiled and thanked her, still blushing, and Elizabeth was glad she'd taken the time to say something. Getting back to business, she pointed at the photo on the back of the booklet. "I'll have one of these, please. A martini." She even felt a little fancy saying it.

"Unlike you."

She passed her a wide-eyed, can-you-believe-it look. "I know. I'm trying something new."

"I'm impressed. Vodka or gin?"

Oh, this was getting harder. "Whatever the house recommends."

"We do a pretty good vodka martini. What brand would you prefer?"

She knew so little. "Um…I'll take the one with the bird on the side."

Irene nodded, apparently impressed with her choice. This was going well. The martini and three sophisticated olives arrived a few minutes later and she took a preliminary sip to get the swing of things. Whoa. Okay. That was…not beer. Or even wine, beer's much more boring cousin. Hell, it wasn't even like the basic whiskey she kept in her truck for special occasions, like Scout's adoption. After a second sip, she sank back in defeat at her failed attempt to bond with this awful-tasting cocktail. At least it came with a snack. The only problem was if she ate those olives now, her drink would look woefully naked and much less like the drink of Ms. Elizabeth Bond when Thalia arrived. She took another sip and resisted the urge to slither under the table in disdain. Instead, she let her gaze drift to the bar. She could people-watch until Thalia arrived, which definitely wouldn't be long now. At this point, she was already eight minutes late. Across the room, Cricket was saying something animatedly to the other members of the cheerleaders—yes, she apparently did still think of them as cheerleaders and probably always would. Coco whooped in response and Heather, the meanest of them all, shook her head and smiled blandly. Devyn stared into her drink, which was a lot more hard-core than Elizabeth's even. Some kind of scotch, maybe? It was nice seeing her out and taking a moment for herself. She'd been so present for Jill since their talk, and it showed in Jill's demeanor. Devyn deserved a moment away…even if those were, sadly, the friends she chose to spend it with.

Another ten minutes went by.

Then another.

Elizabeth tried to stop watching the door. Maybe she should just go. Call it a night. Something had obviously come up in Thalia's world, and that was fine. She was feeling a little tired anyway. But then just as Elizabeth stood next to her booth poised to drop some cash and leave, there she was. Thalia Perkins, who she often called by her first and last name in her head. Jet black hair swept to one side, and a look on her face that said she was happy to be there. It felt a little bit like the world shifted in slow motion. Elizabeth grinned and waved.

But wait, Thalia wasn't alone. There was a woman with her, a redhead with a lot of eyeliner, whispering in her ear, and man with several tattoos and a nose piercing standing next to her. They weren't locals.

Elizabeth waved again, less enthusiastically this time. Okay, so tonight would not include one-on-one time after all. But that was okay. They could do that another time, right?

Thalia spotted her and headed over to the table. "Hey, there," she said, sliding into the booth. She pursed her heavily glossed lips. She had good ones.

"Hi," Elizabeth said, with maybe too much enthusiasm. She should work on that. Ms. Bond should play it more cool and aloof. She forced herself to relax back against the cushion of the booth. That should help. She watched as the two new individuals took their spots. The guy next to Elizabeth, and the redhead next to Thalia. Too close to Thalia, if you asked her.

"I brought Skeet and Mode with me."

She blinked. "Skeet and Mode?"

The redhead raised her hand. "Mode. Nice to meet you. Skeet and I, we go way back with this one." She hooked a thumb at Thalia.

Thalia nodded and glanced around the room as if taking stock. "Massage school," she said, settling back on Elizabeth, then seemed to notice her for the first time. "I like this top. It's adorable in its childlike innocence."

"It does remind me of yesteryear," Mode said sagely. "I love your youthful spirit."

"Mine? Oh, thank you." Elizabeth smiled, not quite sure where that comment came from. "As for the shirt, my friend KC and I found it at—"

"They have a staff here or what?" Skeet asked with disdain, dropping his hand palm first onto the table with a thud.

"Would you chill out and find your Zen?" Thalia asked, shaking her head in annoyance. "I'm talking to my friend, Elizabeth."

"She *is* cute and sweet," Mode said. "You were right."

Elizabeth wasn't sure whether to be flattered or unnerved that they were talking about her like she wasn't present. She focused on the positive. "Well, that's very nice of you to say. Thank you." She turned to Skeet. "Irene is our server. She'll be back in just a moment. She's dropping off food right over there." She sipped the martini. Nope. Still awful. "How was business today?" she asked Thalia.

"Three therapeutic massages, and two facials." Thalia pursed her pouty lips and studied the room again. "Not bad for small-town USA."

"I can't believe you wound up in a place like this," Mode said. "I always imagined you'd open up a shop in Austin or San Fran."

"There's something very chill about the Bay," Thalia said. "I dig its vibe."

Elizabeth smiled. "There really is something special here."

Mode nodded. Skeet glared.

"Okay...well. We should really get going." Thalia stood and passed Elizabeth her killer smile, the one that often left her in a puddle. Not tonight.

Elizabeth frowned, not understanding. "But you just got here." She pointed. "Skeet was about to order a drink."

"These guys traveled in today and we have a reading with a fortune teller at ten. But I want us to get together soon, okay? We need some one-on-one time. You're cute," she said, touching Elizabeth's chin as she passed. Skeet and Mode were hot on her heels.

"But..." Elizabeth turned and watched them leave, confused, let down, and alone with a martini she didn't even like. "That did not go as planned," she whispered to the empty table. She slid the offending cocktail away from her, grabbed her bag, and headed out. She heard female laughter from the bar to her left as she exited the restaurant and stole a final glance at the table of former cheerleaders. At least the more sought-after individuals in the world were enjoying themselves.

Apparently, nothing had changed.

CHAPTER ELEVEN

Good God, it was finally over. The night had been a rough one, but Devyn had somehow pushed through and nodded and smiled in all the right places with her old friends, until she'd finally managed to produce a few well-placed yawns and escape. Given the caretaker role she'd assumed for Jill, the other women were quick to nod sympathetically when she insisted it was time for her to head out.

Finally, able to breathe again, she drove the now-quiet streets of Dreamer's Bay on her way back to Jill's. With the windows down and the radio playing softly she commanded herself to relax. Being back in the Bay among all of her old friends was a head trip, and not a fun one. Alone now, she savored the quiet and the freedom that came from disconnecting from her laptop. Her phone was also tucked safely away in her back pocket. One breath in. One breath out. She released the sounds of her friends' increasingly shrill chatter and replaced it with the sounds of the rustling leaves and ribbits of frogs. The exercise began to work. She turned onto the residential street that led into Jill's neighborhood and paused at the woman walking along the sidewalk. She recognized that easy gait. Elizabeth.

"This is twice in one night," Devyn said through the open window, slowing the tiny car to match Elizabeth's measured pace.

"That is one small car," Elizabeth said, with an interested grin, as she walked. "It suits you."

Devyn balked, mortally wounded. "It so does not. At all. Never say that again." She shook her head. "This car is nothing like me, I'll have you know."

"If you say so." Elizabeth shoved her hands into the pockets of her jeans. The night was a nice one but still a little chilly.

"Can I offer you a ride in the smallest car on the planet?"

"No, thanks. I love walking at night." She glanced up at the trees as if acknowledging friends. "It's why I rarely take my truck places. That, and I get to have a third beer."

Devyn shifted her lips to the side. "I wouldn't have pegged you for a beer drinker."

"No?" Elizabeth asked. "What would you have pegged me as?"

"Maybe something colorful and frozen."

Elizabeth placed a hand over her heart. Her jaw fell in abject horror. "I will have you know that not only do I enjoy a good beer, but I can speak in detail about flavor profiles. Give me a good IPA and I'm a goner." She softened. "But fine, I occasionally indulge in a margarita if it's fruity enough. Fruity is festive."

Devyn smiled. "You have strong opinions on the topic. I saw you with a martini earlier."

She looked horrified. "A total mistake. I have no idea why people enjoy those things. Do you?" She didn't wait for an answer. "Seems like cruel punishment. Even the olives tasted like vodka. A shame."

"Well, they work faster than beer, for one. I indulge in them on occasion."

"I offer my sincere condolences."

Devyn laughed. "Thank you."

They walked and drove in tandem silence, the easy kind. The tall trees swayed quietly overhead, their branches commingling in peaceful underscore. "You going to tail me the whole way?" Elizabeth asked.

"Just making sure Elizabeth Draper, sweetheart of Dreamer's Bay, gets home safe and sound. Can't have the town jewel kidnapped at this late hour. It's my civic duty."

Elizabeth chuckled. "That kind of thing doesn't happen around here. You know that." Of course Devyn did, but Elizabeth was feeling playful, daring, and running with it. After her crash and burn with Thalia, it felt like there was very little to lose. "And not everyone thinks of me as the town jewel. Trust me."

"Well, they're stupid, then." Elizabeth looked like she could use that compliment, and Devyn wondered what had deflated her mood since they'd last spoken. She remembered seeing her talking to a new group after Dexter left the restaurant. "Who were the friends you were with earlier? I don't think I recognize them."

"Thalia Perkins. She owns the Massage and Spa Boutique on First Avenue."

"What's the actual name?" Devyn asked.

"That is the name."

"Creative."

That earned her a slight smile. "It could be better. I agree. The other two are her friends from school. I don't know them."

Devyn just had an inkling that there was more to this Thalia thing than Elizabeth was letting on. "Is she someone you're seeing?"

Elizabeth sighed. "No. She's beautiful and yes, I have a crush, but she's out of my league."

She took a moment with that because it was ludicrous. "She is not."

"Nice of you. But she's many jalapeños."

"I don't know what that means, but your business name alone slam-dunks hers, and you're miles more beautiful." It was true. Thalia looked like Botox might be her best friend, and she had cold eyes. Elizabeth was warm and vivacious. No competition, as far as Devyn was concerned.

She watched as a slow but managed grin appeared on Elizabeth's face. "I won't debate whether it's true or not, but thank you for saying that."

"No problem."

"If you are truly committed to delivering me safely to my front door, it's right up there. Third on the left."

Devyn followed her gaze to a one-story house on the outside bend of the cul-de-sac with the curvy driveway. It was just as she would imagine for Elizabeth. Cheerful, well-kept, and quaint. The house was bricked in white with a pale lavender door and dusty gray shutters. Matching purple flowers with yellow centers had been arranged in two well-manicured flower beds. She could easily picture Elizabeth relaxing with one of her prized IPAs on the covered front porch, watching the world go by and waving to her neighbors. "Your house is pretty," she said to herself as much as Elizabeth. "Great curb appeal."

"From a flashy Realtor like yourself, I say thank you. I love it. One of my favorite things in life is that house." She paused in the middle of that winding driveway and placed her hands on her hips. "Safe and sound. You've done your civic duty."

Devyn nodded. "I can sleep easier now." A pause. "You have a nice night. I'm off to see if Jill finished the book I left her reading."

"Trust me, she did. In fact, she's been flying through them this week. I can't keep up. I swung by the library this afternoon and picked her up some fresh meat. Mainly crime novels and biographies. Her favorite. But I tossed a steamy romance in there just in case."

Devyn stared at her, amazed. "You didn't have to do that. That's not in your job description."

Elizabeth walked to Devyn's car and leaned down to the passenger side window, relaxing onto her forearms. "When are you going to figure out that I'm not motivated by cash? Trust me, if I was, I'd have a lot more of it." She gestured behind her with her chin. "That house won't be paid off until I'm a hundred and eighty-three." She shrugged. "Doesn't bother me."

Devyn swallowed the guilt that crept in for the assumption. "You're a good person, you know that? A little weird. Probably too perky. But good."

Elizabeth tapped the car twice and stood. "Weird, perky, and good sounds like a balanced combo I can live with. I like me." She walked backward a few steps just as the wind lifted her hair. Devyn's breath caught and her stomach flip-flopped uncomfortably. "Night, Devyn. See you in the morning."

"Yeah," she said absently and watched as Elizabeth made her way up the walk and slipped behind that lavender door, a little blown away by how incredibly attractive Elizabeth now seemed. But she must have always been beautiful. Why was Devyn just now truly noticing the magnitude? *Because you've had your face in your laptop or your ear to your phone every spare moment of every day lately*, her brain supplied. She stared at the house, gave her head a mystified shake, and drove on.

What had started out as a pretty abysmal evening had just ended in a refreshing exchange. She smiled at the road, the other cars, the foliage along the way, and the cresting water in the distance. Devyn didn't want to move through life with blinders on anymore. She'd almost lost the most important person to her in the world, but didn't. The wake-up call had been swift and startling. She had a choice in front of her. She could be like the Crickets of the world and worry about petty things like clothes, money, success, and status, or she could be more like Elizabeth Draper and love other people and simple lavender doors. Who did she want to be in this world? That was the question.

As she drifted off to sleep that night, her thoughts shifted to a woman with green eyes, a soft smile, and hair of many subtle shades, and then and there, she knew the answer to the question.

Like Elizabeth, she thought. *Be more like Elizabeth.*

CHAPTER TWELVE

Joaquin, I'm telling you that if she likes 22D, she's going to love the penthouse. Private outdoor space for days and a killer view worth way more than the ask. Plus, if she's an entertainer, the thirty-six-hundred-square foot open-concept that comes with that puppy is going to knock her fucking socks off. My recommendation? Work with your client on her budget and show her the penthouse unit *today*."

A pause. Elizabeth smiled as she listened. It was midday on a Wednesday. She'd already walked Hank, helped load a truck full of flowers for Laurel, the owner of Floral Laurel, and spent the rest of the morning with Jill, who was getting stronger each day. Now it was about time for her to pass the caregiver baton to Devyn and head back to her On the Spot responsibilities. First up was a ballroom dance lesson with Gavin Henry, who'd asked for someone to stand in for his wife, allowing him to surprise her with his dance moves later that month. Next, she would scoop up six-year-old Trip Upworth from daycare and shuttle him back to his mother, Greta, who had a doctor's appointment of her own to attend. That would be fun. She and Trip could sing in the car like they always did. And then maybe a quiet night at home with a beer and some of her favorite game show reruns.

But for now, she took a moment to simply watch Devyn, who talked with her hands on business calls even though the person on the other end would never know. She came with a lot of passion for her job; a spitfire.

"I think we're all on the same page," Devyn told the Joaquin guy. "Let's get her in to see the space and get this deal done." She stood and placed her free hand on top of her head. Elizabeth rolled her shoulders at the unexpected shiver it prompted. She couldn't deny it. Devyn was hot. Beautiful, sophisticated, and confident, though still a mystery to her in many ways. Was she now a different person than she'd been in high school? She was starting to think maybe. Devyn began to gesture again, and Elizabeth relaxed against the doorjamb to watch and melt. She was a wanton woman, wasn't she? Headed to hell in a handbasket woven of lust and more lust that had honestly erupted only recently and with surprising vigor. The word *vigor* prompted further immodest thoughts. She closed her eyes and steadied herself momentarily, shifting so that her jeans didn't press quite so…uncomfortably.

"I swear to you, it's going to be a match made in heaven and you're going to deliver a bottle of high-priced champagne to my office for that really beautiful commission that'll come your way. You'll probably name a child after me. It'll be glorious." A pause. "No, I understand. Have I ever steered you wrong?" Another pause. "Exactly. I'll speak to you soon. My love to Camilla."

Devyn clicked off the call and turned, stumbled, and grabbed her heart. "Holy hell. How long have you been standing there?"

"Holy hell. About three and a half minutes. I was listening to you wheel-and-deal like a boss."

"And?" Devyn exhaled slowly, finding her proverbial footing again.

"I'd say you're pretty great at it. You are, aren't you? You can say yes."

The side of Devyn's mouth tugged. "A lot of people think so."

"I'm more interested in what you think."

Devyn didn't hesitate. An easy smile slid onto her face. "I think I'm damn good at my job. Just hard to do it remotely."

Elizabeth came farther into the room and pointed at the desk where it had all just gone down. "I have evidence that says otherwise. You sold me on that penthouse just now, and I'm not even in the market for one."

"Then I'll send over the paperwork immediately," Devyn said.

"As for working remotely, maybe you should move back to the Bay and find out officially." Why the heck did that just come out of her mouth? Her eyes fluttered closed as she attempted to recover.

Devyn, however, did seem to notice, as she laughed at her suggestion and began to stack the file folders on the desk.

"What? I'm serious. Who wouldn't want the best of both worlds? Small-town charm. Big-city job. Sounds awesome to me."

"Not sure I would survive that," Devyn said flatly. The sentiment stung, because it was a hit on the place she loved most, and Elizabeth had a hard time letting it slide. In fact, nope. She wasn't going to.

She advanced on Devyn, who straightened and powered down her laptop. "What is it about this place that you hate so much?"

"I don't *hate* it here."

"You give off that vibe."

Devyn sighed and leaned back against the desk. "Well, for one, not much happens. Ever."

Elizabeth's jaw dropped. "What are you even talking about right now? We have the silent auction soon, and goat yoga just started on the outskirts of town. Goat. Yoga."

"Well, you have me there," Devyn said sarcastically.

"What else is a problem for you?"

Devyn tilted her head side to side. "In my experience, the people here are laser focused on each other. They nitpick. They scrutinize and find fault."

Something occurred to Elizabeth in that moment. Like a really informative lightbulb, she understood one of the reasons Devyn might have a bad taste in her mouth as far as Dreamer's Bay went.

"You're doing it wrong," she said. "That's totally and completely it. Think about it."

"Okay, but I'm not following."

Elizabeth tucked a strand of hair behind her ear, her brain firing. "Most all of your experiences have happened alongside who?"

Devyn stared at her in confusion, not coming up with the answer quick enough for Elizabeth.

"With Cricket and Heather and those other girls from school, who are *awful*." Hearing herself say that out loud, she quickly covered her mouth. "I didn't actually mean that. They're not awful, they're…not as nice as they could be. In the scheme of things. It's likely they mean well."

"No, they're awful," Devyn said, dividing her attention between Elizabeth and a file folder in her hand. "Last week at Roo's pretty much confirmed it."

"Okay then," Elizabeth said, running with the new consensus. "So, maybe your entire experience was colored a little bit by the company you kept back in the day?" She shrugged in slow motion. "Just maybe?"

Devyn met her gaze. "I suppose there's an outside chance that I equate Dreamer's Bay with my adolescent experience, which was, admittedly, pretty shallow and laced with judgment. The end result? Ignoring who I was for years."

"Ouch," Elizabeth said, wincing. That sounded horrible and pretty hard to come back from.

Devyn raised a finger. "And let's be clear, I can accept my share of the blame. I was no peach."

"Then maybe you need to see this place through new eyes."

"And whose might those be?"

"Mine."

Devyn paused her perusal of whatever was in that folder and met Elizabeth's gaze full on. Her hazel eyes sparkled with interest. "Yours, huh?"

Elizabeth pointed at her. "I'll show you the Bay in all her glory."

"This town is a girl?"

"Yes, yes, she is, and she's awesome, and you're going to see that, and miss her desperately when you go home. But at least you'll *know*."

Devyn regarded her with the most unreadable expression on her face. Had she said something completely stupid? It wouldn't be entirely unlike her, but she stood by her offer. "Why are you looking at me like that?"

Devyn shook her head. "You just have a lot of feelings on the topic. Your whole face lit up and took on this animated quality. It was... something to behold."

"Oh." A pause struck, and they simply stared at each other. The moment was a weighted one, and it reminded her of one from her past that she couldn't quite put her finger on. "Sometimes I can get going," she said quietly. "I'm enthusiastic."

"Oh, I know, Ms. Chicken Suit."

"Mrs."

"Excuse me?"

Elizabeth gestured backward to reference the earlier mention. "The chicken is married and lives in the Midwest. I have a whole backstory for her, but I won't bore you with the details. At least not today. Just know that it makes the telegram feel more authentic if the chicken is."

Devyn seemed amused and confused in equal parts. "So noted."

"What I will tell you is that Jill had her eleven o'clock meds, and we did our morning workout to Celine Dion, and now I have to run, so you're in charge. You got this?"

"I'm on top of it. How are her spirits this morning?"

Elizabeth considered the question. "Holding strong. She's more mobile now that she's using the cane, and I think that gives her a sense of independence."

"I've noticed that, too. She's smiling more."

"And singing. She does a great Celine Dion." Elizabeth laughed and reflected on the conversation. She leaned in. "You realize we're like a couple of parents comparing notes on our kid."

"We are." Devyn laughed and shook her head. "We make a good tag team. You the happy ray of sunshine and me the overly ambitious motivator."

"So, are you free this weekend?" Elizabeth asked. Something propelled her and she wasn't about to resist it. There was an energy to her exchanges with Devyn lately that she didn't encounter that often. Okay, ever, and she didn't know at all what it meant, but she did know she craved more of it.

Devyn looked caught off guard. "For what?"

"Relax," she said, with a smile. "I'm merely asking if I can show you some of the reasons I love this little place."

"Oh." It looked like Devyn was mulling over the offer, which was silly, because what else could she possibly have going on other than more work? Which, let's be honest, had to enter the realm of boring at some point. "Yeah, let's do it," she said, finally.

"Perfect." Elizabeth backed out of the room. "Mark off Saturday in the late afternoon. The other fourth-grade teachers are bringing dinner here for Jill, so she'll be all set."

Devyn met her gaze. "What do I have to lose, right?"

❖

"So, I'm adding the sour cream now or waiting?" Devyn used the back of her hand to wipe the wayward strand of hair from her eyes. She'd been toiling over Jill's potato soup recipe for over an hour now, and the heat from the pot was causing her to melt. She'd already tossed away the button-up shirt she'd worn over her black tank top. If this got any worse, she had no problem cooking this soup in her bra. Jill would just have to deal.

"No," Jill said, from her spot at the kitchen table. Her dark hair had been gently curled with Devyn's help and she now applied makeup while looking into a travel-sized mirror. "Condensed milk, remember?"

"Right. The damn condensed stuff. My bad. Now, where is that again?" She scanned the contents of the pantry and found the needed can and darted back to the pot to keep stirring, apparently one of the potato soup rules. Stir, stir, stir. She felt like one of those witches in *Macbeth*. Not that she minded helping Jill get her big night off to a successful start. She checked the clock. Roughly thirty minutes until Jill's teacher friends arrived. Chips and dip were out, and those little mini quiches would be out of the oven in fifteen. They were going to make it.

It was going on five p.m. on Saturday, and the sun still shone brightly, which only seemed to fuel Jill's good mood. She'd been looking forward to her friends visiting for days now, talking through the menu and making sure there was enough variety. "How's your energy level?" Devyn asked. "You still feeling up to this?"

Jill balked. "Are you kidding? Even if I wasn't, I need to see faces besides yours and Elizabeth's. No offense, but I'm a little sick of the both of you." She smiled and stuck out her tongue just like she used to do when they were kids.

"Fine. I'll stick around to make sure everything is set and ready and then let you take it from there. Give you a break from my boring, stupid face."

"Freedom at last," Jill said, with a Braveheart fist in the air.

Devyn passed her a look. "I refuse to let that hurt my feelings." But as far as Devyn was concerned, nothing could dampen her mood. Seeing her sister make progress, not just physically but mentally, was everything to Devyn, and she knew she'd made the right choice in sticking around, even if it meant sweating it out in the kitchen like underqualified hired help while her career spiraled dramatically out of her control. The bruises that once marred Jill's face and limbs had faded significantly. The broken ribs were still very sore, making upper body movement a painful struggle, but were getting better each day. Her left leg injury was the worst and where they focused much of her physical therapy. She still battled to get around as fluidly as she would like, and her pace was slow and measured. The cane was her go-to, but when she became fatigued, they'd swap it out for a wheelchair. Luckily, that was occurring less and less. Not only that, but Jill's sparkle was back. She seemed lighter, more optimistic about the future. For Devyn, the time she and Jill spent together quenched a thirst she hadn't even known she had. Wasn't that something? Turned out Devyn didn't just love her sister, she *needed* her.

"What do you think about putting out those fresh flowers Elizabeth brought yesterday?" Jill asked, tapping her lips. Elizabeth had developed a habit of arriving with something daily to bring a smile to Jill's face. Donuts one day. Coffee another. A huge bouquet of colorful wildflowers the day prior. She had a generous heart, and even if she was a little quirky, they were lucky for her help.

"Great plan." Devyn scanned the room for the right spot as they prepared for Jill's guests. The handful of teachers from the elementary school had decided on a potluck themed evening of wine and Bunco, a game Devyn had no understanding of at all. She wasn't exactly domestic either, but she asked herself what Noreen, the woman who staged all of her listings, would say. A big overflowing vase of flowers on the kitchen table would add lots of color to its boring brown surface.

"I think the kitchen table would be a great spot for them," Devyn said, seeing imaginary Noreen offering a great big thumbs-up in her head. "They'll look amazing there. The fourth-grade group won't know what hit 'em."

"Well, third grade is coming, too, and a couple from fifth, who we tolerate. They tend to pass each other looks. We ignore the looks, because it's the right thing to do."

"Big of you, Jilly. Keep ignoring those looks. Mom would be proud." She located the flowers where Elizabeth had left them in the kitchen window and moved the vase to the table, taking a minute to admire their beauty. Not a high-end expensive arrangement from a florist but a handpicked variety of all colors, shapes, and sizes combined together for a very jumbled, yet pleasing effect. The bouquet reminded her a lot of Elizabeth herself: beautiful and unique without a lot of rhyme or reason. She smiled as the front door opened and closed behind her.

"Liz," Jill said, turning from her spot. "We were just discussing your beautiful flowers."

"You were?" Elizabeth asked, beaming.

Devyn had honestly never known the meaning of the word *radiate* until Elizabeth Draper decided to walk into her life and demonstrate it daily. Yes, it was a little hokey, but the more time she spent in Elizabeth's presence, the more she appreciated her ability to simply radiate her happiness. Broadcast it to the whole damn world with the flip of a switch.

Jill pointed at the wildflowers. "I'm using them to impress my friends."

"Fifth grade, too?" Elizabeth asked, with a grimace.

Jill deflated. "Let's not get overzealous."

"See? I knew those flowers had a purpose." Elizabeth stole a chip from the chip and dip caddy on the counter and then seemed to reconsider and took three more. Devyn smothered a smile and continued arranging the flowers. "Did you know I'm taking your little sister out tonight?"

Jill raised an interested eyebrow, and Elizabeth blushed, glanced at Devyn, and then quickly away.

"Not *out* out."

"Wait. We're not going *out* out?" Devyn asked, and dropped her arms. "This isn't a date?" She was teasing Elizabeth, on a mission to witness more of that glorious blush. It had already swept down her face to her neck and now approached her chest and the tiny dip of cleavage her navy blue top showcased. Yeah, she owed that top a thank-you note.

"Oh." Elizabeth paused. "I didn't think we…I mean, going out in a way that was more like casual, but not. Really, when I thought about it…" She paused and stared at Devyn hard. "You're messing with me, aren't you?"

Devyn laughed and decided the flowers were good to go. "You make it so very easy."

Elizabeth shook her head woefully. "I've been told so for most of my life. I'd say I'm working on it, but let's be real. I'm just gullible, and that's the way it's always going to be. I once bought a timeshare. An actual timeshare."

Jill slowly made her way to Elizabeth. "You're trusting, and that's a good thing."

"My favorite kind of client." Devyn held up her hands. "But if you're offering to take me *out* out, just let me know."

Elizabeth didn't seem to know what to do with that sentence, opening and closing her mouth as the blush spread.

"Ignore my sister," Jill said. She spun a dish towel and cracked Devyn on the ass with it as she passed. "She's always been the troubled one in the family. She was likely dropped on her head."

Devyn winced and rubbed her ass. "Well, look who's getting stronger by the second. Guess I can head home now."

"Not an option," Jill deadpanned. "Who would stir the damn soup?"

Devyn gasped but did as she was told. "We're resorting to swear words now? My, my, Jilly."

Twenty minutes later, a parade of elementary school teachers in lively colors and patterns invaded Jill's house, chatting a mile a minute. Devyn watched them and their unique communication strategies. Most spoke with their hands in a highly animated fashion. They exclaimed a lot about everything: The snacks they'd put out. The new chair that wasn't there last year—amazing. The beautiful flowers. How surprised they were to see Jill moving so well—not quite herself yet, but she'd get there. Exclaiming happened at a rather high volume, and when all of those teachers got to talking at the same time, the decibel level was really something to behold, and then attempt to escape from.

"I'm ready for that night on the town now," she said quietly to Elizabeth, once the Bunco tournament was under way. The teachers now had a hold of the wine, so she could only imagine what was to come. The exclaiming would undoubtedly turn exponential.

"They seem to be all set," Elizabeth said, nodding with satisfaction. Their job here was done. "Follow me," she said over her shoulder.

With a final wave to Jill, it was time to slip out. Devyn followed Elizabeth to the drive and paused.

"The pickup truck again?" Devyn asked, taking in the big, blue two-door. A little beat up, but with lots of character.

"I call her Sugar or Shug for short. Hop in. She's friendly, but then you already know that."

Devyn planned to hop in but took a moment to watch Elizabeth do so first. Seeing her now behind the wheel of that truck...did something to her. Whatever it was, it sent an overwhelming ripple through her middle section and lower. She touched her stomach and then felt the back of her neck prickle with warmth. She was a professional in her thirties, fully used to high-pressure situations, and little Elizabeth Draper was taking her down? No way. Who was she?

"You coming or what?" Elizabeth called, waiting on Devyn and looking really cute in her overt excitement.

Devyn pulled herself from her lust-laced reaction and smiled back. "Yeah. I was just..." She took a steadying breath, commanding her brain to cut that the hell out. "Yep, coming." She climbed into the truck and dug her fingernails into her palm to bring herself into the here and now and stop indulging in racy thoughts about her old high school classmate. She wondered what it would be like to trace the neckline of that top with just one finger. No! She dug her fingernails in further. *Get it together.* Or maybe just lick that line of cleavage slowly. She slammed her eyes shut and inhaled slowly.

In a matter of moments, they were out of the neighborhood, the main drag of Dreamer's Bay, in all its tiny glory, flying past. The visual distraction helped. Fields, meadows, flowers, trees, the park, the ice cream shop, and the small cineplex that apparently now served wine and beer. "Where are we headed?" she asked, focusing on the task.

"Stop one is the strip mall on Corner Street. Do you know it?" Elizabeth flipped on the dash radio and the truck filled with the sounds of Phil Collins, to which Elizabeth promptly began singing. Loudly.

"We're going to get back to the fact that you're belting eighties music like it's your job in a minute." Devyn shook her head and laughed. Elizabeth never ceased to surprise her. "Are we talking about the strip mall with the flower shop and the bakery and what else is in there now?"

"Mr. Pitts Dry Cleaning."

"No."

"Oh, yes."

"You can't be telling the truth right now." Devyn covered her eyes and laughed. "That's gotta be the worst name for a dry-cleaning place I've ever heard."

"Or the best." Elizabeth tapped the side of her head with her pointer finger. "Think about it."

Devyn did briefly, until she was thinking about the fact that Elizabeth maneuvered her truck like a pro and had a very attractive profile that showcased the subtle dimple in her right cheek. Her gaze drifted down to Elizabeth's neck. God, the skin there looked soft. Devyn would have no problem exploring how soft. A strand of dark blond hair fell across Elizabeth's forehead and covered an eyebrow, while a light brown strand fell just short. She also smelled good, like fresh laundry and cotton pulled straight from the wash.

"Don't you think that's cool?"

Devyn blinked at Elizabeth's question. She had no idea if the thing was cool or not, she'd been distracted, admittedly. "Sorry. Which thing?"

Elizabeth turned the radio down. "Did you hear anything I said just now?"

Devyn shook her head, feeling less in control of herself than she had in years. What was it about this town that stripped her of her hard-earned ability to walk into any situation and own it? Why wasn't she owning it anymore? And where was her assistant when she needed her? Karen always kept her on track and focused. She deserved a raise, now that she considered it. Karen wouldn't let her daydream about women. That's why she had a Karen.

"I was telling you about Saturday nights at the strip mall."

And I was objectifying you in a delicious daydream. Devyn hated herself sometimes. "Sorry. Tell me again. I'm at full attention."

Elizabeth tossed her a glance and flipped on her right turn signal, moving them onto Corner Street. "At the end of the week, the owners of those businesses meet in the parking lot, play cornhole, and crack open a beer or two to celebrate the weekend. Cops look the other way. Anyone can play. Anyone is us."

"We're going to play cornhole in a parking lot with Mr. Pitts and the Laurel Floral woman?"

"Among others. Yes, we are." Elizabeth eased the truck into a parking space and turned off the ignition. "Beer's in the back seat. I really hope you're good." She grinned proudly. "I have a reputation to protect." And with that, she hopped down out of the truck and slammed the door.

"Of course she does," Devyn said to the empty cab.

Fifteen minutes later, with a local IPA in her hand, Devyn found herself smack in the middle of a cornhole tournament as the sun cast the sky with brilliant pinks, oranges, and reds on its descent behind the row of businesses. There were five other teams of two, and a handful of spectators who just stopped by to watch and shoot the breeze on a Saturday night. She knew most of them from her growing-up years and accepted the waves and hugs and pats on the back. Charlie Kielbasa, who owned the liquor store, stood next to her as they did battle with beanbags and holes.

"How's your sister getting on?" Charlie asked. He had a toothpick in his mouth and his hair was spiky, but he was otherwise a decent enough looking guy. He had been a couple grades ahead of Devyn in high school. A former football player. Maybe the kicker. Punter? What were they called? It was hard to say.

It was her turn. She tossed her beanbag and watched it fall short of the game board entirely. Damn. Across from her, Elizabeth winced and stared at the ground. "Jill's much improved. Starting to move with more freedom."

"I need to check in on her more, but she's so dang stubborn."

"More? You need to check in on her more?" Devyn asked. She didn't realize that Charlie the liquor store guy checked in on her sister at all.

He looked caught, stared at the sky, and then crumbled. "Ah, hell. Okay. We're smitten with each other. Well, I think she's smitten with me, but she never says. Bosses me around like she is, though."

Devyn nearly choked on her beer. A beanbag landed on the board in front of her. She shot Elizabeth a thumbs-up for the toss that would earn them a point. "Did you say smitten? You're gonna have to back up."

"Yep." He nodded. Now that the cat was out of the bag, he acted as if it were the most casual thing in the world. "We hook up." Another beanbag landed with a thud on the board in front of them and slid into the hole. Elizabeth raised a fist in victory at the additional three points. Devyn swallowed back the shock at what Charlie had just spilled.

"We're up by three now," Elizabeth called to Devyn, who understood that meant she'd better not blow their lead. She took a moment to watch Elizabeth celebrate with a twirl. She was getting sexier by the second. Why had she not noticed what a killer ass she had until now? She was torn between Charlie's revelation and staring at Elizabeth Draper. Finally, she pulled her gaze away and turned.

"You're hooking up with my sister? Jill. As in Jill Winters? We're talking about the same woman? About this tall? Dark hair? Kind heart?"

"Ah, yep," he said. "Thursday is our day, generally speaking."

"Thursday." She scrubbed her forehead. "You and my sister get together on Thursdays for...alone time. And you're smitten. But she refuses to say that she is." She did her best to assemble the facts. "Do I have it?"

"That's about the long and short of it."

Devyn stared at the painted lines of the parking lot, trying to wrap her brain around saucy Jill's secret Thursday life. She'd been married for a couple of years to a man who'd stormed around the house a lot, worked very little, and spent money like a prince—until she'd eventually had enough and divorced him. Jill had shown zero interest in dating again as far as Devyn had seen, but apparently, Devyn wasn't supposed to *see* at all.

"Oh, golly," a sweet female voice said. "If it isn't little Devyn Winters. From what I've heard, your real estate career sounds incredibly exciting." She turned to see Mary Beth Eckhart standing nearby grinning. She was an old friend of their mom's who would stop by for coffee and a game of cards when the girls were young. Just seeing her made Devyn light up from the inside and remember those lighter days.

She placed a hand over her heart. "Ms. Eckhart, it's so good to see you." Before she could stop herself, her arms were around the woman who took her right back to the comforting thoughts of her mom, which was just the best medicine for missing her.

"Good to see you, too, sweet girl. Now that you're in town for a bit, why don't we get together for some coffee and lemon cake over at my house?"

She remembered her one-story at the end of Tisdale Street well. Ms. Eckhart always had a jar of mints in the entryway. "I'd love that. You always made the best lemon cake in South Carolina."

"Still do." Her eyes crinkled when she smiled, reminding Devyn that time had passed and she'd missed a lot. "It's a date."

"Devyn Winters. Are you gonna toss that beanbag or yammer all day?"

Devyn looked across the parking lot to see Elizabeth's eyebrows drawn in and her game face on. "Wow. You take this really seriously, don't you?" Devyn called back. "And you just said 'yammer.'"

But Elizabeth was too hyperfocused on the board to bother responding. Obediently, Devyn tossed a beanbag and watched it sail slowly across the parking lot and into the hole, to her total and utter amazement. Elizabeth leapt into the air and Devyn couldn't help but do the same, reveling in the victory of her throw. Suddenly, the game had purpose. Their opponents, Chip and Luke from the car wash, were fairly consistent and would not be an easy takedown. However, the game now had possibility. She tossed, Luke tossed, Elizabeth, and then Chip. Over and over. As the number on the scoreboard climbed, so did Devyn's stake in the game. The onlookers cheered and made predictions, calling out their support for one team or the other.

"Take 'em down, Devyn," a pregnant woman yelled from under the awning of Mr. Pitts. She didn't know her, just a friendly spectator, but it made her feel included. All of them did. She smiled and raised her beer, feeling lighter than she had in a very long time. She and Elizabeth took the game in a nail biter of a last round, with Devyn finding her technique more and more as they progressed. They went on to play Mr. Pitts himself, paired up with his wife, Terri, who quite honestly was the better player with a perfect arc to her toss. Wow. Yet she and Elizabeth beat them, too.

"Now listen, this next team is no joke," Elizabeth told her quietly as they waited for another match to finish. "They'll start slow, but once we get comfortable? They'll start to ease in and steal the points." Devyn nodded along, liking the way Elizabeth's breath tickled her ear subtly. Yeah, that definitely did things to her.

"Steal the points, huh?" she asked.

"We can't let them."

She'd never seen Elizabeth so serious about anything other than tragedy, ever. Her blue eyes held fire, and Devyn was not about to let her down. She touched her longneck bottle of beer to Elizabeth's. "Let's do it."

The nine or ten people who remained for what would be the final round clapped as Devyn and Elizabeth took their places on separate sides of the boards. They made eye contact and nodded at each other in solid teammate solidarity. They were up against Lulu and Peggy from the Amazin' Glazin' Donut Shop, and word on the sidewalk was that they had regular practice sessions between frosting batches. Peggy wore a glove on her right throwing hand, and Lulu tied a lucky bandana around her forehead before lining up her shot. Devyn swallowed and rolled her shoulders, flabbergasted at how much this mattered to her.

It was over in a matter of minutes. Peggy and Lulu did just as Elizabeth said they would, allowing them to put a few points on the board before turning the tables and clobbering them completely. Lulu sank nearly every toss into the hole, prompting both women to touch their thumbs to their behinds and making a sizzling sound both amusing and annoying. Peggy's particular skill was knocking Devyn's beanbags entirely off the board with her own. The defeat was solid and devastating. She and Elizabeth accepted the pats on the back from the friends and neighbors who'd gathered, which helped soothe the burn.

"You tell Jill hello for me," Charlie, the smitten liquor store owner, said. "I'm glad she's doing better. Tell her I'll give her a shout soon."

"For a date?" Devyn practically squeaked. She was still trying to reconcile Jill carrying on a torrid affair. It was so…*not Jill*, everyone's favorite fourth grade teacher, watcher of Hallmark Christmas movies. *Meanwhile she's getting down with Liquor Store Charlie on Thursday?*

"For some one-on-one time," he said, with a sheepish smile.

"I'll deliver the message." Devyn tried not to appear as traumatized as she felt.

"Bye, Charlie," Elizabeth said, knowingly, and pulled Devyn away.

Still on a high from the fun they'd had, Devyn walked back to the truck with a smile on her face, chucking her second beer into the trash as they walked. "That was a surprisingly good time for a parking lot."

"I told you. You don't give the Bay enough credit."

Devyn kicked at the rocks on the ground next to the truck and squinted. "Well, technically, you could find a game of cornhole a lot of places."

Elizabeth scoffed. "Not in the parking lot in front of Mr. Pitts with your friends and neighbors cheering you on while you have a couple of brewskis."

"You don't seem the type to use the word 'brewskis.'" Or drive a pickup or have a ridiculous competitive streak, she filled in. But Elizabeth was all of those things in one.

"Well, I do. It's a fun word if you think about it. I like the way it feels on my lips."

Devyn swallowed and took a moment with that one. "Your lips deserve some fun now and then. I can agree."

Elizabeth leaned back against the truck with a side smile that showcased that hint of a dimple. "Are you flirting with me again?"

"No," Devyn said automatically, like a fifth grader incapable of honest communication. She glanced at the ground in mortification of her own behavior because this time there was so much behind it.

Elizabeth dipped her head and caught Devyn's gaze. "Because there have been several moments where I felt like we were flirting."

Devyn placed her hands on top of her head. She met Elizabeth's eyes. "Well, you just put it right out there, don't you?"

"Is that bad?" Elizabeth asked, seeming to not know one way or the other.

"No. I just thought we would play it cool. Let it unravel."

Elizabeth nodded. "We could. Or I could use the two beers I just had to tell you that you're a smoke show." Elizabeth didn't wait for a response. Instead, she pushed off the truck and headed down the sidewalk with her hair blowing in the evening breeze.

"Where are you going?" Devyn called with a laugh. "You can't say that and then walk away, you weirdo."

"Yes, I can," Elizabeth called over her shoulder. "And I'm walking now. Had two beers. Shouldn't drive." She paused and turned back. "Coming?"

Like she had any choice now. Elizabeth and the great time she'd already shown her had Devyn's mood light and her interest piqued. Don't get her started on her libido and how much exercise it was raking in. She hurried to close the distance between them on the sidewalk. "Where are we going?"

"My place. My backyard."

"What for?"

"You'll see. Follow me."

In that moment, she likely would have followed Elizabeth Draper anywhere. "So mysterious." She grinned and her phone buzzed in her pocket.

"I find things are most exciting with a little mystery tacked on," Elizabeth said back. "Don't you?"

"I'm not opposed to it." Devyn finally caught up and pulled out her phone. It was Paul calling, the top broker on her team, likely with updates on Twenty-Four Walker.

"Do you need to take that, Ms. Wheeler-Dealer?"

Devyn stared at the phone and back at Elizabeth. "No. I'm good." She declined the call and felt strangely okay about that. The stars were peeking out from above and the ocean air caressed her face. "It's a very pretty night."

Elizabeth smiled and it made the night even better. "Isn't it?" Her gaze never left Devyn's face. "I can't get over the view."

❖

Elizabeth had goose bumps on her arms. Devyn Winters had given them to her with the long looks she'd cast her way all night. She rubbed her arms now as she looked at herself in the bathroom mirror of her home.

"You have a lot of purple," she heard Devyn say loudly, from the living room. "Oh, and lavender drapes, too."

She opened the door and craned her neck around it. "I've always thought of purple as a calming color. Friendly, too. At least a third of my wardrobe has a touch of something close to it."

"You know? That's true, now that I think about it." She watched Devyn, in her black tank top, having discarded her button-up shirt, make a circle around her living room, taking it in. She exhaled slowly. What was she gonna do with this woman and their very unexpected chemistry? She wasn't sure, but the night felt…alive. In fact, she'd never felt so much energy passing between two people. Surely it wasn't just her, right? The vibrations were palpable.

Elizabeth washed her hands, gave her shoulders a roll, and returned to Devyn, just in time to see Scout emerge from the bedroom with her sleepy eyes on. She must not have heard them come in, which wasn't unusual. Scout, it turned out, was a champion sleeper now that she lived indoors, safe and sound.

"Oh, my gosh," Devyn said, holding out her hand for Scout, who approached her with a lowered head and wagging tail. "I didn't know you had a dog."

Elizabeth smiled. "You didn't ask. This is Scout. She's the best, and will likely curl up in your lap at some point soon."

Devyn knelt and with both hands scratched behind Scout's ears to rave reviews from Scout. "Wait. I've met this dog." Her gaze flew to Elizabeth's in confusion. "From that day. She was at the site of the crash."

Elizabeth nodded. "Yep. She's the reason we found Jill. Felt only fitting to give her a permanent home. Don't worry. I followed the proper channels."

"You adopted the dog that found Jill?"

Elizabeth nodded. "Turns out we make a great pair."

Devyn placed a kiss on the side of Scout's face and spoke quietly to her. "Thank you. I mean that."

Elizabeth felt a pang in her chest at the tender moment. Scout offered a lick and then headed to the couch to curl up on her favorite blanket, content that people were home.

Devyn stood and seemed to shake herself out of the weighted exchange. "I'm glad you did this for her."

Elizabeth shrugged. "For me, too. Are you ready?"

Devyn studied her with a mischievous look on her face that said she had definite ideas. "Oh, I think you're going to have to be more specific, because one could take that a lot of ways."

Elizabeth chuckled but let that one go. Their flirting felt more overt now that they'd acknowledged it. "Follow me."

"You say that a lot." Devyn fell in line behind Elizabeth on the way to her back door. When she opened it and stepped out into the darkness, she heard Devyn's breath catch. Yep. There it was. She paused, allowing Devyn to soak in the sight. "So?"

"Oh, my God. I remember these, just not so many at once. It's gorgeous."

Elizabeth nodded and stared out at the hundreds of lightning bugs that took turns illuminating her yard like tiny lanterns assembling. She would never get tired of their beauty, their peace. She turned to Devyn. "It's really something, isn't it?" she said quietly.

"There are *so* many." She shook her head and stepped farther onto Elizabeth's back porch, looking up into the trees and beyond. "When you live in the city, you forget that all of this is happening at the very same time. Like two entirely different worlds coexisting. And the silence. You forget anything can be this quiet."

"One of the perks of a small town: access to nature and time enough to enjoy it. Milkshake?"

Devyn turned to her. "That's what you offer your guests? Not wine or coffee, but a milkshake as if it were the most natural thing?"

"No, not typically. I'm just in the mood for one, and thought you might be, too. I can pour you wine if that's what you're feeling, though that seems a little boring in comparison to a fantastic milkshake."

Devyn stared at her like she was a unicorn.

"What? Nobody in Philadelphia has milkshakes?"

"No, no. I'm sure they do." She laughed. "I'll take a damn milkshake. Why the hell not?"

"Now you're talking." Elizabeth beamed. "Two homespun milkshakes coming right up."

As Elizabeth blended what would be chocolate milkshakes with extra whole milk, Devyn remained outside drinking in the view. She left the door open so they could converse back and forth.

"Did you know Jill is having a lurid affair with Charlie?" Devyn asked from the darkness.

Elizabeth paused her ice cream progress mid-scoop, not knowing exactly what to say. She had figured that part out, but she hadn't been aware that Devyn had. "Um…"

She heard a gasp. "You did, didn't you?" And then, "That's right. You know all the town gossip. You just refuse to share the good stuff."

Since the cat was already out of the bag, she gave in. "Yes, I did know, but I think Jill likes it better that I pretend not to. I think she would rather the whole world did that. If it helps, I did let the sheriff's department know when she went missing. You know, just in case."

"Well, I appreciate that part."

"It's actually why I was there when you arrived, apart from coordinating with the police on the volunteer efforts." She sampled the ice cream because one had to. "They're kinda cute about it, though. One hundred percent obvious when they're in the same room, passing each other adorable glances, like little smolders, and then looking away quickly."

Devyn stood in the doorway and shook her head at Elizabeth. "Who would have thought Jill capable of clandestine smoldering? Certainly not me."

Elizabeth waited until the blender finished before answering.

"That's the thing," she said, as she poured the milkshakes into separate glasses and carried them outside with Devyn on her heels. "I'm not sure you give Jill enough credit. She's quite the firecracker. Did you know she started a petition to get a more diverse selection of films at the movie theater? She specifically argued for LGBT representation, which makes more sense now that I know you're gay." She handed Devyn her milkshake.

"Or maybe she did that for you, her good friend."

Elizabeth shrugged. "Or for both of us."

"To Jill, then." They touched glasses in shared appreciation.

Devyn took a sip of the milkshake and paused. "I don't normally just hand out compliments, but this milkshake is above average. You know what you're doing."

"Why not?" Elizabeth asked, not understanding the statement. Devyn looked at her, seemingly confused by the question, so she probed further. "What I mean is why *don't* you just hand out compliments? It's a nice thing to do. At least, I've always thought so."

Devyn looked pensive, considering the question. "Well, when you put it like that, I suppose I should. Where I live and in my line of work? It's all about playing the game, staying ahead. Being nice for the sake of it can get you left behind, unless it's a schmooze, and then it's just all fake."

Elizabeth sipped her shake. "That sounds awful. Making someone feel good about themselves has never in turn made me feel like a weaker person or that I was less successful than the next guy."

Devyn exhaled slowly, maybe mulling over Elizabeth's words or maybe thinking they were naïve and trite. "You're too much. You know that? Where exactly did you come from?"

"Your freshman year algebra class, for one. Not that you ever noticed."

They stared at each other, the air around them electric, their movements still.

"Big mistake."

"Ah, flirting again."

"I'm not flirting either. I'm just watching lightning bugs in a friend's backyard with a milkshake." A pause. "Did you know you were gay in high school?"

She could see the flecks of green within the hazel of Devyn's eyes, but just barely. "Nope," Elizabeth said, leaning into the shiver. "That awareness hit in college, making the rest of my life suddenly make sense."

"I knew." Well, that was news.

"You did?"

Devyn nodded. "Freaked me the hell out. I felt like I had this giant secret and that my friends would hate me once they found out. Every party, every social gathering, every football game was excruciating, knowing everything I said and did was false. It's why I ran screaming from this place." This was interesting new information. Elizabeth leaned forward, eager to hear more.

"Here you were, for all intents and purposes the most popular girl in our graduating class, and you were worried about being accepted?"

"Ironic, right?" Devyn shrugged. "Worst time of my life."

"I think they would have understood. At least, I'd like to hope so."

"Things were different back then. My friends? I don't know how they would have taken it, and I was terrified as each day went by that they would see it written all over my face."

Elizabeth nodded. "Yeah, I can imagine. It's unfortunate that those judgmental girls were your measuring stick."

"I think so, too. Now. But that took time to see."

A pause. Crickets chirped quietly, and the warm night air caressed Elizabeth's skin. She watched Devyn get up and wander to the edge of the porch, looking out at the beauty in front of them. "You're nothing like them, you know," Elizabeth said.

"You don't think so?"

Elizabeth picked up her empty glass from the table between their two patio chairs and walked to Devyn, who handed over hers. "Nope. They suck at cornhole."

Devyn chuckled at the unexpected comment, and so did Elizabeth.

It happened without warning. Devyn's hands slid to her waist. Elizabeth still held the two glasses, one in either hand. Their mouths were inches apart. She could see Devyn's eyes from the soft trail of light that emanated from inside the house. She could feel Devyn's soft breath against her lips, and it made her ache. She wanted herself pressed up against Devyn. She wanted to inhale Devyn's sweet scent. She wanted to satisfy every desperate need pulsing through her own body. She wanted. She wanted. Elizabeth knew what was coming, and the anticipation was almost too much. She closed her eyes just as Devyn's lips met hers, accepting the kiss that was soft and slow, and then, because they couldn't help themselves, not that at all. Yes. At last. Her arms moved to rest on Devyn's shoulders as she held tight to those empty glasses, which kept her hands from participating in a torturous, wonderful way. Instead she held them out in the air, lost in space, in some kind of swaying dance that added a nice bit of tension to the already melt-worthy kiss.

Devyn Winters had lips to die for.

Soft, warm, attentive, and smooth. Could lips be smooth? They could. She now knew that with certainty. Devyn took the lead and Elizabeth followed. She asked for more. Her mouth slanted over Devyn's, whose tongue touched her lips lightly, teasing, answering Elizabeth's request, beckoning Elizabeth to part them for her. When she did, heat took over. With Devyn's tongue in her mouth, she went up on her tippy-toes to even out their height difference. Her heart did a somersault. Her body lit up. Her mind went places sexy and alluring.

As they kissed, Devyn's thumbs moved in slow circles against her stomach, scratching at the fabric of her T-shirt. And then it was over. She blinked, as if waking from an unexpectedly wonderful dream.

"What happened?" she asked, feeling a small smile peeking. The tingly feeling she'd had all over hadn't left with the kiss. No, it still hummed across her skin pleasantly.

Devyn brushed her thumb across Elizabeth's lower lip ever so softly. "I think we just stole a moment, and I just learned you have the sexiest mouth imaginable."

She closed one eye. "That's definitely crossing the flirting line."

Devyn chuckled. "I can admit to that. Was totally worth it."

Elizabeth nodded.

There were the crickets again, only now it seemed like they were working together in composition, to underscore this moment. A cricket chorus to go with the firefly light show and the fireworks-worthy kissing. Yes sir, this had turned into quite the evening.

"I didn't plan on kissing you tonight," Devyn said, taking a step back, giving them both a chance to regain their proverbial footing.

Elizabeth used this moment to set the glasses back down on the small table. "Why did you?"

Devyn sighed. "The struggle not to became too much. You were just too sexy tonight with your gorgeous hair, and cornhole grit, and the truck, and then this." She gestured to the quiet backyard. "I haven't seen anything this peaceful in a very long time." She shrugged. "It felt like the right thing to do."

"You smell really good," Elizabeth said. The sentence fell from her lips before she had time to think about it.

"You *taste* really good," Devyn said, not missing a beat. Her eyes were dark, and Elizabeth swallowed hard. Was she out of her depth here? The high school version of herself would have thought so. Regardless, that sentence…did things to her. She shifted, acutely aware of the physical need, nearly uncomfortable now. Devyn was so beautiful, and sophisticated, and important. She had the capability to make a person feel ten feet tall when her attention was cast their way. Elizabeth felt it now. It emboldened her.

"Let's do this again."

"Which thing?" Devyn asked, with a cheeky grin. The confidence was sexy and caused Elizabeth's cheeks to heat. She hated how noticeably she always seemed to blush, but pressed forward, harnessing the conviction.

"Let's go out."

"You mean, *out* out?" Devyn said, with a sparkle in her eyes. "You're going to have to be more specific. Or you could come over here and show me."

Elizabeth steadied herself at the idea of doing just that. Racy images of that possible moment flipped through her brain like the pages of a saucy novel. Where her hands would go, where her tongue would, what kinds of things she'd press against first. She bit the inside of her lip. No. Too soon. She had to slow her roll.

"Yes, *out* out." She bypassed the other offer because further physical interaction would make her body even more uncomfortable than it already was. That was, unless she was willing to go to bed with Devyn right then and there. But that wasn't her style. Damn it. Why wasn't it? What she wouldn't give to be an unrestrained harlot in this moment.

"When?" Devyn asked.

"What about Wednesday?" Four days. Four very long days. That would give her some time to cool off, get her wits about her before they saw each other one-on-one again. She'd be refreshed and breezy. She could laugh casually and appear charming and in control.

"I can wait until Wednesday." Devyn picked up the glasses and headed inside. Through the window Elizabeth watched as she carefully rinsed each one. Even *that* visual affected her. What the hell was happening? She'd found Devyn attractive before, beautiful for days, but it was as if that kiss had unleashed a powerful, new level to her perspective.

She joined Devyn inside and watched as she gathered her bag. "I would have done the dishes, but that's kind of you."

"Well, that wouldn't have been fair. You made the milkshakes." She slid her expensive-looking black bag onto her shoulder. Elizabeth could never pull off a bag like that. Maybe if they made a purple, softer version. Something floral, perhaps.

"You're leaving?" she asked.

"Probably wise. Don't you think? Milkshakes and lightning bugs are hard to fight against. Consider me seduced, and I'm not even kidding about that." She passed Elizabeth a smile that seemed to hold back a lot, and Elizabeth identified. She tried not to think about the night that could have been. "But I would love it if you'd walk me out."

"It would be rude not to." They walked in silence through the darkened entryway to the lavender door. "Sorry I can't drive you home. I'll pick up Shug tomorrow."

"Luckily, I can handle a few blocks."

"You could probably sell four condos in that time."

"No, that's crazy. Six at least." Devyn stepped onto the porch and turned, shoving her hands into the front pockets of her jeans. "Thank you for tonight, Elizabeth from high school. It was unexpected."

"In a good way?" Elizabeth couldn't resist asking, knowing she'd wonder about it later. She leaned against the doorjamb and waited as warmth moved up the back of her neck in nervous anticipation.

Devyn nodded. "In a very good way. I look forward to going *out* out with you. Good night, now."

Devyn headed off down the walk as Elizabeth watched. Nope. This was not a satisfying ending to their evening together. As Devyn turned from the sidewalk onto the street, Elizabeth hurried after her. "For the road," she said, and cradled Devyn's face in her hands for one last thorough kiss.

When she pulled her face back, Devyn shook her head and bit her bottom lip as if still tasting the sweetness of that kiss. Elizabeth sure was. "You are full of surprises. I keep saying that and then you surprise me again. And then again."

Elizabeth took a few steps backward, holding eye contact. "Good."

As she made her way back inside, she felt proud of herself, and also more turned on than she had been in years. She should call KC. Dexter. Somebody she could report this monumental night to.

No. She touched her thoroughly kissed lips, enjoying the slight swell. She would tuck this away for herself for a little while. It was nice to have something all her own to take out and examine whenever she wanted.

Tonight? She'd been kissed by a beautiful and sophisticated woman. She skipped like an idiot into the kitchen and turned off the light. She made her way through the living room, sending the whole house into darkness. Right there, in the spot where she usually watched TV and read books, Elizabeth hugged herself.

Today had been a good day.

CHAPTER THIRTEEN

"We should stop at Amazin' Glazin' on the way home," Jill said, as they turned the corner onto the produce aisle of Festive Foods, the town's one grocery store. Devyn pushed the cart and Jill rode along in one of those grocery store–provided scooters that made shopping a breeze. "Do you know how long it's been since I've had one of their chocolate-frosted with peanuts? Since before the accident. That's too long."

"Those are the ones Mom used to bring home." Devyn lifted her shoulders to her ears at the dose of nostalgia. She remembered how the sight of that bright yellow box would prompt her to dance around the kitchen in her pajamas because Saturday donuts were a special treat on a single-mom budget. "Done. We're stopping. My treat. We'll get two boxes."

"Well, don't break the bank on my account."

Devyn leaned down and placed a smacking kiss on her sister's cheek. "You look super cool on your grocery scooter. Just look at you zoom."

"Don't make fun of me. I do not."

"Do, too. Scooters are trendy these days. Just wait until Charlie sees you. He'll be out of those Levi's in two point three seconds."

Jill brought the scooter to an abrupt halt in front of the bananas, which Devyn thought was entirely apropos. Jill blinked fast and furious before locating words again. "Why are you bringing up Charlie?" She stared in accusation the way she used to when Devyn borrowed her clothes without permission when they were teenagers.

"The question is, why haven't you?" Devyn walked on in nonchalance, pushing the cart down the aisle. She heard the sound of the scooter whirring to life behind her.

"Why would I mention Charlie? He's a friend. I have lots of friends, Dev. We don't talk about them individually just for kicks."

"A special *brand* of friend, I'd say. The *smitten* kind, if I'm quoting correctly, and I am." She glanced to the side and saw Jill close her eyes, acknowledging defeat.

"He told you?" she said.

"He told me."

Jill turned a ripe shade of red right there next to her kindred spirits, the tomatoes. "It's not what it sounds like."

"That you're getting hot and heavy with the liquor store guy on Thursdays? No, I'm sure it's nothing close to that." She made a point to smile. It was rare she ever had reason to tease Jill, who was so levelheaded and together. How could she pass up this opportunity?

Jill glanced around and edged her scooter closer to Devyn, who watched in amusement. "Watch yourself with that thing, speed racer."

Jill ignored her and lowered her voice. "Here's the thing. Charlie's a nice guy. That's really all. And we spend time together, yes. That part is true. Once in a while. On Thursdays."

Devyn squinted. "Thursdays are specific."

"It's...our day, okay? Well, it was before the accident."

"You can still get your Thursday sex groove on, Jilly." Devyn smiled at Jill's across-the-street neighbor as they passed. "Hi, Mrs. Rousch." The elderly woman nodded with a knowing smile.

Jill shaded her eyes and grimaced. "Perfect. Now Mrs. Rousch knows."

"Mrs. Rousch has sex, Jill. Everyone does."

"That's true," an elderly voice said behind them. Devyn turned around in victory and smiled at her new teammate.

"You go, Mrs. Rousch," Devyn said, and tipped her imaginary cap. She was really enjoying this particular afternoon. In response, Mrs. Rousch tipped hers right back.

Jill wilted further. "We're not talking about this anymore."

"Fine by me. What's next on the list?"

Jill paused in mortification. "Eggplant."

"Perfect." Devyn pushed the cart with a playful skip in her step.

"But I'm not the only one getting her groove on," Jill said. "I'm on to you and Elizabeth. The whole town is. Grab a jar of spaghetti sauce. The kind with the mustache guy."

Devyn obliged. "It's not a secret that we're friends and hung out at cornhole the other night."

"Charlie said you were making eyes at her."

"I have no idea what that even means, you weirdo. How does one even make eyes? We need wine." A thought occurred and she brightened. "Maybe we can stop at the liquor store later."

"Stop diverting," Jill said. "Are you setting your sights on Elizabeth Draper?"

"What a great question." Devyn knew that voice well. This time it was her turn to close her eyes. Elizabeth. Of course, it was, right there in Festive Foods, behind them.

"Elizabeth," Jill said, lighting up. Oh, how the tables had turned. "We were just talking about you."

Devyn flipped around to see Elizabeth not only beaming but looking amazing in jeans, white Converse tennis shoes without socks, and a cream-colored blazer that looked better on her than probably anyone on the planet. Her hair was down and around her shoulders. She tossed it back from her eye and regarded Devyn. "I heard. I was waiting on the answer to the question." This girl didn't mess around, but then she never had. There was no playing coy around her. She was a call 'em as you see 'em type, which only kept Devyn on her toes all the more.

"I abstain," Devyn said simply and pretended to shop for an important item on the shelf. *Would you look at that. They sell pasta in the shape of shells at this supermarket.*

"Well, that's disappointing," Elizabeth said, zinging her.

She bit the inside of her lip at the double meaning, just as Jill took over.

"She's a handful, Liz. Always has been."

"I'm learning." Elizabeth took in Jill on her scooter. "You're looking great. All out and about."

Jill posed, fluffing her hair. "Grocery store chic. At least, that's what I'm telling myself. If they ever come out with a women and scooters calendar, I'm submitting."

"You'd land that job in a heartbeat," Elizabeth said, with a hand on her hip. "Well. I'll let you to get back to shopping. See you tomorrow night." She squeezed Devyn's arm as she passed, which pulled a wide-eyed look from Jill.

Tomorrow night? Jill mouthed.

Devyn smiled and glanced at the ceiling. "It's not a Thursday, but it will have to do."

"Stop it already."

"You first," Devyn said, and messed up her sister's hair and they walked on. The next hour consisted of teasing, bickering, and having the best time together. For Devyn, grocery shopping had never been more interesting or fun. She wondered now why she had hers delivered to her back home.

Did she steal long looks at Elizabeth every time she caught sight of her across the store? Maybe. Did she count the minutes until their Wednesday night date? Absolutely. Only twenty-eight hours to go…

❖

What in the world was a girl supposed to wear for a date with a high-powered real estate broker whose gaze she welcomed, whose attention she sought, but whom she didn't want to scare the hell off with how interested she'd become in just the few days since they'd first kissed? This was the question that had plagued Elizabeth since the early afternoon, when she began to anticipate their evening.

She held up a black top and faced Scout. "Too serious? It feels sophisticated, and I'm really not capable of vast sophistication."

Scout walked to her and placed a paw on her shoe.

"Thank you for the support. No black."

She shook her head in frustration with herself. Elizabeth was never at a loss for what to wear. She liked clothes a lot and generally wore what made her feel happy, comfortable, or pretty. Today felt noticeably different. The stakes seemed so much higher. She liked the way Devyn looked at her when her eyes got dark and steamy looking. She wanted more of that, craved it even, and the right outfit might make or break her chances.

"What are you doing?"

"Jesus," Elizabeth said, leaping three feet into the air and grabbing her chest. "Where did you come from?"

KC blinked back at her, adjusting her ponytail. "I let myself in, like I have the nine billion other times I've stopped by. But when I called your name, you didn't answer." She knelt to give Scout some love.

"Oh." Elizabeth paused, remembering KC had just come from a job. "How did things go with Mr. Ivers?"

"He wanted two Big Macs this time. I talked him out of fries because of that new medication. He's gotta watch his salt. Delivered with a smile as always."

"Well done on the fries. I'm making you employee of the month."

"I get a plaque or it didn't happen." KC studied her like a science textbook. "What are you doing? Why are there clothes all over the floor of your normally spotless closet?"

Elizabeth deflated like the sad little balloon she was. "Just looking for something to put on." She raised her arm at the pile of clothes and let it drop. "I don't know what to wear and I'm over it."

"Calm down."

"I can't."

KC tilted her head and dropped her bag. She took a seat on the edge of the bathtub just outside the closet. "Why are you behaving like a fourteen-year-old on your way to a dance?"

"Because that's kind of an accurate parallel. You're going to be a great mom when Gray is older, by the way. Very intuitive."

"Thank you. By that same token, fit throwing will not make the clothes magically march their way onto your body. So, let's talk about the source of your troubles here."

Elizabeth sighed, giving in and recapturing her God-given maturity. "I have a date with Devyn Winters tonight, and I want it to go well. There. I just admitted everything to you and the universe. I hope you're listening," she yelled to the heavens.

KC's smile was slow to start but took up half the room once it got going. "What now? What did you just say?" She cupped her ear. "You're a saucy person who keeps secrets from your best pal."

"I aspire to be that, but my clothes are not cooperating. Look, I'm woefully just a regular person who will never attract a woman."

"And Devyn is the woman you want to attract? Why haven't I been told?"

Elizabeth waved her off. "It's new. She's fun, and impressive, and very pretty, as you know."

"Mmm-hmm. What else?"

"A good kisser."

"I will murder you."

"You should, but not before this date."

A pause.

"Wear a dress. That one," KC said, pointing at the soft blue off-the-shoulder number she'd bought on sale at Drew's Dresses and More. She still didn't know why she'd fallen for that impulse buy. She'd never worn the thing. Not once.

Elizabeth shook her head. "You know I don't do dresses well. I wish I did. I like them."

"We've been over this. You look amazing in dresses but refuse to believe me."

Elizabeth blinked, trying to be open minded and accept her friend's advice. She raised one shoulder. "I guess it can't hurt to try it on again." Her phone buzzed from its spot on the bathroom counter. She glanced at the text message on her screen. Dexter.

Need snax. Coming over.

"Fabulous. Now Dex is on his way over." She hadn't finished the sentence before she heard her fridge crack open in the kitchen. "Correction. He's already come through my backyard and is now eating my food without preamble."

KC lit up. "Oh. Do you have those little cheeses?" She didn't wait for a response, heading off toward the front of the house to find out for herself. With a deep breath, Elizabeth pulled the casual blue dress off the hanger. Six minutes later, she made her way to her living room where Dexter and KC were huddled over a cheese tray.

"What do you guys think of this?"

Dexter paused mid-cracker bite. KC held the cheese knife and turned.

Dexter whistled. "Whoa. Who is this alluring woman?" He turned to KC. "What is happening? Why is my brain melting?"

"Told you," KC said. "You never listen to me." She turned to Dexter. "Does she ever listen to me?"

Dexter looked caught. "I don't even know who this person is, so, no?" KC knocked him in his chest. "No," he said, more firmly. "And she should. Damn. You're killin' it in that dress, Liz."

Warmth infused her cheeks. "It's just a simple dress."

"That shows off your legs." KC shook her head. "How do you have those legs and rarely display them? I'd pay off God for those legs."

Elizabeth looked down at them now, feeling lighter. Pretty, even. She smiled. "You really think so?"

Dexter sat forward. "I'm gonna abstain from commenting so I'm not the creepy straight dude checking out his friend, but listen to KC. Write down everything she says."

Elizabeth came farther into the room and stole a small piece of strawberry Havarti. "Thanks, Dex."

KC threw her hands up in the air as if tragically ignored.

Elizabeth kissed her cheek. "And thank you, Kace-Face."

"Welcome," KC said, grinning up at her. She slapped her ass. "Now go woo your woman."

That caught Dexter's attention. "Who's the woman? The grocery store chick with the spiky hair? Or are we talking Thalia again?"

"Devyn Winters," KC supplied, smoothly.

Without missing a beat, his face morphed into an impressive smolder. "Hit it."

Elizabeth sighed. "I will not be presumptuous about tonight. Not my style. I will hope that we have a fantastic time together. That is all." She turned back to her bedroom, intent on adding the tiniest bit of curl to her hair and maybe a touch of makeup.

"Hit it," Dexter said again, in a deeper voice.

She swallowed back a laugh, because that actually didn't sound like an awful idea.

❖

Devyn arrived in front of Elizabeth's home five minutes after she was scheduled to pick her up for their date. It was a tactic she'd employed when showing up to any negotiating table: keep them waiting on you. Stay just beyond their reach, and they'll want the deal all the more. While she wasn't sure it extended into her love life, or anyone's for that matter, she'd arrived late out of habit. With a final adjustment to her jeans, white sleeveless blouse, and purple and peach Chanel scarf, she knocked on the door with confidence.

Which was short-lived.

When Elizabeth opened the door, she blinked. And blinked some more.

"Hi," Elizabeth said, and waited. She inclined her head to the side and stared at Devyn. "Devyn? I said hi."

"Right. Hi." Devyn rolled her lips in and then remembered to smile. Everything about Elizabeth was beautiful and soft. She wore a blue dress that complemented the vibrant green of her eyes and showed off her bare shoulders. The strappy sandals she wore had a slight heel that made her legs look long and smooth and long again. Devyn tried not to stare but felt fairly certain she'd lost that battle. Elizabeth's hair was down and parted on the side, and she wore shimmery lip gloss that begged to be kissed right off her face. The combined effect of all of the details, and Elizabeth herself, was mind numbing. "Shall we go?"

Devyn was apparently short on words.

Elizabeth quirked her head at Devyn's silence. "We also never decided where."

"Let's go to a nice restaurant," Devyn said, rejoining the program in progress. "A quiet one. Know any like that?"

"Well, there's a new place at the edge of town that specializes in homemade pasta that everyone has been going on about. They have little candles on all the tables. Oh, and white linen tablecloths. It's Seth and Carol's restaurant. Remember Seth? He was the mascot in school. One grade ahead."

"Star Studded Seth with the hair?" That was what they'd called him back in the day.

Elizabeth laughed, and the sight of that smile made Devyn's breath catch. "Yes, that would be him. Now he's elbow deep in pasta dough and pulling in money hand over fist. From what I hear, people from neighboring towns are even driving in. It's been on my to-do list to check it out."

"Okay, settled. Let's go see Seth and eat pasta. But first this." She couldn't stop herself. She stepped in and kissed Elizabeth's lips softly, lingering there and inhaling her fresh cotton scent for a moment before opening her eyes and exhaling. "There. I'm feeling better now, like I can breathe again."

"Are you? I'm feeling...buzzed."

Devyn chuckled quietly. "What does that mean?"

"I have no idea." Elizabeth blinked. "But it's what I am."

She stole one last quick peck. "Shall we go to dinner?"

"Yes, please," Elizabeth said, with a pleased grin.

Devyn wanted to kiss her again but refrained. Dinner was going to be torturous with Elizabeth in that dress, shoulders on display, cleavage slightly glimpsable. She swallowed.

"I'll drive."

Elizabeth looked amused. "In your tiny clown car? We're going to go on a date in that thing?"

Devyn led the way to the Spark. "It's growing on me."

Elizabeth laughed. "I don't know why, but it suits you."

"That's the worst thing you've ever said to me, and you're supposed to be the nice one in this duo." She held the door open for Elizabeth and waited for her to slip inside.

"Are we going to flirt some more tonight?" Elizabeth asked, once Devyn joined her inside. "As opposed to just kissing?"

Devyn paused. "You're not supposed to announce the flirting or talk about the kissing this early. See, that's the thing you keep glossing over."

Elizabeth dialed the radio station to one of the three local ones and away from the Hilton Head station Devyn had managed to pick up. "I can announce them both if I want. Are we going to?"

Devyn looked over at her as they turned off of her street. "I don't know about you, but I'm feeling affirmative."

"Good. Then I love your outfit. It's chic and very Devyn Winters. You look pretty."

"Thank you." Devyn swallowed at the warmth the compliment brought with it. "I would love to know what 'very Devyn Winters' means to you, though."

"I have to keep some secrets or you won't be interested."

Devyn passed her a long look that said *Impossible.*

"If you're thinking about kissing me again, we have an entire dinner to get through first."

First. She filed that word away as her whole body tingled. "Trust me, I'm aware." But inside that car, she felt the sexual tension bouncing off the walls. She was also very aware of the heat from Elizabeth's body as it caressed the right side of hers, one of the few perks she'd experienced from this tiny car in all the time she'd had it. She wanted nothing more than to place a hand on Elizabeth's knee and slide the fabric of that dress upward just an inch, or even a few more. She closed her eyes briefly, gripped the steering wheel, and focused on the road.

"What will you be having?" Elizabeth asked, peering over her menu at Seth's a short time later. The restaurant was small, only a handful of tables. Luckily, it was Wednesday, and the place was able to fit them in. "I'm going for the sweet cream spinach ravioli."

Devyn set down her perfectly made dirty martini. Elizabeth had opted for a Sprite before warming up to an adult beverage. "Maybe the tomato and watermelon salad."

"No. Uh-uh."

"Uh-uh?" she asked, amused. "You're opposed to produce? The menu says it's fresh and *local*, which should make you happy."

Elizabeth tapped the table cloth. "I'm opposed to you not indulging in the homemade pasta at a *pasta place*."

"I guess I've gotten used to salads and eating on the go."

"That's the most ridiculous practice I've ever heard. Eating on the go? Why?" Elizabeth looked outraged. *Downright* outraged, and it made Devyn's stomach flip-flop pleasantly. The fire in her eyes over salads as meals was...everything.

"Ricotta gnocchi it is," she said, placing her menu flat on the table.

"It was that easy?"

"I'm continually surprised by the things you're able to get me to do," Devyn said, with a pretend huff. "It's a little annoying, if I'm being honest. Let's not make this a habit. I've got to retain some control here, okay? It's who I am."

Elizabeth leaned in. "I think you secretly like letting loose. Letting someone else take control for a change."

Devyn's gaze dropped to Elizabeth's lips as she said the words. She imagined Elizabeth in fucking control, and it did wonderful things to her. God, not here. She forced herself to sit up straight and be a normal person in a restaurant.

She painted on a smile. "I'm still not over the fact that I played and nearly won a *cornhole* tournament."

"Don't count us out." Elizabeth tucked a strand of that multicolored hair behind her ear. "There's always this Saturday."

The most amazing thing was that Devyn was excited to hear that, that she could be playing cornhole in a parking lot again this weekend with Elizabeth. What was happening to her and how? Those were the kinds of things she looked forward to now? "I should work on my arc." She acted out the motion.

Elizabeth laughed. "Not bad." She sipped her soft drink. "And how are things going with that big building you're selling?"

"Twenty-Four Walker? We're behind where we should be." She sipped her own drink, feeling herself yanked right back to her day-to-day reality that had nothing to do with beanbags or flirting. A shame. "And time is running out."

Elizabeth sat back to allow the server to swap out her Sprite for the house white wine she'd preordered. Her eyes lit up when the glass was placed on the table. She lifted it happily. "What happens if you don't get it sold?"

"Well, my reputation is shot, costing me other opportunities. Worst of all, I probably won't get another listing from this particular developer, who goes through one major building or reno project after another, which translates to millions in lost commission for me."

Elizabeth's eyes fluttered. "Hold the mustard."

"Like in a deli?"

"Yeah, it's what KC and I say instead of 'phone.' Stay with me. You make *millions* in commission?"

"Yes," Devyn said, dismissing her awe, "but that trickles down to my team and a cut to the firm that houses me, but sure. The initial take from a building like this one is in the multi-millions."

Elizabeth threw back a gulp of wine. She shook her head. "What are you doing here with me?"

Devyn eyed her, confused. "Having dinner." Everything about this woman was becoming adorable to her, right down to her warm-up Sprite.

"I do odd jobs for a living," Elizabeth said, touching her chest.

"And get all the good gossip, apparently. I get very little gossip at work, so on that count you win." Elizabeth took another drink and fanned herself. "You okay over there?" Devyn asked.

"Did I kiss a millionaire? You can just tell me. I won't be embarrassed about it."

Devyn laughed again. "It's possible."

"Oh, Lordy Lord." Another big swallow from her glass. She was going to need another. Devyn signaled the server with a subtle nod to Elizabeth's glass.

"I'd love to hear you say that same phrase in other…more personal scenarios."

Elizabeth's eyes went wide. Her cheeks went pink. And a smile appeared. "I think the flirting just started."

Oh, it had, too.

Dinner was full of it. As Devyn ate what turned out to be the best plate of gnocchi she'd ever been served, they participated in stolen glances. Those progressed to long stretches of eye contact, and the occasional flirtatious compliment. All seemed based in fun, however, which was where Devyn felt most comfortable and in control.

"You know how to rock a scarf," Elizabeth said, over her wine glass. Her eyes danced.

Devyn nodded. "I only have a few skills. Scarf wearing is something I've put a lot of time and effort into getting right."

"Not for naught."

"I'm sorry?"

Elizabeth laughed. "It's the same word spelled differently, with different meanings. Think about it. Not for naught. I like saying it. Basically, it means your efforts were not in vain. You look…very pretty." She took a deep breath. "You always do."

"When you opened your front door tonight, I lost all words. Seeing you standing there in your dress was a surprise."

"Why was that?"

"Because I was already attracted to you. Look, I'm not even going to try and deny that. You know it. But seeing the…shape of your body, and the way the fabric—"

"Hey there, old friends."

They turned. Standing next to their table in a white chef's coat was Seth, complete with the curly blond hair that Devyn had always identified with him peeking out of his cap.

"Hi, Seth," she said, trying her best to smile. "Long time."

"Seth, hi. It's good to see you." Elizabeth beamed. "But not right now."

He quirked his head at her. "Just wanted to make sure you're enjoying your meal."

"More like enjoyed. I killed it." She slid her plate away. "Your restaurant is the best restaurant, and this ravioli will bring me back many more times, but I need Devyn to finish what she was saying to me. Can you come back in ten minutes?" She flashed both palms at him to indicate the number ten.

He laughed, nodded, and moved to the next table.

Well, well. Apparently Devyn wasn't the only one caught in a lustful haze.

Elizabeth leaned in. "You were saying?"

"I was saying you're hot, and I can't stop looking at you."

"People around here don't generally describe me as hot."

"People around here can be stupid. Trust me. They're thinking it. Probably all day." Elizabeth probably didn't even realize she did so, but she licked her bottom lip, which made Devyn want to taste it. "We should get out of here soon."

"I can't sleep with you tonight." Elizabeth exhaled in defeat. "And understand that those words were very hard to say."

"I would never expect—"

"It's not that I don't want to, because God, right now I would be fine with," she leaned in and dropped her voice, "taking those clothes off you in a hurry." Devyn forgot to breathe. "But it's the first date thing I can't get past. I'm not a sex-on-the-first-date kind of girl. And trust me, I've tried to be all night."

"It's kind of our second date," Devyn said. "If you think about it."

"I don't think I'm a second date kind of girl."

"We've also spent a ton of time together at the house, but that still doesn't mean that I—"

"Maybe there's a compromise."

Devyn enjoyed this endlessly. The conflict on Elizabeth's face. The strife. "Second date, second base?"

"Do you think I'm juvenile?" Elizabeth asked. "You can just say it. I feel juvenile with this rule."

"No. That word has not entered my thoughts," Devyn said in sincerity. "You have convictions. Nothing wrong with that."

Something new and informed took over Elizabeth's features. She rested her chin in her hand. "But you'll be headed home soon." She gestured between them. "You live in Philly. I live here."

"And to be clear, I'm not looking for a long-term...anything."

"I imagine not. You live a busy life."

"Very busy. I have no time for much outside of my job. Hence the on-the-go salads."

"This sounds like an opportune time to discuss what's happening here." She gestured between them. "Let's have a summit."

Silence hit and the mood shifted.

"Well, I like you." Devyn reached for a slice of the hot bread from the second basket that had been brought to their table. "We're friends."

"Unlikely friends."

She spread butter on one slice, watched it melt instantly, and handed it to Elizabeth. "Very. But I'm also attracted to you."

"That makes us friends who are attracted to each other." As Devyn buttered a slice of bread for herself, Elizabeth sat back, appearing thoughtful. "I can work with those terms."

Devyn smiled. "I can, too. So, in a sense, we're not negotiating forever."

Elizabeth took a bite of bread and nodded slowly. "We're negotiating right now. So maybe conventional dating rules don't apply to...two good friends who are attracted to each other."

Relief hit. They were on the same damn page. "I really like the way you think."

Elizabeth smiled politely at their server as she passed. "I think we might be ready for our check."

Chapter Fourteen

The room was still. Dexter had taken Scout to his place earlier in the day, since Elizabeth would be out for the night. With her back to Devyn, Elizabeth poured two glasses of wine, because wine was sexier than beer, but she wondered if they'd even get to them. She didn't have to turn around to know that Devyn's eyes were on her. She could feel that gaze across every inch of her exposed skin, causing her temperature to elevate and her brain to go quiet.

Dinner had been an adventure. While she wanted to hear everything Devyn had to say, she also struggled to follow the thread of the conversation because every part of her wanted Devyn. Really wanted her in a primal, very physical manner she'd never experienced. She would have to ask KC about this later, but for now her thighs ached, and the dampness in her underwear had her adjusting uncomfortably. She exhaled slowly. They hadn't even touched.

Yet.

She straightened, standing taller, as she felt Devyn approach. The skin on her shoulders tingled in anticipation as she felt Devyn's warm breath tickle. When the slow kiss landed on her bare shoulder, she closed her eyes and dropped her head back. "Hello," she murmured. Devyn placed the next kiss on her shoulder blade, followed by the side of her neck. Elizabeth's knees trembled. "Are we skipping the wine, then, or…" She couldn't finish the sentence because Devyn's tongue traced a line up her neck that her lips then repeated with open-mouthed kisses.

"Up to you," Devyn said, quietly, continuing to work.

"Wine is overrated." But she didn't recognize her own voice. It was lower and breathier and made her feel outside herself, except she still experienced every nerve ending tingling with overwhelming desire. She turned and slid her arms around Devyn's neck, pressing their bodies together at last. Her breath caught at the heated contact, and she reveled in the sensation of Devyn's breasts against hers. It made her wet. It made her want to be touched.

Devyn didn't revel. She didn't dwell. She seemed to be on a mission, and far be it from Elizabeth to get in her way. She kissed Elizabeth slowly and then fast. She slid her hands from Elizabeth's waist to her rib cage until they found the undersides of Elizabeth's breasts. Elizabeth pulled her mouth from Devyn's to breathe through the sparks that hit when Devyn's hands touched her intimately through her dress. Her hips rocked subtly. She couldn't stop them.

"I love this dress on you," Devyn breathed. "I need to say goodbye to it now."

Elizabeth nodded and watched as Devyn lifted the blue fabric over her head, leaving her standing there in her bra and underwear, the sight of which must have done something to Devyn because she crushed her mouth to Elizabeth's and walked her backward, directionless, as their lips danced, and she clutched Elizabeth's ass.

Bam. Her back met the refrigerator. She instinctively reached to her left and killed the kitchen lights. The small portion of her brain that was still working reminded her that she might not want to give the neighbors a show.

"You're more beautiful than I even imagined," Devyn said, running her hand slowly down Elizabeth's body, over her bra, across her stomach, and slipping gently between her legs. The slight pressure Devyn applied when she pressed upward nearly had Elizabeth out of her skin. She needed that refrigerator. She thanked God for it. The stroking that ensued was heaven, hypnotic and rhythmic, which let her climb and climb. She hissed in a breath, already so very turned on, her underwear already so damp. It wouldn't take much. Her hips moved instinctually, pushing back against Devyn's hand, requesting the release she so desperately needed.

Then Devyn pulled her hand away. Damn it. Elizabeth reminded herself to breathe. She'd make it through this delicious torture.

Dropping to her knees, Devyn went to work. She kissed Elizabeth through the small piece of fabric between her legs, which was lovely, but not nearly enough contact. Then she kissed Elizabeth more firmly, which was, oh good God, so much better. She rocked against the pressure and grabbed the top of the refrigerator behind her with both hands. When Devyn at long last slid the underwear from Elizabeth's hips to her ankles and touched her with her tongue, Elizabeth reached behind her with her right arm and held on to the side of the refrigerator with all she had. She shifted, giving Devyn and her wondrous mouth more access. She accepted it, too.

Her muscles quivered as an even more intense buildup began. The things Devyn did with her mouth astounded. Were those octagons she traced? Her brain couldn't keep up. Didn't matter, they were wondrous, and she was so worked up it was painful. She vocalized her way through it, too polite to ask Devyn to hurry. The moaning turned to whimpering when Devyn pulled her more firmly into her mouth and sucked. She would have doubled over if she didn't have hold of whatever it was she was holding. She didn't really have a concept of her surroundings right now. Wherever she was, her dress was on the floor and her underwear was around her ankles, and her world was being rocked. When Devyn entered her with three fingers, she called out loudly, drunk with pleasure and ready to be set free. With Devyn's fingers driving her, she climbed higher and higher, dizzy and lost, when finally, it all gave way in a burst and she catapulted with a jerk of her hips. She came hot and fast and extra long, riding out the flow of pleasure that overtook her. Devyn's fingers kept the wonderful sensations coming until she couldn't take any more.

"No more," she said, breathless and satisfied. She stilled Devyn's wrist and watched as she stood, smiling and proud of herself. As Elizabeth worked to assemble her thoughts, Devyn kissed her neck softly.

"Amazing," she whispered. "Incredibly gratifying to take you in your kitchen." She wrapped her arms around Elizabeth's waist and kissed the spot where her neck met her shoulder.

Elizabeth tried to catch her breath. "The kitchen. That's right. That's where we are." She straightened and blinked, still regaining her equilibrium. Once she had, she stared at Devyn and realized they were acutely imbalanced. "Your clothes," she said.

Devyn glanced down at her outfit. The scarf had apparently come undone or had been discarded—it was hard to say, but it lay on the floor next to her dress. "What about my clothes?" Devyn asked, stepping back.

"Take them off."

Devyn stared at her, almost like she couldn't believe the command had left Elizabeth's mouth, so she amended it.

"Please."

That pulled a smile, made visible by the soft glow of moonlight over everything. She watched, with now darkened eyes, as Devyn removed the white shirt to reveal a light pink bra that offered a generous glimpse of her full breasts. Elizabeth swallowed. Next, she unfastened her jeans and slid them to the floor, stepping out of them easily. The pink bra had a matching pair of silk bikinis. The color-coordinated set had Elizabeth wet all over again.

She stepped closer to Devyn and, with a hand behind her head, brought her mouth in for a deep kiss. She stepped out of her heels, which she should have done a long time ago, and allowed Devyn the upper hand in the height department because she found it sexy. As their tongues battled, she felt like a kid on Christmas morning, knowing she was going to get to touch Devyn intimately, take her places, and bring her back again. "Want to see my bedroom?" she asked against Devyn's mouth.

All she got back was a nod, which meant things were moving in the right direction.

They didn't travel gracefully, stopping every few steps to kiss or touch or stare. She didn't bother with the overhead light. The small lamp across the room offered a romantic glow. Her hand was between Devyn's legs before they hit the bed.

Devyn squeezed Elizabeth's shoulders as she was caressed. "Just so you know, it's not going to take a lot. I'm already so gone. I'm sorry."

"We'll see about that," Elizabeth whispered. In reality, the idea that she'd turned Devyn on that much was intoxicating and…awesome. It fueled her confidence and made her only want Devyn more.

In a surprise, the normally put-together Devyn was rather vocal when turned on. The sounds affected Elizabeth in a powerful manner. She could feel those sounds move through her as she stroked Devyn softly. The encouraging murmurs when she took off those pink bikinis bolstered her determination. The discarded bra revealed round, beautiful breasts out of a painting. Elizabeth had to kiss each one slowly and lick her way around each nipple. She sucked them softly, then not so soft. Somewhere along the way, Devyn unclasped Elizabeth's bra, prompting Elizabeth to help the cause and toss the thing over her shoulder. She let her full weight settle. Nestling herself between Devyn's legs, she rocked against Devyn purposefully, surprised by how she fit there like a lost puzzle piece.

"More," Devyn said, as she clutched the bedspread beneath her.

All it took were a couple of sharp thrusts of her hips and Devyn tumbled fast and loud. She pulled Elizabeth closer, hanging on to her as she rode out the pleasure. It was perhaps the most satisfying moment of Elizabeth's adult life, not to mention the most beautiful.

"Never that fast before," Devyn managed, finally. "Wow."

Elizabeth kissed her lips softly. "Can I put that quote on my business card?"

❖

"We did a lot of things to each other tonight," Elizabeth said, as she stared at the ceiling. Oh, they had.

It had to be at least three a.m. Her limbs felt heavy and she wasn't sure she could move, wasn't sure she wanted to. Devyn lay next to her on her side, the side of her head resting on her hand and the sheet pulled up to her waist, leaving her amazing breasts on display for Elizabeth. "What's going to happen when I report for work and we see each other?"

"I'm going to say, 'Hi, Elizabeth. The sex last night was amazing.'"

She gasped, turned her head, and looked up at Devyn with wide eyes. "Tell me you won't say that in front of anyone."

"Fine. I won't. But know that it was." Devyn took her hand and threaded their fingers. "This was a good idea. I really enjoyed tonight. You."

"I did, too. Two consenting adults is rather refreshing. No pressure either."

"Have you ever done this before?" Devyn rested their joint hands on Elizabeth's stomach.

She understood her meaning. Sex without the promise of a relationship, even the potential of one. She shook her head. "Have you?"

"I've had one-night stands, but never anything with someone I know. And really like."

Elizabeth appreciated that adjustment. "I like you, too."

Devyn sighed and met Elizabeth's eyes. There was a softness about her that Elizabeth hadn't seen before, as if she were totally and completely relaxed. "What do you want for yourself in life?" Devyn asked. "It can be anything."

"I've always wanted a family. Always, always." She hadn't had to think about her answer. "I want to do things like little league, and backyard barbecues with friends, and then sneak off with the love of my life to have amazing sex and do it all again the next week. In other words, I'm a walking cliché."

"There's nothing wrong with that. If that's what you want, you should have it."

She sighed. "I'm not sure it's up to me, ya know? It hasn't happened for me yet. But who knows? It's what I hope I find one day." She unthreaded their hands and touched Devyn's chin. "What about you?"

Devyn slid down and rested her head on her arm and smiled. "A legacy. I want my name to mean something."

"And how do you plan to make that happen?" Devyn's ambition was wildly sexy to Elizabeth, and prior to this, she didn't realize it was a quality that mattered much to her at all in another person. She continued to learn more about the world and her place in it. What she liked. What she didn't. She wasn't as boring or predictable as she once thought.

"Set commercial real estate records in Philadelphia. Start my own firm with my name on the door, and build my brand from there."

"That simple?"

"Yes. That's what I want."

"I have a strong suspicion you're going to do just that." Elizabeth traced the outline of Devyn's hip until it disappeared beneath the sheet. Her naked body was unreal. If she didn't work out religiously, God had been more than kind. "What about after work?"

"A strong old fashioned with a cherry would be nice, right before I crash for the night."

"You and a drink? That's all?" She frowned. "That's—"

"Not terribly romantic, is it? But it's my kind of day. Doing deals, coming home exhausted, celebrating with a cocktail and collapsing into bed, unable to keep my eyes open until I get up and do it all again the next day."

"Our ideals are so different."

"Not wildly. I actually think your version sounds really nice."

"Just not for you."

Devyn hesitated. "Not what I ever imagined, you know? That's all."

Elizabeth couldn't identify with finding satisfaction in the kind of grind Devyn described. No. In fact, she couldn't let it go unchallenged. Now it was she who propped her head up on her hand. "Devyn?"

"Yes?"

"What about the larger world? The people in it? Where's the time in that kind of schedule for you to enjoy yourself? Sit at a café and read a book?"

"I haven't read a book in a café...ever."

"Oh." A pause. "And that's okay with you?" It wasn't judgment so much as it was curiosity about a life so vastly different from what Elizabeth knew and valued.

Devyn sat up and faced her. "I haven't missed it yet. I like my faster pace."

"Which is why it's killing you to be here."

"Actually, right now it's not bad at all." Devyn wrapped one arm around Elizabeth's waist and pulled her on top. She reached up and held her hair back and just studied her face.

"What?" Elizabeth asked, self-conscious.

"You're so beautiful. It's staggering to me."

"Oh."

"What?" Devyn asked, narrowing her eyes. "You have a hard time hearing that?"

"I love hearing that." She felt her smile dim slightly. "I'm just... not used to it."

Devyn placed a delicate kiss on her chin. "I think I'm gonna have to change that."

When Elizabeth firmly inserted her thigh between Devyn's, she was greeted with wide eyes. "I also like effecting change. That day of yours? It can get better."

"How is that?" Devyn asked, dropping her hands and palming Elizabeth's breasts. At Devyn's touch, she hissed in a breath and her hips rolled automatically.

"You haven't met my mouth yet. Not fully." She tossed away the sheet and crawled down the bed.

"Sweet Jesus."

❖

On that bright and sunny Friday, Devyn sat on a barstool at Jill's kitchen counter with her work spread out like she'd never leave that spot. Contracts everywhere, her laptop, iPad, coffee mug, and signature stress ball surrounded her like a combined comfortable blanket. Across from her, Jill started breakfast, which had to be amazing because the aroma had her nose in heaven. Devyn was feeling energetic and ready for the world, with an extra spring in her step. Maybe it was the fact that spring morphing into summer was a really beautiful sight in Dreamer's Bay. Or that over the weekend, they'd likely pull in a decent number of showings at Twenty-Four Walker. Maybe it was Jill gaining her strength. Who knew? *I do.*

"What are you working on today?" Jill asked between pops and sizzles. Since being homebound and less mobile, she occupied her time cooking, finding new recipes on Pinterest daily. Devyn was not complaining, as she reaped the tasting rewards, which were, eight times out of ten, favorable.

She sat back and ran her fingers through her hair. "We have an offer on 14F, which is a two-bedroom unit with a kitchen, but they're coming in at three point eight, and the ask is four five."

"Four five?" Jill inclined her head to the side as if working out a math problem.

"Four and a half million. So, as you can see, we're pretty far apart."

"You're working on getting them up?"

"I'd like to be, but my guy, the developer, is refusing to even counter."

"And you want him to."

"Yep."

"To get the numbers moving in the right direction," Elizabeth called from the entryway. Devyn turned, unable to glimpse Elizabeth yet but wanting to. She'd had the prior day off from assisting Jill, and they hadn't seen each other, well, *since.*

"The voice without a body is right. If he won't counter, the buyer will assume the negotiating table is closed, and it's not. It's a pride thing, and it's getting in the way of my sellout."

"Gotcha," Jill said, and placed a pile of crispy bacon on the counter. Devyn reached for a strip and got her hand smacked. "Nope. That's for my breakfast casserole. You can eat that, not this."

"You're just like Mom, you know that? Pre-eating is just as important as eating."

"I agree," Elizabeth said and stole a slice for herself.

Devyn's eyes went wide when no repercussions came her way. She pointed. "How is that okay?"

"She's a *guest,*" Jill said, with a shrug.

Devyn turned to glare at Elizabeth, but caught her enjoying the bite of bacon so much that she was forced to smother a grin instead, which seemed to be the case whenever carefree Elizabeth was around. Yes, she was super easygoing and, okay, very easy on the eyes as well. The other night had certainly shored up that particular notion. She flashed briefly on Elizabeth looking over at her in bed, naked, and radiating. She hadn't slept at Elizabeth's place that night, feeling that might have been too intimate for a "two consenting adults" scenario, and they hadn't exactly discussed if there would be a repeat encounter. She'd slipped out somewhere in the wee hours and crept back to her own bed, careful not to disturb Jill.

"What?" Elizabeth asked, staring at her now, suspiciously.

"Nothing." Devyn went back to her contracts. Or pretended to.

Jill stared at the two of them. Correction. She stared at Devyn and then at Elizabeth and then back at Devyn. Finally, she exhaled, shook her head, and went back to her recipe. Yep. She knew.

"We have PT in half an hour," Elizabeth said.

Jill offered a salute. "I haven't forgotten. Just enough time to pop this casserole in the oven for later. We'll call it brunch."

"Perfect," Elizabeth said brightly. "Do you mind if we swing by the flower shop on the way? Floral Laurel's got a bunch of old doorknobs she wants to have melted down and has hired On the Spot to do it."

"How are you going to melt doorknobs?" Devyn asked, unable to work with such information at play. Industrialized Elizabeth had her interest piqued and her libido firing. Just when she thought she knew everything...

"I'll use a blowtorch," she rattled off and turned back to Jill as if it were the most everyday thing in the world. Meanwhile, Devyn was imagining that very sensual image of sweet Elizabeth wielding fire. The duality had her fantasizing almost instantly.

"Where'd you go?" Jill snapped her fingers.

Devyn flinched. "What do you mean? I'm sitting right here." Lies. In actuality, she was in a garage, unzipping the coveralls Elizabeth wore to reveal nothing underneath.

Jill pointed. "Well, your phone is going off, and you're ignoring it. You never ignore your phone. In fact, we'd have to pry it from your cold dead hands to get it away from you."

Right. There were things to do. She sighed, putting pause on her delicious fire fantasy, clicked onto the call, and headed to the bedroom to reason with her seller and get that counteroffer. Attractive friends with blowtorches would have to wait, and wasn't that a damn shame.

❖

"I don't know if you saw, but the Springaling is tomorrow." Elizabeth said it and waited for Devyn to turn around from the desk in the spare room. She and Jill had just returned home from PT, which had worn Jill out. She was resting comfortably in front of the TV with a plate of her brunch casserole as a reward for her hard work.

"Do the firemen still make pancakes in the middle of the afternoon with their shirts off?" She turned in her chair and raised an eyebrow.

"They do."

Devyn grimaced, and Elizabeth laughed. "All for a good cause, you know. They donate that money to the animal shelter, including those fifty-dollar tips from the women's bridge club. Martha McCray stuffed a twenty down one of the probies' turnout pants last year."

"Martha McCray has always been a tenacious old woman. She's still around? And is her hair still slightly purple? God, I pray it is."

Elizabeth gasped. "Stop that." She paused. "But yes, and yes."

"See? I know this town better than you think." Tiny lines around Devyn's eyes crinkled when she smiled, and forced Elizabeth to roll her shoulders and focus.

"Do you know what else the Springaling has? Live music and dancing and fried food and flowers everywhere, and me, to teach *you* how to enjoy it all." She eased a strand of hair behind her ear. "Sometimes I think your enjoyment mechanism gets jammed. I like giving it a good hard slam."

"Good thing I have you slamming me," she said with a knowing look. Elizabeth chuckled. "Though that does sound painful."

"You'll live. I'm good for you. Cornhole and homemade pasta places and a little action in the kitchen." She winked, not sure if it landed. She'd never been an expert winker and should probably just embrace that. Maybe pointing would be more in her lane. She'd work on it and see.

"You make a good point, because that's quite a decadent list. I should probably…explore more. Of Dreamer's Bay." She didn't wink back, but Elizabeth felt like it was probably implied. Maybe they weren't quite done with each other in the benefits department yet. Was it wrong that she really hoped not? She'd replayed the events of two nights ago several times over. No, Devyn wasn't forever material, but she was certainly an unexpected blip on the radar.

"Excellent, because I'm taking you. Jill can come, too. All part of your education on why this town is so amazing."

"It has its perks."

Elizabeth wasn't sure if that was a nod to their tryst, or a general endorsement. "That was flirting again, or…?"

"What am I supposed to do with you announcing the flirting every step of the way?"

Oh goodness. Elizabeth had definite ideas of what Devyn could do with her. Right on cue, that magnetic pull appeared again, the one she'd begun to feel whenever she was in close proximity to Devyn Winters, who she didn't even think about as *that* Devyn Winters from high school anymore. Nope. She felt like a whole different human being. Yes, Devyn was caught up in her own life, but she wasn't nearly as shallow or cruel as her old group of high school friends still were. She'd run into Cricket-Jones-now-McMahon at the bank the other day. She'd said hi and smiled, to which Cricket had nodded quickly and moved on. Not a word. Almost like Elizabeth was invisible, not worth her time. Devyn was nothing like that. "I feel like the announcing just gets it out there, you know? Puts all the cards on the table."

"Oh, it's out there. You can rest easy." Devyn smiled a relaxed smile that mirrored the sentiment nicely. "So, the Springaling tomorrow. Yeah, okay. Let's do it. Why the hell not?"

"Yes." Elizabeth clapped. "This will be great. We'll eat all the food. Play some games."

"Announce any and all flirting."

"Not in front of Jill," she whispered.

"I can hear you, you know," a voice called from the living room. Elizabeth froze. Devyn laughed.

"Well, now you've done it. Jill knows we *flirt*." She tossed an exasperated hand in the air and let it drop. "But we know about Liquor Store Charlie and Thursday nights, so I think all is well."

"Hey," Jill yelled. "That's personal."

"Just keeping you in line." Devyn yelled back.

"I'm gonna knock you in your head."

"I'm gonna tackle you right back if you do. And I'm not the one using a cane. Who do you think is gonna win?"

"Bully."

Elizabeth smiled at the sisters doing their thing and realized how lucky they were to have each other, and what a shame it was they lived so far apart. "You guys are still twelve."

Devyn grinned. "That will never change."

"Good. Meet me at the entrance to the park at noon tomorrow?"

"We'll be there," Devyn said. She hooked a thumb behind her. "Can I get back to work now or do you want to check me out some more? Totally your call. I'll just be here, trying not to look devastatingly sexy." She gave her hair a toss.

Elizabeth was pretty sure that Devyn had meant it as a joke, but the effect actually was incredibly sexy. Elizabeth swallowed the flutter it caused, instead making a show of glaring at Devyn and turning playfully on her heels.

"Work it," Devyn called. "I like the sass you have going. Yes, girl."

Elizabeth shook her head but kept walking, putting an extra swing in her hips, hoping Devyn was checking out her ass and secretly loving every minute of it.

CHAPTER FIFTEEN

Devyn had never seen more flower arrangements in her life. And not just the kinds in vases. Bountiful Park had been outfitted to the gills with wreaths, strings of bursting blooms, flowers in the shape of happy townspeople, animals, objects. It was quite simply overflowing with color, and even Devyn, who found the whole concept of the festival to be a little hokey, could not deny how breathtaking the place looked. The organizers of this one must have worked tirelessly the day before.

The weather had shown up for the festival, too, cresting in at an even seventy-six degrees, complete with a comfortable breeze that rustled the many trees shading the festival grounds just inside the park. She and Jill waited patiently at the ticket table, while pretty much everyone who passed raced up to Jill to check on her status.

"I should be back at school officially next month," Jill told some of them with a warm smile. "I'm doing so much better. Thank you for asking. Not quite myself yet, but I'm getting there," she told others. They'd made a pact that they would go slowly through the festival grounds and allow Jill to rely only on her cane this trip, leaving whenever she felt too tired to keep going. A quick call to her doctor had concluded that this kind of outing was actually very good for her.

Meanwhile, Devyn scanned the arriving faces, but no Elizabeth. When it hit ten minutes past the hour, she began to get antsy. "Where could she be?" Devyn asked, getting ready to text her.

"You know Elizabeth. She doesn't have a lot of downtime. She's probably finishing up a job somewhere before heading over."

"You looking for Lizzie?" an older, grouchy-looking fellow asked. He didn't wait for an answer before pointing behind him into the festival. "Last I saw her she was hurling softballs at the dunking booth. Knocked the mayor off his perch twice from what I saw. She's a ringer."

"Of course she is," Devyn said, confused and intrigued by this information. "And you are?"

Then as if summoned, by the mention of her name, Elizabeth raced out of the park entrance and landed in front of Devyn. Her face was flushed and glowing. "Hi," she said, first to Devyn and then again to Jill. "I got a head start. Couldn't sleep last night with all the anticipation of today." She made a silly face as if realizing how ridiculous she was. Only Devyn didn't think so. Her enthusiasm only made her likable. And cute. Yep. Her friend was very cute. And fuckable. She shook her head at that last part.

Jill laughed and slung an arm around Elizabeth. "Should have known. The pleasure seeker was off enjoying herself."

"Don't worry," Elizabeth told them. "I saved all the best stuff. Do you want to start with the fried Oreos or the miniature Ferris wheel, which I have to admit could be more exciting."

"Gonna pass on the Ferris wheel," Devyn said. "Small rides can be dicey. I've seen the news."

"Fair enough. But let me warn you, we're doing the three-legged race at two. Jill, you should maybe sit that one out."

Jill nodded. "Probably a wise decision. Happy to watch and cheer you two crazy kids on, though."

"Well, look at this. You're here." It was Charlie. He ambled up all smiles in his short-sleeve plaid shirt that he'd tucked in. Bless his heart. His sneakers gleamed, too. "I wondered if you'd make it." It was like he couldn't take his eyes off her.

"Hello, Charles," Jill said, blushing.

Charles?

Riveting.

Please let there be more. Jill had been divorced for years now, and this was the first time Devyn'd had the privilege of witnessing her reacting to a man. It was something to see. Jill stood taller and fluffed her hair. She also glanced away a lot, clearly affected. The pink cheeks were adorable and drew arrow signs over the affection she must have carried for Charlie—sorry, *Charles.*

"Been a long time. I wish you'd have let me stop by." He hadn't stopped grinning.

Jill glanced furtively at Elizabeth and Devyn, as if she didn't want to discuss any of this in front of them. Thereby, Devyn remained respectfully quiet. "Just wanted to gather a little more strength first. Can't have you seeing me laid up."

Devyn smothered a cough.

"Just glad you're here now. Come on," Charlie said. "I'll buy you a cone."

"Okay," Jill said automatically.

Well, that hadn't been hard at all.

She turned to Devyn. "You two gonna be okay on your own?"

"I think we'll manage," Elizabeth said sweetly.

Devyn turned to Charlie, shifting to protective younger sister mode. "You realize that she can't walk very fast, and she needs to use her cane all of the time? Not just once in a while to handle some of the weight on that side. All the time."

"Yes, ma'am. I do."

She turned to Jill. "Do you have your cell phone in your back pocket so you can call if you need us?"

Jill patted her left cheek. "Right here."

Devyn hesitated and exhaled slowly, wondering if this was such a good idea. "When will I see you again?" But the two of them were already heading off in the direction of the festival.

"Let's play that by ear," Jill called back.

Damn it. She hoped Jill would be okay.

Elizabeth patted her shoulder as they watched. "They grow up so fast."

"Don't they, though?"

"C'mon. There's exploring to do."

Devyn smiled and vowed to keep an open mind. "You lead the way."

First stop was the face-painting booth, in which Elizabeth immediately zeroed in on a sunflower for her cheek. "What about you?" she asked Devyn.

"I think I'm just going to watch."

"Suit yourself."

But after she'd said it, Devyn felt a little bad about not participating in something that Elizabeth seemed to think was a lot of fun, remarking to the people around them. helping them find exactly the right design from the book the artist laid out.

"Jimbo, you need to get the peace sign," she told the teenager in line behind them. He smiled noncommittally but seemed flattered to have been spoken to by Elizabeth, who was, after all, very pretty.

"What about me?" the older woman flipping through the catalog asked. "I like rainbows."

"I was just about to suggest a rainbow for you, Midge. You look amazing in multicolor."

"Maybe a giant building for you," she whispered to Devyn.

She opened her mouth to answer but Elizabeth beat her to the punch.

"Or a refrigerator. We could ask the artist if she can do one."

The words died right there on her lips. She pivoted. "You're trouble."

"I could be a lot of trouble for you."

Devyn laughed off the sentence, refusing to take it too seriously. She could handle Elizabeth and what they had going. If she was capable of a multimillion-dollar sellout in one of the largest cities in the nation, Elizabeth Draper was a walk in the park. And not just literally. "Nothing I can't handle."

"Can you handle a ladybug? 'Cuz it's the smallest one they have and it would look very attractive right there," she said, and touched a spot on Devyn's cheekbone. That brief contact left her cheek warm and her stomach uncomfortable, making said ladybug hard to resist.

"Fine."

Elizabeth beamed. "A small victory for the country mouse."

"Does that make me the city mouse?"

She closed one eye. "A retired country mouse."

Devyn balked. "I sound geriatric. I'm in the prime of my damn life and showed you so just the other day."

"Shh," Elizabeth said, leaning into her, but she was laughing, which only encouraged Devyn.

"Do you need another demonstration?"

Midge raised an amused eyebrow and made a point of looking away respectfully.

Elizabeth's eyes danced. "I wouldn't rule it out," she said quietly in Devyn's ear.

That did it. Her "friend" Elizabeth had her wet and turned on in a crowd of hundreds with the day stretched out in front of them. Perfect. The very least she could do was submit to a ladybug on her cheek.

"I'm starving," Elizabeth said thirty minutes later, showing off her newly sunflower-adorned cheek. Devyn snapped a photo.

"Think they have any salads?" Devyn asked, and received a death stare.

"Everything you're eating today will be fried. Prepare for that."

"I'll notify my arteries to prepare for battle."

As they waited in line for fried Twinkies, Devyn received a call from one of her brokers, who was having trouble getting a potential buyer to put in an offer because the only floor they could afford at Twenty-Four Walker didn't come with a stellar view. "Well, what have you tried?" she asked her guy, Damon.

He sighed. "Everything. I've pointed at the other perks the unit does have, the high ceilings and the chef's kitchen, the one-of-a-kind designer fixtures—"

"Yeah, but they're hung up on the views, right? You want to emphasize the bright spots the outdoor area does offer. Have you shown them the outdoor living space?"

"In the initial showing."

"Get them back into the unit, but not before you spend a little money to get the outdoor area staged. Pipe in some music on the sound system and have a sommelier there with a selection of wine. Tell Karen that I authorized the purchase. They'll be putty in your hands." She held up one finger to Elizabeth, who stood there holding two cardboard trays with fried Twinkies and strawberry sauce. "Damon, I gotta go. Let me know what happens with that offer. Don't sleep until it's done."

Elizabeth quirked an eyebrow. "Don't sleep? That seems strict."

It was a phrase she'd said a number of times to her team, one that had always seemed within bounds and status quo. Away from it all now, though, in the midst of others enjoying themselves and their Saturday, it did seem a little extreme. She accepted her Twinkie from Elizabeth. "I suppose you don't say that to any of your On the Spot employees?"

"Can you imagine? Patch that tractor tire by midnight, KC, or never talk to me again."

"KC works for you? Best friends and coworkers?"

"Just here and there." Elizabeth nodded. "I trust her implicitly. In fact," she scanned the rows of booths, "she should be getting off her shift about now. The daycare hosts a funnel cake booth as a fundraiser and the parents all take turns manning it. Over there. By the polka band."

"A polka band? Well, hell, why didn't you say so?" Devyn joked.

Elizabeth slid her a sideways glance. "You like all of this more than you're letting on."

"Maybe," Devyn said, through a mouthful of an amazing hot, battered Twinkie.

KC was off her shift, just as Elizabeth had predicted, and standing in front of the booth holding a toddler. Lots of curly blond hair and a couple of teeth.

"Liz, why don't you have a beer in your hand?"

"I'll get there," she said.

"You remember Devyn. High school dancer turned commercial real estate ninja."

"That's what they call me," Devyn said, nodding.

KC smiled. "I can't believe this is the first time we're running into each other. So glad to hear Jill is on the mend. And that you two have been spending...*quality* time together."

"It's good to see you again, KC. This little guy is adorable. Yours?" She decided not to finish the remainder of the Twinkie, knowing there would likely be more fried objects to come, and she wanted to save room. Apparently, she now cared about such things.

"Yep, this is my little guy, Gray," KC said. "You met my husband, Dan, at the hospital."

"Yes. He checked in on us multiple times, even once the orthopedic guy took over. He's great." Just as she discarded the last bit of her Twinkie, two tiny arms reached for her.

"Whoa," KC said, glancing from Devyn to the toddler. "Gray doesn't usually go for strangers."

"It's okay," Devyn said, accepting the toddler into her arms and feeling crazy nervous about what to do with him now that she had him. Oh, and would you look at that? His hands were sticky. She decided, in fear of the answer, not to ask why. Gray studied her face with a deeply furrowed brow. She studied him right back. That mop of bright blond hair, large blue eyes, and a pouty bottom lip. Then something crazy occurred. He broke into a luminous grin, the kind that was unabashedly joyful, and she did, too. "Hi, there," she said.

"Hi," he said back, simply.

"Would you look at that?" Elizabeth said, enjoying this. "I think you have a new best friend."

She wouldn't have predicted this, but the next half hour only solidified her point. They walked with KC to the kiddie rides and watched as Gray circled around and around in the tiny little cockpit of an airplane. Each time he passed, it was Devyn he waved and yelled to. "Look. Look."

"I see you," she yelled back. "You're in an airplane."

He threw his head back and laughed as if it were the funniest thing. When they moved on to the next ride, he held her hand as he toddled back and forth, chattering nonsensically. All the while, she could feel Elizabeth watching her, and it made Devyn feel like she could take on a world full of toddlers. She liked that feeling very much.

"You doin' okay?" Elizabeth whispered as Gray worked on a cotton ball art project at the kids' station.

Devyn smiled. "More than okay. Thank you. It's one of those days where the world just seems a little easier." Hearing the words coming out of her mouth made her feel ridiculous. Her cheeks heated.

"What?"

Devyn turned to Elizabeth. "I'm starting to sound like you."

She shrugged. "I don't see the problem."

KC tossed a gleeful Gray over her shoulders like a sack of potatoes. "I gotta get this kid home and in a bath before the sugar crash hits. Nap time looms. You two have all the fun." She flipped her body around so they could see Gray's face. "Tell your friends goodbye."

"Bye-bye." he said with a huge grin spread wide across his face. He continued to wave as KC walked him out of the park, and they continued to wave back until he disappeared in the throngs of festival attendees.

"Now what?" Elizabeth asked.

"Three-legged race is starting."

Elizabeth's eyes went wide. "We haven't even talked strategy. I got caught up with a two-year-old and now we're going in blind. There's a grocery gift certificate on the line." There was that competitive streak Devyn enjoyed so much, out in full force the second a race was mentioned.

Devyn shrugged, attempting nonchalance to calm Elizabeth's nerves. "What do you say we don't necessarily try to win? Let's just have fun with it." She dropped her voice. "If I remember correctly, we work pretty good pressed up against each other."

Elizabeth blinked as if the thoughts had just been plucked from her head. Finally, she said, "Okay."

"Okay? Perfect."

"Five minutes until the three-legged race," a man on a microphone proclaimed.

"We should probably head over there," Elizabeth said, but she now had a dreamy, faraway look in her eye, and Devyn knew she was thinking about sex, which had her keyed up all the more. This plan had backfired, but then again, maybe not. They were about to be tied up together.

"C'mon, let's go."

As they stood at the starting line minutes later, middle leg tied together and with an arm around each other, Devyn found herself acutely aware of Elizabeth's body heat and the way she smelled heavenly of fresh cotton. "What lotion do you use? I need to buy it."

"I'm not wearing lotion," Elizabeth said, turning her face toward Devyn's neck. Her breath tickled the skin there and sent a chill straight from Devyn's spine to her center.

"Then why do you smell so good that I want to do things to you?"

A pause. "What kind of things? Tell me."

"Go, Liz and Devyn," a voice yelled from the group gathered in the grass to watch. She glanced over at Jill sitting next to Charlie with a stick of fluffy blue cotton candy in her hand. Apparently, she wasn't the only one having a good time today. She offered a wave with her free hand and turned back to Elizabeth.

"Really, really slow things. With my tongue. My lips."

"And go," the race official yelled. Beside them, twenty other teams took off, bound and determined to make it to the finish line first and collect the hundred-dollar gift card to Festive Foods. Devyn and Elizabeth hadn't moved.

"We have to run," Elizabeth said, as if on delay. But they were a disorganized mess now, and after only four steps, fell over in the grass. Elizabeth folded in, partially on top of Devyn. "Uh-oh," she said. "That didn't go well."

"Damn," Devyn said, staring up at Elizabeth, who amusingly enough made no attempt to get up. The weight of her had Devyn's body awake and craving.

Elizabeth frowned. "We should probably concede defeat and congratulate the winners."

"Whatever you say."

They held eye contact for a heated moment, and Elizabeth's hands moved to Devyn's hips, where they squeezed lightly. Finally, as Elizabeth pushed up and off her, she made a point of grazing Devyn's crotch very slowly with her knee and flashing a smile. Devyn's eyes fluttered closed and she took a steadying breath as the pinpricks of pleasure hit and died. She shook her head at Elizabeth and assisted her with the untying process.

"Three-legged races as foreplay never occurred to me." Devyn freed the rope.

"And now we'll never look at them the same way again." Elizabeth, the town goody-goody who had just brushed against her intimately in public, now offered her a smug smile as she sauntered over to Peggy and Lulu, who had taken down the rest of the competition with triumphant flair. As Elizabeth walked, Devyn stared at her ass, her legs, and the always perky energy she carried with her. God, she wanted to do things with her. To her. She also wanted to buy her a cupcake and watch her face light up. How was it that those two thoughts existed in the same space over the course of 2.3 seconds?

What was she going to do with Elizabeth Draper? And why did such a question deliver her all sorts of exciting options? She laughed as she crossed the field to find her. Sex and cupcakes. Devyn's new reality.

❖

The Springaling Festival might just have been Elizabeth's favorite to date. Everyone's smiles seemed brighter, the food was more exciting, and the vibe was, at all times, cheerful. Did it also have something to do with the fact that she had Devyn with her, and seeing it all through her eyes added to the appeal? Maybe. She couldn't discount the pull she felt whenever Devyn was in her vicinity, friend or no friend. She was on a high and loving every second of it.

"Hi, Mr. Rotowski," she said to her old algebra teacher, who really should just shave off that last tuft of hair that clung to his head for dear life.

"Hi there, Ms. Draper." He high-fived her as they passed, tuft a-blowing in the breeze.

"Was that who I think it was?" Devyn stared off after him. "Roto-Rooter?"

"In the flesh. I wholeheartedly enjoy that I'm still friends with my teachers."

"Only you, Draper. Only you."

They walked on, side by side, as the temperatures dipped a bit with the descent of the sun. "What was it like to be popular in high school?" Elizabeth asked. "To go to all the parties and have invites thrust your way everywhere you looked. People wanting to be you. Hang out with you."

Devyn shrugged. "Way less exciting than it sounds, if I'm being honest."

"Well, that's a shame."

"I look back at that time and remember how unhappy I was underneath all the bravado. Not ready to tell the world who I was yet, and wasting all of my time with people who were uninterested in knowing the real me anyway. What I should have been doing was spending time with my mom, who wouldn't be around forever, you know?" She glanced away. "She loved things like this. You know, when the whole town came together?" She touched her heart, where the pang of longing clearly hit.

Elizabeth nodded. She hadn't known too much about Devyn's mother, who had been well liked in the community and was definitely gone too soon. "I'm sorry you lost her."

"Thank you. You lost yours, too, right?"

She shifted uncomfortably and took a deep breath. "Nope." She nodded to a spot about twenty-five yards away. "She's right over there."

"What?" Devyn quirked her head. "I had no idea. I thought your dad raised you."

"He did, and he was wonderful. I miss him every day, much like you and your mom." She decided she should maybe explain. "My mother left us when I was in the second grade. Rode out of town on the back of a motorcycle with some guy she deemed infinitely more exciting than we were. A tourist named Todd."

"God, I've always hated that name," Devyn said, as if she had a bad taste in her mouth. "All the more reason."

"Right?" She sighed. "She showed back up fourteen years later with a husband, not Todd, and now lives with *him*, raising his two daughters. That's them next to her at the jewelry booth. Twelve and fourteen now."

Elizabeth stopped short of explaining that though her mother claimed to have come back to town to be near *her*, they rarely spoke for longer than three minutes in any given stretch.

"Hey, there, Lizzie-Loo." It was almost as if they'd summoned her. Elizabeth cringed at the use of the childhood nickname, unique to her mother. Kristine Lockwood, her married name, raised an energetic hand from where she stood shopping. "Good to see you, sweetie," she yelled in her sassy Southern accent. Elizabeth used to try to mimic it when she was little. Not so much now.

They walked toward her, and a pit arrived in the center of Elizabeth's stomach right on time. "Hi, Mom. Having fun?"

Her mother, who wore her bright red hair up and tall today, brightened. Her makeup was flawless as always, if a little thick. "Looking for something special for these sweet girls. They've both gotten good grades this term, and I promised them we'd pick up a special treat."

"How great," Elizabeth said, wondering what that must be like, to have a mother care about your grades, or even know what they were, for that matter. It wasn't that she wasn't happy for Mika and Milla—they seemed like nice enough girls—but somehow, they'd landed a stepmother who was fifty times the mother Elizabeth had had. She couldn't help her envy.

"Who's your friend, sweetheart?" her mother asked, gesturing to Devyn with a smile.

"Oh, right. Forgive me. This is Devyn Winters. She's an old high school classmate in town from Philadelphia."

"Well, welcome back to the Bay," Kristine said, with a hand on her hip. "I left and came back, too, ya know. Just couldn't stay away from those gorgeous beach views. Our house has beach access."

"Which shot your property value up by at least a third," Devyn said, and then winced. "Sorry. Force of habit."

"She's in real estate," Elizabeth offered.

"Well, isn't that as exciting as a pig tussle?" Kristine had always enjoyed a good, nonsensical phrase.

"This one." Milla picked up a silver necklace with an infinity sign and held it up. "Mom, what do you think? I'm thinking this would look awesome sauce with my navy top. Oh, hi, Elizabeth," the young teenager said with a hint of polite enthusiasm.

"Hey, Milla. Looks like a good choice to me." She tried to smile but found it hard. All of a sudden, she just wanted to be anywhere but right where she was. "We're headed home, I think." She exchanged a look with Devyn, who nodded as a concerned expression creased her features.

They said their goodbyes and her mother instructed her to stop by sometime "for some iced tea or something"—which was about all she ever said in the way of invitation. Nothing concrete. Nothing that would ever actually happen. The idea of Elizabeth in her life was really just that: a nice thought, but probably too much work.

She and Devyn walked the streets of Dreamer's Bay quietly, tired from the day, or in their own thoughts. Likely, a mix of both. She found herself a little introspective after the run-in with Kristine. It happened frequently enough that she should have been used to it by now, but old wounds take a long time to heal.

"Things seemed…a little strained with your mom," Devyn said delicately.

"Oh, they are." She smiled. "You don't have to feel weird about that. It's been a thing since I was seven."

"Got it. Her daughters are your sisters, then?"

"No. Well, stepsisters technically, but we've never really embraced that relationship. They live their lives and me and my dad lived ours. Until I lost him."

"That had to be rough. I'm sorry." A pause. "Wanna walk down to the beach?"

Elizabeth turned, liking this idea. "What's prompted this suggestion?"

"You look like you could use a little bit of calm. When I was a kid, finding a spot on the pier and just relaxing used to help. In a small town, it's hard to find a truly quiet spot."

Elizabeth shook her head. "I did the exact same thing. Still do. I guess we're not as different as we thought."

"Um. Let's not get carried away," Devyn said, holding up a finger. "We're very different, Ms. Chicken Serenade."

"I could serenade you right now," Elizabeth said, leaping into the road and making a sweeping gesture with her hand.

"Oh, no. Please don't." Devyn glanced around to see how many people were watching. There were decidedly several, including Mr. Lowes, who was watering his begonias, which only encouraged Elizabeth more.

"Happy birthday to you," Elizabeth bellowed.

"Oh, dear God." Devyn shaded her eyes. "It's not my birthday. Pretty sure it has to be your birthday for that. Objectively. You're breaking rules right now."

"Doesn't matter. Happy birthday to youuuuuu." Elizabeth opened both arms wide. "Happy birthdayyyy, dear Devyn Winters from here now Philadelphiaaaaa…"

"Please stop." But she was smiling, and Elizabeth was becoming addicted to the image.

"Happy birthday." She returned to her spot at Devyn's side as she sang. "To you." And booped her nose for good measure.

"Well," Devyn said, walking on, eyes forward. "That was certainly a sound sensation."

Elizabeth squinted, her spirits already lifted from where they were just five minutes earlier. "What does that mean? I'm feeling suspicious."

"A friend once taught me that when you're not quite sure what to say to someone, you simply use the word *sensation* somewhere in the sentence. That overly seasoned casserole that left you racing for water? Why, it's certainly a taste sensation. The ugliest house you've ever seen? Whoa, check out the architectural sensation. Works every time."

Elizabeth stared hard. "I think you're insulting my song."

"No, I'm not. It was a true sensation." Devyn grinned widely.

"You are the worst." She had to bump Devyn in the shoulder for that one. Behind all the balking and kidding, she really did appreciate how different they were. Devyn mystified her and kept her on her toes. The fact that she was also hardheaded and a total challenge also had Elizabeth hooked. Who knew she liked the difficult ones?

"I am the worst. I can totally admit that," Devyn said. "I'm not even sure why you're walking the streets with me."

"Someone has to, and I do perform odd jobs for a living. I'm probably the best candidate."

Devyn gasped.

"What if you fall in love with me?" Elizabeth asked. The stupid words were out of her mouth before she had a chance to run them through her brain. It had always been a problem for her, the unfiltered what-you-see-is-what-you-get side of herself. At least she said it in a semi-playful tone, right? That was something. She held her breath, ready to deflect.

"I won't," Devyn said, with a soft, self-assured smile. But the words, as expected as they were, still packed an awful punch. She'd set herself up for that one, hadn't she?

"Good. I can't be breaking hearts all over the Bay." Elizabeth added a chuckle for effect. It sounded hollow, mirroring how she suddenly felt.

"Hey," Devyn said, squeezing her hand as the water, bursting with color, came into view at the end of the street. "Doesn't mean I don't have a good time with you. You're a ton of fun. I like you a lot."

That was her. Lots of laughs. "I have fun with you, too. In many different ways."

"Now who's flirting?"

"Now who's *announcing* the flirting?" Elizabeth went up on her toes to see the pier better. "C'mon. Jimbo's ice cream cart is out."

"You can still eat?"

"Well, no, but it's *ice cream*."

"I guess there's no arguing that."

They sat side by side with their legs dangling off the pier. The water wasn't high enough to reach them today, but the serenity of its lapping was a nice contrast to the more boisterous atmosphere of the festival.

"Did you have fun today?" Devyn asked. She licked her lime sherbet cone. Elizabeth stopped to watch a moment before returning to the question.

"It was a best day."

"A best day. That's a thing?"

Elizabeth nodded, nearly halfway through her chocolate sundae swirl. "Some days just reach their own level of greatness. A best day kind of day. Today was that. A best day." She looked over at Devyn feeling uncharacteristically shy. "Confession. I like hanging out with you. I know you've been to all kinds of festivals here before, but I felt like maybe you saw a new side of the fun today."

"I did," Devyn said. She pointed at the ladybug on her cheek. "The evidence cannot be ignored." She stared out at the water. "Confession right back. When I'm with you, I do a lot of things that would never occur to me otherwise. I ate fried Coca-Cola today. That actually happened."

"I've never been prouder."

Devyn turned to her, her expression now dialed to serious. "What are you doing tonight?"

Elizabeth shrugged. "No set plans. Usually on a Saturday I see what Dexter is up to, or KC, if she's free. Or both. We're kind of a three-person friend group." She paused. "Unless I had another offer." She licked her cone and watched the water, acutely aware of Devyn's gaze on her.

"I'm offering."

Elizabeth pulled in a slow breath as her body shivered. "You could always come over later. I'll need to shower first and get all this festival off me."

"I don't see why that has to happen on your own." Devyn continued to lick her cone, and it was the most amazing thing Elizabeth had seen since FaceTime was invented. "Seems like a waste." Elizabeth exhaled in an attempt to steady herself, because do you know what wasn't wasted? The image of Devyn's tongue circling the ice cream. God.

Elizabeth didn't understand how Devyn was able to affect her so potently, with her having zero say in the matter. Yet here she sat, so turned on she was uncomfortable. "Huh. You make a decent point."

"I should come with you, then?" Devyn smiled proudly at that one.

Elizabeth felt the blush. She opened her mouth, closed it, and shook her head. "You said that on purpose."

Devyn took a last lick of that cone and tossed it in the nearby trash can. When she turned back, her eyes shone brightly with a look of determination. "I'm feeling very purposeful."

❖

Devyn had never been more ready to touch another person. To be touched. Heart raced. Desire rippled. She throbbed endlessly and loved every damn second of it. Elizabeth made her feel like a kid on Christmas morning, and there was no better feeling.

Elizabeth fumbled behind her, holding her around the waist with one arm and turning the shower knob at the same time with the other. If Devyn hadn't been so acutely turned on, she would have been impressed. They'd shed their clothes one piece at a time as they stumbled, hopped, and bumped into random pieces of furniture, walls, and lamps as they traversed her house on their way to the master bathroom. Devyn flung her bra behind her and watched as Elizabeth's gaze dropped immediately to her breasts, for which she was learning Elizabeth had a thing.

Elizabeth stepped backward beneath the stream, and Devyn followed her there, catching her mouth again, dancing the way they did with lips and tongues and just the right amount of cling. Her hands slid down Elizabeth's body, over her round breasts, now wet from the spray, the perfect curve of her hip, to the outside of her thighs. She felt the pressure between her own legs near its peak, aware of Elizabeth touching her intimately there. She suspended her exploration of Elizabeth's body when the sensations became too much. Her back was against the shower wall, hair wet as they stood face-to-face, water dripping from their chins. Elizabeth's hand continued to stroke her rhythmically as her legs shook. She was headed toward a major release, and the need was almost unbearable. She bucked her hips and pressed her hands against the now-heated tile of the shower wall as pleasure arrived hard and wonderful, racing through her like a bullet train. The sounds she heard were definitely emanating from *her*. Lost and delirious and riding out an orgasm that had to have been building since the damn three-legged race, she allowed herself to revel in every moment of decadent gratification. She'd never come so hard in her life and it was all thanks to unassuming Elizabeth, who was not unassuming at all, it turned out. With soaked hair and slick skin, she found her breathing as Elizabeth continued to touch her softly, circling her most sensitive spot as the water fell.

"What the fuck?" she breathed, allowing her head to fall forward onto Elizabeth's shoulder. "How do you do that? Did you take some sort of class?"

Elizabeth kissed her neck, melding herself to Devyn's body. "It wasn't hard at all with you standing here without clothes. Look at your body. Unreal." Elizabeth ran her hands down Devyn's torso. Devyn caught them and placed them against the opposite shower wall. She dipped her head, caught a nipple between her lips, and sucked. Elizabeth whimpered.

"Prepare to call out my name," Devyn said in her ear.

"Yeah?" Elizabeth bit her bottom lip with a grin.

"I have some creative ideas I think you might like."

"Creative things are my favorite," Elizabeth breathed, as Devyn kissed down her body.

❖

Dawn hadn't broken, but Elizabeth lazily glimpsed the first hint of orange through the tree branches outside her window and watched in captivation as the small light grew. Inside, Devyn lay in her arms sleeping soundly, their limbs intertwined, their clothes still scattered throughout her home wherever they'd dropped them, forgotten and not at all missed. Scout slept peacefully near the door, snoring quietly. All felt right and calm.

She'd had shower sex. She, Elizabeth Draper, who lived a fairly mundane existence, had had sex not only in her kitchen but now her shower, too. They'd stayed in there until the water had run cold. What in the world was happening? She wasn't sure, but it scared her. She kissed the forehead of the woman in her arms and vowed to slow the emerging feelings that would only get her heart into trouble. *Focus on the great sex*, she told herself. *Don't think about how it feels to hold her this way. To inhale her scent. To feel her warmth as the morning creeps in.*

Devyn certainly wasn't dwelling on those things. She was too in control to allow those feelings to percolate, and honestly, Elizabeth probably wasn't even that noteworthy a partner. She closed her eyes, knowing that wasn't true. She saw firsthand the effect she had on Devyn, and it was potent. At least physically.

"Good morning," a scratchy voice said. Elizabeth smiled as Devyn kissed her neck softly in greeting. "I stayed the night. I'm sorry about that. I hope that's okay."

Elizabeth pulled her in further, her fingers threaded through the back of Devyn's hair. "I'm glad you stayed."

"Really? I wasn't sure if that was crossing some sort of line we hadn't—"

"Devyn."

"Yeah?" She smiled.

"We've crossed so many lines that I can't see them anymore."

"Good point." Devyn smiled and stole a kiss. "I checked in with Jill before falling asleep. Turns out you're not the only one with overnight company."

Elizabeth raised her eyebrows. "Does that mean Charlie had a good night, too?"

"Mmm-hmm. And it's not even Thursday."

Elizabeth smiled at the ceiling. "You go, Jilly."

"What about me?" Devyn asked, raising her head from the pillow she shared with Elizabeth. Her blond hair was tousled. Her lips were perfectly swollen. She had never been more beautiful. Elizabeth's heart filled and grew. "Should I get out of your way now?" The sheet only came up to Devyn's belly button, and Elizabeth stole a glimpse of her right breast, which had her hungry and ready to take it into her mouth.

"You stay right where you are." Honestly, it was shocking how perfectly their bodies fit together. She'd never slept so comfortably with another person in her entire life. Just as the thought hit, Devyn pressed against her, sliding a thigh between hers. The hint of stimulation grew to full blown. She blinked and rolled her lips in to steady herself. Her arousal didn't pass. She wiggled the tiniest bit, pressing intimately against that thigh, which seemed to alert Devyn to her predicament. She eased the thigh upward and studied Elizabeth's face.

"I love it when you get that look. I know exactly what it means and exactly what to do about it." Elizabeth didn't have time to answer or ask what the look consisted of. Devyn placed a soft kiss on her cheek before disappearing under the covers on a very welcome mission.

Elizabeth inhaled sharply as her thighs were parted, and twisted her head against the pillow at the sensation of Devyn's tongue.

Sweet heaven.

Morning had arrived.

CHAPTER SIXTEEN

"Would you look at what we have here," Jill called from one of the quaint rocking chairs on her front porch. The morning was a nice one with just a hint of a chill in the air, but the sun was beginning to make itself known. Jill sat outside in her robe, rumpled hair and all, with a cup of tea she hopefully hadn't had to work too hard to make.

Devyn wound her way sheepishly up the sidewalk, wearing the same outfit she'd worn the day before. "Yeah, yeah. Make fun of me all you want, Jilly Donut, but I'm not the *only* one who spent the night with someone."

Jill pointed at the rocking chair next to hers. "Sit down and spill your guts, and maybe I'll do the same. I made you a cup, too, just in case. Coffee. Black and boring the way you like it, you weirdo."

Devyn stole the cup and brought it close to her face, enjoying the heat and the potent aroma. She glanced behind her and lowered her voice. "Liquor Store Charlie gone?"

Jill squinted. "Can we just call him Charlie? Or Charles."

"I mean…we *can*. It's less fun, but I can make that sacrifice if it makes you happy." She reset herself in time, and brightened. "Hey, is *Charlie* gone?"

"Left a half hour ago." Jill wasn't able to hide the smile in the slightest, and her cheeks and neck turned rosy red.

"You are smitten with him, aren't you?" Devyn said, leaning over and poking Jill a million times on the arm. "You are a schoolmarm by day and sex kitten by night and very few people suspect it. Even your *ears* are pinking up right now. Look at you go. What would Mom say?" She was teasing her sister because it was part of who they were, but underneath it all she was thrilled to see Jill light up the way she did when Charlie's name came up.

"She would be pleased, I think."

"She would interrogate the hell out of him and then make us all set the table so she could invite him to dinner."

Jill smiled at the characterization. "She would. She might even use the guest dishes." She paused. "But we're forgetting the more surprising story."

Devyn cradled the warm coffee mug. "And what is that?"

"I'm not the one who waltzed into town and set my sights on the very sweet and most innocent of townspeople."

"Neither did I. There are no sights set."

Jill sipped her tea and looked straight ahead to the front yard. "Liar. You have feelings for Elizabeth you didn't expect. It's written all over your face when you're around her, Dev. That goofy grin when you came up the walk? That told me all I need to know."

She balked. "We're killing time together. Nothing more than that. Trust me. She's nice enough, and yeah, I find her very, very attractive."

"If you say so." Jill drank her tea.

"I do." She took a swig from her mug and burned her tongue, which only made her think about Elizabeth and their morning and the cute sounds she made while in the throes.

"Why are you grinning like that?" Jill asked. "What's going on in that head of yours?"

She banished the smile from her face. "I was just ruminating on the fact that you let Charlie stay the night on a non-Thursday." *That's right. Toss it right back to her.*

"So I did."

Devyn shifted to sincerity because there was something different about Jill this morning. She seemed lighter and heavier at the same time. Maybe she was more serious about Charlie than even Devyn realized. "Do you love him, Jill?"

Her sister took a moment with the question before slowly nodding. She shifted her lips to the side and stared at Devyn, seeming unsure of what to do or say. Yep. She loved him, but it scared her. That much was clear.

"It's a good thing, you know. Falling in love. I'm happy for you."

Jill sighed. "Thank you, but love's not all sunshine and rainbows. I've tried it before, remember? You were my maid of honor. Didn't work, and I was left to pick up the pieces."

"Frankie was an ass from the start. You just decided to ignore half his personality because he was good looking. Is Charlie an ass?"

"I give him a hard time, but no. He's a really good person, Dev. He treats me like I'm somebody special even though I'm just me."

"Stop that," Devyn said, with maybe more force than she intended. "You're probably the nicest, most deserving person I've ever met, but you always sacrifice your happiness for everyone who is not you. You've got to stop taking the smallest proverbial slice of pizza for yourself. You deserve the big pizza, okay? If Charlie gets how awesome you are, and you happen to think he's awesome right back, then I say throw Thursdays the hell out the window and be happy every damn day of the week."

Jill nodded. "You know, I'm warming up to the idea." She pursed her lips together and seemed to make a decision to share more. "I can't believe I'm telling anyone this, but last night was the first time he's slept over."

Devyn made a point to remain casual so as not to frighten this new open and honest version of Jill. "And how was it? Having him here."

Jill scrunched her shoulders together in an adorable show. "I liked it. And he was so attentive and careful with me because of my injuries, you know? Offered to get everything for me. Do all the cleaning up after dinner."

Devyn tapped her coffee cup. "His stock is rising in my book."

They drank their tea and coffee and watched the neighborhood wake up slowly. An orange cat ran up a nearby tree. The across-the-street neighbor put out his trash can and waved. She had to admit, the slow pace was incredibly soothing. In fact, she couldn't remember feeling this relaxed in…well, ever. Her mind drifted to the events of last night. The hot shower scene was one that was burned into her brain and body for all time. But more prominent was something Jill had just touched on herself. Waking up wrapped around Elizabeth was the nicest of discoveries. Her warmth, her sweet cotton scent, and the manner in which she held Devyn close resonated. She shook her head at the fullness of her heart. She was apparently in some sort of weird mood to let something that mundane affect her. The back of her neck prickled as she distantly considered that maybe it wasn't so mundane after all. Maybe this was a big deal.

"Have you ever been in love, Dev?"

She studied Jill and grappled with how to sidestep the personal question, but then realized that Jill had opened up to her. She should try doing the same. She met her sister's friendly brown eyes. "No."

Jill continued rocking. "You're like me. You don't let people in easily. My walls went up after my divorce, but you know something? Your walls have always been up. Why do you think that is?"

Devyn let a little time pass before tackling the question, deciding it was easier to just dodge it altogether. "Probably because I'm married to my career. In fact, I should be on the phone right now, selling my ass off. Shaking my international contact list and seeing what falls out." She stood, more than a little uncomfortable with the direction of the conversation. She didn't do well in the spotlight.

Jill nodded sagely but didn't comment right away. Instead, she watched Devyn walk to the front door. "You hide behind it, you know? Your career."

Devyn scoffed, her hand on the doorknob. "I do not. It happens to be what makes me happy in life."

"That's what you tell yourself so you can justify not having to get too close to anyone. If you live a fast enough paced life, you won't notice what's missing." She tapped her temple. "You forget how well I know you."

"It's not like that." It was a lame argument, but it was all Devyn had.

"Let her in, Devyn. You might just be surprised."

"Who are we talking about?" she asked, knowing full well and dodging the acknowledgment. She let herself into the house and spent the rest of the day making calls abroad and organizing a brokers' open the likes of which the city of Philadelphia had never seen. Emotional vulnerability was the best motivation.

When she finished her to-do list for the day, she sat back at her desk with two fingers of whiskey, watching the trees sway through the window as dusk fell. Jill's words still rattled around in her head, annoying and loud. She was afraid to let anyone in? She'd never quite considered that and wondered now about the accuracy of the statement, fearing its validity. She'd always blamed her passion for her job for her lack of any real, close-knit personal relationships. She was too busy to get wrapped up in another person. She questioned the logic now.

Because she *could* make time for someone important. She *should* make time for that person. So why didn't she?

Devyn took a slow pull from her glass, pondering. Maybe Jill was right, and maybe it was time to take down some of her walls. Wouldn't be so hard if she just put her mind to it.

But if that was true, why did the idea scare the living hell out of her?

❖

"That one is not your friend," Elizabeth said the following Wednesday, giving Hank's leash a tug. "Uh-uh." He stood nose to stinger with a brightly colored bumblebee, and it was up to her to save his precious life and nose. She gave him a whistle along with a second tug and he happily trotted on, leaving the potential friend behind. "You really made the right call with that one, Hank. He would have hurt you in more ways than one."

The energetic doggo, seeing he was close to his own street, picked up the pace, which prompted Elizabeth to match his speed and gusto. The late May sun beat down on her shoulders, making her happy she'd gone the tank top and sandals route. She adjusted her aviator sunglasses and took a deep inhale of the familiar fresh coffee aroma that particular street always served up.

The sound of a car to her left pulled her focus. "Delivery," a voice called. She turned to see a tiny green car, and Devyn ducking her head low and holding a to-go cup through the passenger side window.

Elizabeth pulled Hank to a stop. "What in the world? You brought me coffee? Seriously?"

Devyn shrugged and glanced away and then back. "Not a big deal. I remember you saying that the Hank walks always made you want a cup, and since you walk Hank on Wednesdays…"

"And you know my schedule." Elizabeth tapped her cheek. "Interesting."

"I happen to pay attention when you speak. It's the polite thing to do. I also like it when you do that thing where you just talk a lot."

Elizabeth winked. "My nervous rambling. Let's just call it what it is."

"We can. Regardless, I like it."

She studied Devyn, who had her hair pulled back today. "So, you thought you'd do something nice for me?"

"I don't know. I suppose I did."

This wasn't the kind of thing Devyn did or was comfortable with. It was a simple gesture, but the effect it had on Elizabeth was anything but. Someone as important and as busy as Devyn had gone out of her way because she was thinking of *her*. She walked to the car and accepted the warm cup. "Thank you." She gestured to her charge. "This is Hank, by the way. Not as calm as Scout, but just as friendly." He whined softly, wondering why in the world they would ever stop walking when there was so much to explore between here and his home.

"Nice to meet you," Devyn said, with perfect professionalism.

Elizabeth laughed. "Want to walk with us?"

Devyn smiled at her, and for a moment, that was all they did. Smile and stare, unwrapping each other. Finally, Devyn pulled them out of it, giving her head a wake-up shake. "Can't. Though I'd really, really like to. Especially if that tank top is sticking around."

Elizabeth glanced down and grinned. "It's probably better I keep it on, I'm thinking. Neighborhood sidewalk and all. And why is it you can't join us? Hank would love to lick your hands, face, and shoes. Still not clear on why the last one is important to him, but it is."

"I'm sorry to miss that very specific initiation, but I have a call with my developer." She leaned in farther toward the passenger window. "This, however, was a nice way to break up my morning."

"What? Me?"

"Yeah, you. Stay out of trouble, Liz. Maybe I'll see you later if you're not busy?"

"I'm hoping so." Elizabeth raised her coffee cup in the air and watched as the tiny Chevy Spark headed off down the street, leaving her on a high.

A text from Thalia hit her phone. She stared at the message:

Drinks tonight at Twill's? Just you and me.

A month ago, a sentence like that from Thalia would have sent her over the moon. She rattled off a reply:

Unfortunately, I've got other plans.

She turned to Hank as they headed off down the street. "That was Devyn. She makes life better."

❖

How was it already approaching five? The workday for Elizabeth had been a busy one. After helping with Jill, who had honestly made so many wonderful strides that she really didn't need much assistance any longer, she'd come back to On the Spot headquarters, also known as her converted garage, and started fielding job requests like a maniac. Business certainly wasn't hurting, and she knew that part of it had to do with her relationship with the community. Remaining upbeat and hospitable, even in the midst of a difficult job, certainly went a long way, and she wondered why more people didn't take advantage of how far being nice would get you. She scanned her oversized day planner, which she much preferred to a laptop. That afternoon she had Genevieve and Haley, both sophomores at the community college up the highway, out on errands. Her two part-time employees, Drake and Brent, were delivering mulch in a very large quantity to the fire station, and she was already into scheduling the next day and the next.

"Excuse me. Is this place open for business?"

Elizabeth glanced up and smiled, already recognizing the voice. She hadn't had more than a fleeting conversation with Devyn in the past three days, and damn it, her heart leapt at the welcome sight of her. "Well, hi. We are open. What can I do for you?" Elizabeth stood from her desk and watched as Devyn approached with a smile. She wore jeans, a short-sleeved navy blue T-shirt, and light gray Converse, dressed more casually than Elizabeth had ever seen her. A tingle flowed through her and she leaned into it. Devyn looked more than good.

"Do you offer kissing services?"

Elizabeth swallowed. She was caught off guard by the pointed question, but listen, she wasn't complaining. Neither was the rest of her. The parts of her that hadn't touched Devyn in a handful of days now. They usually took a few moments to warm up to lines like that, but today felt different. Devyn did, too.

"Um. Well. You wouldn't have guessed this from our very professional reputation at On the Spot, but we do on occasion offer such services for special cases. Yes."

"Is it very expensive?" Devyn walked farther into the garage until she stood, face-to-face, with Elizabeth. She smelled amazing. Cucumber and citrus. All Elizabeth could do was steal glances at her lips. She loved the bottom one especially, and the way Devyn used it to punctuate so many of her expressions. She probably didn't even realize she did it.

Elizabeth nodded. "We're running a special."

"This is a really great coincidence I came today, of all days, then."

"Isn't it, though? Let's get started." Elizabeth leaned in and pressed her lips to Devyn's. They stayed that way for a moment, in the bliss of just that initial contact, until Elizabeth readjusted, parting her lips to deepen the kiss. She heard Devyn murmur against her mouth, which was, without question, incredibly hot. They were a hot couple. Had she ever been part of such a hot couple before? She forgot the question altogether because, sweet Jesus, Devyn's tongue was in her mouth and she could no longer feel her own legs.

"You taste really good." Devyn wrapped her arms around Elizabeth's waist and, oh man, with their bodies pressed together and their lips dancing, there were things happening lower that Elizabeth couldn't quite find words to describe. The more time she spent with Devyn, the more she craved her, thought about her, and wanted more time. She wanted that opportunity. She wanted to explore what they were like…as a *them*. It was the first time she'd admitted that to herself.

"The clock is ticking," she said, breathless, as she pulled her mouth away from Devyn's. The words were out in the universe before she realized it. Why did she do that? Her arms still rested on Devyn's shoulders with her fingers laced behind, but now she felt awkward and nervous. Why did she have to go there? Just enjoy the moments they had. That was all she had to do.

"What clock?" Devyn asked, glancing around the garage.

Elizabeth bit the inside of her lip. Well, she might as well say it. She'd already half gone there, like an idiot. "Ours. Is it crazy that I'm suddenly very aware of it? That our time together is dwindling?"

Devyn rolled her lips in and appeared to figure out how to tackle this one. "I know. How do we set that knowledge aside?"

"I'm not sure. Jill is getting better, which is exactly what I want to happen, but that comes with a chain reaction, the implications of which…make me sad. I don't want you to leave."

Devyn nodded and kissed the underside of Elizabeth's jaw before moving away. "I don't know what to say to that." She placed her hands on top of her head. "It's not like I'm disappearing off the planet when I head back to Philadelphia."

"That's true."

"We'll still be…"

Elizabeth could tell she had no idea how to finish that sentence. She took control of the conversation. She had to. "At first we were just friends who flirted. Then, we were friends who hooked up." She paused, musing. "I've never said 'hooked up' before."

A grin spread across Devyn's face. "I'm really proud of you. Another milestone for today. That, and the kissing special."

She tilted her head, getting right to it. "Are we still just *hooking up*? It's okay if we are, I'm just…needing to know, for my own piece of mind."

"I like you, Elizabeth Draper."

"Why do you so often call me by my first and last name?"

"You would rather I didn't?"

"I call foul. That's two questions in a row you haven't answered."
She smiled. The lighthearted tone that had settled over the conversation
somehow made all of this easier.

"You're very observant and very beautiful. Especially in your
element like this." Devyn gestured around them.

"And now you're trying to charm me off the topic. Focus."

Devyn scoffed. "I wouldn't do that. I'm a straight shooter. I just...
don't have the answers you're looking for. This is new territory for me,
okay?" For the first time, Devyn appeared a little bit vulnerable.

Her answer made sense but still frustrated Elizabeth. She dropped
her head back and stared at the ceiling, studying the splatter of paint
that had somehow made its way up there. What did she expect Devyn to
do? Profess her undying love, quit her job, and move back to Dreamer's
Bay, the one place she couldn't stand? She sighed. "I'm overthinking,
aren't I? I should relax."

Devyn walked back to her and took her hand. "You're not. You're
being a normal human with feelings and concerns. Generally, all things
that would send me running and screaming." She raised a finger. "That's
a new discovery for me, by the way."

"That feelings terrify you?" She laced their fingers and studied
their intertwined hands. "You don't have to be afraid of me, Dev. I'm
probably the most harmless person on the planet."

Devyn paused, letting the comment land. "I like it when you
shorten my name."

"You lengthen mine, and I shorten yours." Elizabeth laughed and
stepped in. "How about Big D? Even better?"

Devyn covered her face. "Uh-uh."

"Hot D? Spicy D? Demolition D."

"Not even a little bit. No."

"I think it's an honest-to-goodness nickname sensation."

"At the very least." Devyn glanced at the driveway through the
open door. "Let's get outta here. Go for a drive. Pretend we have
everything figured out."

Elizabeth eyed her and glanced at the desk. "I have scheduling to
finish. You, of all people, being the self-aware workaholic that you are,
probably sympathize."

She gathered her blond hair into a bunch and let it drop. "I'll wait
over there." Devyn took a seat in the deep purple arm chair across from
Elizabeth's desk, picked up that day's edition of *The Dreamer's Bay
Tribune*, and pretended to immerse herself.

Hesitantly, very aware of Devyn's presence, Elizabeth continued to pencil in job requests that had come in via the porthole she'd had set up online—the portion of technology she'd embraced—for her clients and began matching up tasks to appropriate employees. Drake would be perfect for the lawn mowing Mrs. Davidson needed. KC could handle picking up the Dawson kids from soccer practice. She would be more than happy to bring two Big Macs for lunch the next day to Mr. Ivers, who'd at least taken a few days off from fast food. She glanced up to see Devyn grinning.

"What?" Elizabeth asked. "What's so amusing?"

"You're cute when you work. You get so serious and there's a little line that forms right here." Devyn gestured to the spot in the middle of her forehead. She shrugged. "I like it."

"You do?" Elizabeth was caught off guard, but in the best way. She felt warmth on her cheeks as she worked, enjoying the quiet company, and Devyn's appreciation. "What are you reading about?" she finally asked, some fifteen minutes later.

Devyn peeked at her over the top of the open paper. "Well, you're not going to believe this, but RayEllen Mink has been bowling for over thirty years, and is now in first place in the seniors league. She might lose her standing, though, if she can't work on picking up the three-ten split more of the time."

Elizabeth nodded. "RayEllen is not to be messed with. I was actually excited when she moved up to the seniors league."

Devyn went back to her paper and then peeked back over the top. "Will you wear your bowling shirt for me later?" She bounced her eyebrows.

"No, because you're making fun of me."

"You in a bowling shirt and wearing not another stitch of clothing is nothing to make fun of. God, now I can't get that image out of my head. Dammit. I did this to myself."

Elizabeth sucked in a breath. "Maybe we can revisit the issue later."

"Thank God." She dropped the paper. "Ready for our drive? Maybe we can even swing by the bowling alley. You can show me your skills."

Elizabeth found the keys to Shug in the top drawer of her desk and tossed them to Devyn. "Lead the way."

CHAPTER SEVENTEEN

With vintage Stones blaring from the speakers, Devyn drove them along the shoreline, windows down, the last of the sunshine filling the truck. Their hair blew around with wild abandon as Devyn accelerated on the open road, and Elizabeth stared out at the waves. "No time of day is this beautiful," she said. "Just look out there."

Devyn did, taking in the golden glow that enveloped most everything as the sun crept to bed. Beneath it, the tide rolled in, encroaching on the beachgoers, who moved their towels and shrugged into hoodies as the evening temperatures crept in. "There really is nothing like it."

It was officially summer in South Carolina, and with school getting out, the town would see more and more visitors renting houses, apartments, and guest cottages. The boogie board place near the beach that sold key chains, T-shirts, and snorkel gear would bask in the glory of the impending summer rush. Devyn remembered the summer culture all too well and surprised herself with the excitement she felt. Well, until she realized she likely wouldn't be a part of it.

Since when did she care about missing anything in Dreamer's Bay? So much new was happening.

"Do you go in the water much?" Devyn asked.

Elizabeth looked over at her, and the sun caught those green eyes and amplified their color. "Maybe once or twice over the course of a given summer. I'm more of a likes-to-sit-and-stare-at-the-water kinda girl."

"I get that about you." Devyn paused as an image settled. "A bottle of wine with you on the beach at sunset would be nice." And now she was romanticizing the place. But Devyn shoved down that voice in her head and enjoyed the newfound inclination, because it felt refreshing and more natural than she would have guessed.

"I'd love that." Elizabeth hung an arm out the window of Shug the Truck. "Though I might smuggle in a beer."

"Of course you would. I would be shocked if you didn't." Because she simply wanted to, Devyn leaned over and stole a quick kiss before refocusing on the road. "Where to next?"

"I gave you the keys, remember?" Elizabeth, the tour organizer, had given her control.

"Let's go all over."

Elizabeth pressed her cheek against the seat and smiled at Devyn, who never wanted the night to end.

They bowled a game next, and Devyn spent more time checking out Elizabeth from behind than she did trying to win the game, which was ridiculous because Elizabeth was a pro.

Devyn stared at the overhead screen. "You almost rolled a two hundred without even warming up. Who does that?"

"A one seventy-eight is hardly a two hundred. But to answer your question, someone who takes her bowling career very, very seriously," Elizabeth said, as she approached Devyn in one of the chairs. Her hands immediately went to Elizabeth's waist, and Elizabeth stared down at her tentatively.

"So, we're doing this?"

Devyn understood what she was getting at. They'd not exactly engaged in public displays of affection. Ever. Their relationship and its confusing status had been something they'd kept to themselves because it was likely to be temporary. But maybe all of that didn't matter. Devyn shrugged, her hands still on Elizabeth. "I don't care if you don't."

That earned a smile. Elizabeth bent down and skimmed Devyn's lips with hers. It took everything Devyn had not to pull her back down because the tiny kiss sent shivers. Actual shivers. She leaned into the skid, allowing herself to relish and enjoy it.

"Just a preview of coming attractions," Elizabeth said.

Devyn loved the teasing. Another new piece of information she was learning about herself. As Elizabeth stepped out of the way and took a seat at the console, Devyn's gaze landed square on Cricket's, six lanes over. Her eyes were wide and her mouth formed the shape of an O. Knowing Cricket's undying love of gossip, the fact that she and Elizabeth had just kissed in the bowling alley would be all over town before they had a chance to settle their bill. Maybe it was time to do a little damage control by playing nice. "Be right back," she said to Elizabeth.

Cricket brightened on cue as Devyn approached. Her smile was too big, and she acted too surprised to see Devyn, which was clearly her attempt to pretend she didn't even know they were there. How crazy. A farce. Devyn knew Cricket too well for that. She pushed her hands into the back pockets of her jeans. "Hey, there," she said, with a friendly wave. "You guys out for some fun?"

"We are," Cricket crowed with over-the-top enthusiasm that had arrived out of nowhere. The two young boys Cricket had with her were her spitting image—clearly the sons Devyn had heard so many glowing stories about. One purposely dropped a bowling ball on the other's foot, prompting a wail. Cricket didn't seem to care. She stood and pulled Devyn into a hug, which was how all of the cheerleaders greeted each other in high school. Even if that had meant sixty hugs a day. In every class, there was a hug. Lunch, hugs. Arriving at practice. Leaving practice. Hug, hug, hug. It was obnoxious. She saw that now.

Devyn gestured behind her. "We're just having a bit of a free night. Exploring the town."

Cricket pursed her lips and nodded as if she knew all too well what that was like. She did it all the time. "I didn't know you two... were close. You and Elizabeth."

"Because we kissed?" Why not just jump right to the point?

"Well, that was surprising. Not that there's anything wrong with it," she rushed to say.

"The gay thing, you mean?"

"No," Cricket practically shouted. "Absolutely not." She placed a hand over her heart. "I'm an ally. I make donations."

"That's wonderful," Devyn said, trying to mask the hint of sarcasm and probably losing.

"I just meant, there's nothing wrong with *Elizabeth*. She's not who I imagined you with. But she's a hard worker, and she's very nice."

"She is." A pause. "We're just out enjoying the night. That's all."

Cricket's expression took on a serious quality and she lowered her voice. "A booty call? You can tell me, Dev. We've all been there. We've all needed a little special attention. Lord knows."

Devyn closed her eyes. "Nope. Just bowling. We like each other and like spending time together." She glanced at the boys, who were studying a handheld video game as if the world might be ending. "You guys enjoy yourself."

"Don't you two get into too much trouble, you hear me?" Cricket called after her like they were a crazy couple of kids who tickled her endlessly. She gave it sixty seconds before Cricket was on some kind of group chat with Heather, Coco, and Lisa, and by midnight the whole town would be staring at them knowingly for the rest of time. It was how things worked here. Oh, well. She wasn't going to stop living her life because the rumor mill would erupt.

"Want to get out of here?" Devyn asked, when she returned to their lane.

Elizabeth studied her, off-kilter now. "Did Cricket say something to upset you?"

Devyn glanced back and minimized the interaction, refusing to believe that Cricket had the capacity. Yet the younger Devyn still seemed to be in there somewhere and let friends like Cricket get under her skin. Elizabeth was a *hard worker*? Why would she lead with that? It was laced with judgment and pretention. "She didn't upset me. She's just being Cricket, which is always a little unfortunate." She ordered herself to leave the exchange in the past and smiled at Elizabeth. "Where to now?"

Elizabeth considered the question and checked her watch. "Well, it's soccer season."

It certainly was, and when they arrived at the old high school field, Devyn was pleased to see that they'd spent the money to install fluorescent lighting to allow for evening games. The stands were packed and the aroma of popcorn and Frito pies permeated the air. She smiled at the snow cone line and remembered her own affinity for the lime ones, in their neon green greatness. Some things never changed. They waved to Jill and Charlie, who sat on the bottom bleacher in the accessible section, and found a spot for themselves on the grass alongside the stands.

"I didn't bring a blanket," Elizabeth said in apology.

Devyn shrugged and touched the spot next to her. "I hear grass never killed anybody."

Elizabeth grinned. "I appreciate your practical mind. Though the Devyn I met a couple months back had higher standards, if I remember correctly. Had assistants for everything. Didn't even do her own grocery shopping."

"She did live a certain catered-to lifestyle, didn't she? Maybe someone is rubbing off on her."

Elizabeth stared at the darkening sky. "I don't know who that person might be."

"She's weirdly into purple and knows how to wield a fucking blowtorch."

Elizabeth chuckled. "My kind of person."

Devyn nudged her. "Mine, too."

The moment was not a monumental one, but Devyn noticed it. More specifically, she noticed the lightness in the air, the smile that had been on her face for the past few hours—ever since she'd picked up Elizabeth in her garage office—and the way she hadn't thought about work in hours, which left her less stressed than she could ever remember. There was something to all of this, something to *Elizabeth*, who made her undeniably happy.

"There you go, Milla," Elizabeth yelled, leaping to her feet.

Devyn stared out at the field and saw Elizabeth's stepsister steal the ball and dribble down the field. She jumped up and clapped alongside Elizabeth.

"She's not bad for a freshman," Elizabeth said, with a small smile. She wasn't comfortable with her family, no matter how nice they tried to be. There was a lot of complication there, Devyn could tell, and it made her sad for Elizabeth. She was on her own and didn't have to be.

The match continued with one team scoring and then the other. Devyn's adrenaline pumped as the clock ticked, the game pulling her in. The Stars were down by one and had to make something happen in the final two minutes. They yelled, they cheered and, in the end, had their hearts broken when a shot by Milla was blocked effectively by the goalkeeper on the opposing team. The Dreamer's Bay fans sighed collectively.

"Do you want to stay and speak to Milla?" Devyn asked, as they stood.

"Um…" Elizabeth wrapped her arms around her midsection, literally closing herself off at the mention. "She probably has other people to talk to." But the way she said it indicated that she was unsure.

"No, I think we should," Devyn said, leading off toward the team's bench. Parents and friends gathered around to help rally the players and get their hugs.

"Devyn, wait."

"Why are you dragging those feet? C'mon. Let's say hi." Devyn gave her head a follow-me toss and, shortly after, felt a reluctant

Elizabeth on her heels. When they arrived in the large grouping, Devyn made her way straight to Milla. "You did great out there," she said, and then stepped out of the way for Elizabeth.

The teenager thanked Devyn and smiled at Elizabeth, who smiled back. "I'm so happy I made it to one of your games."

Milla's smile only grew. "I know. I hope it was a good one. I just wish we could have pulled it out in the end. Sucks." She shifted her weight to her other foot. Aha. The kid was nervous, too.

Elizabeth knocked her one on the shoulder. "Trust me. You'll get 'em next time."

They stepped aside to let the next batch of well-wishers through and came face-to-face with Elizabeth's mother. "Well, hey, there, baby girl," she said, in her bright blue Stars T-shirt. "I didn't see you in the stands."

"Just caught the last half." Elizabeth's usual perky demeanor seemed to dim every time they encountered Kristine. Devyn hated watching it happen.

Kristine nodded. "Well, I couldn't be prouder of this one," she said, pulling Milla into a playful headlock. "Hey, I'm making my famous tuna casserole tomorrow night. You used to love it when you were a tiny tot. You should come by for supper. Six p.m."

"Oh, I wish I could," Elizabeth said, automatically. "I have work."

"I understand." Her mother's enthusiasm waned. "What if I came by your place a little later after supper, then? I could bring you a to-go portion. Enough for lunch the next day, too."

"You don't have to do that." Devyn gave Elizabeth the tiniest of nudges and saw her close her eyes briefly as if pausing to regroup. "Well, I guess that might be nice."

The expression on Kristine's face shifted from friendly to ecstatic. Regardless of what events made up their past, Elizabeth was wrong about her current intentions. She clearly *wanted* Elizabeth in her life. "Well, that's just the best news since Thanksgiving dinner hit the table." She turned to Devyn. "I adore turkey and all the fixin's. Loved it since I was a little girl in Alabama."

"It's a great holiday," Devyn said. "I can agree."

"Same," Elizabeth said conservatively. The grin on her face when she turned to face Devyn was frozen in place and seemed to scream "get me out of here now, please."

She could accommodate. "Well, I think we better head out. I've had the longest day and need to get some rest."

That sent Elizabeth into an overexaggerated stretch. "Agreed. Yes, sir, I'm ready for some relaxation." They really needed to work on their acting skills.

Elizabeth's mother hadn't stopped celebrating her victory and beamed at them while she slung an arm around Milla's shoulder. "Well, you kids go enjoy your night. I'll be by with that casserole after suppertime."

"Sounds good," Elizabeth said, and practically dragged Devyn away. Once they were on their own, she passed her a wide-eyed glance. "So, that was crazy."

Devyn raised an eyebrow. "How was that crazy? We said hello, and now you're in for some free homemade casserole. Sounds like a win every which way."

"No, no, no. We don't do that kind of thing, she and I. The casual swinging by. Never have."

"Is it a bad thing that you try it?"

Elizabeth exhaled. "I guess not."

"I can't think of too much that could go wrong. I doubt she's going to shoot up your house or anything."

"You're hilarious."

Devyn paused. "No one's ever thought so, and that is the damn truth."

Elizabeth squeezed her hand as they split to climb into the truck. "It'd be more like her to just not show up and then apologize profusely for the next two weeks, fall all over herself."

"But if you're already planning on that, what's the worst that could happen?"

Elizabeth shut the truck door and considered the statement. "There's a certain logic there, I guess."

"Funny *and* logical? I'm racking it up tonight." She gave Elizabeth her best set of puppy dog eyes. "I should be rewarded."

"Agreed." Elizabeth leaned across the console and pressed her mouth to Devyn's without hesitation, her hand on Devyn's chin. Why was that hot? The chin thing? But it so was. In fact, her head spun until the world slowed down, bringing a smile to her face.

"You always grin when you kiss," Elizabeth whispered, inches from her face.

"Do not," Devyn said, and continued to kiss Elizabeth, feeling the grin appear. "Maybe a little," she murmured against Elizabeth's mouth. "I know other things that make me grin."

"Trust me, I do, too. Shall we?"

"God, yes." Devyn faced forward, buckled her seat belt, and flipped on the radio. She was a model passenger. Anything to accelerate them to the moment Elizabeth's clothes hit the floor.

Twenty minutes later, she was nearly there. With a close-to-naked Elizabeth straddling her in the armchair of the living room, Devyn kissed her breast through her yellow bra.

Elizabeth cradled the back of her head, her hips pushing against Devyn's stomach. This was what she'd been thinking about all night.

"Are you grinning right now?" Elizabeth said, her breathing quick.

"How could I not be?"

Elizabeth couldn't sleep, which never happened. Her thoughts were a jumble. Reliving the awful details of Jill's disappearance and accident, her confusing feelings for Devyn, her relationship with her mother all wound together into a knot she couldn't quite untie. She stood in the pitch black of her kitchen, sipping from a cup of decaf tea she'd managed to make while fumbling around blindly and listening to the clock on the wall tick quietly. Devyn was asleep in the other room with Scout curled up in the bend of her knee like they were best friends, and she didn't want to wake her by turning on a light. In fact, it would have been a crime. She'd never seen anyone look so beautiful when they slept. With her blond hair in shambles from Elizabeth weaving her fingers through it, one arm thrown behind her, and the other one tucked underneath her cheek like a second pillow, she made it hard for Elizabeth not to stare.

It hadn't escaped her that she was now sleeping with the captain of the cheerleading squad. Elizabeth smiled as she drank her tea, thinking of all the things she enjoyed about Devyn. She loved the way she had entire conversations with Scout when she thought Elizabeth was out of earshot. The night before while she brushed her teeth, she'd heard Devyn explain the concept of commission to her dog and all the ways to increase earning potential. She caught sight of them in the mirror and saw Devyn massaging Scout's ears as she talked to her. They were quickly becoming a pair.

She placed a hand over her chest because the sweet recollection caused actual pain. Why? Because she wouldn't have those moments for very much longer. Though they had shelved talk of Devyn's impending return to Philadelphia, she was wildly aware that they'd reached no real conclusion. They hadn't decided that things would necessarily end, but then they hadn't decided they wouldn't, either.

The *either* really resonated.

"What's going on? You okay?" Devyn asked in her raspy sleepy voice.

Elizabeth turned in the darkness. She couldn't fully see Devyn but could tell she stood across the room, near the entrance to the hallway. "Just having some tea."

"At 3:24 a.m.?"

"Seemed like a good time for it."

"Really?"

She could tell Devyn was moving toward her now, intermittently illuminated by patches of dim moonlight. She wore Elizabeth's favorite worn-out army green T-shirt that said *No Frills* across the front. No longer any reason for the darkness now that Devyn was awake, she flipped on the small lamp she kept near the kitchen table. It had been her father's favorite lamp to work by at night. She distinctly remembered the sound of the switch going on and off. Off meant time to play. On meant quiet time for Elizabeth until he was done for the night.

"So, what's going on?" Devyn asked, bleary eyed and blinking as she adjusted to the new light.

"Oh, you know me. Someone who likes to have all her *t*'s crossed."

Devyn blinked several more times and ran a hand through her hair as if trying to piece it all together. "We're an uncrossed *t* for you, aren't we? This is about the conversation we had earlier?"

Elizabeth wrapped her arms around herself. "No. Well, yes. That and I was…thinking about my mom." That was actually the truth. "I think tonight brought up some memories. She left in the middle of the afternoon. I didn't realize as I watched her pack that she'd never be back. I would have paid more attention to the moment. Standing here now, I'm missing parts of how it played out. What color her shirt was, and what the actual time was in the afternoon. Two o'clock? Three? I'll never know."

Devyn leaned against the counter next to her. "Maybe it's better that you are missing some of it. I'm not sure a moment like that is one you want to revisit with too much clarity."

"It seems important, though, you know? To who I am? Someone who was left. That's me."

Devyn studied her profile. Elizabeth wasn't looking at her, but she could feel that gaze caress her cheek with what? Sympathy. She didn't love that, but at the same time it felt nice to have Devyn there to talk to. "She didn't leave because of you, you know. If I had to guess, maybe she was just running from her life or from something within herself that she wasn't comfortable with. Who knows?"

Elizabeth turned and met Devyn's gaze. "Sure felt like she was leaving *me*."

They stared at each other for a moment. No one broke eye contact. "We're not just hooking up," Devyn said, finally. The words were everything. "I should have made that clear earlier today. So, I'm saying it now."

Elizabeth knew as much in her heart. There was too much tenderness in the way Devyn touched her and too much meaning behind her eyes for Elizabeth not to matter to her. But hearing Devyn say so made all the difference. "I had so much fun with you tonight. It was the best night I've had in a long time." She bit her lip and shook her head. "Maybe ever. That's a bad thing."

"No, it's not." Devyn placed her hands on Elizabeth's waist and leaned back against the counter.

"Not yet. But we're building a pretty impressive tower that has the potential to crash to the ground in what could be only a few weeks, for all I know."

"Which means you cease to exist?" She searched Elizabeth's features.

She shrugged. "No. I'll be here."

"Good. I want you to always exist." She pulled Elizabeth to her and nuzzled her hair. "We took the first step by talking about it, twice now today, which gets us bonus points. Especially since I'm not someone who talks about feelings."

"I know. Thank you for indulging me."

"The thing is, I don't think we have to have all the answers, and maybe, over the course of time before I leave, we'll find them. It's my hope that we do."

Elizabeth wrapped her arms around Devyn's neck and pressed her forehead to her chin. "When we're together like this, it feels like everything else fades. That we're the only two people. Is that just me?" She met Devyn's beautiful hazel eyes, her voice shifting to a whisper for the next part because it was the only way she'd get the words out. "I want so badly to believe you feel it, too."

Devyn nodded. "I feel it. It's powerful, and all encompassing."

"You don't have to just say that because I did."

"Would you stop?" Devyn disentangled herself and took a few steps back to better see Elizabeth. "I'm in this, too, you know. You don't have the monopoly on feelings, and I happen to be just as out of my depth as you are. But I know this: I'm a little crazy about you."

"You are?" Elizabeth asked, trying to understand but not yet daring to believe. The passion she saw flare said something, though. Maybe Devyn really was as invested. She allowed that news to comfort her and didn't push for more. She'd done enough of that, and knowing they were in this together was enough. "Then come back over here and take me to bed so I can find a way to switch off my brain."

Devyn allowed a grin to blossom. She walked slowly back to Elizabeth, the T-shirt brushing the tops of her thighs. She took Elizabeth's hand, intertwined their fingers, and brought them to her mouth for a kiss. "We're going to need a nap tomorrow."

"You're really pretty," Elizabeth said.

Devyn frowned. "Are you saying that as some kind of farewell? Like you're memorizing my face? If so, then stop it. Because I will still be here in the morning."

"You're right." Elizabeth nodded and tucked a strand of hair behind Devyn's ear. She wasn't just pretty to Elizabeth, she was lose-your-thought-mid-sentence beautiful, even in the dead of the night, sans makeup, sans wardrobe, stripped down to just her. Part of that had to do with the person underneath and the bond they'd formed. She tried not to think about how much more there was she still wanted to do with Devyn. See movies, have a picnic, and maybe that bottle of wine on the beach at sunset. What would it be like to come home from a long day and just make dinner together? She had a feeling they'd complement each other really well. Nope. Too much to process for close to four a.m.

As she snuggled into bed again, Devyn tucked herself behind Elizabeth and held her close. Scout, at the end of the bed, grumbled at the disruption. "Want to see a movie this week?" she whispered. "I can't tomorrow because of my mom coming by, but maybe the day after? If Jill is okay?"

Devyn kissed her cheek. "I'd love to see a movie with you."

CHAPTER EIGHTEEN

The doorbell chimed at 7:36 in the evening after Elizabeth had knocked off work for the day and straightened her house. You know, just in case. She'd stolen glances at the clock every few minutes, in spite of how much she hated herself for doing it. Her mother mentioned that she'd be by "after suppertime" which, quite honestly, could mean a lot of things. The most likely scenario would have been her not showing up at all, but that apparently wasn't the case. Hence the knock that had her heart hammering. Why did she care at all? That part irked her.

Elizabeth walked to her front door and smoothed her jeans and blouse. Yes, she'd put on an actual ribbed pullover that she felt made her look a little more put together than a T-shirt. You know, just in case there *was* company.

Her mother smiled brightly as she opened the door. "Hey, there, Lizzie." She'd always been a little heavy on the energy and exuberance, which was probably overcompensation on her part for all the years she'd been absent. Her red hair had been curled and styled and she wore a mauve lipstick that matched her shirt. Randomly, she wore heels in the middle of the evening, but then she was always out to impress whoever she could.

"Hi, Mom." She stepped back. "Come on in."

"Sorry we missed you at dinner, but I think you're really gonna like how this batch of casserole came out. I added the extra cheese you used to love."

Elizabeth didn't remember ever asking for extra cheese, but it seemed like something she might do. She accepted the covered dish and placed it on the counter of her kitchen.

"Really nice of you to drive it over here."

"Anytime, sweetie." She took in Elizabeth's living room. "Would you look at this sweet place? I love what you've done with your home. The lavender accents really make the room so cheerful. I'd love it if I lived here."

"Thanks." She slid her hands into her pockets, not really sure what else to say. They'd now done the casserole drop-off. Checkmark. Weren't they done now? There didn't seem to be a guide for dealing with family members who'd abandoned you and then popped back up for niceties and gifts of casserole.

They stared at each other. Then did that some more.

What was probably three seconds in reality felt like twenty, until finally Scout rounded the corner from the bedroom and perked up at the sight of a new human, her tail picking up speed as she lowered her head in submissive hello.

"Would you look at that." Her mother turned to her. "You got yourself a furball. C'mon over here, sweet baby."

"This is Scout," she said as her mother knelt, allowing her face to be licked like crazy. It was kinda nice to see someone appreciate her dog. A lot of people didn't enjoy dogs kissing them on the face the way Elizabeth did. Who knew her own mother wasn't one of them? A nice surprise.

"Hey. I heard you and that friend of yours from last night are heating things up."

"Mom." Estranged or not, it was weird to hear your mother say *heating things up*. "We're just spending time together."

She gave Scout a final scratch behind both her ears and stood, pushing off the ground like it wasn't as easy as it used to be. "Well, she seemed nice, and don't get me going on how pretty that face is. Wow. She should model."

"She's beautiful. We can agree on that. The whole world does."

Her mother dipped her head. "But she lives someplace else?"

Elizabeth nodded and leaned against the kitchen counter. Talking about Devyn seemed to ease some of the tension. She tried to not smile overtly at the thought of her. "Philadelphia. She's just here for a short time to help her sister get better after her car accident."

"Look at you, all pink cheeks and sassy eyes."

"Sassy eyes? I don't know what that even—"

"Excited for life. Full of zest. This woman's got a hold of you, I can see it a mile away. We may not be close, but I'm your mama and I know things."

"Oh. Well. Maybe."

"Makes my heart swell."

Elizabeth smiled shyly at the countertop. "Mine, too, if I'm being honest. She's pretty great. She didn't used to be, but people change." Talking about Devyn seemed to have broken the tension.

Her mother paused as if she were making a decision. "Honeypot, I know our relationship hasn't always been easy-breezy, and I take full responsibility for that. I was mixed up when I was younger, and selfish."

"I know," Elizabeth said. They could agree on that part.

"I want us to change things between us. We can take baby steps at first if you want. Like two gals in therapy together." Elizabeth stared at the ground, because it was hard to buy in. "I know I should have done more for you when I moved back." Her typical smile faltered. "I was nervous being around you again, if I'm fessing up. Don't much like the way it feels to see how much of your life I missed. At first, well...I wasn't sure how I could ever make that up to you, so I just didn't." She sighed and pulled on a strand of red curly hair. "Then I tried, but not enough."

"You have a lot on your plate," Elizabeth said. In this moment, she could convict her mother of everything she'd ever done to make Elizabeth's heart hurt, explain to her all the ways she'd failed and do so quite easily. Yet Elizabeth just couldn't bring herself to go there. Not when she stood in front of someone who looked so sad, so vulnerable. She just didn't have it in her to lash out.

"Not too much for you." Her mother gestured to the casserole. "You'll be getting more of those, since this is the first time in a while you've accepted an overture from me. Yes, sir. I think I found my ticket. Casserole will be comin' out of your ears, missy." She laughed nervously, and Elizabeth softened. She couldn't help it. She'd always had a bleeding heart.

"Thank you for bringing it by." A pause. "And for the chat."

She watched as a smile sprang back onto her mother's lips, as if it radiated from the inside out. "You might have just made my whole week." She swatted away the sentiment. "I'll get out of your hair now. Know when to quit while I'm ahead, and who wants old ladies getting soft in their kitchen anyway?"

Elizabeth chuckled and walked her out. "Drive safe, okay? It's getting dark."

"Will do. You take care of that sweet pup and that head turner you're running around with. Still can't get over that face. Not that it has anything on yours."

"Thanks, Mom." She gave Scout, who pressed against the outside of her knee, a head pat. "That's my plan." With a final wave, her mother was headed home. She stood there, stuck in her entryway. She had just survived a one-on-one visit. No, not just survived. Dare she say she'd flourished and enjoyed their small exchange, even? She wasn't ready to jump back into any kind of deep mother-daughter relationship, but to be paid this little bit of attention actually felt nice.

"What did you think of her?" she asked Scout, who now lay on her back, four paws in the air, as she scrunched and slid around on the carpet. "You seem more interested in that back scratch you're giving yourself. But I do know someone who I want to share this with." It took her only a moment to place the call.

Devyn didn't even say hello, jumping right to the point, which surprised Elizabeth. She wasn't even sure if Devyn would remember the plans she'd made with her mother. "Did she come?"

"Surprisingly, yes. And…it wasn't awful."

"Well, not awful is an improvement, isn't it?"

Elizabeth smiled and joined Scout on the floor. "It is. She didn't stay very long, but she met my dog and complimented my house, which made me feel good."

"I'm so happy it went well. I was prepared to lay down my life in apology if it didn't. I've been sitting over here nervous as hell."

Elizabeth grinned and stared at the patterns of her ceiling. "You deal with millionaires daily and this makes you nervous?"

"Well, yeah, because it's you. The idea of you sad makes me…"

As she trailed off, Elizabeth's grin grew. Those kinds of confessions didn't come naturally to Devyn, but Elizabeth could feel how much she was truly trying.

"I know," she said. "I feel the same way."

They talked for an hour, which was silly because they were literally moments away from each other in two separate houses in the same small town, but Elizabeth enjoyed talking to Devyn on the phone. The more they talked, the more they laughed, and the more they confessed. There was a safety there, in not seeing the other person's face.

"I've been trying to remember everything I can about you from high school," Devyn said. "I still wish I'd known you better then."

"Oh, I remember a lot about you," Elizabeth said. "You and your friends would always make your weekend plans in Mr. Maguire's precal class. I would listen in."

"Really?"

"It's true. You guys would always head to that sand pit near the beach, and someone would volunteer to bring the wine."

"Usually Cricket."

"And there would be boys invited. It sounded so sophisticated to me. My Fridays involved my dad, the television, and occasionally a sleepover at KC's. Not that those weren't fun. Some of my best memories."

Devyn paused. "If I knew myself then the way I know myself now, I would have spent that time with you instead. I missed out."

Elizabeth's heart fluttered pleasantly. It had to be one of the nicest things anyone had ever said to her. "Well, we know each other now."

"I consider myself lucky." Another pause. "Are you going to give her a chance? Your mom?"

Elizabeth, feeling on a high from the events of the evening, considered the question. "I'll be cautious, but…yeah. I think I might crack that door open a touch. And, Devyn?"

"Yes?"

"Thank you for pushing me the other night. I'm not sure I would have let her come by otherwise, but somehow you knew it's what I needed."

"You're welcome. I just want to see you happy. That, and I miss my own mom and thought, if there was a way for you to have yours back, maybe it was worth exploring." Devyn's voice got quieter on that last part.

"I hadn't thought of it that way. You must miss her a lot."

"Yeah. Being back was really hard at first because of it. One of the reasons I'd stayed away. But now? It's like I can feel her all around me. I stumble onto a new memory of her almost daily, prompted by a location or a person I hadn't thought about in years. It's been surprisingly nice."

"I feel like I've watched the world fall off you since you've been here. One layer at a time until it's just you standing in front of me. I can see you so clearly now, Devyn. Who you are."

"That's exactly what it feels like, too." Silence hit. "Liz, can I ask you something?"

"Anything."

"How do you feel about company tonight?"

Elizabeth laughed. "Well, that depends. How fast does that little car drive?"

"I'm betting money on NASCAR status if that answer is yes."

"Get over here and kiss me," Elizabeth said, and hung up the phone. She laughed and looked at Scout, who sat up at attention, already aware that her favorite playmate was on her way.

"Today has been a really good day," she said to Scout, embracing the happiness full on. "Let's memorize it, okay?" With her eyes closed and a hand on her heart, she took a moment to do just that. She'd had a lot of good days in her lifetime, and she cherished each one, but today was different. Today she felt special, and that was a feeling worthy of commemoration. "I matter to some people," she said to Scout, through tear-filled eyes. "Me."

❖

"I feel like a guy would never actually say those things, you know, outside of a Hallmark Christmas movie."

"What are you talking about?" Elizabeth asked in exasperation, as they meandered from the darkened movie theater back into the lobby after their rom-com let out. She took a deep inhale of the freshly popped popcorn, prepped for the late show. Even after devouring their own giant tub, she still loved the aroma. "A *sensitive* guy absolutely would say all of that. What?" Elizabeth asked. "Don't look at me like that. I know things."

"About men?"

"Well, not a ton of firsthand experience in the romance department, but I'm a citizen of Earth. I observe. I feel like Dexter would profess his undying servitude."

Devyn considered this with a laugh. "Gotta love that guy. You might be right. I ran into him at Festive Foods when I was grabbing a yogurt for Jill, and he was all starry-eyed about some woman he was seeing later that night."

"Misty. She's his forever person, I'm thinking. I've never see him focus so fully on just one woman. It makes me happy."

"I think when you meet someone that you just click with, it's hard to look away." She stared at Elizabeth for several seconds before looking ahead again. Elizabeth grinned and bit the inside of her cheek, because the insinuation was clear. They clicked. They really,

really did, in spite of their many differences. And maybe it was the differences themselves that created this very palpable chemistry she'd never experienced with another human. Devyn met her gaze. "But the movie was good outside of the sentimentality."

"Do you know what I think?"

"Tell me."

"I think you're more of a softie in there than you let on."

"Maybe."

"I think you liked that film deep down, even the overly sentimental part. You might have been weeping inside."

Devyn raised her shoulders. "Steel yourself because I'm about to make a confession."

"Give me a minute," Elizabeth said, and bounced a couple times in the darkened parking lot.

Devyn laughed. "I want to make fun of you for that, but it was too endearing. How do you do that? Make the most ridiculous stuff seem awesome all of a sudden? Stop it already."

Elizabeth wrapped both arms around Devyn's waist as they approached the car. "It's one of my two gifts in life: being a dork and organizing things and people."

"Really?" Devyn said, glancing down, her eyes dark. "Because I can think of a couple of other notable talents that have stuck with me."

Elizabeth's mouth fell open as she pretended to be scandalized. "And now I'm blushing and you're diverting. Get back to the confession."

Devyn leaned back against Shug. "I do feel all soft inside lately." She shrugged. "For a while I was convinced it was my taking the town back. You know? Coming back in and making new memories that would replace the harder ones?"

She shook her head and glanced over at Elizabeth, who felt her heart squeeze. She didn't know where this confession was going, but Devyn was letting her guard down, which didn't always happen. She wanted to be present for this moment.

"The more I'm around you, the more I feel myself opening up. Changing. It's exhilarating on one hand, but unnerving on another." She turned to face Elizabeth more fully. "What if I'm a big ole softie when I try to sell? I'm known as a ballbuster. What if you broke me?"

Elizabeth grinned. "Trust me when I say that the ballbuster side of you is very much intact. I heard you on the phone just two days ago."

"Yet I didn't close that deal."

"I'm sorry."

Devyn shrugged. "It doesn't bother me the way it once would have. That might be a problem."

She didn't dare hope. Except that was a lie. Elizabeth was hoping with all of her heart that this change in Devyn might have greater implications for the two of them. They were closer than they'd ever been, spending pretty much all of their free time together. Devyn slept at her place several times a week. She missed her desperately on the nights she didn't. Yes, Devyn had a life back in Philly, but maybe the life she was finding here, just maybe, would be enough to sway her to stay. Elizabeth didn't utter those words, though. They were too delicate. Instead, she held on to them tightly. Hoping…

"Do you think this new you is a good thing?" she asked, tentatively.

Devyn didn't answer her with words and instead kissed her. She felt the customary grin through the kiss. "I think it's safe to say that I'm starting to like her a lot," Devyn said, quietly, and went back for more.

Elizabeth's eyes fluttered closed and she slid her hands into Devyn's hair, sinking into the kiss. Her heart soared, and the night felt vibrant and awake. She shimmied her shoulders as her skin prickled pleasantly. She'd never felt so happy. In her head, she saw glimpses of dinners at home, date nights at the beach, or lazy Saturdays walking through town. Maybe a game night with Jill and Charlie. She exhaled slowly as Devyn pulled back from the kiss and smiled.

"Let's go home."

Devyn might have meant the word in the generic sense. She probably had. But it resonated with Elizabeth all the same.

Home.

CHAPTER NINETEEN

This is the problem I'm having." Devyn closed her eyes and walked across the spare bedroom she used to work. It was sunny outside, and that in no way matched what she was going through with her client. She'd been on the phone with Wyatt Lowe two other times this week, and each time he was less happy than the last. "You wanted a showroom?" he said. "I invested the money and now you have one. You pushed for a lower price point. I worked with you on that."

"I know you did, and it was the right move. Everyone is talking about the building." That part was true. It was the talk of downtown, but sales had been slower than she'd hoped. And yes, she had a good idea why.

"All I asked for was a four-month sellout. We're at just over three months now, Winters, and I'm still sitting on nearly sixty percent of my inventory. That's unacceptable."

"I get that. I just need a little more time is all. It's a big building, which is what's fantastic about it."

"No more time. I signed on with *you*. Not your team. And who's this Ricky guy who called me last week? Wasn't he some random guy trying to learn the business when we met? The redheaded guy? Now he's selling my building? Fuck no." Wyatt was more worked up than she'd ever heard him. She wasn't sure what to do about that. She'd pulled Ricky onto the project when she'd had to step away, hoping his eagerness would transfer into a few extra sales. He was not supposed to have contacted her client directly. She'd have to speak with him about that. Damn it, Ricky.

"He did a couple of showings for us."

"Anything under contract?"

She sighed. "No."

"I want him off the project."

"Done." She pinched the bridge of her nose, feeling backed into a corner. She'd send Ricky a giant thank-you basket. He'd understand. "Listen, Wyatt, it's been a rough time for my family, and I was unexpectedly pulled away. I explained that. This is in no way reflective of my work ethic or my ability to sell. I'm just asking for your patience."

He didn't hesitate, still talking a mile a minute. "We all have personal stuff, and I'm really sorry about whatever you have going on with your sister, but I've invested millions in this project. You understand that, right?"

"I do."

"So get your ass back here and sell these units."

"I'll do my best."

"Not good enough. I have a senator and two celebrities who want to see the place this week. Either you're back in the morning to handle them personally or I'm pulling the listing. Just business."

She closed her eyes. "Understood."

She clicked off the call to see Jill standing in the doorway, staring at her with wide eyes and a worried brow. She held her cane and wore a brace on her injured leg, a reminder that Devyn was still needed right where she was. But maybe that was an exaggeration, one that had made Devyn feel more comfortable with her decision to remain in Dreamer's Bay. The reality of the situation was that Jill was now quite capable of living entirely on her own, and with the tricks her PT guy had shown her, she could accomplish most anything if she took her time.

"That was my guy in Philly. He's going to pull the listing if I'm not back and ready to go to sales war by tomorrow."

Jill exhaled slowly. "I see. We knew this was coming, I guess."

Devyn tapped the phone against her opposite hand in a metronomic rhythm. What was she supposed to do here? Two months ago, she wouldn't have thought twice about racing back; now she felt... reluctant. What was that about? Who exactly was she becoming? She shook her head, hating how weak she felt. Indecisiveness had never been part of who she was. She'd let herself be vulnerable. She'd let herself get attached, and now look where she'd landed. Her career was on the brink of destruction and she didn't recognize herself in the mirror. She inhaled. One way or another, she had to get it together and fix this thing.

"I'll be okay, Dev. I can move around fine on my own, if a little slow. I can drive, so that's not a problem. Plus, Elizabeth can still help me out, and there's, well, Charlie now."

"Yeah, I know." She rolled her bottom lip in and out again. "I was just expecting more time, you know, with you…and…"

"Elizabeth."

Devyn met her sister's gaze and smiled sadly. "Yeah." She scrunched her shoulders and did what she could to harness the version of herself who took no prisoners when it came to getting her job done. She was known as cutthroat for a fucking reason, and it was time to reclaim her identity. She hadn't been that woman for a while now, but that was likely the point Wyatt was trying to make. She was still in there, though, that firecracker, and Devyn could get this building sold if she reined in her focus, shelved her emotions, and packed her damn bag. Still, it didn't feel good. But that would be the trick to getting through this, turning *off* the feelings and not letting herself fall into this trap ever again.

"When will you fly out?"

"Tonight, I guess."

Jill shifted and her gaze dropped to the floor, like she'd just been dealt a blow. "It's been so nice having you here. For a little while, I thought you might…" She didn't finish, but Devyn knew what she was about to say. She'd secretly hoped Devyn would stay. It wasn't that she hadn't envisioned it briefly herself, but the Bay, as happy and relaxed as it made her lately, had created some kind of "vacation version" of herself that she hated now that she faced the consequences. Her real life was back home, and it was time to pull up her bootstraps and face the reality of that. Living with her head in the clouds had been ill advised.

"I'll be back soon. Give me a few days to get things back on track. A week or two tops, and I'll visit. Check on you."

Jill nodded, but the look on her face said she was unconvinced. "I hope that's true."

"And you need to come to the city and hang out with me. We can have a girls' night, and I can show you this amazing building I'm selling. Don't get me started on the martinis they make in the bar next to my place." She tried to brighten and make it all sound like tons of fun when, in reality, she was struggling.

"It's a deal."

Her arms were around Jill a few moments later, delicately, as she still dealt with some pain. They stood like that in the doorway for several emotion-packed moments, as the realization hit that this time together, this very unexpected and important time for both of them, was coming to an end.

"You need to find her and talk to her," Jill whispered.

Devyn nodded. "I know." The phone call with Wyatt had been rough, but saying goodbye to Elizabeth was something she wasn't sure she could go through with. Yet her feelings for Elizabeth had landed her in this spot in the first place, and she bristled against them now. This crazy emotion she felt had thrown her life into a tailspin in just a few short months. What further damage might it inflict? She swallowed against the fear. Her instinct was to run as far away from it as she possibly could. To hop on a plane, avoid the painful goodbye altogether, and rejoin her life. Six months ago, she would have done exactly that.

But no. At the very least, Elizabeth deserved a face-to-face.

Devyn would do what she had to, to get through it and move forward. There was no other option.

❖

"Are we seriously doing this?" KC asked. "This might be the best On the Spot gig yet! I'm stoked."

"Couldn't agree more." Elizabeth placed another glazed donut on the far side of the donut pyramid they'd been building for the last half hour. "Lulu was quite serious when she handed over a hundred of these bad boys. They're apparently going to also give away a free hot donut to every guest tomorrow as part of their twenty-fifth anniversary. So, show up."

"I'll take mine now." KC took a bite of one. "Nice of her to let us eat while we work."

"Isn't it?" She stole a bite from the donut in KC's hand. They built the anniversary pyramid in the corner of the Amazin' Glazin' dining area as one table of customers looked on with interest. Given that it was just Mr. Henry and Mr. Learner from the gas station, Elizabeth didn't let the audience bother her. "Don't get any ideas, Mr. Learner. These donuts are for looking at. No eating once we're through with this masterpiece."

He heartily dunked the last of his own donut into his coffee. "No promises, Lizzie." He popped the soggy thing in his mouth and grinned.

"Speaking of someone's favorite dessert, incoming."

Elizabeth followed KC's gaze to the glass door where she spotted

Devyn making her way up the walk, blond hair swaying gently, aviator sunglasses in place. Elizabeth passed KC a look.

"What? Just because I called her dessert does not mean I'm not a fan. I've never seen you smile the way you have lately."

"Really?" she asked, quietly, knowing it was true.

KC nodded. "It's the best."

The door swung open and Devyn walked in, removing her sunglasses and allowing her eyes to adjust from the sunlight. Her gaze landed on Elizabeth, and she moved toward her with purpose.

Right on cue, Elizabeth's chest flooded with warmth and she grinned. "This is a nice surprise. Are you here for a donut?"

Devyn glanced at the half-built pyramid and raised her eyebrows. "Oh. Um, no." Her focus returned to Elizabeth. "You. You didn't answer my texts, so I drove around a bit until I saw your truck."

"Has anyone ever called you resourceful?" She glanced at KC. "Then again, we do live in a small town."

KC pointed at her in agreement. "It's pretty hard to hide."

Devyn didn't look amused and seemed to ignore their exchange altogether. "Do you have a minute?"

She was put-together Devyn again. The one Elizabeth had met when she'd first returned to town. Huh. Interesting.

"Of course," She stood and pulled off the plastic baggies she'd been wearing as gloves. "Donut pyramids, man. You know how it is." She smiled. "Hard to operate a phone." The lighthearted comment fell flat. Devyn smiled briefly, but it seemed like she didn't have the emotional energy to sustain it, and that pulled Elizabeth's focus. Her spidey sense fired, and her stomach muscles flexed. "What's going on?"

Devyn eased a hand into the back pocket of her slim-fitting black pants. She was dressed nice. Too nice. Another clue. "I talked to my client this afternoon. Either I head back to Philly for good or he's pulling the listing on the entire building."

"Oh." She took a moment to process. "So you'd lose it all."

"Everything. Which would be catastrophic in the scheme of my career. It's not my call, but it is what it is."

Elizabeth nodded while at the same time felt like the world was crashing to the ground all around her. "Okay. So how much time do you have?"

Devyn shifted and hesitated.

Oh no. This wasn't good. She felt the blood drain from her face. She clenched and unclenched her fists.

"I'm actually on my way to the airport now. I already said goodbye to Jill."

"As in *right now* right now?" Right then and there, everything in Elizabeth downshifted. Her thoughts didn't formulate correctly. She couldn't keep up with what was happening.

Devyn nodded. "I'll be back at some point. Just need to get this project back on track somehow. Really buckle down and focus, the way I used to."

Elizabeth's brain sputtered and stalled. She'd already picked out her outfit for dinner with Devyn that night, and this weekend they were going to take a day trip to Hendersonville because it was known for some cool secondhand furniture stores. Then they were going to stop at that cute wine bar Elizabeth had heard so much about. They wouldn't get to do those things now, and that felt so very wrong. Not unjust, just inaccurate. Was that weird? She wasn't sure. What about Scout? Would Scout get that Devyn, her favorite person, her champion snuggler, was just *gone*? She ordered her brain to shut up and stay focused so she could think about the here and now of the moment. "I don't want you to go." The words came easily, because there were none more true.

"I know, but I have to," Devyn said, and smiled apologetically. Her guard was in place. Elizabeth could see that clear as day.

"Don't. Just forget all about that building." She made sure to add a playful tone to her delivery to muffle the desperation. Yet that was exactly how she felt: desperate, helpless, and as though she was about to lose something too valuable to even articulate. What could she do to stop this? Everything in her cried out.

"You take care, KC," Devyn said, and walked over and gave her a hug. She turned back to Elizabeth. "Walk me out?"

Oh, God. This really was it, wasn't it? Pain arrived hot and fast right in the center of her chest, and her legs felt like lead as she followed Devyn to her rental. She smiled one last time at its ridiculous smallness. Devyn could have traded it in at any point in her trip but had admitted that she felt bonded to the little car after all they'd been through together.

Devyn fumbled with her sunglasses before raising her eyes to Elizabeth's. "Jill is okay because of you. I need you to know that. You have my eternal gratitude. You're a good person, Elizabeth."

"Not just me. No. Everyone was—"

"It was because of *you* we found her. You and that wonderful dog of yours. I will never be able to repay you for that, but there's so much more I have in here to say." She touched her chest. "But maybe it's for the best that I don't."

"Okay," Elizabeth said, catching her wrist. "The next time we see each other, maybe."

Devyn nodded and popped her sunglasses on, blocking Elizabeth's window into her emotional state. "I'll call you soon."

Soon. It was so noncommittal. It wasn't tonight, or tomorrow. Who knew when they'd next speak? "Okay. Soon, then."

Devyn took Elizabeth's cheek in her hand and brushed her lips to Elizabeth's briefly. There was no lingering, no drawing it out. Devyn pulled her into a quick hug and dropped her lips to Elizabeth's ear. "Goodbye for now. You take care of yourself."

Elizabeth didn't want to take care of herself. She wanted Devyn to take care of her. "Goodbye, Devyn," Elizabeth said, still stunned that this was it.

Devyn slid into the driver's seat and, with a final wave, pulled away from the shopping center.

This wasn't real, was it? Elizabeth glanced back at the donut shop where she happened to be in the middle of a job. Was she supposed to just go back in there and pick back up like her life hadn't just blown up in front of her? She walked slowly back to the shop in a sad daze. How could that be?

"You okay?" KC asked, standing. She shifted uncomfortably. Her eyes were mournful and full of empathy, and Elizabeth's embarrassment crept in.

She shrugged and stared at the pyramid, trying to focus on stacking strategy, anything to not crumple into a teary-eyed mess. Didn't mean her heart didn't hurt. The lump in her throat seemed to grow bigger as the moments passed. Somehow, she managed to answer. "She's leaving." A pause. "I'll be fine. Nothing I didn't know was coming."

KC winced. "Still."

"Yeah." They stared at each other. Elizabeth didn't know what to do with herself. She needed direction and someone to tell her what to do. KC innately got it.

"Let's focus on this project for now, knock it out, and after this we're getting drunk. Dan isn't on call tonight. He can watch Gray."

The tears pooled, but Elizabeth knelt and got to work. She focused intently on the donut in her hand, laying it gently on top of an established row. "You don't have to do that," she said on a shaky breath, reaching for another donut. "I'll be fine on my own. That's what I do, right?"

KC didn't hesitate. "You don't have a say. We're doing it. That's final. I'm calling Dexter."

"Okay," Elizabeth said quietly, ignoring the first tear that fell and then the second. She kept her face to the side, careful that no tear touched or interfered with her work. If she didn't allow the brunt of what just happened to fully infiltrate her brain, she could get through this, and then the next thing, and the next. She was Elizabeth Draper. She was used to being left.

❖

Devyn kept her sunglasses on and the music loud as she drove straight out of Dreamer's Bay for the open highway. She passed the strip mall where the weekly cornhole tournament would take place that Friday and Saturday. She didn't glance over, keeping her mind carefully blank. Bountiful Park flew by on her right, and shortly after that Festive Foods, where the high school band's booster club was taking down their fund-raising table in front of the store. There was a grill out front, and the aroma of something amazing wafted into her car. Probably brisket tacos, the same they'd sold last week. She kept driving. Turned up the music even louder and blinked hard to steady herself and to hold off any and all emotion. Nothing good ever came of it.

She had all of this under control.

The only way Devyn had gotten through that exchange with Elizabeth was to wall everything off, and that was the state she planned to remain in for as long as she needed. It was a pretty impressive trick, pushing your emotions to the back, stuffing them right the hell down, but it was a skill she'd refined to perfection over the years, leaving her the successful machine she'd grown to count on. In fact, she thrived under those conditions. She'd survived her self-loathing teen years by doing just that, and then again with her mother's death. She didn't connect with too many people in Philly for the same reason. People made things…messy. Love was even more destructive. She'd be fine if she could just get through this transition phase. Once she was back in her old life, she'd forget what she'd left behind. Time healed.

The wall didn't feel good anymore, though. She'd have to work on that.

She stuttered, and stumbled, and stole a glance at the service station, knowing full well that the owner, Mr. Henry, was enjoying his afternoon off at the Amazin' Glazin' and likely had Alton, one of his three employees, running the place in his absence. Even saying goodbye to the service station tugged at her. No. Damn it. She gave her head a shake. The wall went back in place as she focused on the road, ignoring what she knew was next. Two straight miles of some of the most gorgeous shoreline in the country. She didn't plan to give it so much as an appreciative nod.

Elizabeth would be fine. So would Jill. They were the kind of people everyone loved, and they'd look out for each other.

She'd be fine, too.

As she stood in line to board the plane two hours later, her emotions were at war. She'd lost the control she thought she'd established and nearly gave in to the urge to scrap this whole plan and drive straight back to the Bay, pick up some burgers from Ronnie Roo's, and eat them on the floor of Elizabeth's living room over the coffee table. Could they make that happen? Was that possible? She had money. She didn't need this job. But it wasn't the job that kept her moving forward. She was terrified and she damn well knew it. She wasn't in control anymore and had allowed her feelings for Elizabeth to take over everything. Her heart raced and the air seemed scarce. She had to find her way back to in charge.

Her phone buzzed. Sheldon, her personal assistant. "Hi, Shel. Flight's on time."

"Perfect. I have Gary to pick you up at your gate when you land. Just calling with an update."

She sighed, letting go of her delusions, ready to find solid ground again. "I'm ready."

"Your kitchen's been stocked fully, the cleaning crew just left, and the temperature in your condo is an even seventy-two, ready for your arrival. The mail has been sorted and anything pressing I already took care of."

The image of her world coming back to life snapped her into the here and now. "What about flowers? Can we do something to soften the place up?"

"Soften?" Sheldon asked, probably not recognizing the sentiment coming from her.

"I just think flowers are nice to…you know what? Never mind.

Thank you, Shel. I'll call you tomorrow and we can get my dry cleaning prepped. I have a busy week ahead."

"Right. I remember and am on top of it."

"Thanks, Sheldon."

She clicked off the call and handed her boarding pass to the gate agent with a renewed determination. She just needed some space between herself and this whole experience. Once she was home, she'd rebound. She would find her way again. She sighed. Somehow.

❖

"Here's the thing," Elizabeth said, gesturing with her glass. She wasn't even sure what was in it, something KC had brought back from the bar, but after hating it for a while, she actually found the brown liquid quite nice. Okay, a little strong, but welcome at this point. "I'm going to be fine. You know? Back to status quo. Nothing wrong with my life before Devyn Winters and her ability to kiss like a goddess."

"I know you'll be fine," KC said. "Doesn't mean you can't be sad right now. It's okay to acknowledge that this hit you hard."

"The problem is that I thought she might be my one, ya know?" She was feeling the alcohol after only two brown things. She twirled the liquid in a whooshy circle. "She's not. I don't have a one. I'm Elizabeth Draper, boring, perpetually alone, and owning it."

KC sighed and studied her from across the booth. "Devyn could be back, ya know. Didn't she say she'd be back?"

"Isn't that what they're supposed to say?"

Dexter slid into the booth next to Elizabeth and looked over. He seemed like a shadow of himself. "Sorry, Liz. KC told me Devyn left, and that fucking sucks."

She nodded. "I like that you said 'fucking.' It fits."

"Let's get trashed."

"Word." Elizabeth squinted. "Do people still say that?"

KC shrugged. "Sure."

Dexter signaled the bartender and called for a double bourbon after gesturing to their glasses. Huh. So that's what she was drinking. She wondered what was up with him. His eyebrows hung low. Seemed like more than friend sympathy.

"Where have you been?" KC asked, incredulous. "I texted you two hours ago."

"Misty and I had a blowup. Think we're done. I need this as much as you do." He picked up the bourbon the server set down, tossed back a good portion, and gave his head a single shake, letting it settle.

Elizabeth winced. "Take it easy."

"Gotta catch you, slugger." He stared hard into the glass. "I don't know why we get mixed up with 'em. I know better."

Elizabeth nodded. "They just hurt us."

"Leave us high and dry."

"Hearts slashed to pieces."

KC shook her head. "Nope. This isn't a Love Sucks club. We're nursing a specific broken heart, but we're not punching love in the damn face and telling it to get off our lawn."

"Yes, we are," they said in unison, and clinked their glasses.

"What did yours do?" Elizabeth asked Dexter. When she blinked he turned into two Dexters but only briefly, which meant she could keep drinking, one of the benefits of living close enough to walk home. KC was right. This getting drunk thing did take the edge off. She should try it more often.

He shook his head. "Here's what happened. I wanted to talk about getting a place together, and she went deer in headlights and had to run errands."

"Then what?" Elizabeth asked, eager for the rest of the drama, and happy for the shift in focus.

"That was it. Rebuffed."

She and KC exchanged a look and KC leaned in. "You're walking away because she got nervous about moving in together? A lot of people might do that. Misty's been so nice. She's settled you down."

"Domesticated you," Elizabeth added. "Your house is clean and you do laundry at least twice a month now. She has a right to be cautious about the next big step. You gotta chill, I think. Word."

"You're not using it right anymore," Dexter said.

"Damn."

"Give her time," KC said, ignoring them. "Not everyone moves at the same pace."

Conflicting emotions crossed Dexter's features, and he turned his glass in a circle. It looked miniscule in his hands. "I thought we were both *there*, ya know?"

KC grabbed his hand across the table. "Doesn't mean you won't both be there next month. If she's the one, Dex, you gotta put in the time. Be patient. Take it at her pace."

"At least she didn't *leave*," Elizabeth said, and took another swig. She liked the word *swig* and the way that photo of a beaver on the wall seemed to be smiling at her. She waved at it. Friendly little beaver.

KC glanced behind her in confusion and then back. "Who are you waving at? Please say Thalia didn't just walk in. That is not at all what we need tonight."

Elizabeth sulked. "That would not be helpful when I'm drinking the brown stuff. No. Plus, I have no interest in Thalia, not after experiencing—"

"Love?" KC asked. Elizabeth shut her mouth. She refused to say that word, to acknowledge the strength of what emanated from smack in the middle of her chest like a beacon. It was too much, and verbalizing it would push her over the edge. "Are we not going there?" KC asked apologetically.

"Nope," Elizabeth said, and tossed back the rest of her glass. "We're not. Are we doing another brown? I'm in."

Dexter hopped up. "This round's on me."

An hour and a half later, once Elizabeth tried to take the beaver photo off the wall and home with her forever, her friends insisted on walking her there, during which she cried. "Was it real?" she asked, quietly, staring up at the trees as if they held the answer. "I think maybe I romanticized the whole thing."

"Of course it was," KC said. "I saw it firsthand. I'm just sorry for how abruptly she left. She has some things to work through, I think."

"I'm not even sure she gave it a second thought. Bam. She had a building to sell and was *out*." Elizabeth held her arms out like an airplane to steady her balance. It was also way more fun than she would have imagined. "Do you think she hesitated even a little? I'd like to know, ya know? I should ask that beaver." She blinked hard to clear her damn vision. "He seemed wise."

"Nah, you're wise," Drunk Dexter said. He got quiet when he drank, only piping up occasionally. Sometimes he made sense. Luckily, KC had cut herself off three rounds ago and had taken charge of getting everyone home safely and at a reasonable hour. "You know she was into you. Hell, the whole town did."

"She was into me," Elizabeth said, needing to hear the words. "Didn't matter, though. She left. Career was more important. People always leave me. Have you noticed that? It's part of my life. If anyone writes a book about me, that's what they'll call it. *Leaving Lizzie*." She stared blankly at her friends as the world spun. "Or maybe *Lizzie the*

Unlovable. Something with an 'L' because that alliteration pops." She made a few popping sounds with her lips.

"C'mon, Liquored Up Lizzie," KC said, angling an arm around her waist. "I think it's time for bed."

"Alone."

"Nope. You have a dog now, remember?"

She brightened at the thought. "Scout. Oh, that's the best news ever. We'll snuggle."

They arrived at her place, and the high she'd been on just minutes before, the one that let her push through the pain to make jokes and ride the alcohol wave, seemed to drop her harder and faster as the minutes ticked by. The reality of her broken heart busted through like the Kool-Aid Man through a brick wall, prompting her to struggle with her own self-worth. "Good night, guys," was about all she could manage as she closed the front door on her two concerned friends. "I'll take it from here," she called through the barrier. Once alone, she walked slowly into her living room, blinked several times, and slid to the floor, doing her best to muffle the sob.

This wasn't where she wanted to be in her thirties.

Not even close.

CHAPTER TWENTY

Devyn hadn't eaten lunch. She hadn't eaten breakfast either. If she remembered correctly, she'd managed a few forkfuls of a blackened chicken salad in a to-go container Karen had brought to her desk for dinner, but most of it had landed in the trash when the phone took precedence. She only had a few short weeks to turn this project around, and she damn well planned to succeed. She'd exhausted her Rolodex of clients and brokers and had her team going hard at her international contacts, trying to stir up more interest abroad. The strategy had been fruitful and they'd received contracts on six more units in the past two days alone, with more on the way. She hadn't had a proper night's sleep in days either, but that was nothing new.

It had just been a rough time, and every part of her body felt it.

A quick glance at the clock told her it was close to three that afternoon. She picked up her desk phone's receiver. "Hey, Karen? Any chance of a cappuccino before I leave for the next showing?" She'd taken to handling as many of the showings as possible in person. There was no time to lose, and she'd given her team plenty of opportunities to prove themselves. It wasn't that they hadn't done a decent job, it just hadn't been fast enough. Not everyone could close the way she could. It's why the listing was in her name.

"It's already here," Karen said. "I sent Billy ten minutes ago."

"This is why we make a good team."

"About that raise?"

Devyn laughed. "On my to-do list. Building sold first. Karen's raise next."

"Speaking of selling the building, Carrington's, the department store, is looking for a unit, preferably on a high floor, for an executive who is relocating to open up a downtown store here in Philly. Their agent called this morning."

"Then I have the unit for them. A penthouse, in fact. Set up a showing? I'll handle it myself."

"Consider it done."

Devyn replaced the receiver and inhaled as she looked over the pile of contracts. If nothing else, they'd kept her mind busy and off other topics. Just the way that limiting her time in bed kept her from dwelling on how empty it felt. She gave her temples a rub to free her head of the image of Elizabeth's eyes gazing into hers from one pillow over. What had she done to herself? She shook her head.

"Not doing this," she muttered, and took a trip across the room, hoping the movement would knock her out of that mode.

The trip home to Dreamer's Bay seemed so far away now, yet it had left an indelible mark. She'd felt bad about not calling Elizabeth when she got herself settled in. She couldn't. Too dangerous. Too terrifying. Elizabeth had become incredibly important to her in just the span of one season on the calendar. But she hadn't called, because if she had, she'd crumble. She'd lose her focus, her momentum, herself all over again. She couldn't very well leave one foot in Dreamer's Bay if she planned to fully reestablish herself into her old life, which was where she belonged. She had to be realistic about all of this. Once the building was sold, she could relax. Maybe she'd call then.

For now, it was full steam ahead.

❖

Elizabeth had waited patiently. The days since Devyn left had crept by one at a time. They were up to six. She hadn't expected to go six whole days without hearing from Devyn. She'd left the ball in her court, but that had proven not only disastrous but telling. Maybe Devyn didn't miss Elizabeth as much as she missed Devyn. No. That didn't seem possible. There had to be another explanation for Devyn not calling, and maybe it was time to test the waters. The thought had her more nervous than she would have anticipated. This was just Devyn, after all. Yet at the same time, this was *Devyn*. The stakes were high.

It was now or never. Why hadn't she had a beer first?

She picked up her phone, sucked in a deep breath, and placed the call. The line rang once. Elizabeth's heart thudded. Twice. She glanced up at the ceiling, forcing a smile so that her voice sounded chipper, unaffected when Devyn answered. A third ring. She swallowed. A fourth and voicemail. Here went nothing.

"Hey, there. Just calling to see how you're doing." A pause. "I haven't heard from you, so I'm guessing you're pretty busy with work. At least I hope that's the reason. Okay. Well…" Another pause. "Give me a call if you get a chance. I miss you."

She clicked off the call and lowered the phone.

Hollow. That was how she felt, and very, very small. She scratched her dog's ears. When Scout looked up at her with such love in her eyes, she crumbled a little. "She'll probably call," she told Scout. "I think she will."

❖

It was after midnight when Devyn, bleary eyed and exhausted, slipped out of her heels as she arrived back home at her apartment. She shrugged out of her suit jacket and dropped it over the back of her couch. Sheldon had the place in pristine condition and had left her a note on the counter that said there was Chinese take-out in the fridge for heating up, should she be hungry. She was and she wasn't. There was a voicemail waiting for her. It was all she could think about. The third from Elizabeth since she'd left the Bay, and no matter how hard she tried, she couldn't bring herself to listen to it. The other two had paralyzed her, and she couldn't take that kind of setback, emotionally. Elizabeth's ability to yank her right out of the here and now was too powerful to combat, and Devyn needed to feel whole again. Listening to that message was a bad idea.

As she heated the cardboard container of chicken fried rice, did her overexhausted brain wonder what Elizabeth was doing? Yes. Did she picture her in her home, reading a book, or tugging on a toy with Scout? Sigh. Absolutely. The quieter moments, when she found herself on her own, were the hardest. She took out her phone and stared at the voicemail notification, her thumb hovering over the Play button. She couldn't do it. Didn't have the emotional strength.

Devyn was a coward, and hated herself for it.

❖

The annual Summer Solstice Dine and Dance was off to a boisterous start at the Bay's Convention Center. Round tables in white linens were topped with floating candles with adorable yellow napkins at each place setting. Plates had gone for a hundred dollars a pop, and Elizabeth was happy to see that attendance was even larger than last year. The community clinic could use the extra supplies, and they were going to get them.

She'd been assigned the silent auction portion of the fund-raiser and was pleased with the bountiful donations she'd managed to snag from local businesses. Even Thalia had donated a free champagne facial for two. Elizabeth walked the space, smiling at those she passed, even Cricket and Heather, two of her least favorite people.

"Hi, guys," she said, and kept walking.

"Elizabeth?" She turned back at the sound of Heather's voice. She hadn't walked fast enough, apparently. "I haven't seen Devyn around." She made a big show of looking around the room. "Is it true she left?"

Elizabeth smiled. "She's gone back to Philly. Her job."

"Oh," Cricket said sympathetically.

Elizabeth wanted to return it. She didn't want Cricket's pity.

"She didn't really have much of a choice, or she'd lose a very important client." Elizabeth nodded several times, feeling the need to say more. "Which would lead to other lost clients. It's a whole... thing."

Heather nodded. Cricket nodded. They exchanged a look that said "sure."

Elizabeth didn't appreciate that look. It hurt her feelings. No, more than that. In fact, it irked her. That's right. *Irked.*

"Hey, guys? What does that mean?" she asked, forcing a follow-up smile. She should have let it go, and the Elizabeth of any other time period in her life would have. This one, heartbroken, missing Devyn, and still licking her wounds, needed an explanation. "Why did you look at each other like that? You did it very quickly. But I saw it."

Cricket sent her another poor-thing smile. "I'm sure she *did* have to get back. If it weren't for her job, she'd be here. With you."

"Oh." A pause. "I see. You think she just told me that, to what, get away from me without any drama? She wouldn't have had to lie." But it was starting to seem like she had. Elizabeth didn't share that part.

"No," Heather said, and then passed Cricket a look again. She eased her too-long blond hair behind her ear. "Of course not. We would never assume."

"There," Elizabeth said. "You did it again. See? Why do people have to do that?" She was off her own self-imposed leash now and could feel herself let go. "Can't we just support one another without judgmental glances? I think that might be a nice thing."

Cricket squinted and touched Elizabeth's forearm. "I feel like you're having a hard night."

"Well, yeah. Objectively. But that's not why you should be nice to people. You just should, that's why."

"Everything okay over here?" She turned at the sound of a friendly voice and exhaled slowly at the sight of Jill moving toward them with her cane in one hand and Charlie not far behind.

"We're not sure," Heather said in an overly delicate voice. "We'll let you two talk. Seems like maybe there are some unresolved feelings at play."

Elizabeth gasped audibly as Heather and Cricket turned and walked away in unison, almost the way the cheerleading squad would exit the field, walking in step.

"Hey, you all right?" Jill asked quietly.

Elizabeth nodded. "Just don't understand why people have to be mean. It makes no sense to me."

Jill gave a head shake and rolled eyes combo. "They used to stay the night at our place growing up, and it was all I could do to stand them for one night. Those girls would spend the whole time trying to one-up each other while wearing green face masks and watching *America's Next Top Model*. It was awful."

That made Elizabeth smile, which helped. So did seeing Jill, who was such a kind soul. "How have you been?"

"Started back at school this week. The first day took a lot out of me, but I'm getting into the swing of things again. The kids have been so gentle and take such great care of me."

"You have a good group. And everything else?" *Do not ask. Do not ask. Do not ask.*

Jill softened. "You mean Devyn. Well, we talked last night. Sounds like she's burning the midnight oil to make the sellout happen. They're getting close."

Elizabeth nodded enthusiastically. "Very cool. I'm so glad to hear that." She wasn't glad to hear it. It crushed her. She'd not heard from Devyn. Not once, and she'd left a handful of hopeful, pathetic messages. Yet she was calling her sister. The message was clear. Confirmed. Devyn was done with her, and she was not only heartbroken but horribly embarrassed for having believed... She couldn't finish the thought. Everything inside her crumbled.

"She asked how you were," Jill said gently. Elizabeth nodded again, not really finding her voice very strong in the moment but trying her best to appear upbeat. She wondered how that was going. "Look, Liz," Jill stared off to the side, as if to zero in on the right words, "I don't know what she's told you, but you made an impact on my little sister. Like no one has before."

"Yeah, well, I'm not so sure about that myself," she admitted. It was an understatement.

Jill squeezed her hand and caught her eye. "I'm sorry. But maybe, give her time? She's new to this whole vulnerability thing."

She nodded and heard the words but couldn't hang on to them. Devyn had gone off the grid. As much as she had hoped for a different outcome to all of this, the writing was on the wall. They'd had their fun and now it was over. Elizabeth just had to figure out how to go back to being the person she was before. It actually didn't seem possible.

She looked down at her green off-the-shoulder gown, and at the people scurrying around the silent auction table. She'd keep herself busy, go through the motions, until eventually the pieces of her heart came together again. She'd forget Devyn Winters had ever set foot in Dreamer's Bay. Picking up her skirt, she headed over to the auction table.

Life had to go on. She'd make sure of it.

Seven exhausted faces looked back at Devyn from around the conference room table. She didn't blame her team for their fatigue, but this was the home stretch. They had a huge event coming up that could take this thing home for them and allow Devyn to walk away victorious, on to more projects with fewer complicating factors. She'd been back for a little over three weeks now and was beginning to find her stride.

"Sixteen units remain," she told them. "One of them is a penthouse."

"Seventeen," Donna said with a wince. "The funds from the all-cash offer on 14F fell through. They just called."

Devyn closed her eyes briefly but didn't flinch. "Seventeen units. Doesn't matter. We can handle this."

Her team nodded. They were prepped for a lavish cocktail hour in the very penthouse they needed to sell, and no detail could go unattended to.

"Ashley, you'll be there at six to let the caterers in?"

"I will."

"Sven, did you make sure the Ketterman Group will be in attendance? I hear they have several buyers up our alley."

He nodded. "Talked with them this morning, and they're excited to see the unit."

"Perfect." With the details in place she could relax and prep her notes for the event. She would make a brief speech and then spend the evening schmoozing and giving tours. If all went well, their inventory should cut itself in half within the next forty-eight hours.

Once the meeting wrapped up, she turned to Karen. "Did my sister call back?"

Karen winced. "Not yet."

"I've left her two messages. It's weird."

"Want me to try her again for you?"

Devyn eased her attaché onto her aching shoulder. "Please."

As her car service drove her to Twenty-Four Walker, she ruminated on her last conversation with Jill two nights prior when she'd been on a high from the Summer Solstice fund-raiser.

"You should have seen the ballroom," she'd said excitedly. "Decorated to the hilt with yellow and orange fabric drapes schwooping from the ceiling."

"Schwooping, huh?" Devyn tried to imagine it and not wish too badly that she'd been there herself.

"Yes. The place felt entirely summery. I loved it. They also employed this specialty lighting concept that effected a very specific glow. It looked just like sunshine. You should have seen it."

"That sounds amazing. I need that for one of my brokers' opens."

"You do," Jill said. "Oh, and Elizabeth wore a beautiful green gown that was not only gorgeous on her but radiated in the midst of all of the summer décor. Have you talked to her recently?"

"I haven't. I need to." Devyn closed her eyes tight. She could see Elizabeth just as Jill described. She'd kept her as far from her mind as she could, but the second she let the tiniest thought invade, she felt the squeezing in her chest. It was near painful how much she missed her. She'd still not called her back and hated herself for it, but the fear of backsliding into an emotional shambles had her walls firmly in place. As the days crept by, she wondered how she'd ever explain herself now. Hearing Elizabeth's name alone brought it all rushing back in a breathtaking gut punch.

"Shall I drop you in front of the building?" her driver asked. "Or would you prefer the side entrance?"

"The front would be great."

She checked her phone. No return call from Jill, which was so unlike her. She shrugged it aside and forced herself to brighten as she exited the car. No telling who could be watching, and it was important that she walk with confidence and grace, no matter how much turmoil shifted inside her, no matter how much she dreamed of a woman in a green dress, radiating.

❖

Buzz. Buzz. Buzz.

Devyn swatted the bee away from her face, turned to Elizabeth, and laughed. "Man. I think he's got a thing for me."

Elizabeth grinned and raised an eyebrow. "You know what? I don't blame him at all." She leaned in for a kiss just in time for: Buzz. Buzz. Buzz. Devyn bolted upright, disoriented. She blinked and looked around, running a hand through her damp hair. She was sweating. She was also in her bedroom. Sunlight streamed in from the picture window. She closed her eyes and swallowed, her throat dry. That's right. She'd taken a long morning after the party to give herself a chance to catch up on sleep. She glanced at her nightstand where the phone continued to buzz.

"Yes?" she said, without bothering with the readout.

"Devyn. It's Charlie."

She searched her brain for which of the brokers had been named Charlie. "How are you, Charlie?" she said, already on and in professional mode. "What can I do for you?"

"I'm calling about Jill."

Devyn went still, and her brain stuttered, trying to catch up. If nothing else, the mention of her sister's name woke her up entirely. This was Charlie Charlie. *Liquor Store* Charlie. "Is everything okay? Jill hasn't returned my calls."

"That's not good." He paused on the line. "I was calling to see if she was in Philadelphia with you. Haven't seen her in a couple days."

She blinked. "No. She's not."

"Okay." Another pause. "Just checking. Let me know if you hear from her. I'm sure she's fine." Devyn wasn't. What if she'd fallen somewhere with her cane and needed help? What if she'd run off the road a second time? It could happen. Lightning had been known to strike the same person twice, after all. She didn't even hesitate, threw off the covers in a panic and looked for her bag. *Not again. No, no, no.*

CHAPTER TWENTY-ONE

Devyn didn't notice the scenery this time. She didn't allow nostalgia to weave its way to her that afternoon. She was all action and adrenaline. Maybe suffering from PTSD from that last time she'd almost lost Jill, Devyn drove faster than she should have, hell-bent on a mission.

She'd called Charlie's phone again, but he'd not picked up. Jill's voicemail box was full. Panicked, she'd even tried Elizabeth but clicked off the call the second it went to voicemail. She just had to get there, plain and simple.

When she pulled in front of Jill's house nearly three hours after leaving Philadelphia, it was dusk. She exited her car and stared in confusion at the house. It wasn't dark and closed up the way it had been last time. No, in contrast, a warm glow of light emanated and she could glimpse Jill's form in the kitchen moving about. Relief arrived like air to the suffocating. She placed a hand on her chest and waited for her heart rate to slow. Once it did, confusion layered in.

She shook her head in mystification and made her way up the walk, not even bothering to knock as she entered the house. Jill turned and did a double take once Devyn appeared in the kitchen. She was dressed nicely in jeans and a yellow tunic and had a full face of makeup. She was perfectly fine in every way.

"Devyn?" She glanced at Charlie in surprise and back again, as if shocked. But there was the problem: She overdid it. That was Jill's tell, the overacting. "What are you doing here?" she asked loudly.

Devyn stared at her, exhausted and frustrated. "You haven't returned any of my calls. Charlie couldn't find you," she said, gesturing in annoyance at the guy standing *right there* in plain sight of Jill. "So, you're fine, then?" she asked, just for complete clarification. "Totally okay?"

Jill nodded.

"Then what the hell, Jill?" Devyn practically fell onto the floor in exasperation. What a total clusterfuck this whole day had been.

"I'm so sorry. I must have had my phone turned off," Jill said, with a wince.

Charlie nodded vigorously. "She did. And when I also didn't get an answer this morning when I knocked on her door, I tried you."

Jill raised her shoulders apologetically. "I was doing some early-morning grocery shopping. I sometimes like to avoid the rush."

Devyn didn't believe these two for a second. "Were you trying to get me back here? Is that it?" She studied both of their faces.

Guilt hung from Charlie's features like an uncomfortably crooked painting. He looked away and she sighed.

"Someone want to tell me what's going on? I'm hanging on by a thread here. I was terrified for you and just abandoned everything I had on my schedule today to get here. I got on a damned plane. I need to understand—"

The doorbell chimed and Jill leapt into action. "Sorry, Devyn. We have dinner guests. You're welcome to stay. I made that garlic chicken you love. Charlie, grab an extra chair from the front room."

Panic struck Charlie's face, and his eyes darted to the table in question. Devyn followed his gaze where she saw that he'd already brought in a fifth chair, which really just said it all. Yep. This had been a setup. She heard voices from the entryway. Elizabeth and Dexter. She only had a second or two to prep herself but the wistfulness was upon her immediately, blocking that endeavor.

She turned and her gaze landed on Elizabeth, who froze.

Her lips parted slightly. She carried a six-pack of longnecks in one hand and a bouquet of flowers in the other, a gracious guest as always. "Oh." A pause. "Hi."

"Hi," Devyn said, and shifted. She was instantly aware of her appearance, and closed her eyes in mortification. Jeans and an unironed white button-down shirt she often wore for work. Maybe it was buttoned correctly. Maybe it wasn't. Her hair had been finger-combed in the car at best. She probably looked like someone who'd been out on an all-night bender while she stood facing the woman she loved.

And there it was. The word had been on the tip of her tongue more than once.

She didn't resist it in this moment the way she had shoved it aside anytime it tried to make an appearance in her head. Yet standing in this kitchen, staring at Elizabeth, who was everything that was good and worthy in this world, the feelings were too overwhelming. She let them wash over her like a flood.

"I didn't expect to see you here," Elizabeth said, and looked to Jill as if to find out why she hadn't been told.

"She just showed up," Jill said with an excited smile as she carried a big bowl of potatoes to the table. "Isn't this a nice surprise? I had no idea."

"That's a lie." Devyn blinked and pointed at her sister. "She faked her own disappearance and gave me a virtual heart attack to get me here to check on her."

"Oh, damn," Dexter said, the smile fading from his face.

Elizabeth's brow furrowed and she set down the beer.

Devyn wasn't done with Jill. She rounded the island after her, and the anger came through in her voice. "Using your well-being as *bait* is so far out of bounds, Jill, that I don't even know what to say to you right now. You know what your accident did to me, and you used my own trauma like a weapon against me. The ultimate manipulation."

"How about we have some dinner? We can do that instead of this," Jill said, trying to dodge the accusation.

"Not until you explain yourself."

"Maybe you two could talk after dinner," Charlie said. He looked caught, and he damn well should feel that way. He was a part of this.

Devyn whirled on him. "And you're no better, calling me so concerned like that, doing her bidding."

Jill waved her off. "Don't beat up on Charlie. I made him do it."

"So, you admit it. Unbelievable," Devyn said, throwing her hands in the air. She stalked into the living room and placed her hands on her hips, back to the room as she seethed. "Who does that to someone?"

It was quiet. But only for a moment.

"Who does that?" Elizabeth repeated quietly.

She turned. "Yeah."

Elizabeth pulled her face back, amazed, shocked. "I could ask you the very same question, so don't you dare get mad at Jill, who has been nothing but kind. *You* bolted from this town the second you were called and never looked back. *You* never returned my calls. *You* never sent a text. An email. *You* disappeared off the planet, as far as I was concerned. By choice." The intensity rose in her voice as she spoke. "Maybe I'm inconsequential to you, but I'm a person, Devyn. I have hopes, and fears, and a family, and feelings. I matter."

"I know that," Devyn said, quietly. "Of course you matter." But underneath she knew exactly what she'd done to Elizabeth and how awful it was. Who does that, indeed? She deflated, hating herself more than she'd ever hated anything.

"Then why did you vanish, huh? Why did you treat me like dirt beneath your shoe?" She was advancing on Devyn now, fire in her eyes.

Devyn had not seen this version of Elizabeth and couldn't stand that she'd hurt her in this way. Every justification she'd come up with when she'd been back in Philadelphia felt selfish now and was dismissed from her brain in that instant. She'd been so very wrong.

"Why aren't you saying anything?" Elizabeth asked, face-to-face with her now. She was on the verge of tears but held them back admirably. Anger was king, holding court. Devyn swallowed and Elizabeth poked her shoulder hard with one finger. "What you do to people is not okay. I don't know who the hell you are. Maybe I never did." She turned back to the room and paused, trying to soften. "I'm sorry, everyone."

"You don't need to apologize," Jill said.

Dexter shook his head. "Nope."

Charlie rocked back on his heels, looking uncomfortable.

"I'm the one who should be apologizing," Devyn said, finding Elizabeth's gaze. "Could we maybe step aside? Talk for a minute, just us?"

Elizabeth gestured to the table. "No, I don't think we'll be doing that. Time to eat."

❖

If they could bottle discomfort, they'd all be very rich. Elizabeth had never sat through a more tension-filled dinner in her entire life. She was determined to hold her head high, though, and not show Devyn all the new cracks in her emotional armor, the ones Devyn had inflicted. She wouldn't give her the satisfaction. Silverware clinked against plates in a sort of unfortunate underscore. She received more than one check-in glance from Dexter, who took it upon himself to try and keep conversation afloat, with Jill acting as his only real teammate in the effort.

"This weather, though," he said. "This is my jam. I've been working out outside more. I'm not like most people. I welcome the summer heat. Gets me going."

"I'm the complete opposite," Jill said, as if it were the most interesting topic in the world. "When the thermometer climbs over eighty, I'm a compulsive indoor dweller."

Dexter laughed too loud at what wasn't even really a joke. Jill joined him. The rest of them nodded. New clinking commenced.

When the dinner from hell came to a close, Elizabeth helped clear the plates from the table, all the while acutely aware of Devyn's gaze on her anywhere she went in the room. She found it irritating. Why was Devyn so interested now after weeks of nothing? She ignored her and focused on the task at hand. Stack the plates. Accept the serving bowl from Charlie. Resist Jill's attempts to get her to stop helping. One foot in front of the other until she'd stayed long enough to seem reasonable. At last, that moment arrived.

"Thank you for having me," she told Jill, as she pulled her into a hug. "Your culinary skills continue to impress."

Jill squeezed her hands. "You sure you don't want to stick around? Have a beer on the back porch? Charlie and Dexter are already out there."

Elizabeth shook her head, knowing she needed to get out of there. "Please tell Dexter I decided to walk home. I don't want to pull him away. He should enjoy himself."

"I get why you're angry. You should be. Just…keep an open mind, okay?" Jill sighed and walked her to the door. "I'm sorry if you felt ambushed tonight. Forgive me."

"Noting to forgive. You were trying to help."

"I was. But maybe I misjudged this one." She scratched the back of her neck in guilt.

"I did, too. Good night, Jilly. Call me soon and we can go school supply shopping. You know it's my favorite."

Once the door closed behind her, Elizabeth shrugged out of her open plaid shirt, leaving just the maroon spaghetti strap top beneath. She needed to free herself from that whole experience, and the less that encumbered her, even physically, the better. The summer evening air on her skin helped. She paused at the end of the driveway and took a deep, steading inhale.

"I think I really fucked up." She turned around and saw the most beautiful woman in the world walking toward her. Devyn's hazel eyes carried worry. No, maybe that was fear. "Amend that. I know I did. Seeing you…I can't describe it, but it's made everything snap into focus."

"I'm happy I helped with that." She turned to go.

Devyn raced forward. "But before you leave, try to understand that I'm not good at any of this."

"You've mentioned that. You were right."

Devyn nodded, accepting the barb. "I was planning on calling when I got back to Philly. I honestly was, but I was scared. What you and I had changed me, and I've never felt more terrified of anything in my life. It became easier to just avoid dealing with the concept of us altogether. I ran, and I'm an ass for that."

"Ya think?" Elizabeth wrapped her arms around herself. She was aware of the intense effect of being near Devyn. She felt her all over, and what she once cherished, she now hated. Devyn's power over her apparently hadn't changed, only it was no longer a good thing.

"It was awful of me. I'm awful." A pause. "But you're not. God, Elizabeth, I'm so sorry."

Elizabeth nodded. "Thank you for saying so. I'm gonna go. Please let me do that." She headed off down the sidewalk, the conversation just a bit too much for her in her present state. She was just a few blocks from home and could have made it there in no time flat. Instead, she walked a little farther, meandering through town, or at least pretending to. The evening was a comfortable one and she smiled at her neighbors, some of whom walked dogs, while others watered their lawns. Crickets chirped. She scrunched her shoulders, very much lost in her own depressing feelings. She didn't notice when the tears made their way onto her cheeks, but they'd apparently done so at some point. The doorstep she eventually landed upon seemed only a minor surprise.

Her mother answered after a lengthy pause. "Well, I'll be. Elizabeth." The smile was immediate. She wore no makeup and her normally glamorous persona was MIA. The woman before Elizabeth was stripped down and looked much older than she was used to. She wore baggy jeans and an untucked high school T-shirt. There were no heels, only bare feet with red polished toenails. "Come inside. This is an unexpected surprise."

She'd been in her mother's home before, but it'd been a while. It smelled homey, like maybe they'd had fried chicken for dinner that night. *Jeopardy* was on the TV, and there were a couple of pairs of tennis shoes abandoned on the living room rug. A soft-looking plaid blanket sat unfolded on the couch, and she could hear the girls' voices upstairs. It felt like a real home, and though it wasn't hers, she took comfort.

"I was on a walk. I almost passed by, but I don't know. I decided I'd stop and say hello."

Her mother tossed her hands in the air. "Of course you should have. I'm thrilled as a tick on a piglet. Here, sit." She caught sight of the blanket and immediately set to folding it. "I was making me some black brew. That's what I call coffee. Want some black brew?"

"Sure. I'll take some."

"Coming right up. Two cups of brew for two weary gals."

Elizabeth felt lost and didn't know what she was doing there, but the comfort that seeped in felt pleasant and very much needed. She sank into the comfy couch and exhaled as her mother prepared coffee in the kitchen to her left. "I tell you what, I just had the trickiest of days. One of those rough ones where it feels like nothin' much is going your way and you might as well just put on your comfy pants and watch Alex Trebek." She gestured to the television, and Elizabeth smiled.

"I didn't have a great day either. Devyn showed up after weeks of not speaking to me."

"Oh yeah?" Elizabeth could hear the coffee being stirred, though she didn't look over. "She blew you off after heading back to the city?"

"Expertly."

"Well, that's no good," her mother said. She came around the couch and handed the warm cup to Elizabeth, who cradled it in both hands. "What do you think happened there?"

Elizabeth took a moment. "Hard to say. Maybe she just wasn't that into me."

"You really think that's it?"

Elizabeth blew on her coffee, and the warmth blew back against her face. "No."

"Nah, me neither. She was all starry-eyed when I met her. Couldn't stop looking at you like you climbed a ladder and hung the moon on a hook in the sky. She was gone on you."

"I'd started to believe that, too." She shook her head and humiliation overcame her. "Maybe we can talk about something else?"

Her mother nodded. "Yep. How about I bore you with the details of how my entire roundup of groceries was left at Festive Foods this afternoon with a stock boy named Johnny standing guard, and then we can watch some *Jeopardy*?"

Elizabeth smiled, actually liking that idea very much, as surprising as that was. "Tell me about Johnny and the groceries."

And she did. They spent the evening trading stories as Elizabeth warmed up to the give-and-take a little bit at a time. Two hours later, the devastation of Devyn had been replaced with a solid kernel of hope for her relationship with her mom. No, she didn't dare put too many eggs in that basket, but they'd had a good night…for the second time in a row.

"You've been more than hospitable," Elizabeth said, as she washed her cup in the sink. "I'm gonna get out of your way now and go throw a rubber monkey for my dog. She's obsessed."

"More exciting than the rest of my night folding laundry." They walked to the door. Her mother looked at her with sincerity, the usual energy in her voice gone. "Lizzie, I can't say how happy it's made me that you stopped by. Made my whole week."

Elizabeth nodded. "Yeah, well. It was nice. To talk a little bit."

"For me, too." A pause. "Don't punish her too bad if she's truly sorry. Some of us struggle when it comes to knowing where we belong in this world. Not makin' excuses for her or for me, just sayin' it might take her longer to know what you always have, sweet girl. Does that make sense?"

"Maybe. But I'm not sure I'm ready to hear it quite yet."

"I know." Her mother opened her arms for a good-night hug, and without even thinking about it, Elizabeth moved into them. The familiar scent of products she remembered from childhood bombarded her senses and she relaxed into the comfort. This wasn't a sad hug, but rather a fortifying one that left her ready to stand tall and face her troubles. She'd found her strength on that couch, with *Jeopardy* on the TV, from one of the most unlikely sources. Would wonders never cease?

"Good night," she told her mom. "And keep an eye on those groceries from now on. Make sure they're in your trunk before driving away next time."

"Trust me, never again. Night night, Lizzie."

She walked home then, back in her open plaid shirt, hands stuffed into the pockets of her jeans. The wind lifted and released her hair in spurts. Her mother might be a little too loud, and gaudy, and into attention, but there seemed to be something well-intended at her core. Maybe she *had* grown and changed and learned from her mistakes.

Maybe that kind of thing was possible after all.

❖

"I did it for you, ya know," Jill said.

Devyn nodded into the night, her gaze never leaving the small expanse of their backyard. It was the lightning bugs that held her attention most, transporting her back to one of the most wonderful and carefree evenings she'd ever experienced. It was the night she'd really gotten to know Elizabeth beyond all the stress of Jill's accident.

"How do you figure?"

"I knew when you saw her, you'd realize what you were giving up."

Devyn tipped back her scotch. "A wake-up call. Is that what you were after?"

Jill took her spot next to Devyn in the Adirondack chair just beyond the back porch. "Well, I wanted to see your face as well, so that was certainly a bonus."

"Consider your mission successful, because my head is beyond fucked up now. Cheers."

Jill winced at the swear word the way she had when they were kids. She'd never quite been a rule breaker, which was why this little stunt was so unexpected. They let the silence linger. Devyn drank her scotch. Jill sipped from whatever the hell dessert drink she'd thrown together. Baileys? Frangelico?

Jilly turned to her. "You're in love with her, you know."

"I know." She sat forward, leaving her glass resting on the thick arm of the chair. "But am I supposed to just toss everything aside and move to the Bay and mow my lawn on Saturday?"

Jill blinked several times as if absorbing. "It's kind of insulting the way you say that, because I happen to like my life. And yes, lawns have to be mowed. There are no assistants here. The lawn is part of it, Devyn. Geez."

Devyn pinched the bridge of her nose and self-recrimination flared. "I heard how that sounded and I hate myself. It's the person I've been for the past fifteen years, elitist. And selfish. I don't like her either, Jill, trust me."

"She definitely takes some patience." Jill gestured with her triangle-shaped cocktail glass. "It's like your walls are up all over again."

"Say it. It's nothing like who I was when I was with Elizabeth."

Jill nodded. "I can agree with that, too. I'm telling you right now, little sister, she brought out the absolute best in you. You were vibrant, happy. You slept in on weekends, for goodness sake." Jill twirled the creamy contents of her glass, and it honestly made Devyn a little jealous. Why did she feel the need to be so serious all of the time? A fun drink like that might actually be really nice. More than nice. It could be everything, if she just considered having one for herself. Scotch just seemed so much of an overkill right now.

"There has to be something to that," Devyn said finally.

"There is."

"I'm not sure it matters. I'm not cut out for any of this. Love is… too daunting. I'm better off sticking to buildings."

"Because they love you back. Right. That makes sense."

Devyn sighed. Another valid point. "You're right. Maybe I miscalculated." A pause. "No. I definitely did."

"So, what are you going to do about it?"

"What can I do?"

"Nothing mundane, that's for sure. Are you ready for drastic?"

Devyn looked her sister square in the face. "I don't know." She pointed at the frothy drink. "But can I try one of those and we can talk about the details?"

❖

Devyn popped a second bottle of champagne as her team applauded and cheered. It had come down to the wire, but they'd sold every last damn unit of Twenty-Four Walker, making Wyatt Lowe not only rich but a record breaker in Philadelphia real estate. They were all exhausted, proud, and ready to celebrate.

"I have to give you credit," Wyatt said, as Karen took the bottle from Devyn and went around the room filling glasses. They stood in the now-completed lobby of the building itself, savoring the moment and knowing that they'd accomplished the nearly impossible. "I wasn't sure you'd pull this off, but you've lived up to your reputation. I'm impressed."

Devyn touched her glass to Wyatt. "Thank you for saying so. It was a tall order, but I'm thrilled that I was able to deliver for you." Because she was good at what she did, she tossed him a no-sweat smile.

Wyatt pulled a sheet of paper from his pocket, unfolded it, and handed it to Devyn. "A deal's a deal."

She studied the paper, which turned out to be a high-end rendering of a gorgeous building. The lines alone had her drooling. "What's this?"

"My next project. Eighteen stories. Towering ceilings. Amazing views. Top-of-the-line finishes. It's going to blow this town away. It's all yours."

"You're serious?" She blinked.

"You've earned it." He sipped his champagne and lifted the glass in the air. "I think we can do great things if we stick together, Devyn."

She closed her eyes to enjoy this moment. Nothing got her blood pumping like a brand-new, beautiful building, and knowing Wyatt had faith in her meant everything. She handed him the rendering. "I love everything that you're saying to me right now. You have no idea how much."

"Send me the paperwork. Let's get started."

Devyn smiled. "I have to decline."

Wyatt blinked. He wasn't the kind of guy people turned down. "What are you talking about?"

"I have somewhere else I need to be for the next sixty years or so, but can I make a recommendation?" She turned around and spotted Ricky chatting with a group near the 3-D model. She signaled for him to join them. "Wyatt, I think you should have a conversation with Ricky. He's got a lot of fantastic ideas I have a feeling you're going to like."

Ricky beamed. Wyatt shook his hand.

Devyn smiled at the future stretched out ahead of her. She had a lot of work to do, but then she'd never been afraid of hard work.

It was time to get serious.

CHAPTER TWENTY-TWO

This should be interesting.

Elizabeth had agreed to the meet-up with Thalia on a last-minute whim. She'd spent each night alone in her house watching *Dateline* marathons and wondering how she'd gotten so dark. She also looked at husbands a little differently now, because had anyone run a ratio report of how many times they were their wife's killer? She made a note to tell KC to watch out for Dan just in case. You could never be too careful.

"Hey, there, cutie." Thalia slid into the cozy little booth at the back of the bar at Ronnie Roo's. It was a slow Wednesday night, and they had the section virtually to themselves. Any other time in her life Elizabeth would have been thrilled about the invite. Tonight, she just wanted to get out of the house before husband #293 finally confessed to investigators.

"Hey, Thalia." She didn't remember Thalia ever calling her *cutie* before. She went with it. "Good week?"

"Fantastic. The fund-raiser gave the spa some much-needed attention, and I saw a twenty percent uptick in appointments."

"Very cool." Elizabeth smiled and bopped her head to the music coming in through the speakers above them.

"How about we split a bottle of that Pinot Gris from this little winery up north? I heard Ronnie took a shipment after I recommended it. It's this charming little place where all the people harvest the grapes in the nude and live off the land."

"Interesting. I'll take a Sam Adams."

Thalia grinned and approached the bar with a very obvious sway of her hips. Elizabeth also noticed her short skirt for the first time. She sighed and studied the pattern on the wooden table.

"You seem down tonight," Thalia said, and slid Elizabeth the beer before taking a seat next to her on the same side of the booth. Their arms were touching. Elizabeth glanced at her out of the side of her eye.

"I've had better months. I can be honest about that."

Thalia nodded sympathetically. She was as gorgeous as ever. Her large blue eyes blinked in sharp contrast to the paleness of her smooth skin. "This is about Devyn Winters. I heard you two had a thing. I'm sorry if you're sad, Elizabeth. You know, I was hoping I could help." She touched the back of Elizabeth's neck and gave it a soft squeeze.

Aha. That's what this was. Now that she'd been seen with Devyn, who was objectively rated higher on the desirable scale, Elizabeth was suddenly more interesting to Thalia. Unfortunately, being with Devyn had done the opposite for Elizabeth, because Thalia, even the idea of her, now fell flat.

"You know, I'm not up for this," Elizabeth said apologetically. She moved her neck away from Thalia's touch.

"Not up for drinks? We can skip them if you want."

"And do what?" She blinked back at Thalia.

"Go somewhere a little quieter. A little more personal. We keep saying we need some one-on-one time." She sent her a sexy-eyed look.

It was ironic how much that sentence and that look did not affect her, when she would have given anything for either of them just a short time before. "You know? I'm going to pass. I've followed you around like a puppy dog for a couple of years now."

"A very cute and sweet puppy dog."

"That's a little condescending, but I'm going to move past it." She turned so she could fully face Thalia. "The problem is that you treated me really poorly throughout that time. You canceled plans, dismissed me, and behaved as if I had no feelings, which I do."

Thalia chuckled as if reminiscing about the good times. "But that's just part of the game, isn't it? People circle each other until they finally find that moment to click."

Elizabeth studied her. "Yeah, this isn't that moment. In fact, I don't think there's one on the calendar for us. I also don't enjoy playing games." In spite of Devyn's insecurities and the fact that she'd left Elizabeth and never looked back, she'd shown her what kindness and support meant in a relationship. Not only that, but Elizabeth's feelings for Devyn had been genuine, deep, and real. Nothing like she felt for Thalia. She could see that now as clearly as she could see that Thalia's nose ring was red and possibly infected. She pointed. "You might want to get that looked at. In the meantime, I gotta go. *Dateline* is looking better and better."

"I'm sorry?" Thalia said, standing to let Elizabeth out of the booth. "I'm really not. Have a nice night."

She walked out of Ronnie Roo's with her head held high and her confidence on the rebound. She held on to that confidence when she walked to Dusty McCurdy's real estate office the next morning to finally see about taking On the Spot to a more professional space. Working in her garage had been convenient and necessary, but with Elizabeth's ambition bolstered, and business so fruitful, it was time to professionalize. Only the hanging sign for McCurdy's was gone from the front of the small office building. She stared up at a man on a ladder painting the exterior of the doorframe. The rest of the building had also been given a fresh coat of paint, which really elevated the look of the property.

She shielded her eyes from the sun. "Any idea what happened to McCurdy's? The real estate company that used to have an office here." She hadn't been down this particular street in a while, and wondered how long they'd been gone. Admittedly, she'd been out of her usual gossip loop.

The man looked down, removed his hat, and wiped away the sweat on his brow. Summer was almost on its way out, but the temperatures remained quite warm. "I heard he sold the place. New tenant moves in next week." He gestured with his chin to the dusty-blue sign propped against the side of the building, ready for hanging. In elegant script, it read: *The Winters Group*. Elizabeth stared at it, not comprehending, and glanced up at the man for answers. He shrugged, clearly just there to paint.

Elizabeth didn't move. She couldn't. Unsure what this all meant and feeling unsettled, she took a seat on the curb and watched the cars go by. Everything in her felt numb.

To her right, another car engine whirred and quieted. She turned and watched a black Mercedes, a two-seater, pull up to the curb about twenty yards from where she sat. It wasn't a familiar vehicle to her, but then the Bay was growing with each passing day. The driver exited the car and came into view. Elizabeth swallowed. Devyn Winters, wearing a pinstriped navy business suit that must have been hand drawn for her body, came around the front of the car. Her blond hair was down and bounced against the white collar of her starched shirt. She took off her sunglasses and paused.

"What's going on?" Elizabeth asked from the curb. She didn't stand. She didn't move. She couldn't until she had more information. Her heart hammered away almost painfully, the un-ignorable reminder that she was nervous as hell.

Devyn gestured to the building with her aviators. "I bought the building."

"Why?"

"Well, to start with, it was for sale. I saw it hit the MLS and snatched it up. It needs some renovating and a new coat of paint, a nice new floor, and replaced windows, but I've always liked its location. Close enough to the heart of town, but far away enough to feel peaceful."

"Why does that matter?"

"Because I'm going to be working here." She gestured to the building. "This is my new office."

Elizabeth knew her mouth was hanging open and made a point to shut it. "You're, uh, moving back to the Bay?" She scratched her cheek casually, because that's all this was, a casual conversation.

Devyn nodded. "It's taken me weeks," she inclined her head from side to side, "okay, months, to make this decision, but sometimes you have to follow your gut, or in this case your heart."

"Your heart?" Did she really just say that? What was happening?

"Yes. My heart." Devyn paused and looked up at the building. "But this is the right move for me. I know that now."

Elizabeth tried to assemble the pieces but came up short. "I don't understand. What about your job, all the million-dollar buildings?"

"Been there. Done that. I may take a listing in the city here and there, but my day-to-day work can be in the Bay and the surrounding towns. Poky little Realtors are great, but maybe what this town needs is someone who can shake it up."

"Maybe," Elizabeth said, proactively working to not react to this news. This was the woman who'd neglected her, broken her heart, and she would not allow her in a second time. She couldn't. "I guess it will be nice to have a new friend in town." She made a point to emphasize the word.

"Just a friend?" Devyn raised a sculpted eyebrow. The question, clear as day, hung in the air between them.

"Yep," Elizabeth said, using Devyn's shoulder to stand. "You can never have too many of those. Good luck with the new business." She glanced over her shoulder at the two-story structure. "I have a feeling a lot of folks are going to be thrilled with your services."

"I hope you're one of them."

"Is that a euphemism? Because I'm over those. Been there. Done that, ya know?" She was finding her strength again, and held on to it.

Devyn blinked at the blow and stood, reminding Elizabeth how well she filled out that damned business suit. "Well, I don't fault you. Maybe over time I can change your mind."

Elizabeth simply shook her head, leaving Devyn and the power she once carried on the curb behind her.

❖

Devyn had expected business to start slow and pick up over time as she established a presence in Dreamer's Bay. That had not been the case. In fact, since she'd opened her doors in early September, nearly three weeks ago now, a steady stream of calls and walk-ins had prompted her to hire a receptionist sooner rather than later. Barb, who now sat in the small lobby of the building, seemed to be the most qualified.

"Ms. Winters, would you like to see today's paper?" Barb asked from the doorway. She was likely in her sixties, with a cheerful disposition and the ability to type seventy-two words per minute with a pencil in her hair. The fact that she'd once known Devyn's mother also carried a lot of weight. The partnership somehow seemed ordained. Not only that, but Barb knew every soul who walked in the door and could give Devyn a heads-up about who she was dealing with.

"Sure, I'll take the paper. I have a little time before my ten a.m., right?"

"Quite true," Barb said and carried over that day's edition. "But remember what I told you about Mr. Reynolds, the ten a.m."

"I will. Indecisive, but loaded. I will keep those facts tucked away."

"And he likes food, so I'm having donuts picked up and delivered by On the Spot. After all, you said the more we use them, the better."

Devyn grinned. "Perfect. I'm glad you're calling on them so much." She'd made it part of her plan to use Elizabeth's company as much as possible, which would hopefully give them a little face time. She had a lot of ground to earn back after the way she'd behaved, but she vowed to spend each and every day making it up to Elizabeth, if she would only give her the chance. For the food deliveries and courier services she'd ordered, Elizabeth had sent one of her younger employees each time, thereby dodging run-ins with Devyn. Today, however, it was Elizabeth walking up the sidewalk with a box from Amazin' Glazin'.

Devyn stood and smoothed her white blazer. She'd found she could go more casual in the Bay and had swapped out her dress pants for a dark pair of jeans and modest heels. Professional, but approachable.

"Hey, Barb," Elizabeth said from the lobby. "You called in a delivery order for a combo dozen?"

Barb tossed her hand up in celebration of Elizabeth's arrival. "Yep. Special client coming in this morning."

Elizabeth leaned in. "Let me guess. Moneybags Reynolds."

"That would be the one."

Devyn came around the front of her desk and smiled through the open French doors. Seeing Elizabeth already made her day ten times better, and it had already felt pretty great. "Hey."

"Hi. Look at you, all settled in." Elizabeth was at least attempting to be friendly, which was something. She walked the expanse of Devyn's large office with the high ceilings and picture windows. "Wow. The natural light in here is beautiful."

Devyn nodded. "I had the windows put in two weeks ago."

Elizabeth smiled. "It's perfect."

"Thank you."

"I've been meaning to ask you something."

"Anything."

"Maybe someday I could set up an appointment to talk about office space. I'm not in any real hurry but looking to upgrade from the garage. Was going to ask McCurdy but—"

"He moved to Charleston."

"Right. So, would you be willing? Maybe in a month or two."

Devyn met Elizabeth's gaze and held it. "More than willing. I already have a couple of ideas." Then she remembered herself. "Oh, and I got you something."

"You did?" Her brow furrowed.

Devyn opened the top drawer of her desk and pulled out a small box. "I was shopping the other day at the outdoor market off the Circle, saw this, and thought of you." She handed Elizabeth the square box with the ribbon. "With autumn pretty much here, I thought you could maybe use one of those."

Elizabeth opened the box to reveal a purple and black checkered scarf that would look amazing on her. She stared at it and held it in her hands for a moment, her expression unreadable. "Purple." Was that a sigh? "This was very thoughtful. You shouldn't have done it, but thank you all the same."

"She's wooing you," Barb sang.

Elizabeth glanced from Barb to Devyn and appeared nervous, which made total sense. She was surely terrified of Devyn after how she'd behaved, and had every right to be. Who wants to open themselves up to heartbreak twice in a row? Now it was up to her to put in the time and prove to Elizabeth that she knew what she wanted and wasn't going anywhere ever again. She'd play the long game if she had to, because women like Elizabeth Draper didn't come around too often, or ever, and she was not going to blow her chance a second time. Her stubborn, stupid head had already gotten in the way once.

"Want to grab a drink sometime this week?" she asked as casually as possible.

"I'm slammed, sadly, but you guys enjoy those donuts. Make sure Moneybags buys lots of property."

"That's the goal," Devyn said quietly, and watched as the most wonderful woman in the world left to go about her day.

They saw each other here and there over the next few weeks. In a small town, it was hard not to run into each other. Devyn wasn't complaining. She used each opportunity to steal a few extra moments with Elizabeth to hear about her day or what Scout had gotten into, often the trash. The most recent run-in happened at the enormous pumpkin patch the Bay set up each October. Devyn lined up for a cup of warm cider behind Elizabeth, realizing that she couldn't have planned it better herself. The weather was gorgeous, the pumpkins extra orange and cheerful, and the air held excitement for the new season.

"You're buying a pumpkin?" Elizabeth asked, dubious.

"I'm buying two, actually. Wouldn't want one to be lonely. They'll be a pair."

"That's a nice idea." Elizabeth nodded. "Make sure the second one sticks around, though. Knows how to use a phone."

Devyn sighed at the obvious reference. "I will stay on top of that."

They shuffled forward in line. Elizabeth finally glanced back at her. "That's nothing like you."

"What isn't?"

"Pumpkin buying."

Devyn pulled her face back. "I'm a person, you know. People congregate with other people and partake in holiday traditions."

"No. You don't get involved with little things. You're a bigger-picture type of person. Why are you different?"

Devyn scoffed. "People can change. I work on it every day, actually."

That seemed to snag Elizabeth's attention. She absently chewed on her bottom lip. Turned around in line and then back again, as if she simply couldn't resist. "I know people can change. Of course I know that."

"You just don't think I can." Devyn held up a hand. "It's okay. You don't have to. Plus, the slower pace at work is actually really nice. Gives me time to focus on things like finding myself a good pair of pumpkins. I already have a few contenders."

Elizabeth turned back and faced the cider truck, appearing uninterested. Again, it didn't last. She whirled back around. "What is going on with you? I mean, specifically." Her eyebrows were pulled in and her lips were tight in an accusatory manner. Devyn didn't mind getting under her skin. Anything was an improvement over silence, and it meant that she still affected Elizabeth.

She shrugged. "Nothing is going on with me. I'm just living my life, trying to enjoy myself more. Take in the little things." She looked skyward. "If I remember correctly, that's what someone once thought I should do. Turns out, she was pretty wise, and I'm feeling lighter by the day."

"Good for you," Elizabeth said with forced cheer. "You seem lighter. Happy, even." She turned back around for a final time.

"That's the goal."

Oh, yeah. Devyn was making an impression.

She just hoped she hadn't waited too long.

❖

There were two adorable mugs, one green and one lavender, and a bag of chocolate-flavored coffee in a basket with a bow on Elizabeth's doorstep that second day of November. She didn't have to read the card to know who had left them for her. She sat down on her step, opened the door so Scout could join her outside, and picked up one of the oversized mugs. At first, Devyn's continued advances annoyed her because where had that mentality been when she'd disappeared off the face of the Earth? Why now, all of a sudden, when Elizabeth was finding her way back to being a person? Lately, though, the little gestures seemed…sweet. Maybe it was the holidays approaching. Goodwill toward men and the Christmas spirit and overflowing hearts seem to be the norm this time of year. But it wasn't just the gestures that resonated with Elizabeth. Devyn herself seemed more open, more engaged with other people than she'd ever seen her. She smiled a lot, attended events, looked more relaxed, and was actually out there living life, rather than being chained to her email. She wasn't sure what to do with that information.

Scout licked her nose and whined softly. "You still miss her?" she asked her dog, who stepped one foot at a time into her lap. "You realize you're about four sizes too big to be a lapdog?" She stared in amusement at Scout, who spilled well beyond Elizabeth's crossed legs. "That can't be comfortable, you goof."

KC, who was scheduled to stop by for a beer, pulled into her driveway fifteen minutes early. "I'm an adult out in the world without a child." she yelled, arms outstretched. "I raced over. Where are the snacks? It's after five. Feed me promptly."

"I have baked brie assembled that I was going to toss in the oven, but you're early."

"You're not listening. I'm childless. I have to be early. Oh, I love those," she said, taking a mug from Elizabeth's hands and marching into the house as if she owned it. In many ways, she did. Scout scampered after KC, but Elizabeth paused before following them in, stealing a moment for herself because she was feeling off-kilter. Devyn's staying power surprised her. Despite all of Elizabeth's rebuffs, she hadn't backed down or given up in the slightest. While part of her was, well, impressed, the larger part still viewed Devyn as an unreliable threat to her emotional well-being. She couldn't let someone like that back into her heart, even if she wanted to. She sighed, thinking about their most recent encounter just that morning. She'd been three blocks into her walk with Hank, this time with Scout along, too. She'd turned after hearing footsteps approach from behind to see Devyn, hair in a ponytail, out for a jog. She wore skintight black athletic leggings with a blue stripe down the side and a matching spandex top. Elizabeth blinked. The image of Devyn in sleek athletic wear that showed off so much of her…physique wiped her mind clean of thoughts. She couldn't even recite her address, and she tried.

"Hey, funny running into you here," Devyn said as she came up on them. She smiled widely and jogged in place, waiting for Elizabeth's response.

She eventually located the ability to operate her brain again and stood up tall, bracing against the dogs that wanted to pull her forward. "Hi." She quirked her head. "You're a runner?"

"I am. I used to run late at night on the treadmill in the gym in my building. Now I embrace the sunshine. Turns out that fresh air is much better. Gets my mornings started right. I don't think I'll ever go back."

"Fresh air *is* nice," Elizabeth said, as Hank got the better of her, pulling her forward a few steps.

"Are you having a nice morning?"

"I'm having a *great* morning," Elizabeth said automatically. She forced herself to smile to show off just how great. She was having an amazing time. Just look at her. Walking dogs and such. "Probably one of my best." Okay, that might have been overkill. She sucked at projecting confidence. Always had.

"Really? Well, that's a strong endorsement. I was hoping you were." The jogging in place turned into jogging backward in front of Elizabeth as she continued the dogs' walk. "Not sure if you know, but I made a purchase."

"What kind?" Elizabeth asked, pretending to be extra interested in what Hank was sniffing.

"The house at the end of Mockingbird Point. The one with the giant oak in the front lawn?"

"Oh. I really love that house. You're going to live on the same street as Jill?"

Devyn nodded, still jogging. "I need someone to borrow a cup of sugar from. She's great about that stuff. Plus, the street holds a lot of great memories for me." Her ponytail bouncing. Other things, too. Elizabeth wanted to slam her eyes shut and free herself from this torture.

"I was going to try that new café near the water tonight. I'm told their clams can't be touched. Wanna come along? Very casual."

Elizabeth exhaled. Every part of her wanted to go, but her brain overruled her pesky and less intelligent heart. Not that this new Devyn didn't leave her curious. Wondering. Interested. "I'd love to, but I'm probably going to take tonight to stay in with Scout. Relax."

Devyn nodded, though her smile dimmed a small amount. "Well. I like the sound of that. Scratch her behind her ears for me, okay?"

"I will do that."

"I hope I see you soon, Liz." She turned and jogged off, leaving a gawking Elizabeth to watch the very impressive show.

With the mug and coffee in her hands now, she pulled herself back into the present and headed inside for snacks and drinks with her best friend, wondering distantly what this new version of Devyn Winters thought of that café by the water. She felt her resolve cracking ever so slightly and pondered maybe, just maybe, calling her sometime to find out.

CHAPTER TWENTY-THREE

Good God, this town never tired of festivals and events. It wasn't that Devyn was complaining, but there really was an unending stream of them. The people of Dreamer's Bay were deep celebrators, and who was she to take issue with that? In actuality, the community gatherings made her feel more and more at home in the Bay, beyond what she ever would have thought possible. Dare she say she actually enjoyed them?

"Hello there, Devyn. You are a stunner in navy," Mary Beth Eckhart said in her ear. Devyn glanced down at her jeans, navy sweater, and tall brown boots, hoping her outfit blended with the masses.

She smiled at her mother's friend, who wore a shimmering silver top and pearls. One of the better dressed attendees. "I was hoping to blend in with the locals." She'd heard of the event, interestingly named *Red, White, and Turkey*—yes, really—but had never once attended. For twenty dollars a ticket, a person could sample a variety of wines from multiple vendors on one side of the pavilion. On the other, they staged a turkey cook-off, in which local restaurants battled for the most votes on their turkey preparation. There was roasted turkey, fried turkey, traditional turkey and gravy—and don't get her started on the turkey cheese balls she didn't quite understand—all in preparation for Thanksgiving, now just two weeks away. The chill in the air gave the event a true holiday feel, and she snuggled into her sweater even more. The townspeople mingled in the large outdoor pavilion surrounded by a variety of vertical heaters. Barrels of wine flanked the perimeter to give the event a rustic feel, and a bluegrass band played on the small, erected stage.

Mrs. Eckhart regarded her knowingly. "Well, you're a local yourself now. A new home. A business. I'd say we're keeping you."

"All part of my plan," she said, and sipped her hot mulled wine.

"You have a good time, now," Mrs. Eckhart said, patting her shoulder. "I'm gonna see if Mr. Ivers wants to scoot around the dance floor with me." She demonstrated a couple of moves and sashayed away.

Devyn smiled and called after her. "Who could say no to you?"

"From your lips," she called back. "Coming over next week?"

"I'll be there."

She'd taken to stopping by Ms. Eckhart's house every other week or so for a chat, or just to see if she needed any help with anything around the house. She found the visits healing, and a way for her to feel closer to her mom. Plus, Mrs. Eckhart made that amazing lemon cake that had Devyn jogging a few extra blocks to make up for it.

On her own now, she walked the different booths and inhaled the amazing aromas drifting over from the various grills and on-site ovens. She bopped her head to the music, feeling content with her life choices for the first time in...well, ever. Who knew she'd not only enjoy small town life, but actually thrive? She had hobbies now and time to genuinely take in her own surroundings without leaping from one listing appointment, to a showing, to the negotiating table, only to repeat it all again fifty times a week. She exhaled and grinned.

"What has you smiling so wide?" Jill. She turned to see her clad in jeans, a black top, and a red puffer vest, holding on to Charlie's bicep for support. Gone was the cane, which was a gigantic milestone in her recovery. In its place was Charlie, always at the ready to help Jill with whatever she needed. Devyn had watched their relationship take one tentative step forward at a time until they'd become practically inseparable. Seeing Jill so happy, she couldn't help but root for them. They were *that* cute.

Devyn shrugged and held it. "Just enjoying tonight. Realizing I made the right decision coming home. I feel that reassurance in the air all around me." She held out a hand. "That may sound crazy, but it's happening."

"It's not at all crazy." Jill placed a hand over her chest and exhaled. "I mean, I thought that would be the case, but I'm so relieved to hear you say it."

"You don't miss the big city?" Charlie asked, accepting two cups of mulled wine for himself and Jill from his store's very own booth.

"Part of it, sure," Devyn said. "But I'll get back there every now and then for an occasional listing. I made it clear to my clients that they could call on me for the special projects. But on a daily basis, I'll work from the Bay."

"We all set to check on some beachfront properties, Ms. Winters?" Jerry Dill, from the mayor's office, asked from behind a turkey-and-cranberries-sandwich booth.

She pointed at him. "On my calendar. I have four options, and you're gonna have a tough time choosing."

"That's what I like to hear."

"Well, well," Elizabeth said, joining their group. "Sounds like business is picking up." Her green eyes were bright and they complemented the scarf she wore, the purple and black one Devyn had given her, perfectly. She blinked, trying to understand what that could mean. Maybe she just enjoyed the style.

"Business is great," Devyn said, and swallowed. Elizabeth looked beautiful. Her hair was pulled back loosely on the sides and cascaded down her back. The scarf accentuated the black turtleneck she wore perfectly. The short black booties added an inch to her height. She looked stylish and cozy, and it was all Devyn could do to not let her thoughts wander to those more intimate in nature. But no, she was content just to be in Elizabeth's presence and enjoy a little bit of the evening with her. Her heart ached for more, but she knew the state of things and could be patient. "Almost ready to find that new office?"

"I was planning to give you a call after the holiday. Maybe find a place by Christmas and in time for the new year."

Devyn nodded. She'd been watching the market to see what kinds of things might potentially open up. "I think the timing of that is spot-on."

"Great. And thank you for the front porch delivery."

She said it with a smile, which was a step forward. The usual annoyance had receded, and something in Devyn quieted and sighed in relief. She didn't want to be pushy, and at the first sign that she was being received that way, she would back off.

"You're welcome. I hope you enjoy the blend on that roast. I had it specially made, given your sweet tooth."

Jill and Charlie looked from one of them to the other, as if gleeful spectators at the most entertaining of tennis matches.

"I love it," Elizabeth said.

Oh, wow. Look at that. The polite smile melted into a genuine one, the very smile Devyn hadn't seen in a long while and missed more than she thought possible. Her stomach tightened and flip-flopped, because this was the first sign that there was maybe a true chance for them. She stared into her cup to not give away the happy tears that threatened. She'd come so far, and made so many awful mistakes along the way, and this very slight encouragement...mattered to her.

"Well," Elizabeth said, and looked from Jill to Charlie, then back to Devyn. "I'll let you all enjoy your evening. Gonna go find little Gray and give him some overdue kisses. Did I mention I'm going to give wine a shot tonight?"

"Who are you and what have you done with beer-loving Elizabeth?" Jill asked.

She shrugged happily. "Change is in the air."

Devyn raised a hand in farewell and offered a smile. Seconds later, once they were alone, Jill slugged her, nearly toppling her mug of mulled wine.

"What in hell, Jill?"

"She was giving you the eyes," her sister said, and then let her jaw drop in surprise. "I wasn't sure you'd ever get there again with her, after how heartbroken she was, but I felt an actual spark."

"Ah, yep. I felt something there, too," Charlie said. "Wasn't sure what, but if that's called a spark, then yeah, okay. Works for me." He looked at her. "There were sparks, Devyn."

She nodded, playing it cool. "So, it wasn't just me hoping?"

"She loves you," Jill said earnestly, and shrugged her shoulders to her ears and held them there.

"Then we're a matching pair, because I love her so much, Jilly." She squeezed her cup to ground herself and live in the warm truth of those words, because they were everything.

A voice interrupted the moment and they turned to see Bobby Delacore, the young, debonair mayor of the town, on the microphone. Devyn remembered him as Jill's class president and found it fitting that he transitioned into politics. "It's the time in the evening, folks, where we turn to the Turkey Tell-All, which has become a town tradition. Those of you familiar with the Tell-All know it's about the celebration of the short story, the tall tale, or a heartfelt confession. We already have a line forming to my left, so if you've got a tale to tell, we'd all love to hear it."

It would be a bold move, the grandest and most public of gestures, but his words landed square on her heart. Feeling encouraged by her earlier exchange with Elizabeth, Devyn found the confidence to take the leap. Because Bobby was right. She did have a heartfelt tale to tell.

"Hold my mug?" she asked Jill, who stared at her in mystification. After a story from a ten-year-old about a lost pet that was found, and the tale of Mrs. Eckhart winning two thousand dollars in the state lottery, she was up. She took the microphone in her hand and found her poise. She'd always been a confident speaker, a skill required for her job.

"My story isn't full of twists and turns, but it's a story of one person changing the life of another. I hope you'll indulge me." A room full of interested faces perked up. Many nodded their encouragement. She saw her old high school friends in a clump eying her with intense curiosity. Elizabeth, at the back of the pavilion next to KC and her family, blinked in apparent disbelief. "There was once a jaded out-of-towner, used to the hustle and bustle of a fast-paced world, where people didn't take a lot of time for one another. Transactions mattered, and convenience was everything. She didn't know, that particular out-of-towner, just how much of life she was missing until she met someone who was much wiser than she was. The wiser woman also came with the biggest heart the out-of-towner had ever seen. She put other people first. She looked after her neighbors and made friends everywhere she went. Slowly but surely, the out-of-towner fell in love, but it terrified her, and she didn't give into it, which is a horrible thing to do." There was some nodding in the crowd. She took a moment to gather herself.

To cover the silence, someone yelled out, "You got this, Devyn."

She smiled nervously with gratitude and continued. She hadn't looked in Elizabeth's direction since she'd started her story, but she did so now. She was attentive, and listening, but her expression was unreadable. She pressed on. "No one should ever run away from love, it's the reason we're all here. So that out-of-towner plans to do everything she can to be a better person, to enjoy each and every moment life has to offer. The wise woman taught her to. It was the best decision she ever made. She didn't want to be on the outside looking in any longer." She smiled at the people in the crowd. "You probably get that the person I'm describing is me. I'm happy to be a resident of Dreamer's Bay again, and all I hope to do in the world is to make her happy from today until forever." As she set the microphone back onto its stand, she was met with applause as people turned immediately to Elizabeth, who blinked back at them with a reserved smile. Cricket looked like she'd been hit with a two-by-four of shock and awe, which Devyn derived a good bit of satisfaction from.

She descended from the small stage, and Thalia Perkins caught her by the arm as she passed. "So, I guess what you're saying is that I blew it?"

Devyn met her gaze. "You have no idea how much. But I'm eternally grateful for your oversight and loss." She smiled and headed off in search of Elizabeth, needing to see her face, look her in the eye, and say the words directly to her. It was time. But when she found KC at the back of the pavilion, she and her family stood alone.

"She left, Devyn," KC said, looking uncomfortable. "I don't think she's capable of putting herself out there again. I'm sorry. She's been through a lot, you know."

Devyn nodded, feeling like she'd been hit in the chest with a ton of bricks. The speech had been a bad idea. Elizabeth wasn't where she was, and maybe wouldn't be again. "Ah. Well…" Her gaze found the ground. "A swing and a miss."

"It was a good speech," Dr. Dan said, with an apologetic smile.

She nodded her thanks. "You all have a nice night."

As she worked her way through the crowd to the exit, she felt all eyes on her. She wasn't embarrassed or ashamed that she'd spoken her truth in front of hundreds of friends and neighbors. No. She was only concerned with the reaction of one person, and now it was feeling like maybe she'd been wrong all along. Elizabeth had been friendly and polite in response to all of her efforts to win her back, because that was what Elizabeth did. It was who she was as a person. It was time for Devyn to step back and understand that maybe there was no coming back from her behavior.

"You all right?" Jill asked as she passed.

There was a lump in her throat but she found her way around. "You know me. I'm always okay." She squeezed her sister's hand, offered Charlie a pat on his shoulder, and took her leave.

She'd be better on her own tonight.

She sat alone in her darkened living room, taking stock of who she was, who she wanted to be in this world, and where she was headed. Whatever came her way, she would face it. She would take life by the horns and make sure she lived it to the fullest. Maybe she couldn't have everything she ever wanted. She'd find a way to settle for less and savor the simple things.

She was half asleep when a foreign sound jolted her back. She blinked and stared into her darkened bedroom, wondering what in hell. But there it was again. A loud kerplunk from across the room. Her fuzzy brain attempted to process and identify the sound. Again.

Only this time it carried more of a bang. The window. She got out of bed and made her way there, just in time for a decent-sized rock to smash against it, sending a jagged crack zigzagging down the glass. Realizing her house was being vandalized, she threw open the window in indignation, ready to stop the attack in progress. She pulled up short when she saw Elizabeth and Scout standing beneath her second-story window, looking up. Elizabeth's hand covered her mouth.

"Oh, no. Did I break it?"

Devyn glanced up at the marred glass now above her head. "I would say definitely. Are you throwing giant rocks at my house?"

"I am so sorry. I was looking for pebbles to toss at the window, but there weren't any down here. You always imagine the pebbles will just *be* there, you know, but they weren't." She tossed up her hands. "I was just trying to…I love you." She stared up at Devyn in earnest.

Silence.

Devyn was afraid to move a muscle. She didn't want to do anything to disrupt this moment and the exact feeling that landed smack in the middle of her chest at hearing those words. She savored them, turned them over in her heart, and basked. "You do?" she asked hesitantly.

Elizabeth nodded. "I'm terrified, and nervous, but that part I know is true. I love you."

"I love you, too," Devyn said. "It's the whole reason I moved back. For you. For the slightest chance that we could work our way through this crazy world together."

A pause. "Maybe also a little bit for the Saturday cornhole tournaments?" She smiled.

"Purely bonus." They stared at each other. "Elizabeth, I've never been more me than when I'm with you."

"What now?" Elizabeth asked.

That was the big question, wasn't it? "I don't want to rush you, or push you, and maybe that's what I did tonight with that stupid story idea."

Elizabeth shook her head. Devyn couldn't tell if those were tears. She was too far away. "It wasn't a stupid idea. It was a wonderful story."

"But you left."

"Because I'm scared, and when I felt myself crumbling and wanting so badly to put my arms around you and not let go, I panicked." She nodded several times and then tilted her head to the side. She looked so very beautiful standing there beneath Devyn's window in the moonlight. "But I think you're scared, too. I could tell when you told your story."

"I am. This is a big leap I've made. Leaving everything I know behind me. It's the right decision, but it's still terrifying."

"It's not just the move, Devyn. I'm not standing here because of the little gestures either. Though those have been very nice."

"Then why?"

"There's a difference in you, and I kept waiting for it to fade away, but I don't think you're going anywhere."

"That's because I'm not." Devyn smiled. "Let's just say I realize now what's important. You helped me do that."

Elizabeth shook her head slowly. "I don't think I've ever seen you fully before. Until now. I saw a glimpse here, another there. But lately, it's like you've stepped out of the shadows, and you're standing in front of me. I can see all of you." Devyn nodded but didn't interrupt. "So here we are. We're both scared. The thing is, I was thinking that maybe we could be scared together."

Devyn steadied herself. "We could. You don't know how much I'd like that." She laughed through the thick emotion. "Why are you still so far away? I'm coming down."

She took the stairs two at a time and opened her door to find Elizabeth standing there with a watery smile. Scout calmly walked inside in search of a comfy place to sleep.

"Come here," Devyn said, taking a step back and tugging Elizabeth into the darkened entryway of her home. Elizabeth didn't hesitate, allowing herself to be tugged. They stood there face-to-face, understanding the importance of this moment. In a span of five minutes, they'd become an us, and the world would be forever changed for the wonderful.

Elizabeth reached out and touched Devyn's cheek. "I've missed you. And I don't know what you're wearing, but you look amazing." She blew out a slow breath.

Devyn smiled and glanced down at her pink striped pajama pants and the pink camisole that she'd always filled out nicely, happy now that she'd worn it. "First of all, I'd say I've missed you, too, but it would be such an understatement. Second, you could always take it off me if you wanted."

Elizabeth kissed her slowly on the mouth, then her cheek, and then moved until her lips were next to Devyn's ear. "Oh, I want," she whispered, sending a shiver through Devyn she'd likely never forget. She kissed her neck slowly as they stood there in the faintly lit room, pulling an unexpected moan from Devyn's lips. She shrugged out of her jacket, and when the moonlight crisscrossed her features, Devyn saw the determined desire in her eyes. She loved Elizabeth on a mission. They came back together more aggressively, Devyn catching Elizabeth's face in her hands as she approached and pulling her in. Their lips and tongues did battle as the temperature climbed, their heat undeniable, as always. Elizabeth pulled her mouth from Devyn's, her gaze dropping. She pulled down the front of Devyn's tank top, exposing her breasts, which spilled out, no longer restrained. With a murmur of appreciation, she dipped her head and aggressively took a nipple into her mouth, holding Devyn in place at the waist. She entwined her fingers in Elizabeth's hair, craving more, and now at the mercy of the pulsing ache between her legs.

"Take me to bed," she said, breathless.

Elizabeth nodded, settling on her mouth once again.

They made love that night slowly, memorizing each other, not because they had to this time, but because they wanted to. Eye contact was plentiful, and each touch felt like an important promise. Once they lay satisfied, spent, and tangled up in each other, Devyn allowed the full brunt of her happiness to land. "There's a house on Sunset Hill, the street on the east side of town, not far from the water."

Elizabeth propped her head up in her palm and looked down at Devyn. "There is, huh? Are you the listing agent?"

"No, but I could see us living there."

Elizabeth's lips parted as she took in the information. A smile formed. "We can't buy a house yet. Are you crazy?"

"I will accept the *yet* part of your answer. Honestly, it would be perfect for us down the line. I'm going to keep my eye on it." Elizabeth's eyes went playfully wide. "When we're ready, of course," Devyn amended, reaching up and touching a silky strand of Elizabeth's hair. "I want you to fall asleep in my arms tonight. I've been dreaming of you there."

Elizabeth slid down and rested her head on Devyn's shoulder. She traced a circle around Devyn's nipple, causing her to tense. "I'd like that very much, and I think we should do just that."

"Good."

"But I don't think you're ready for sleep."

"I actually think I could sleep pretty hard, now that all is right with the world again. Do you want to go to the café for breakfast tomorrow? Say yes."

"Yes." Elizabeth circled the nipple a second time and watched Devyn shift uncomfortably. She did it once more and smiled at the intake of breath. Devyn was wet again and turned on from that simple a touch. But she had to even things out. She shifted and turned until they were facing each other, reached down, and traced a very similar circle between Elizabeth's legs and watched as her eyes slammed closed in surrender.

"Not playing fair," Elizabeth said, though she moved into the touch.

Devyn accepted the invitation, slid her fingers inside, and smiled as Elizabeth's hips began to move rhythmically, slow at first, and then faster. When the payoff hit, Elizabeth's gaze met Devyn's. This was her forever, this wonderful woman. She'd never been more sure of anything in her life. She had found her spot in this world in the most unexpected of places, Dreamer's Bay, and she was never leaving again.

When she awoke the next morning, hints of sunlight peeked through the window. The room was chilly but the warmth pressed against her reminded Devyn that last night hadn't just been a magnificent dream. "Good morning," she whispered and kissed Elizabeth's forehead.

She stirred in Devyn's arms and lifted her face. After blinking a few times, she ran a hand through her hair, lifting it off her face, which blossomed into a heartfelt smile. "Hi."

"Hi." Devyn pulled her face down for a good-morning kiss. "I'm taking today off. Put me to work."

"You're gonna run errands for me? Do my bidding?" Elizabeth asked playfully and snuggled into Devyn.

"For the rest of my life if you'll let me."

"Let's start with you taking me out for those pancakes you promised, so I can make eyes at you across the table."

Devyn laughed, and her heart soared. "We'll start with pancakes."

EPILOGUE

One Year Later

"I'm nervous," Devyn told Jill as they worked, side by side, in Jill's kitchen. Devyn was on green bean duty and Jill checked on the turkey. Thanksgiving dinner would be a festive one this year, and even though Devyn demanded Jill take it easy now that she'd entered the second trimester of her pregnancy, Jill was having none of it.

"It's good that you're nervous. It means today is important."

Devyn nodded, grateful she'd insisted on coming over in the early morning hours in advance of Elizabeth, using the excuse that Elizabeth should take the morning for herself to relax after such a busy workweek. When she'd left the house at just before eight, she'd kissed Elizabeth goodbye as she read a book on the couch, snuggled up to Scout.

"What if she says no?" Devyn asked, gesturing with the spatula-spoon combo thing. "Will that spoil Thanksgiving for everyone? That could be awkward with her friends here." KC and her family, along with Dexter, would be joining the four of them for dinner around lunchtime. "I mean, not to overshadow the heartbreak and embarrassment I will feel, but I don't want to ruin everyone's day."

Jill held up a hand. "Devyn."

"Yes?" she asked.

"You and Elizabeth are two of the most in love people I've ever seen in my life. You're inseparable, you're considerate of each other, and more than once I've had to look away out of respect because you blatantly show affection all the time."

Devyn relaxed into what felt like a dreamy grin. "We do that, don't we?"

"She's not going to say no, and if she does, then something has gone really wrong with the world."

Devyn nodded but held on to that last bit, because what if something had gone wrong and she'd missed it? She scrunched her shoulders to release some of the tension and focused on the seasoning of her green beans. The time would be here soon enough.

❖

The long table draped in white and covered with a variety of Thanksgiving dishes was a raucous one. With glasses of white wine flowing, everyone at their Thanksgiving dinner was full of smiles and participating in lively conversation. Elizabeth looked from one person's face to the next, forever grateful for each one, until she settled on the one she never got tired of staring at. Devyn had her blond hair up today and looked elegant and chic. Elizabeth loved how she vacillated between homebody in jeans to professional in Prada when she needed to. The last year had been the best of her life, and she still woke up every day amazed that the life she was living was hers. Unassuming Elizabeth Draper had finally found her person.

Devyn Winters had proven to be the true love of her life, and she wanted nothing more than to make her happy every single day. So far, so good. She squeezed Devyn's leg underneath the table, and they exchanged a private smile as Charlie explained that Dreamer's Bay seemed to be more of a bourbon town than a scotch one.

"Wouldn't have guessed that," Dr. Dan said.

KC squinted. "Well, write that down for your future moonshine business. We gotta give the people what they want. Are there more of those buttered rolls?"

Jill happily passed the basket.

Just then, Devyn picked up her spoon and touched it to her glass three times, which was just enough for everyone to look her direction. Elizabeth quirked her head in curiosity.

"First of all, I want to say thank you to Jill for this fantastic meal."

"Please. You helped with all of it."

Devyn shook her head. "Not true. I was probably more trouble than I was worth in the kitchen."

"You often are, but you make me laugh trying."

"Fair enough." She turned her attention back to the larger group.

"I wanted to say how much I've enjoyed my first Thanksgiving back in the Bay. If I'm being honest, this year came with some major changes for me. New home, new job trajectory, new friends and family." She smiled at Charlie on that one. Elizabeth nodded, waiting for Devyn to wrap up. She had things on her mind, too, and this might be the opportune time to express them. "But nothing changed my life the way this woman next to me has."

Elizabeth felt the warmth as the blush crept onto her cheeks.

"I want every year to be just like this one."

"In that case, I have something to say." Elizabeth stood, seizing the opening. Devyn turned to her with wide eyes.

"You do?"

"Marry me. Those are the only two words that I have in my head these days. I don't have a speech, because it's all right here." She placed a hand over her heart. Instead of getting on one knee, she got on two and took Devyn's hands. "This year can be every year."

In her peripheral vision she saw KC cover her mouth. Dexter slid his chair back from the table in happy shock. Jill took Charlie's hand and waited.

"Oh. I almost forgot." Elizabeth pulled the ring she'd purchased with pretty much her life's savings from her pocket, where she'd practically sewed it in place. Her nerves got the best of her, causing her to fumble with it a moment. When she looked up from her hands, she found Devyn on her knees across from her, holding an open ring box of her own. The oxygen left the room. Elizabeth attempted to speak but wasn't clear on words anymore. She shook her head instead until they returned. "Wait. What? Are you..."

Devyn smiled her killer smile. The one that made Elizabeth's knees weak. "Marry me right back."

Dexter stood, hands on his head and turned in a circle. "You guys better stop it right now."

"I bought the house on Sunset Hill," Devyn said.

"What?" It didn't make sense. "The one by the water? It wasn't on the market."

"I made them a desirable offer, and they accepted. I want us to live there."

To her left, Elizabeth saw Jill vibrating with joy. KC covered her mouth, but even that couldn't hide her grin.

"Yes," Elizabeth whispered finally, and nodded. "I will marry you. I want to live in that house and wake up to you each and every day."

"That's a yes from me, too," Devyn said to the room, which pulled another laugh in the midst of damp faces.

Then came the emotion that swelled like a giant wave, gaining momentum in the ocean. It crashed and spread, culminating in a reminder of the feelings she had for Devyn that started with a twinge of something important the day they graduated from high school and grew into the greatest love she'd ever known. She reached for Devyn, unable to keep her hands to herself a moment longer, and pulled her face in for a kiss.

"I'm ready for forever," she whispered.

About the Author

Melissa Brayden (www.melissabrayden.com) is a multi-award-winning romance author, embracing the full-time writer's life in San Antonio, Texas, and enjoying every minute of it.

Melissa enjoys spending time with her family and working really hard at remembering to do the dishes. For personal enjoyment, she throws realistically shaped toys for her Jack Russell terriers and checks out the NYC theater scene as often as possible. She considers herself a reluctant patron of spin class, but would much rather be sipping merlot and staring off into space. Coffee, wine, and donuts make her world go round.

Books Available From Bold Strokes Books

Beautiful Dreamer by Melissa Brayden. With love on the line, can Devyn Winters find it in her heart to stay in the small town of Dreamer's Bay, the one place she swore she'd never remain? (978-1-63555-305-5)

Create a Life to Love by Erin Zak. When sixteen-year-old Beth shows up at her birth mother's door, three lives will change forever. (978-1-63555-425-0)

Deadeye by Meredith Doench. Stranded while hunting the serial predator Deadeye, Special Agent Luce Hansen fights for survival while her lover, forensic pathologist Harper Bennett, hunts for clues to Hansen's disappearance along the killer's trail. (978-1-63555-253-9)

Endangered by Michelle Larkin. Shapeshifters Officer Aspen Wolfe and Dr. Tora Madigan fight their growing attraction as they work together to destroy a secret government agency that exterminates their kind. (978-1-63555-377-2)

Incognito by VK Powell. The only thing Evan Spears is focused on is capturing a fleeing murder suspect until wild card Frankie Strong is added to her team and causes chaos on and off the job. (978-1-63555-389-5)

Insult to Injury by Gun Brooke. After losing everything, Gail Owen withdraws to her old farmhouse and finds a destitute young woman, Romi Shepherd, living in a secret room. (978-1-63555-323-9)

Just One Moment by Dena Blake. If you were given the chance to have the love of your life back, could you ignore everything that went wrong and start over again? (978-1-63555-387-1)

Scene of the Crime by MJ Williamz. Cullen Mathew finds herself caught between the woman she thinks she loves but can no longer trust and a beautiful detective she can't stop thinking about who will stop at nothing to find the truth. (978-1-63555-405-2)

Fear of Falling by Georgia Beers. Singer Sophie James is ready to shake up her career, but her new manager, the gorgeous Dana Landon, has other ideas. (978-1-63555-443-4)

Daughter of No One by Sam Ledel. When their worlds are threatened, a princess and a village outcast must overcome their differences and embrace a budding attraction if they want to survive. (978-1-63555-427-4)

Playing with Fire by Lesley Davis. When Takira Lathan and Dante Groves meet at Takira's restaurant, love may find its way onto the menu. (978-1-63555-433-5)

Practice Makes Perfect by Carsen Taite. Meet law school friends Campbell, Abby, and Grace, law partners at Austin's premier boutique legal firm for young, hip entrepreneurs. Legal Affairs: one law firm, three best friends, three chances to fall in love. (978-1-63555-357-4)

The Last Seduction by Ronica Black. When you allow true love to elude you once and you desperately regret it, are you brave enough to grab it when it comes around again? (978-1-63555-211-9)

Wavering Convictions by Erin Dutton. After a traumatic event, Maggie has vowed to regain her strength and independence. So how can Ally be both the woman who makes her feel safe and a constant reminder of the person who took her security away? (978-1-63555-403-8)

A Bird of Sorrow by Shea Godfrey. As Darrius and her lover, Princess Jessa, gather their strength for the coming war, a mysterious spell will reveal the truth of an ancient love. (978-1-63555-009-2)

All the Worlds Between Us by Morgan Lee Miller. High school senior Quinn Hughes discovers that a broken friendship is actually a door propped open for an unexpected romance. (978-1-63555-457-1)

Falling by Kris Bryant. Falling in love isn't part of the plan, but will Shaylie Beck put her heart first and stick around, or tell the damaging truth? (978-1-63555-373-4)

An Intimate Deception by CJ Birch. Flynn County Sheriff Elle Ashley has spent her adult life atoning for her wild youth, but when she finds her ex, Jessie, murdered two weeks before the small town's biggest social event, she comes face-to-face with her past and all her well-kept secrets. (978-1-63555-417-5)